HIGH TREASON
AT THE
GRAND HOTEL

HIGH TREASON
AT THE
GRAND HOTEL

A Fiona Figg Mystery

Author Photo Credit: Vanderbilt Photo Studio

First edition

ISBN: 978-1-947915-90-9

Cover art by B&P Design Studio

This book was professionally typeset on Reedsy.
Find out more at reedsy.com

For Lisa

Contents

Praise for the Fiona Figg Mysteries

PRAISE FOR *HIGH TREASON AT THE GRAND HOTEL*

"A clever mix of humor and espionage that will keep you turning the pages and laughing all the way!" — Dianne Freeman, author of the award-winning Countess of Harleigh mysteries.

"The Fiona Figg mysteries are a perfect blend of wit, fun, and intrigue. With Fiona's ever-changing outfits and innovative methods of spying, author Kelly Oliver has created another winner with her well-written *High Treason at the Grand Hotel.*" — Debra Goldstein, Author of the Sarah Blair Cozy Mysteries

"On assignment in Paris, during The War, novice spy Fiona Figg wears disguises to broaden her information-gathering net. Soon she's up to her fake eyebrows in intrigue, jewel thieves, invisible ink, double agents, and master spies. Lushly layered in period detail, Book Two of the Fiona Figg Mystery captivated my attention. Fiona Figg runs on moxie, heart, and stunning hats. This historical mystery delivers twists and turns in a lighthearted tale of suspense and derring-do. I can't wait for the next one!" — *Muddy Rose Reviews*

"Oliver offers another whimsical World War I espionage escapade featuring a file clerk/spy-in-training working for British Intelligence. In between murders and speculation about double agents, Oliver treats readers to an often amusing romp through upscale 1917 Paris, where the partying stands in stark contrast to the squalid conditions that the protagonist experiences in a Parisian jail. A fun diversion with an entertaining female lead." — *Kirkus Reviews*

"A delightful romp through WWI Paris, rich with period detail, effervescent with British resourcefulness, and full of gentle humor reminiscent of early Hollywood zany comedies. A refreshing lark." — Keenan Powell, author of the award-nominated Maeve Malloy Mysteries

"*High Treason at the Grand Hotel* is a tale marinated in feminist sensibility. Underestimated, condescended to, oft overlooked, Fiona is easily the better of her confederates and is the novel's only true match for the diabolical Fredericks... If you're a habitué of the continent of cozy, if you want your excitement without *too* much blood on the wall, if you enjoy a resourceful heroine who (mostly) saves herself, then you'll find a great deal to enjoy." — *Paul Eberly Reviews*

PRAISE FOR *BETRAYAL AT RAVENSWICK*

"Take a plucky sleuth, a handsome soldier, a shady stranger, add mystery and a dash of espionage, shake well, and you have *Betrayal at Ravenswick*. Fans of traditional mysteries will root for Fiona Figg as she navigates the treachery of London and a seemingly bucolic English country manor at a time when everything in England was changing." — Liz Milliron, author of The Homefront Mysteries

"I truly enjoyed reading *Betrayal at Ravenswick*. Fiona's self-deprecating humor and unspoken asides connected me to her from the start. The story is filled with memorable characters, and it is wonderfully suspenseful. I am awestruck by how seamlessly Oliver has woven in researched material. What great details—from medical treatments of the time to facial glue! I'm glad this is a series, and I can look forward to more." — Lorraine Lopez, PEN Faulkner Award-winning author of *The Darling*.

Warning to the Reader from the Author

Many of the characters in what you are about to read are based on real people. For the sake of the plot, I've altered the timeline of some events. For a brief description of the real people and the correct chronology, see my afterward. In the meantime, I hope you enjoy this *entirely* fictional account of some real adventures.

Chapter One: A Dangerous Mission

"Fiona is a good girl, but trailing Fredricks is a dangerous mission." When I heard one of the code-breakers use my name, I couldn't help eavesdropping. *Not very polite, I know, but jolly informative.* I put down my pencil and craned my neck. I couldn't see around the partition separating my desk from the rest of the office, but I knew who was speaking all the same.

"I can't believe the upper brass is sending her, a mere file clerk, and a woman no less." I recognized Mr. Knox's booming voice. "Espionage is no job for a woman." Dilly Knox was a former classics scholar at Cambridge and one of the best code-breakers in Room 40, the heart of British Intelligence. Despite his old-fashioned views, I couldn't help but like him.

"Shame about her husband. Widows get up to all sorts of things these days." *Steady on, Mr. Grey, with your high-pitched little whine.* And here I thought Nigel Grey was more broad-minded than most of the men in Room 40. Mr. Grey, the grandson of the fifth Lord of Walsingham studied several languages at Eton College and then went into publishing before being recruited as a code-breaker.

"But spying on the bloody Germans? Surely that's a man's job." Mr. Knox again.

Come on, chaps, it's 1917, not the dark ages. Can't you see, thanks to this bloody war, women are carrying the world?

The men in Room 40 may have been incredulous that I, Fiona Figg, "a mere file clerk, and a woman no less," would be crossing a war zone to pursue a fiendish South African huntsman cum war correspondent who was most certainly also a German spy, but the upper brass in the War Office must have confidence in me. Otherwise, why send me to Paris after Fredrick Fredricks?

I didn't want to admit it, but I knew the answer. Not because I was a good spy, or even qualified—apart from my two-week crash course in espionage. No, I was a last resort because they were blooming desperate. All able-bodied men were busy fighting at the front, so they turned to able-bodied women. And what my body lacked in ability I made up for in determination. Fredricks had gotten away from me once. He wasn't going to do it again.

"Fredricks isn't German. He's South African," Mr. Grey said. "Anyway, she's just following Fredricks. She's not going to fight at the front."

"True. And Fredricks is nothing more than a cad who's bedded half of the English aristocracy," Mr. Knox said. "And now he's moving on to the well-heeled beauties of Paris."

Thanks to my recent reconnaissance at Ravenswick Abbey, the upper brass didn't agree. Fredricks's conquests weren't just limited to the bedroom. I'd given them proof that Fredrick "Apollo" Fredricks was actually the infamous Black Panther, one of the deadliest agents in Kaiser Wilhelm's espionage unit.

"Who can blame him?" Mr. Knox's pot-belly preceded him into the threshold of my alcove. Once inside, he began singing a song in French, "*Les Amis de Monsieur...*" My French was good enough to know the song was about an adulterer and his wandering eye. Mr. Knox should know. He was the king of the wandering eye—an incorrigible flirt who chased dancing girls, war heroes, and everything in between.

"Good luck, old girl," Mr. Knox said raising his eyebrows. "You'll need it." When I scowled at him, he laughed.

"Oh, come now, Fiona, you know you'll miss me." He winked.

Cheeky devil. Winking at me and using my Christian name.

"Quit pestering Mrs. Cunningham." Mr. Montgomery came to my rescue. Mr. William Montgomery, a former Presbyterian minister and an expert translator of German theological texts, was the head of cryptography. But with his pinched face and spectacles, he still looked more like a preacher than

2

one of Britain's premier code-breakers. He still called me Mrs. Cunningham even though Andrew, my ex-husband, had divorced me to marry his secretary and then gone and got himself killed. "Have you broken the code on that telegram yet?" Mr. Montgomery asked the other two men.

I'd overheard that British Intelligence had just intercepted a telegram between Berlin and the German embassy in Spain.

"We broke that code months ago." Mr. Knox scoffed. "Even the frogs have figured out how to read it."

"They used *that* code?" Mr. Montgomery said.

"They did." Mr. Grey joined his associates at my desk. "So you're off to Paris, Miss Figg." Mr. Grey's mousy nose twitched. "Maybe you can find out why the Germans are using a code they know we've broken."

All three men peered down at me.

"Is this related to Fredrick Fredricks?" I asked.

The head of the War Office, Captain Reginald "Blinker" Hall, had given me strict instructions to keep my distance from him, find out whatever I could about his mission in Paris, and report back as soon as possible. I checked my watch. Just over nine hours until my departure on the midnight boat train to Paris. I pulled my ticket out of my handbag. Leaving July 1st at midnight, arriving July 2nd at nine in the morning.

"No, not Fredricks," Mr. Grey answered. "Apparently, the Germans have a lady agent in Paris. They call her H21. She's seducing French officers to get military secrets."

Mr. Knox chuckled. "Officers have all the luck." He patted his ample stomach as if he'd just eaten a tasty pudding. He got a mischievous look on his face. "Is that what you'll be doing in Paris, old girl? Seducing officers?"

Even Mr. Montgomery laughed at that.

"Don't be ridiculous." I waved him away. No amount of face paint or padding would make me irresistible to officers or anyone else. I would have to resort to other sorts of disguises to get the information I needed.

"Anything for the war effort, eh, Fiona?" Mr. Knox said, snickering. He enjoyed tormenting me.

I waved him off.

"What?" Mr. Knox gave me a cheeky grin. "A girl like you, in her twenties—and not bad looking—could have a smashing good time in Paris." He chuckled.

"What's so funny?" The familiar lanky figure of Captain Clifford Douglas appeared on the threshold of my cubicle. As usual, Clifford looked smart in his khaki uniform. Chivalrous, loyal, and a bit too old-fashioned when it came to women, Clifford was the epitome of English manhood.

"Speak of the devil," Mr. Knox said, raising his eyebrows. "If it isn't an officer. Fiona, work your magic."

My cheeks aflame, I glared at the impudent fellow.

"I say, what's this all about?" Clifford glanced around at the other men and smiled awkwardly. The men were used to him coming to fetch me for lunch. He worked on the second floor, but spent as much time in Room 40 as in his own office.

"Fiona is off to—" Mr. Knox started to say.

"Dilly, come with me." Mr. Montgomery shook his head. "We have work to do. You too, Dormouse." They called Mr. Grey "Dormouse" for obvious reasons.

Once again Mr. Montgomery had come to my rescue. No one outside Room 40 or the upper brass of the War Office was supposed to know about my top-secret assignment, especially not Clifford Douglas, who was a good friend of mine but also a great friend of the notorious huntsman—and an incurable blabbermouth.

"I've come to say goodbye." Clifford moved closer to my desk. "I'm catching the afternoon train. Off to the Grand Hotel in Paris for a couple of weeks. My brilliant friend Fredricks is there on a journalistic assignment for the Americans, you know. Darn good journalist too—"

"The War Office will miss you," I interrupted before he could continue his dissertation on his *brilliant* friend Fredricks, who in Clifford's opinion could do no wrong. I put away a pencil in a slot in my top desk drawer. As I too was leaving for who knew how long, I needed to straighten my desk and get my files in order. My father liked to say, outward order conceals inward turmoil. If so, my soul must be a cyclone. And if the reverse were true, the slobs in this office had the souls of monks.

"And what about you, Fiona?" Clifford sat on the corner of my desk. "Will you miss me?"

I hoped he wasn't about to propose again. He had the odd habit of proposing to women of his acquaintance, especially those he deemed damsels in distress.

"That depends."

"Depends on what?" He face was so earnest, it made me want to crank him up a bit.

"Whether you tell me what you're really up to, meeting Fredricks in Paris." With his open countenance and old-fashioned chivalry, I doubted Clifford Douglas was also a spy for the War Office, but these days one never knew. I mean, who in their right mind would ever have suspected me of spying? Anyway, Clifford was probably far too gullible for espionage. Given his susceptibility to a pretty face, however, he would be the first officer lined up for seduction by the mysterious agent H21.

"Fredricks is on assignment for that New York newspaper. He's their star war-correspondent, you know." He gave me a quizzical look. "Why, what do you think he's doing?"

"And I suppose you're going to tag along to learn his investigative methods?" I shouldn't have been so snide about Clifford's admiration for the Great White Hunter. He had no idea Fredricks was a German spy. Surely if he knew, he'd change his tune about the man.

"Well, I..." Clifford stammered. "He *is* a darn good investigator." Clifford picked up a pencil off my desk and fiddled with it. "Fredricks believes humans are animals like any other and act according to instinct." Clifford loved to waffle on about applying Fredricks's hunting techniques to human beings, as if you could track a criminal simply by following his footmarks and checking for scat. "Of course, I'm perfecting his methods." Clifford fancied himself a true-crime writer, a detective of sorts.

"Of course you are." I grabbed the pencil out of his hand. "How'd you persuade the War Office to let you go to Paris?" If Clifford was on assignment too, I wanted to know. Although if he really was a spy, he certainly shouldn't be telling me.

"They've given me an extended leave." He touched his leg. "My war injury, you know."

I nodded.

"May I write to you?" he asked sheepishly.

"Nothing would delight me more." *As long as you tip the wink on your friend Fredricks.* I stood up and finished filing the few remaining papers on my desk. "There," I said with a sense of accomplishment. Now I was ready to tackle Fredricks.

"And you'll write back?" He smiled.

"Of course." *Hmmm. If I'm off to France too, how will I get his letters?* I pushed my chair into the desk and checked to make sure everything was in its place. "But you know how dodgy the post can be with the war on."

"Everything is dodgy until this beastly war ends." He adjusted his cap to cover his receding hairline.

"Do you have time for a cup of tea before you go?" I asked. "I need a pick-me-up."

"Me too," Mr. Knox chimed in from the other room.

Is the blighter eavesdropping? Of course, I'm a fine one to talk....

"I'd take a cuppa too... that is, if you're making some anyway, Miss Figg," Mr. Grey added.

Sigh. I was about to go on a top-secret espionage mission, and I was still expected to make the blasted tea. I scooted around my desk and past Clifford and headed out of my alcove. The balance of Room 40 was filled with rows of tables where men and women worked deciphering telegrams. Luckily, the kitchenette was at my end of the long, narrow space.

Clifford followed me into the kitchenette.

As usual, I was met by a stack of unwashed dishes and the smell of feet. Since no one else in the office ever bothered doing the dishes, in my absence, I expected the health department to condemn the place. Disgusted, I couldn't make us tea until I tidied up the sink. Soapy sponge in hand, I dumped day-old coffee and scrubbed the stains from ceramic cups.

No doubt realizing the tea-making would take some time, Clifford removed his cap, took a seat at the small table, and picked up a piece of paper from a pile strewn across the tabletop. I'd have to attack that mess of papers next.

"I say, listen to this." He glanced up at me. "French battalions are refusing to fight. They won't leave the trenches."

Suspecting he'd gotten a hold of something confidential, I wiped my hands on a towel and went to see what he was reading. I snatched the white paper from his hands. "Who left this here?" I stuffed the notice into a pocket of my skirt. "This is classified. We can't let the Germans find out."

"Of course not." Clifford looked indignant. "Good Lord. You don't think I'm a spy, do you?"

"You never know." I went back to the stove and the kettle. I still had a sandwich in the icebox from yesterday. I'd have to throw it out or eat it. To avoid being wasteful, I decided on the later.

"Really, what's wrong with those soldiers? Sheer cowardice, if you ask me." He shook his head. "Our Tommies would never refuse to fight."

"I suspect if our Tommies were asked to charge to their deaths on empty stomachs, they might balk too."

"But we are." He said proudly. "I was always hungry in those bloody trenches. Tinned beef for weeks on end."

"As Napoleon said, an army marches on its stomach." Unwrapping the waxed paper from my margarine sandwich, I offered Clifford half. "Well, at least we will march on margarine."

He accepted the day-old sandwich with a smile. I quickly poured him a cup of tea lest he choke on the first stale bite. Taking the milk from the icebox, I poured a splash into my cup. Clifford may like his tea black, but I preferred mine a little sweeter.

"Do you know why we drink our tea with milk?" He sat back in his chair, holding his mug. "Cups used to be so fragile, boiling water would crack them. That's why you put the milk in first. To keep the cup from breaking. That reminds me of a funny story. Once, when Fredricks and I were hunting in South Africa—"

"I thought you had a train to catch," I interrupted before he could launch into another one of his endless stories.

He played with his cap. He didn't seem in much of a hurry. I was beginning to worry that Clifford might be booked on the midnight boat train too. Given the clandestine nature of my assignment, it would be jolly awkward spending the trip dodging the dogged captain. It was bad enough that we'd both be in Paris... and at the Grand Hotel, where my quarry, Fredrick Fredricks, was holed up at this very minute. I sat at the table and took a bite of margarine sandwich. What I wouldn't give for a nice slice of cheese and a tomato.

"Are you in a hurry to get rid of me?" Clifford gave me that hangdog look of his.

"I do have a lot of work to do."

"Is the tea ready yet?" Mr. Knox called from the other room.

"As you see," I said, waving a bread crust in front of Clifford's face. "I'm crucial to the war effort."

"Just so." Clifford laughed. "Someone's got to make the tea to keep the code-breakers in tip-top form." He drained his cup. "I'd best be going." He stood up, replaced his cap, and adjusted his uniform. "I'll miss our lunches together, old girl."

"Me too." It was true. Clifford could be deuced annoying at times, but I had to admit I would miss his company... if not his nattering on about his *great* friend, the *brilliant* war correspondent and *world's best* big-game hunter.

He held out his hand.

I smiled at his formality, stood, and shook his hand. Then I leaned in and kissed him on the cheek.

"I say..." He blushed and gazed at me with smiling eyes.

When he reached the threshold to the kitchenette, he turned back. "Promise you'll write to me. Grand Hotel, *Chomps El Leasy.*" *Blimey.* His accent was worse than mine.

"I will." At least I'd been practicing my French by listening to Bizet's operas, especially the scandalous *Carmen*. Its title character seduced officers and, like all great women of opera, was killed for being too clever. "Bye." I waved.

As soon as the good captain was gone, I gobbled down the rest of my sandwich and gulped the dregs of my tea. I prepared a tray to take out to the pesky Mr. Knox and the other men. The sooner I served them their tea, the sooner I could get on with my own preparations.

* * *

An hour later I was filing the last stray documents someone had carelessly left out on the kitchenette table when Mr. Montgomery interrupted me. "Captain Hall wants to see you upstairs." He pointed at the ceiling.

Drawer half-open, rifling through the alphabet, I quickly filed the telegram I was holding.

"Now, Miss Figg," Mr. Montgomery said. "You don't want to keep the captain waiting."

I felt as if I were being called to the headmaster's office. I hoped Captain Hall hadn't come up with a reason to ground me. I was so looking forward to my adventure in Paris... or anywhere other than here. Since my divorce, I'd taken any opportunity to get out of London, where everything reminded me of Andrew. After his death, every place we'd ever been together felt haunted.

The hallway leading to Captain Hall's office seemed to go on for miles. The clicking of my heels echoing through the long hallway, made me feel as if I were walking to face a firing squad. On tiptoe, I continued toward the open door at the end of the corridor.

His receptionist invited me to take a seat. My pulse was racing at such speed, it was difficult to sit still. *What could Captain Hall want at the eleventh hour?* I glanced at my watch. I needed to get home, finish my packing, and decide on my disguise. *Should I travel on the train as myself or someone else? What disguise could I wear?*

Growing up, I'd wanted to be an actress but was told I wasn't pretty enough. Fortunately, my espionage exploits didn't require beauty, but rather cunning and a modicum of talent... and the right disguise. Luckily, I'd studied theater at the all-girl North London Collegiate School and knew how to apply spirit gum and a good mustache.

"Captain Hall will see you now," the receptionist said, waving me into his office.

Sitting behind his mammoth wooden desk, eyelids flicking, the petite Captain Hall looked like a turtle encased in its shell. Unlike the desks of the men in Room 40, his was neat and tidy. From the perfectly aligned books on the bookcase to the evenly spaced matching chairs across from his desk, everything in his office was just so. I approved and wished the other men would follow his example.

"Miss Figg, are you ready for Paris?" Captain Hall gestured toward a chair. "Please sit."

"Yes, sir." I sat, smoothing out my skirt. "I hope so, sir."

"I've heard a rumor about you." He opened a file folder. "I'd like to find out if it's true."

I couldn't imagine what kind of rumor he'd heard about me. It couldn't be the silly gossip from Ravenswick, could it? Blast it all. Had Clifford told him about my clandestine involvement in the murder case? I'd been sent to Ravenswick disguised as Dr. Vogel, a fictional physician pretending to be on holiday while I tracked the Great White Hunter. That is where I met Clifford, though he had no idea—and still has no idea—that Dr. Vogel and I are one and the same. While we were there a murder occurred. Captain Hall had expressly forbidden me from getting involved in the investigation. And I'd disobeyed orders... a necessity at the time. I suppose in a military outfit like this one, that meant court martial or at least the sack.

Eyelids tapping out some sort of Morse code, Captain Hall held up a sheet of paper. "This is a telegram we intercepted recently." He passed it to me. "Take a good look at it."

I took the paper and examined it. It was a combination of German words and numbers. I had no idea what it meant. "I'm sorry, sir." I glanced up at him. "I have no clue..."

He held out his hand. "Of course not." He wiggled his fingers, prompting me to return the telegram.

"Please have a seat at that table." He pointed to a small table in the corner. I did as I was told.

Carrying the file folder and several sheets of blank paper, he joined me at the table. He set a piece of blank paper in front of me and handed me a pencil. "Please transcribe the telegram."

Was this some kind of test? "May I see the telegram again?"

"No. Just write down what you remember." He nodded encouragingly.

Good heavens. Did he really expected me to reproduce a page of numbers and foreign words I'd only glanced at? Pencil in hand, I stared down at the sheet. Unfortunately, my mind was as blank as the page. I closed my eyes and tried to conjure the telegram. Numbers and letters began to appear before my mind's eye as if I were still looking at the document. With my eyes still closed, I put pencil to paper and sent my fingers moving on automatic. I opened my eyes and scrawled down everything I saw before the words and numbers disappeared.

"By God, it's true." Captain Hall looked over my shoulder. "I heard you have a photographic memory. Very impressive, Miss Figg." He chuckled. "Very impressive indeed." Eyelids fluttering, he rubbed his hands together. "A photographic memory could come in very handy. Yes, the War Office can make good use of you."

I didn't like the sound of the War Office *making use* of me. It gave the impression I was disposable. Too many young lives had been lost already in this bloody war. I was as patriotic as the next file clerk, but I didn't plan on dying because I'd memorized some German commander's laundry list.

"Besides trailing Fredricks, we may have another special assignment for you in Paris." Captain Hall paced the length of his office and then turned back to me. "If you succeed in this assignment, we will consider making you a permanent agent."

Now I was blinking. "What's my code name and cover this time?"

Captain Hall narrowed his brows. "No code name. No cover. You're Miss Fiona Figg, who has just lost her husband and is visiting her great-aunt in Paris." He handed me a slip of paper.

The reminder of what I'd lost was like a slap in the face. I touched my practically stinging cheek and then glanced at the paper. On it was written a name and address: Madame Bovary, 29 Rue Vernet. *Was this a joke?*

11

Madame Bovary, another clever woman from literature who had to die for her ambitions.

"Madame Bovary is one of our sleepers in France. She will be your contact." He cleared his throat. "We may be reassigning another agent to work with you. He will contact you if necessary and fill you in on the details."

"How will I know him?"

"I can't tell you any more yet. He will contact you when the time comes."

"Is my assignment still following Fredrick Fredricks?"

"For the time being, yes. But we may have something bigger for you too. In the meantime, you're simply Miss Figg, visiting your great-aunt."

"Fiona Figg visiting my great-aunt," I repeated. "Yes, sir."

"Under no circumstances are you to be anyone else. No silly costumes this time." His lashes were beating a mile a minute. "And don't call attention to yourself."

"No, sir." I shook my head. Back in my flat, my suitcase was already chocked full of clever disguises I'd bought at Angels Fancy Dress shop. *Would I have to return them or leave them behind?* I hoped my disappointment didn't show on my face.

"This mission could be dangerous." Captain Hall's voice cracked, which did not inspire confidence. "Can we count on you, Miss Figg?"

I nodded and swallowed my fear.

Chapter Two: The Javanese Princess

As I exited the Old Admiralty Building and strode toward Westminster station, a motorized lorry sped past, spraying my ankles with mud. I'd only made it two blocks when the sky opened up and dumped buckets. By the time I reached the station I was soaked through and must have looked a sight.

Was I the only person in London who'd forgotten her brolly?

A crush of commuters in damp overcoats exacerbated the oppressive smells of the train car. A squat man standing next to me allowed his umbrella to drip onto my shoes as he swayed to-and-fro munching on a biscuit. Why do men always think they have a right to drip on women's accessories? I held my arms out on either side of my body like two rigid planks in hopes he'd be forced to back off. It didn't work.

I got another dose of foul London weather walking the five blocks from the station to my flat. Summer rain squalls were the worst.

I wonder what the weather is like in Paris. My only other trip to Paris had been in April 1915, a two years after Andrew and I got married. He'd been sent on a business trip for Imperial and Foreign Corporation and took me along as a sort of second honeymoon. While he'd worked days, I'd visited every fashion house on *Rue de la Paix*—window shopping, mind, since Andrew didn't approve of my addiction to hats. Okay, I admit, I couldn't resist buying a delicious plum corduroy cloche with a golden silk sash and an ivory-tipped dagger of a hatpin.

Daydreaming about those divine Parisian nights spent dining, dancing… and doing other things… I walked right past the entrance to my flat and had to turn around. My marriage to Andrew had been the best—and the worst—part of my quarter century of life.

I dripped my way upstairs to my—previously our—second-floor flat. Anxious to finish packing and prepare for the trip, I wasn't paying attention and nearly slipped down the stairs. Luckily, I caught myself before I tumbled spout over teakettle. The last thing I needed was a broken leg... or worse.

Once inside the flat, I ran a hot bath and stripped off my wet clothes. First things first. *Ahhhh, lovely.* As I shut my eyes and melted into the warm water, for some inexplicable reason, I remembered Archie Somersby, a young soldier I'd met at the hospital the night Andrew died. I wasn't thinking of the letter we wrote together to his mother, not of the telegram he sent from South Africa telling me about Fredrick Fredrick's family, not even of that lock of wavy chestnut hair that so temptingly fell across his forehead. No, what I remembered was the warmth of his embrace as I cried myself to sleep. I'd never slept next to a man—other than Andrew, of course.

I stepped out of the bath and shook the memory from my mind. After all, it was inappropriate to crawl into hospital beds with shirtless soldiers, especially if your husband—ex-husband—just expired from mustard gas... even if the shirtless soldier was deuced handsome. Toweling off, I concentrated on my wardrobe instead of daydreaming about a soldier I'd never see again anyway.

All of my clothes were at least three years old, except for the dress I bought to wear to Andrew's funeral. Andrew once told me that soldiers risked their lives running into no-man's-land to retrieve silk parachutes for their sweethearts to make a new blouse or a fancy pair of knickers. I didn't have any Tommies pining after me and risking their lives for a piece of silk. And I hadn't purchased any new clothes since the war started... unless you counted the disguises from Angels Fancy Dress shop. But those were for business, not pleasure.

Captain Hall had forbidden me from wearing any "silly disguises." I packed them anyway. I mean, you never knew when a pair of men's trousers or a mustache would come in handy. It may not be the dark ages, but there were still plenty of places a respectable woman couldn't—or shouldn't—go on her own.

I stared into my wardrobe. None of my outfits were chic enough for Paris. *What are the latest fashions? Fiona, get a grip. You're not going to Paris on blooming holiday.* No, I was going to Paris to tail Fredricks to prove he was working for the Germans. I knew it, of course. But for some unfathomable reason, the War Office needed even more proof he was a traitor. So which of my outfits was most appropriate for trailing a German spy? Practicality won out over vanity, and I chose two skirt sets with matching blouses. There was a war on, after all.

Not knowing what I'd encounter on the night train to Paris, I decided on a plain ankle-length skirt with handy pockets and a striped sailor blouse with a red silk tie. I rolled up my stockings, polished my scuffed Balmoral boots the best I could, and laced them tightly. I packed my sturdy oxfords as backups. I may need to be quick on my feet, and my favorite Mary Janes just wouldn't do. Too bad I didn't buy those ridiculous new rubber lace-ups called "sneakers." In my new line of work, I might need to do some sneaking. Next trip to Liberty, I'd have to look for a pair.

I checked the insole of my oxford for Archie Somersby's telegram. *Balmy, I know, but that's where I keep it.* That telegram was my only memento of the handsome lieutenant. Just because I may never see him again didn't mean I had to forget him.

I rested against my wardrobe door, wishing I could bring some nice dresses and of course more hats. But my suitcase was full. *Ah well.* I leaned into my overflowing case and pushed the air out of the neat stack of clothes. *This will have to do.* With the sacrifices so many others were making, the least I could do was sacrifice my vanity. On impulse I snatched the corduroy plum cloche from the top shelf and tucked it under my arm. Who knows, maybe its six-inch hatpin would come in handy. I'd pricked myself on it enough times to know it was as sharp as a dagger.

With all the costumes taking up so much room in my luggage, I had to sit on my case to get it latched. So much for Captain Hall's insistence on no disguises. I smiled to myself. If he discovered I was gadding about Paris dressed as a dance-hall girl or parlor maid, that would really get his blinkers going.

Yet after my performance as Doctor Vogel at Ravenswick Abbey last month, I'd come to realize that I felt more comfortable as someone else. In any case, my hair still wasn't quite long enough for a finger wave, so a wig was an absolute necessity, even for the persona of Miss Fiona Figg. Luckily, since my last assignment, my assortment of wigs had become almost as extensive as my collection of hats.

Now which wig should I wear to chase the Great White Hunter, Fredrick Fredricks, across the continent? I never could find a wig to match my own auburn hair. The closest I'd come was too orange and too puffy, and it made me look like I was wearing a pumpkin pudding atop my head. I'd already packed my favorite, a strawberry-blond bobbed number... along with several extra hairpins, which I'd learned in my espionage course came in handy for picking locks.

Touching each of my four remaining wigs in turn, I settled on a lovely brunette hairpiece with soft curls around the face and a chignon on top. I tugged it into place and examined myself in my hand mirror. The effect was startling. For a moment, I saw my great-aunt Mable staring back at me. Mable was never considered a beauty and eventually joined a convent. Whatever happened, I vowed not to do the same.

I took one last look at the flat where Andrew and I had spent four happy years, before Nancy, the husband-stealing tart, came along. She was another reason to get out of town. I still dreaded running into the second Mrs. Cunningham. Seeing their baby, little Georgie, at Andrew's funeral had pulled at my heart, both out of pity for the poor little orphan, and because Andrew and I never were able to have a baby. If we had, maybe he wouldn't have left me. I suppose little Georgie was living proof my body and not Andrew's was defective in that regard.

Sigh. No matter. Brushing imaginary dirt from my hands, I turned my back on my life with Andrew and headed for the door. *Remember, old girl, what your body lacks in ability, you make up for in determination.* If I couldn't be a mother, I might as well be a spy. I strengthened my resolve to catch Fredricks in the act of espionage and prove myself to Captain Hall.

Without looking back, I picked up my suitcase and stepped out the door to my flat and into the hallway. Goodbye, London. Hello, Paris.

* * *

At Victoria station, the platform was crowded with men in khaki uniforms. The few women with their colorful coats and frocks stood out like daffodils and bluebells against the bombed out remains of a Zeppelin raid. I picked at the fingers of my gloves and waited for the train. To calm my nerves, I closed my eyes and took a deep breath, which I immediately regretted. The fetid smells of garbage mixed with unmentionable bodily fluids and coal smoke assaulted my nostrils.

A few minutes later, the South Eastern and Chatham Railway train screeched to a stop, and arriving passengers jostled against those waiting to get on. A large man with titanic cases in each hand pushed his way through the crowd. I had to jump backward to avoid getting run over. As I steadied myself and rearranged my skirt, I saw a familiar lanky form board a second-class car. *Blast! Not him. I thought he was taking an afternoon train. He'd blow my cover for sure.*

I shielded my eyes with my hand and peered at him from across the station. No doubt about it. Captain Clifford Douglas had just boarded my train. *Think, Fiona. Now what?* The overly eager captain would blow my cover for sure. It was too late to rifle through my luggage and get into one of my disguises. I'd have to avoid him at all costs.

The cost turned out to be exactly eighteen shillings and three pence, the price of upgrading to a first-class ticket, which, I must say, did considerable damage to my pocketbook. *I wonder if the War Office could give me an expense account?* At least if Clifford Douglas stayed put in second class, I wouldn't have to worry about running into him during the eight-hour trip. Still, I'd have to be especially careful when transferring to and from the ferry boat.

I'd never ridden in a first-class train car. Instead of uncomfortable bench seats, cushioned wicker chairs sat on either side of the carriage. I found myself in a long, narrow sitting room featuring wood paneling, chandeliers, and heavy curtains adorning cut-glass windows. A porter helped me with my suitcase, and I took a seat in the back corner next to a small table upon which sat a lovely little vase with three pink roses. They stood out against the darker burgundy carpet. All in all, a jolly agreeable room.

I'd barely removed my gloves when a waiter appeared with a glass of champagne. I took a sip. When I thought of all those going without, a pang of guilt chased away the pleasure of the moment. *Sigh.* Well, perhaps not entirely. I finished my drink and marveled at the furs and feathers of the first-class world. The disparity between the luxury of this world and the wartime scarcity of my everyday existence was like the difference between a scone with clotted cream and a margarine sandwich on stale bread.

The conductor came through and asked to see my ticket and my passport. I guess even the wealthy can't escape wartime security protocol.

My passport still had *Mrs. A. Cunningham* scrawled in blue ink across its cover. We'd been happily married when I got it, and seeing Mrs. A. Cunningham on an official document had made my heart soar. Now, it made my heart ache. My marriage was gone and so was Andrew.

After the conductor moved on, I leaned my head back against the upholstered headrest, clutching my passport as if my life depended on it. In spite of my excitement about the journey, the champagne combined with the train's rhythmic jostling and the late hour made it difficult to stay awake.

* * *

The uncanny sensation of a human presence nearby woke me up to find an elegant woman bending over to brush off her gorgeous beaded pump. When she saw me watching her, she slinked into a seat across from me and glanced around. Her catlike movements gave the impression she was stealing away from someone. She was dressed as if she'd just come from the opera, with a fur stole around her shoulders and a voluptuous velvet turban hat pinned to her raven locks.

I wrapped my cotton jacket more tightly around my chest to cover the inadequacy of my plain skirt and blouse.

When she glanced at me again, I realized I'd been staring and looked away, but not before she caught me with her mesmerizing cocoa eyes.

"Are you traveling to Paris?" I asked. Stupid question since it was a train to Paris.

"Yes," she said in an accent I didn't recognize. She draped her fur across the back of the seat.

"From London?"

She nodded with such grace you'd think she was on stage.

"Are you going home?"

"In a manner of speaking," she said, tugging one at a time at the fingers of her long gloves. She removed her gloves and laid them across her lap. "Don't *all women* who run away from their husbands go to Paris?"

Perhaps even this dark beauty was a wronged woman whose philandering husband had fallen into the arms of his secretary.

"Lady Gresha MacLeod." She held out her slim hand as if she expected me to kiss it. A jade ring on her index finger sparkled in the light.

Not another countess. My past experience with countesses was tragic.

"Fiona Smith," I said, disappointed at my lack of imagination. Hadn't Captain Hall told me not to use an alias? Only an hour into my assignment, and already I'd disobeyed a direct order.

"Pleased to meet you Miss Smith. Or is it Mrs.?" she asked with a mischievous grin. When she smiled she looked like a twenty-year old, but under all her make-up, I suspected she was well over thirty.

"I'm afraid *all women* pretty much sums me up." Truth be told, I too was running away to Paris to escape a husband, or at least the haunting memories of one.

She gave me a knowing nod, opened the velvet purse that was dangling from her wrist, and pulled out a bonbon wrapped in foil. "Would you like a chocolate?"

"You have chocolate?" I hadn't seen chocolate since before the war broke out.

"From one of my admirers." She held out her hand, the little gem sparkling in her palm.

"Thank you." I took the sweetie, picked open the wrapper, and popped it into my mouth. I closed my eyes and savored the dark, rich bit of heaven. What a treat. "The only thing an admirer ever gave me was a head cold."

Her laughter was as sweet as the chocolate.

"Do you have many admirers?" I asked, hoping her handbag was filled with more goodies.

"Now that you mention it…" she leaned closer and whispered. "There's my longtime *friend* Émile Guimet, who gave me my start at the Musée. He's very wealthy and spoils me. And the famous lawyer Édouard Clunet, perhaps you've heard of him? Or Louis Renault, the car manufacturer?"

I shook my head.

"Crown Prince William, you've heard of him, surely," she said with a twinkle in her eye, and unwrapped another bonbon. "I'm not one to kiss and tell, but boy could he kiss. Beyond that though, he's worthless." She popped the treat into her rosebud mouth.

I gaped at her like a schoolgirl hearing about the birds and the bees for the first time.

Even with her hand in front of her mouth, I could see she was amused at my naiveté.

"A beautiful girl like you must have many lovers too, *n'est-ce pas?*"

My face burned. I lowered my gaze but didn't answer. Andrew was the first and only. What was a virtue to others must seem silly to this worldly woman.

"No matter." She waved away the clouds of embarrassment. "All that will change when you arrive in Paris." She put her hand to her bejeweled bosom and sighed. "You haven't lived until you've sampled the delights of Paris."

The memory of Archie Somersby's bare chest ambushed me, followed by a wave of guilt. I twisted the wedding ring around my finger. Even though Andrew was dead—and had left me—I couldn't take it off. I guess that ring offered a kind of protection. "I expect with this horrid war, even the delights of Paris will be scarce."

"You'd be surprised what a resourceful woman can do." Lady MacLeod touched the pearl necklace around her throat.

"Many women feel all resources are best used to help the war effort," I said and immediately regretted my abrupt tone. But the lady's flippant attitude toward the war was grating. She obviously hadn't spent time in a military hospital tending to those poor broken boys.

"If anything, the war teaches us to savor the moment." She tightened the strings on her purse.

Maybe she had a point.

"Think of all those unfortunate women on the Titanic who waved away the dessert cart." She winked.

I burst out laughing. I had to admit, Lady Gresha MacLeod was a charming woman. I could see how men might find her irresistible. Her playful but forthright manner calmed me considerably as I embarked on the adventure of my life.

"What do you miss most from before the war?" she asked.

"Strawberries, lovely ripe strawberries." *I don't know why I said strawberries. Of all the things to miss.* "And lemons. I miss lemons and a cool glass of lemonade."

She pulled at her purse strings, and for a moment I thought maybe she was going to pull fresh produce from her handbag. "Sweet and sour," she said. "You're a woman of deep contrasts, a sign of intelligence. I think I'll call you Miss Lemons."

* * *

I stayed close to Lady MacLeod as we made our way onto the ferry boat. Again the first-class section was decked out like a posh lounge. If it weren't for the rocking, the fog horn, and the plume of smoke as we set sail, I wouldn't have known I was at sea. But as the journey progressed, the wind whipped up the waves, making it harder to ignore that I was on a boat. I didn't fancy boats. I never had. Even as a child, I hated the water. My father insisted I learned to swim, but I did my best to defy him and always managed to sink like a rock.

I gripped the arms of my seat and willed myself not to be seasick.

Lady MacLeod didn't seem bothered by the roiling seas. "Champagne," she said, giving me a look of pity. "Best cure for seasickness." She ordered a bottle of some fancy French bubbly and then forced me to drink it.

I really didn't trust putting anything into my mouth at the moment, but I obliged the lady by taking small sips until I'd finished the glass. *By golly, maybe she's right.* I did feel a bit better. She took the bottle out of the ice bucket and refilled my glass. I suspected this was a case where too much of the cure could be worse than the disease.

When Lady MacLeod noticed I hadn't touched the second glass, she asked, "May I?" and drank it herself. "I hate to waste good champagne."

I guess the war had made us all more frugal, even posh ladies like Gresha MacLeod.

Despite the lady's effective cure for seasickness, I was glad to soon be back on solid ground. Together, she and I disembarked the ferry and boarded the train for the final leg of the trip to Paris. I took the porter's outstretched hand for support, and took a big step up onto the train. As I did, I glanced down the platform. *Crikey.* I could swear I saw a man who looked exactly like Fredrick Fredricks. *Must the champagne going to my head.* Fredricks was already in Paris at the Grand Hotel.

Lady MacLeod and I settled into another wonderfully comfortable first-class compartment. She ordered more champagne, saying, "Nothing like the duo of champagne and a nice traveling companion to make a journey pleasant."

"Indeed," I agreed. I was falling under the charming lady's spell. But even she couldn't compete with my need for sleep. I kept nodding off, and eventually gave in. Sometime around dawn, I awoke to the clattering of a tea cart.

Out the window, the farms and forests we passed were bathed in a misty violet hue.

A waiter came round with the cart and offered tea and scones with real butter and thick-cut marmalade. I'd been eating stale margarine sandwiches for so long, I'd forgotten the pleasure of a warm scone slathered in butter and marmalade. Amazing how such a simple pleasure improved the quality of one's life. More amazing how the privileged few still enjoyed the simple pleasures while so many went without.

Lady MacLeod extended a delicate pinky finger and sipped her tea as gracefully as she did everything else. She reached into her handbag and pulled out a lipstick. A playbill came with it and tumbled onto the floor.

Across the top, it read "Mata Hari, Poetry in Motion," and across the bottom it said "Javanese Princess. Star of Dance." In between was the photograph of a dark beauty wearing an ornate copper breastplate, sheer silken veils, and not much else. The Javanese princess had a crown on her head that looked like some sort of bejeweled antler. *Did Lady Gresha MacLeod go in for that sort of thing?*

Good heavens. I nearly choked on my scone. I glanced from the photograph to the lady sitting across from me. They were one and the same. Lady Gresha MacLeod *was* Mata Hari. What a strange name. I'd seen it some place before. But where?

My cheeks burned and I turned away. I'd never considered myself a prude, but if stripping off their petticoats and dancing behind veils was what wealthy ladies did in Paris, I was glad I wasn't a lady, not an official one, anyway.

"Tickets and passports," the conductor called as he entered the train car.

I hauled my handbag out from under the little table. When I glanced up, Lady MacLeod had disappeared. I opened my purse and rummaged around for my passport.

"That's okay, miss, I remembers you," the conductor said. "I seen your passport and ticket when we set out last night."

I grimaced. I realized that was the last time I'd seen my passport and my ticket too. I looked around my seat. Nothing but crumbs from breakfast. When the conductor had passed through the car, I knelt down and felt around on the floor. *What happened to my passport?* It was nowhere to be seen.

I remembered showing it to the conductor shortly after we'd left London. Then I fell asleep and woke up when Lady MacLeod—aka Mata Hari—was brushing her shoe... *Blast it!* She wasn't brushing her shoe. She was picking up my passport. But why would Mata Hari steal my passport?

Chapter Three: Mrs. Douglas

As the distance between villages shortened, my heart quickened, anticipating our arrival in the City of Light. I'd searched the entire train car and no passport. I'd searched both first-class compartments and the dining car and no Mata Hari. Without my passport, the French authorities would send me straight back to London... either that, or lock me up.

My first international assignment and I'd already bungled it.

At the risk of running into Clifford Douglas, I steeled my nerves, steadied myself, and headed for the second-class cars. The first I entered was a sea of brown uniforms and weary faces all turned in my direction. I quickly scanned the car for Clifford's receding hairline and angular face. Perhaps there was a car reserved for officers. After all, he had been recently promoted to captain.

Fortifying myself to traverse the swaying train, I continued down the aisle. Unlike the first-class compartment, the second-class cars had rows of upholstered benches, which looked deuced uncomfortable for an overnight journey. Listen to me, already spoiled by seven hours in luxury.

The next car was much like the last. Uniforms, haggard men, and an occasional feather or bit of colorful felt on a woman's hat. But not the red velvet turban and contrasting raven locks of Lady MacLeod, aka Mata Hari. Could she have changed her hat? *Blast.* Perhaps she'd disembarked at the last stop. Again, I asked myself why would she want my passport? Given the extent of her travels, she must have one of her own. Didn't her wealthy paramours provide passports along with bonbons?

Even if she disrobed and gyrated in public, the idea that Lady Gresha MacLeod would take my passport was absurd. It must be somewhere under my seat or hiding in my handbag.

I did an about-face and marched back to the first-class car to search behind and under my seat yet again. If I didn't find it, when we arrived in Paris, I'd have to rush off the train and stake out the station. It shouldn't be too difficult to spot Lady MacLeod, gorgeous as a peacock, amongst all of the brown sparrows.

As we pulled into the station, a cloud of smoke enveloped the train and the wheels screeched bloody murder. Bracing myself against the side of the car, I was the first in line to exit. When the train jolted to a stop, I bounced off the wall and my suitcase smacked into a corpulent lady whose face was veiled.

"Apologies," I said, holding the handle of my case with both hands and trying to regain my balance.

When she grunted in response, I had the strange feeling I knew her from some place. I allowed her to depart ahead of me. She gripped the porter's hand as she took the stairs one at a time.

Once she was out of the way, refusing the porter's assistance I hurried off the train. I glanced around the platform looking for Lady MacLeod and my missing passport. Streams of brown uniforms flowed onto the platform. Other passengers pushed past me. Swarms of bodies buzzed all around me. Hissing and clanking from the trains drowned out the chorus of voices on the platform. Head spinning and disoriented, I tried to get my bearings.

Even at five foot seven, I wasn't tall enough to see over the heads of the soldiers surrounding me. My heart was pounding. The crowd was closing in on me. I'd never find Lady MacLeod now. My passport was a lost case. With pungent smelling bodies pressing again mine, all I could think about was getting outside into the fresh air.

At both exits, guards were checking passports and long lines had already formed. I would never get out of here unless I retrieved my passport. No matter which prince or colonel was her latest intrigue, Lady MacLeod would have to wait in line like everyone else. Surely, I'd be able to spot her red turban.

The crush of bodies and smoky station made it difficult to breathe. So far, the air in Paris was not much different from that in London. Foul and thick. Although, I had to admit the air was drier in France and the absence of fog made it just a bit less vile.

The weight of my suitcase was pulling my arm out of its socket. I wedged it between myself and the soldier next to me and tried to set it down.

"Would you like me to carry that for you, miss?" the soldier said, a smile on his ruddy face.

"How kind." Thank goodness for chivalry.

As we inched our way to the exit, we made small talk about his family back in Dorchester, and the food in Paris, and the heat of the station, anything but the war.

"You remind me of my mother," he said, moving another step closer to the exit.

That stopped me in my tracks… either from his melancholy tone or the comparison to a woman no doubt old enough to be *my* mother.

He must have noticed my puzzlement. "Your voice, I mean."

I nodded and snapped open my fan. For only nine in the morning, it was beastly hot. After a night of little sleep—even in first class—I desperately wanted a cool glass of lemonade and a bath. Of course, I hadn't seen a lemon since before the war. I wondered if any of Mata Hari's suitors gave her lemons. When I found her, I'd allow her to buy my silence with a tall glass of lemonade… and a chocolate covered biscuit… and a beef steak covered in sautéed mushrooms. My stomach growled.

We inched closer to the front of the line. Perhaps if I hid behind the kind Tommy carrying my case, I could sneak past the guard without a passport. *What else could I do?* The moment of truth was upon me. I glanced around the station for any hidden exits I might have missed. Nothing but a battalion of soldiers jostling to get outside, no doubt in order to sample the "delights of Paris."

"Next," the guard called out.

"After you," the Tommy said. He handed me back my case.

Heart racing, I searched my imagination for any possible story to explain my missing passport. My father always said, "You can't go wrong with the truth." Maybe he was right. After all, my passport was stolen.

As I approached the officer, I flashed my most innocent smile.

"Papers, madame." He held out his hand.

"I'm afraid my passport was stolen on the train."

He scowled. "No passport, no entry."

"But I must. You see—"

"I'm sorry, madame." He gestured toward all the others waiting. "Can you step aside please?"

"Certainly there must be something I can do. The embassy. Can I contact—"

He cut me off again. "Sorry, madame." He shook his head.

I was about to give up and step aside when a hand caught my elbow and a familiar voice exclaimed, "Fiona, is that you?"

I turned to see Clifford Douglas smiling down at me, his blue eyes bright. "I say, your hair." His face fell.

"You don't approve?" I patted the brunette bun on the top of my head.

"But you had such lovely auburn hair." He gave me a puzzled look.

"Please step aside," the officer said in French in a rather gruff tone.

A spark ignited in my brain. "But officer," I said, taking Clifford's arm. "This is my husband. He can vouch for me." I gazed into Clifford's eyes, trying to send him a secret signal with my brows. "Right, Clifford, dear. Tell the policeman how my passport was stolen on the train."

"Stolen," Clifford stammered. "Husband. Fiona, what are you on about."

I pulled him closer and kicked him in the shin.

"Ouch!" Clifford gave me his puppy dog look. "Why did you do that?"

"Clifford, dear," I said through my teeth. "We really must get to our hotel and freshen up. Please show the officer your passport so we can go." I shoved my suitcase toward him with my foot.

"Why yes, I see. Of course." Clifford fumbled with his passport and eventually managed to hand it to the officer.

"Lieutenant Clifford Douglas," the officer said, looking Clifford up and down. Luckily, Clifford was wearing his uniform.

"Actually it's Captain Douglas now," Clifford said beaming.

"Captain Douglas," the policeman repeated. "And this is Madame Douglas?"

"Yes," I said. "That's me." I discreetly kicked Clifford again for good measure.

"Yes, that's right," Clifford squeaked. "This is my wife, Miss Fiona Figg."

I kicked him again.

"Er, Mrs. Fiona Figg… Douglas, Mrs. Douglas, my wife. I mean, yes. This is my wife, er, Fiona Douglas."

I pointed at my suitcase and Clifford picked it up. He was still waffling on when the guard waved us through the gate.

Once outside the gate, I let go of his arm. "Thank you."

"Does this mean you've reconsidered?"

I grabbed my suitcase. "See you around."

"Steady on." Clifford caught my elbow. "Mrs. Douglas, I rather like the sound of that. What about you, old girl?"

"I'm sure Mrs. Douglas will be a very lucky woman, whoever she may be. But she won't be me."

"Why not?" His countenance darkened.

"Really, Clifford. Not again." I grasped the handle of my suitcase with both hands and did my best to carry it as I walked away.

"Let me," he said, taking my case. "What are you doing in Paris?"

"What were *you* doing on the midnight train? I thought you left yesterday afternoon."

"Bloody afternoon train left right on the dot." He blushed. "I missed it, you see, and had to take the overnight."

I should have known. Clifford had a peculiar sense of time. He always was a wee bit slower than most.

"You can walk me to the taxi stand, but then I really must be going." I was glad not to have to carry my heavy suitcase.

"But you haven't told me what you're doing here. I say, you weren't following me, were you?" he asked with a mischievous grin.

"Don't be daft."

"You were." His eyes lit up. "You were following me."

"Believe whatever you want." I waved for a hansom cab.

"Where are you going?"

"To visit my great-aunt… Mable."

"Where does Aunt Mable live?"

"On the Champs-Élysées near the *Arc de Triomphe*." My voice cracked. I didn't dare tell him I too was staying at the Grand Hotel. I knew that's where he was meeting Fredrick Fredricks.

"I say, that's where I'm headed too." He smiled. "You *are* following me!"

I smiled back. Let him think that if he wanted. It would be better than telling him the truth. If he knew I was working for British Intelligence as anything other than a filing clerk, he'd spill the beans. He wouldn't mean to, but he would. He was as loyal as a beagle, but as talkative as one too. I should know. Besides the famous literary detectives Sherlock Holmes and Auguste Dupin, my constant—and only—companion growing up was Bentley the beagle, who was as devoted as he was chatty. Always howling at every cricket or ant to cross our threshold.

"Do you fancy a cuppa?" I asked, hatching a plan to pump Clifford for information on why Fredricks was really in Paris. "I'm famished."

"What passes for tea in this city may turn you into a coffee drinker yet," he said, slinging his military-issue duffel bag over one shoulder and grabbing my suitcase. "I know just the place. Come on." He put a hand on the small of my back. "Ready for an adventure, old girl?"

"I was born ready," I said, wriggling away. That wasn't exactly true. I was a sickly only child, raised on barley bread and strict discipline.

It felt good to be off the train and out walking in this bustling city on the arm of a British officer, even if that officer reminded me of my pet beagle.

Once we walked a few blocks from the station, the smoke cleared and the sky was a brilliant blue, so different from the perpetually dull grays of London. Even the air felt lighter. And the world radiated an underlying vibrance I hadn't seen since before the war. Sure, the streets were filled with soldiers in uniform, but the French royal blue and scarlet were much cheerier than the drab English khaki.

When we turned a corner, Sacré-Coeur Basilica's brilliant stained-glass peeked out from under protective wooden braces. Charming boutiques, their windows crisscrossed with paper tape, were still inviting. And even heaps of sandbags around the bottom of *Monument de la défense de Saint-Quentin* couldn't diminish its grandeur.

"Here it is," Clifford said, pointing at a graceful steel archway. "Saint Quentin, the oldest open-air market in Paris."

The building looked like an elaborate cake with a layer of stone, and then one of brick, topped off by a crown of steel and glass.

Inside, natural light flowing in from all sides illuminated sparse rows of colorful fruits and vegetables, fish glistening with their watchful dead eyes, and fresh-cut flowers. I'd never seen such an abundance of vitality and delicious produce. Farmers in France must be doing better than those in England. I couldn't imagine what the market must be like when it was operating in full force. Spectacular.

I clapped my hands together. "Oh Clifford, it's marvelous."

"I knew you'd like it." He smiled from ear to ear. "Come on. You haven't lived until you've tasted Moroccan food."

No doubt before the war, Clifford and Fredricks had enjoyed riding camels and killing Barbary lions together in Morocco.

"Since Morocco became a French protectorate five years ago, Moroccan food in Paris is almost as good as in Marrakesh." Clifford led the way through the crowds in the market. "Fredricks and I hunted cats in Morocco."

"Barbary lions, no doubt." *Killing animals for sport is not very sporting if you ask me.*

"There's no animal Fredricks can't track. You know, once…" Clifford nattered on about the Great White Hunter all the way through the market.

Finally, after we passed by dozens of vendors and what seemed like a mile of bits and bobs, we landed at a corner stall with two small café tables.

"Here," Clifford said, dropping his duffel bag and my suitcase, and then pulling out one of the café chairs for me.

As I sat down, I inhaled the savory aromas of cinnamon and cardamom.

My mouth watered in anticipation. I hadn't had a good hot meal in ages... not since the fateful dinner at Ravenswick the night the countess died two weeks ago. I shuddered and pushed the bad memories from my mind.

The waiter told us they only had one dish on the menu today—something called trid—which was just as well since I had no idea what to order.

"Two orders of trid then," Clifford said. "And two teas please."

"What's trid?" I asked when the waiter left.

"We ate it daily on our hunts. It's kind of like toad-in-the-hole only with broth and meat poured over the bread instead of inside it."

I hoped it tasted better than it sounded.

The waiter delivered tea in glasses adorned with sprigs of mint instead of in cups with milk the way I usually took it. *Ouch.* The glass was too hot to hold. Perhaps Clifford was right, Paris would make a coffee drinker out of me yet.

A minute later, the waiter reappeared carrying two piping hot plates of soggy bread topped with dodgy chunks of meat. Even toad-in-the-hole was more attractive.

I picked up my fork and took a tiny bite. *Golly.* After a few seconds, an explosion went off on my tongue... cinnamon, ginger, and clove with hints of roses and lavender. Delicious. I tucked in to my plate with the appetite of a hungry Barbary lion.

"You know," Clifford said between bites. "Among Barbary monkeys, the fathers care for the babies while the mothers groom each other."

"Sounds like a sensible arrangement."

"I thought you'd approve."

"Wait." I dropped my fork. "Don't tell me we're eating monkey."

Clifford laughed. "Monkeys in Paris?"

I narrowed my eyes at him. "You and Fredricks didn't kill monkeys, did you?"

He shook his head.

For the next few minutes we ate in silence.

The stew was so scrummy, and I was so busy eating, I'd forgotten to grill Clifford about Fredricks. Since I planned to ditch Clifford at the hotel and then go undercover, this would be my last chance, so I'd better get to it. I decided on the direct approach.

"What's Fredricks doing in Paris?" I asked.

"I told you. He's working for that American newspaper." He smiled in a way that suggested there was more to it.

"And what else?"

"Well." He glanced around as if Fredricks might be sitting at the next table eavesdropping. "He's meeting his friend Zelle." The way he said *friend* suggested she was a very good friend. He leaned closer and whispered. "She's an exotic dancer. Her stage name is—"

"Wait. Let me guess..." *No. It couldn't be.* "Mata Hari?"

His face fell. "How'd you know?"

This was a very small world indeed. "Just a second," I said more to myself than to him. *That's where I'd seen the name.* "Room Forty has a file on her." I remembered filing it a few months ago. "Why would British Intelligence have a file on Mata Hari?"

"And you've seen it?" Clifford looked impressed. "What does it say?"

I bit my lip. I'd already said too much. Clifford was rubbing off on me. "I only filed it. I didn't look at it." That wasn't quite true. Mata Hari was such a strange name, I might have glanced through the file. But I didn't make much of it at the time. Now, if I could only recall what it said.

"Why not? I jolly would have."

"What do you take me for?" I said a bit too harshly. "A spy?"

The wheels of my brain were awhirl. Both Fredrick Fredricks and Mata Hari were persons of interest to British Intelligence. And they knew each other. But what did the fiendish Fredrick Fredricks have to do with the passport-stealing Mata Hari? Were they both spying for the Germans? I was determined to retrieve my passport and find out.

Chapter Four: The Telegrams

With Clifford's help, I disembarked from the hansom cab on the Avenue des Champs-Élysées a couple blocks away from the Grand Hotel. The grand boulevard was bustling with life. You would have never known there was a war on.

Clifford insisted on carrying my suitcase up to Aunt Mable's flat. Obviously, since Aunt Mable was a ruse, I couldn't allow that. Unfortunately, I had to get quite cross with him before he'd leave me on my own. I promised to have dinner with him Wednesday night across the street at *des Ambassadeurs*, provided he keep my presence in Paris a secret from the Great White Hunter. Clifford knew I didn't think highly of his friend, and we left it at that.

I ducked into a nearby café to wait until the coast was clear. After Clifford disappeared into the hotel, I dragged my suitcase up the boulevard and around the corner to Rue Vernet and the address Captain Hall had given me for my contact, Madame Bovary. I still chuckled at her code name. I hoped my contact didn't meet the same fate as her literary namesake, a painful death at her own hand by arsenic poisoning.

The pretty brick building at 29 Rue Vernet had an awning and a doorman. Wiping my brow with my handkerchief, I asked for Madame Bovary. The doorman gave me a strange look. "No one here by that name, Mademoiselle," he said in French.

I examined the slip of paper to make sure I had the right address. "Is this 29 Rue Vernet?" I was glad for Mrs. Boucher's French class at North London Collegiate School for girls.

"Yes." He nodded. "But no one by that name lives here."

Either the doorman was lying or Captain Hall had given me outdated information. Just in case she returned, I scribbled a note indicating I'd be at the Grand Hotel.

I had no choice but to lug my suitcase back to the café and wait. Now I had no idea how to get a hold of my contact. I was completely on my own.

Hot and sticky, I was dying for a lemonade, but I doubted that even in Paris such simple pleasures were on offer any more. I plopped into a café chair and fanned myself with my hat. Wearing a wig in this heat was blasted uncomfortable. I gulped the first glass of water the waitress brought and asked for another.

I would allow another half an hour to give Clifford enough time to check in, and then go to the hotel and get myself checked in and hidden away in my room before Clifford or Fredricks spotted me. I could pop into the washroom at the café and put on my clever disguise, but then I wouldn't be able to check into the hotel as Fiona Figg, or Fiona Smith, or any other woman for that matter. *Blast.* I should have made the reservation under another name.

After forty-five minutes sipping insipid tea, I settled my bill and headed for the hotel. It was deuced difficult to sneak anywhere dragging my heavy suitcase. I should have packed lighter. By the time I'd lugged the thing the three blocks to the hotel, I was drenched in sweat and my face was burning hot. I wasn't used to direct sunlight. In London, fog and smoke combined to provide a protective shield from our shared solar orb.

If I hadn't been so overheated and anxious, I could have enjoyed the wonders of the glorious Grand Hotel with its golden glow and jasmine scent. The clacking of the heels of my boots on the marble floor made me self-conscious, and I lightened my step as I gawked around. From the velvet curtains pulled back to reveal picture windows, to the plush carpet and carved banister of the grand staircase, the lobby of the hotel screamed opulence.

When I reached the registration desk, I dropped my suitcase and wiped my sleeve across my brow. *Whew. I made it.*

As he handed me my key, the grumpy hotel clerk gave me a disapproving look. I snatched up the key and blew my sticky hair out of my face. I glanced around, hoping someone could help me with my bag. My right arm had stretched an inch already from carrying the bloody thing around for the last hour.

"We're short staffed or I'd get someone to help you," the clerk said. "All the able-bodied boys are fighting and the girls up and get married and disappear. You just can't find reliable help anymore." He shook his head and sighed. "If you have any valuables, please leave them with me to put in the safe. I'm sorry to say, we've had some unfortunate incidents lately."

"Incidents?"

"A diamond ring was *misplaced* last night."

"Misplaced?"

He shrugged. "*Oui.*"

A luxury hotel with girls getting married and disappearing and stolen rings. What kind of establishment is this? I limped off carrying my suitcase.

Nonchalantly dragging the case up the stairs was an impossibility. I lugged it, bumping up one step at a time. *Is there no bloody lift in this hotel?* Thankfully, the stairs were carpeted or the thuds would have echoed through the cavernous lobby. A well-dressed couple held their noses in the air as they passed me on the grand staircase. *Come on, Fiona, old girl, get it together.* Rattling up the stairs like a locomotive was not the best way to be discreet.

"Madame, *Je peux vous aider?*" a baritone asked from the bottom of the stairs.

My hat had slid so far down my forehead, I could barely see out from under it. I turned to make out who was addressing me. The voice was familiar. *Bloody hell.*

Fredrick Fredricks, the last person I needed to see, or more accurately, to see me. He'd only met me once when Clifford tricked me into having dinner with the scoundrel after the Ravenswick scandal. But given that I nearly accused him of murder over our pudding, he probably hadn't forgotten me.

In his jodhpurs, tall boots, and loose white shirt, he looked ready for a hunting expedition. Long black curls poked out from under his slouch hat. I had to admit, he was a striking figure.

I kept my head down. *"Non, merci, monsieur,"* I squeaked in the highest range and best French accent I could muster—Fredricks had heard me speak before, but in the lower register I'd used for Dr. Vogel—and then hastened up the rest of the staircase as best I could. When I reached the landing, I glanced back, but the Great White Hunter had vanished into thin air. Hopefully, he didn't recognize me.

Once I was safely hidden away in my room, I hurriedly disrobed. Dropping my sweat-drenched clothes on the floor, I ran a bath. Never in my life was I so happy to see a warm bath. What a luxury, a hotel room with a private bath. I shivered with anticipation as I dipped my toe into the... COLD bath water. *Blimey.* It seemed even the Grand Hotel had to make wartime sacrifices. Why couldn't they have given up butter or beef instead of hot water? I shivered exiting the bath too... only now it was from freezing to death.

A towel wrapped around my torso, I set about remedying the catastrophe that was my hair. Without my wig, I looked like a hedgehog with spikes of striped hair sticking straight up. The roots were my natural auburn and the ends were jet-black from my last— or should I say, first—assignment as Dr. Vogel. Luckily, I'd packed a coal-tar hair dye to initiate the transformation into my newest persona.

Leaning over the sink in the lavatory, I applied the thick paste. Waiting for it to take hold, I thought of its inventor, the English chemist William Perkin, who intended to extract the malaria drug quinine from coal tar. Instead he created the color mauve. I was aiming for a nice chestnut brown. Hopefully I wouldn't have to settle for mauve... although I did have a lovely mauve frock with white lace trim back at home.

My eyes burned from the fumes, and I rejoiced when the time came to wash the foul smelling stuff from my hair. After rinsing half a dozen times with cold water, my scalp was numb. I rubbed it vigorously with a towel and then went to the dressing table to inspect the results in my hand mirror. I moved a lamp closer to get a better look. *Good heavens. Don't they ever dust in this hotel?* There was a circle where the lamp had sat. Warm water obviously wasn't the only wartime sacrifice.

I wiped the table with my towel and then braved the hand mirror. Now, instead of a hedgehog, I looked like a drowned rat. I applied a dab of brilliantine and combed my short hair straight back from my forehead. Like magic, the spitting image of my uncle Frank appeared in the mirror.

All I needed now was to paste on the bushy eyebrows and toothbrush mustache—oh, and my favorite, the plain-glass wire-rimmed spectacles—to complete the transformation. As much as I hated the dreaded spirit gum with its offensive turpentine stench smeared right under my sensitive nose, I had to admit, in the end, I made a passable young man.

I opened my case and pulled out the clever disguise I'd selected especially for the Grand Hotel. I bound my chest with a wrap bandage—not that there was much to worry about in that department—and then slipped into new underclothing *sans* corset. The pants hung off my narrow hips and I had to cinch up my belt to keep them on. My boots were two sizes too big, but I wore extra thick socks and stuffed the toes with tissue paper. The collared shirt and short-cut double-breasted jacket finished my ensemble, except for the crowning feature, a porter's purple pillbox hat. I tapped the hat onto my brilliantined head.

Voilà. Harold the helpful bellboy was born.

I'd gone from plain old Fiona Figg to a porter at the Grand Hotel, who happened to resemble Charlie Chaplin's Little Tramp... either that or an overgrown organ grinder's monkey. In any case, no one would recognize me in this *getup*—as Captain Hall called my disguises. Now I just had to work on lowering my voice an octave. As I'd recently learned on my assignment at Ravenswick Abbey, I had quite a range when necessary.

Since I wasn't really a porter at the Grand Hotel, the next step was to nick a key to Fredrick Fredrick's room, wait until he was out, and then search for clues. *What is the real reason the huntsman cum journalist is in Paris?* I was going to find out. Mr. Knox had his doubts, and Clifford all but worshiped him, but I knew the blackguard was a German spy. And I planned to prove it to him and everyone else. After I retrieved some dirt on Fredricks, there was still the little matter of my passport and the devious Lady MacLeod, aka Mata Hari.

I peeked out my door. After glancing both ways down the hall, I stepped out into my new role as Harold the bellboy. Tugging on the bottom of my tight-fitting jacket, I strode toward the staircase. Relieved of my heavy case, and wearing trousers and practical men's boots, I was confident I could conquer the monster staircase. On the second flight I made the mistake of gawking around the grand lobby. Two-sizes-too-large boots can be a tripping hazard. I gripped the banister and caught myself before I went tumbling down spout over tea kettle.

I'd just reached the bottom, very proud of myself too, when the pinched-faced clerk shouted from behind the registration desk, "*Garçon, garçon*," in my general direction.

I twisted my head to see who he was shouting at.

"Come here at once," he said in French, staring right at me.

"Me?" I put my finger to my bound chest.

"Who else?" He shook his head.

I trotted over to the desk, trying not to trip over the long toes of my boots. "Yes, sir." I stood at attention.

"Take those cases up to Lady MacLeod's penthouse," he said, pointing to two huge trunks.

My eyes widened. "*Oui, monsieur.*"

So Lady MacLeod was staying at the Grand Hotel too, in a penthouse no less. She must have some fancy sugar daddy in Paris to set her up at the top of one of the poshest hotels in the city.

Turning circles around the lobby, I searched for the bell stand in hopes of finding a cart or a dolly for the giant cases. Lady MacLeod's mammoth trunks made my heavy suitcase seem like a handbag.

"Boy, what are you doing?" The hotel clerk growled. "Get those cases up to Lady MacLeod on the double or I'll dock your pay." That wasn't much of a threat since I wasn't actually on the payroll.

I quickened my pace, and, to my great relief, stumbled upon the bell stand, behind which was a luggage cart on wheels. I gasped. *Good heavens!* A bearded man lurking under the stairs was leering at me. He smiled and tipped his hat, revealing his bald pate. I gave a weak smile in return and continued on my mission.

I had a devil of a time holding the cart still while I heaved the trunks aboard. Finally, when both cases were balanced precariously on either edge of the cart, I carefully pushed the unwieldy monster toward the lift. *I wish I'd used this lift when Fredricks saw me thudding up the staircase like an African elephant.*

Maneuvering the trunk-laden cart through the small lift doors was a feat of engineering. I almost got the blasted thing inside, but couldn't get the door shut because the corner of one of the trunks was in the way. I pushed on it. Stubborn thing wouldn't budge. Leaning against the wall of the lift for leverage, I used my foot to apply pressure. One foot wasn't enough. I stepped up onto the edge of the trunk with both feet and pushed. *Bang.* I landed on my bum on the floor. But at least it had worked.

Brushing myself off, I got up and closed the lift gate. Now which button for the penthouse? The top button was marked *A. For attique? L'auvent? L'appartement au dernier étage?* I ran through the translations for *penthouse* in French. I pressed the button. My mustache twitched with excitement, and I pressed on it to make sure the dodgy thing wasn't coming detached.

I'd never been inside a penthouse. But as the lift arrived on the top floor, my eagerness turned into anxiety. If Lady MacLeod recognized me, the jig would be up. I just had to hope for the best.

Putting my weight into it, I pushed the luggage cart out of the lift and across the foyer to the door of the penthouse. I adjusted my cap, tugged on the hem of my jacket, and knocked.

"Just a minute," a familiar melodious voice said. "Who is it?"

"Porter, ma'am." My voice cracked. "With your trunks."

When Lady MacLeod swung the door open, my cheeks caught fire. She was striking in a sheer black negligee, black satin slippers, and a red silk headband wrapped around her jet-black hair. A web of light from the windows behind her created the eerie effect of a black widow spider stalking a defenseless fly.

"Set them in there." She pointed across the spacious sitting room toward a set of French doors. "In the bedroom."

Leaning into the luggage cart, I pushed it across the thick carpet, admiring the striped satin upholstery on the chairs and sofa as I went.

"Put them up against that wall." She pushed opened the French doors and then followed me into the bedroom. "My lady's maid is off today." She smiled and struck a suggestive pose. "Might you be a dear and unpack them for me?" She seductively stroked the sash on her robe. "I'll make it worth your while."

"Yes, ma'am." I stared at my oversized boots. Certainly she couldn't mean what I thought she did. *Really.* Princes and officers were one thing, but bellboys too? Where did she draw the line? Newspaper boys?

"Wonderful," she purred and sashayed from the room.

Now was my chance. I could look for my passport as I unpacked the trunks. While I lifted chiffon veils, velvet turbans, and silky evening gowns from the first trunk, I tried to recall the Room 40 file on Mata Hari. After laying out all the gorgeous pieces from the first trunk on the gigantic bed, I listened for movement from the other room. Ear cocked, I overheard Lady MacLeod talking on the telephone. I moved closer and hid behind the French door, which was slightly ajar, to eavesdrop.

"What time does your wife go to play bridge this evening?" Lady MacLeod giggled. "When the cat's away…"

Of course, under ordinary circumstances, I would never dream of eavesdropping—almost never. But I made exceptions for thieves and husband-stealing tarts… not to mention matters of national security.

Speaking of husband-stealing tarts, the memory of Andrew in the arms of his secretary attacked unbidden. My hand flew to my heart. *Why did it still sting so much?* The brass buttons down the front of my jacket reminded me of the task at hand. I was Harold the bellboy and not sappy Fiona Figg, the jilted wife. I tucked my feelings away and slowly backed away from the door. I had best take advantage of Mata Hari's diverting telephone call to look for my passport. Rushing to one of the night tables, I began my search.

Keeping my ears open, I systematically examined the contents of the small drawer of the night table. Cigarettes, perfume, mineral oil, a sleeping mask, but no passport. I dashed around to the other side of the bed and checked the drawer of the second night table. Cigars, a silk sash, and more mineral oil. Obviously, the lady worked hard for her keep.

An overnight case sat on top of the nightstand. Glancing around to make sure Mata Hari was still home-wrecking in the other room, I snapped open the clasp.

Aha! A piece of paper... though not my passport. The corner of a telegram was sticking out of a pocket on the inside lid of the case.

I slipped it out and carefully unfolded it. *Golly.* A telegram in German. Why would Mata Hari have a German telegram? My pulse quickened. Already, I had something to report to Captain Hall. *See, my disguises came in ruddy handy.* I took a mental picture and refolded the paper. Underneath was another folded paper. Another telegram? This one was blue... and in French.

My French was better than my German, which wasn't saying much since my German was nonexistent. *"Vos informations sont inutiles."* Your information is useless... or was it useful? I committed it to memory for future re-examination and chastised myself for not paying more attention in my French classes at North London Collegiate School. Luckily, I seemed to pick up languages fairly quickly. My drama teacher, Mrs. Benson, always said I had "an ear," which she hoped might compensate for my lack of much else.

I continued my search through Mata Hari's overnight case. The contents included a pot of rouge and blotting papers, a jar of kohl, face powder, and a small tin of something called *Lash-Brow-Ine.* Curious, I turned the tiny tin over in my palm. *Maybell Laboratories.* Whatever it was worked so well for Mata Hari, I made a mental note to purchase some for myself.

"Boy, what do you think you're doing?"

Blimey! I dropped the tin back into the case, snapped it shut, and stepped away from the nightstand. Wiping my sweating palms on the seat of my trousers, I waited for my defenestration.

Chapter Five: The Invoice

Mata Hari had accused me of being a thief, and then blustered around the suite threatening to report me and get me sacked. I'd hightailed it out of there before she could do anything worse. Although the hotel couldn't fire me because technically I didn't work here, they could boot me out or blow my cover. And then how would I find out what Fredrick Fredricks was doing in Paris? Hopefully Mata Hari's bark was worse than her bite. *Blast.* Now I'd have to alter my disguise. I'll run out of costumes at this rate.

I hurried back to my room to write down the contents of the telegrams while they were fresh in my mind. I needed to get word to Captain Hall as soon as possible tomorrow when the embassy opened. It was already closed today. And Captain Hall had instructed me to use the embassy telephone to call him when I had news. Wouldn't he be pleased if I routed out two spies instead of just one?

Back in my room I resisted the urge to tear off the horrid mustache, which itched something terrible. Sitting at the small corner desk, I took up paper and pen. I closed my eyes and allowed the contents of the German telegram to appear before my mind's eye. Closing my eyes just made me realize how knackered I was. After the overnight train trip, sightseeing with Clifford, missing Madame Bovary, transforming myself into Harold the helpful bellboy, and then finding these telegrams in Mata Hari's penthouse, I'd had quite a day.

Concentrate, Fiona. You've got to get the telegrams down on paper while they're still fresh in your mind.

I could see the telegram paper and the words, even though I didn't know what they meant. I reproduced it one letter at a time. *"Mata, meine geliebte, ich vermisse dich. Mein Bett ist kalt ohne dich. Heinrich."* If only Mr. Knox were here to translate for me.

In spite of my exhaustion, I retrieved my Cassell's German-English dictionary from my suitcase and thumbed through the Bs. *Bett* meant bed. Then the Ks. *Kalt* meant cold. *Geliebte* meant beloved. And *vermisse* meant miss. As best as I could make out, the telegram read something like, "Mata, my beloved, I miss you. My bed is cold without you." Could it be some kind of code? Or was it just a note from one of her lovers?

I glanced at my watch. No wonder I was so tired. I'd been awake for almost forty hours. As much as I wanted to get to the bottom of Mata Hari's telegrams, I was desperate to sleep. It was all I could do to remove my mustache and fall into bed.

* * *

The next morning, even before dressing, I took up pen and paper and went back to Mata Hari's telegrams. My transcription of the French telegram was interrupted by a knock at the door. *Good heavens. Who could that be?*

I patted by pajama front to remind myself of my identity and adjusted my voice accordingly. "Who is it?"

"Le femme de chambre," a tiny voice answered.

"Plus tard, si'l vous plait," later, please, I called back. If she was the one dusting—or should I say *not* dusting—my room, it wouldn't matter when she came back.

Her voice was a reminder that I'd best get dressed and circulate through the hotel looking for Fredricks before the grumpy clerk caught on and tossed me out on my ear. After all, the War Office sent me to follow Fredrick Fredricks and not Mata Hari.

To be safe, I visited my recently acquired mustache tray. Fingers twitching, I examined my caterpillar collection and exchanged my toothbrush model for a thin pencil number in a slightly lighter shade of brown. I found some matching eyebrows, and, gritting my teeth, I pulled off the old and replaced them with new lighter brows. I really should learn not to sleep in my eyebrows. I traded my wire-rimmed eyeglasses for a sturdier pair. I was tempted to do without, but I couldn't risk Clifford Douglas or Fredrick Fredricks recognizing me. While my brown eyes weren't exactly distinctive, they were mine.

First things first. I needed to find out which room was Fredricks's.

After rechecking my disguise from head to toe, I headed for the hotel lobby, where I planned to stake out the registration desk until I saw Fredricks leave or retrieve his key. *Who knows?* He might even need assistance with his luggage. *Can I hide behind the stairs and only come out when I saw Fredricks? Will the grumpy clerk see me lurking and ask me to help someone else? How will I find Fredricks and avoid the clerk?*

In the hallway, before I'd even reached the stairs, a young maid blocked my path with her cart. She batted her eyelashes at me.

"*Avez-vous une cigarette?*" she asked with a mischievous smile.

"*No, je suis désolé, je ne fume pas.*" I was surprised the hotel management would allow her to wear that much makeup. Her plump cheeks were painted with rogue and her eyes dark with kohl. And certainly she wasn't allowed to smoke on the job. Smoking was not an attractive activity for a man or a woman.

"You're new here aren't you?" she asked in broken English, her hands on her hips. "Where you from?"

Is my French that bad? I suppose my accent was obvious.

"Wales," I lied. Not that it mattered.

"Cutie, would you like meet me later?" She slid around the side of her cart and sidled up to me.

I took a step backward and landed up against the wall.

She giggled and stroked my face. "Soft like baby bottom." She put her arms around my neck. "I love you." She'd obviously practiced that English phrase.

Good heavens. I pressed myself against the wall. Were all French girls this forward? No wonder our Tommies raved about their leaves in Paris. It was

45

a wonder they didn't all come back with the French disease.

"Excuse me, mademoiselle, but I must get to work." I slipped out of her grip.

"Want hanky panky *avec moi?*" She toyed with the heart-shaped locket around her neck.

At that, I nearly broke into a run.

"My name's Berthe," she called after me. "What's yours?"

I hurried through the hall and galloped down the stairs. Beads of sweat formed on my forehead. From the exertion in this heat? Or my genuine fear of the stocky young maid? I didn't know.

I took a few deep breaths and from the landing scanned the bustling lobby below. Ladies with parasols at the ready whirled in and out of the revolving door. In clumps of brown and blue, soldiers smoked cigarettes and laughed. Smoking aside, it was heartening to see them enjoying themselves for a change.

On the lookout for Fredricks, I drifted into the stream of visitors and took a turn around the lobby. The same bald-headed, bearded man wearing a bow tie caught my eye. Why was he always lurking around the lobby? Was he a guest? Something about him gave me the creeps. I quickened my pace.

My boots glided across the marble floors as I scoped the scene, looking for my prey. Half a revolution yielded results. I stopped in my tracks behind a potted fern. Clifford was nattering on about some hunting trip while Fredricks smoked a fat cigar and none other than Lady Gresha MacLeod, aka Mata Hari, smiled seductively, giving the men her rapt attention. I ducked behind a grand column and cocked my ears.

Clifford was describing some ghastly safari he and Fredricks had gone on in Africa. Mata was glowing, and at one point in the story put her hand on Clifford's shoulder. Clifford blushed and smiled, obviously enjoying the attentions of the renowned beauty. Frankly, the whole scene turned my stomach. No doubt, Clifford would be down on one knee at any minute.

"Garçon," a rough voice came from behind me. "Get back to work."

I turned to face the surly hotel clerk, M. Jacques according to his nametag. He glowered at me, and I straightened up and stood at attention.

"Go to the break room and fetch that good-for-nothing Berthe and tell her to clean the penthouse at once. The lady wants it cleaned while she's out."

I stood there blinking like an idiot. I didn't know where to find the break room and I didn't fancy another encounter with Berthe.

"Well?" The clerk clicked his heels together. "What are you waiting for, world peace?"

"Yes, sir," I said, snapping out of it. "I mean, no, sir." I took off in the direction of the registration desk, hoping the break room was nearby.

"Where are you going?" The clerk tugged on the back of my jacket and nearly pulled me over. "I said the break room, you idiot." He pointed to an alcove behind the grand staircase.

If I weren't undercover, I would have given him a piece of my mind. Instead, I adjusted my jacket and scurried away.

The break room was more like a closet under the stairs. Unlike the rest of the hotel, it was dark and dank. Berthe was sitting with two other young women in maid's uniforms. All three were smoking like chimneys while they giggled and pointed at a magazine laying in the middle of a rickety wooden table. I approached the trio like a hare entering a coyote den.

"Say, Cutie." Berthe looked up at me. "Would you ever put an advert in a magazine to find a girl?" She pointed at the magazine.

I moved closer and peered down at a full page of notices in *Le Journal*. One circled in red caught my eye, and I picked up the magazine. "Widowed businessman seeking wife to join him in the pretty colony of Tunisia."

"You girls don't plan to answer this ad, do you?" I asked. I knew men were scarce due to the war, but still, answering ads in the lonely-hearts section of a magazine seemed extreme.

"Why not?" Berthe said. "Better than cleaning up other people's messes for the rest of our lives."

"Tunisia, how romantic," a freckle-faced redhead said with a sigh. I recognized her voice. She was the parlor maid who'd knocked on my hotel room door earlier. The one who didn't know how to dust properly.

"If you fancy malaria and sunstroke," I said.

The girls gave me a queer look and then burst out laughing.

"Actually, we already did," Berthe said. "We're both meeting him and then we're going to see who he picks to marry."

"I have more to offer," said the redhead. "He'll pick me. I'll make sure of it."

"I have a lot to offer too," Berthe said with a wink. "Right, Cutie?"

I knew better than to step on that landmine.

"Look at this," the redheaded girl said, holding up a second magazine called *La Vie Parisienne*. "Advice on what to wear in an air-raid shelter."

"What a cute skirt," Berthe cooed.

I peered over her shoulder at the magazine. "And that hat is lovely."

The redhead furrowed her brows. "So you go in for ladies hats? Maybe play dress up at home?"

Crikey. That's right. I'm supposed to be Harold the bellboy. "I appreciate a nice hat, that's all. I just meant it would look lovely on Berthe."

The girls giggled. The phrase *thick as thieves* came to mind.

"Berthe, I came to tell you, Mr. Jacques wants you to clean the penthouse right away." I clicked my heels together, imitating the grumpy old clerk.

Berthe blew out a series of smoke rings and then crushed the rest of her cigarette into a saucer. "Cutie, wanna help me make the bed?" She twisted a lock of hair around her index finger.

My heavens, she was a saucy thing.

It occurred to me that she could get me into Fredricks's room. *But could she be trusted?* Probably not. Anyway, at this point, I was afraid to be alone in a room with her.

By the time I disentangled myself from Berthe and returned to the lobby, Mata Hari was sitting at a café table near the large front windows chatting up a distinguished older gentleman, her gloved-hand placed not-so-discreetly on his knee. The bounder probably had a wife and a dozen grandchildren at home. His besotted countenance said it all. *Men. If geese can mate for life, why can't we?*

Fredricks and Clifford had vanished. If only I knew Fredricks's room number, then I could take advantage of his disappearance to search his room.

And I can try out my newly acquired lock-picking skills. My two weeks crash course at the War Office just might come in handy. I patted my hair where I kept an extra pin for just that purpose. As I took another turn around the lobby, I pondered how I might find out. A neatly folded newspaper laying abandoned on a bench gave me an idea. I picked up the paper and headed for the registration desk, hoping the cranky old clerk had gone home.

No such luck.

"What are you doing loitering, boy?" The clerk glared at me over his pince-nez. "Don't you have work to do?"

"Yes, sir." I held up the newspaper. "Mr. Fredricks asked me to deliver this paper to his room. But he didn't tell me the number."

"And you didn't ask." The clerk shook his head. "Stupid boy." He did an about-face and examined the key cupboard. "Room three-five-nine. But first, there is a cart full of luggage waiting for delivery. Take care of that luggage and then get Mr. Fredricks's paper. Now get going. No dillydallying, you hear?"

"Yes, sir." I left the bad-humored clerk and went to find the luggage cart. It was laden with cases. Geez. This could take me an hour. I examined the room numbers and made haste to deliver the bags so I could get into Fredricks's room before he returned.

After I delivered the cases, I bounded up the stairs. I knew the room number, but how was I going to get inside? I could either try my hand at lock-picking or cajole Berthe into using her passkey. Since my linguistic creativity outstripped my mechanical abilities, I ducked into the lift and pushed the button for the penthouse. Hopefully, I'd find Berthe still cleaning Mata Hari's suite. Maybe I could convince the little flirt to let me in.

Outside the suite, I put my ear to the door. I heard shuffling inside. It couldn't be Mata Hari back already from her assignation with the distinguished gentleman, could it? I took a deep breath and knocked. The rustling inside the room stopped and all went quiet. I knocked again. Nothing.

"Berthe?" I knocked louder. "Open the door, it's..."

I realized Berthe didn't know my name. She just called me "Cutie." I wasn't about to say, "open up, it's Cutie." For a smart woman, I really didn't think things through.

"Berthe, are you in there?" I knocked again. "It's Harold, the bellboy."

Horsefeathers. Either she wasn't there or she wasn't answering the door.

Perhaps I'd imagined noise coming from inside the room. Maybe the sounds were from downstairs or outside. I listened again. Nothing.

I was on my own. At least I wouldn't have to fight off Berthe's advances. As I turned to go, the door to the penthouse opened a crack and a little nose peeked out. I pressed myself up against the wall and waited.

The freckle-faced chambermaid who'd been giggling over the lonely-hearts column darted out of the room, tore across the foyer, and disappeared behind a door marked *Sortie,* exit. *My word, why is she in such a hurry?* Apparently, so much so, she didn't notice me. Perhaps my red-and-blue uniform blended into the foyer's Chinese wallpaper with its crimson flowers, cobalt petals, and colorful rare birds. Or maybe she just had bad peripheral vision.

I heard noises again. This time coming from the lift. Blast. I frantically glanced around for a place to hide. The foyer was small and exposed. Besides the lift and the door to the penthouse, the only other way out was the door marked Sortie. I dashed across the foyer, opened the exit door, and quickly slid behind it onto the stairwell landing.

The elevator door opened.

Holding my breath, I quickly shut the exit door, all but a crack. Hiding in the stairwell, I peeked out into the foyer and listened.

Mata Hari floated out of the lift. She turned back, talking to a man and pulling him by the hand. I stifled a gasp when I saw the chunky gold ring on his pinky finger.

Instead of the distinguished old gentleman from the lobby, the Great White Hunter emerged from the lift. Wearing an open-collared sheer white shirt, his broad chest was on display. As usual, his pencil mustache was waxed to perfection and so were his knee-high black boots. *Why was he always dressed as if he were tracking lions in the bush?* He carried his swagger stick and slouch hat in one hand and let Mata Hari lead him into her suite with the other. He was tracking a feline all right, but one more dangerous than any he'd find in the South African bush.

What was Fredrick Fredricks doing with Mata Hari? Perhaps they were both German spies. The way they were touching and carrying on, I suspected they were exchanging a great deal more than information. At least I knew Fredricks would be occupied for the foreseeable future and it would be safe to visit his room.

I didn't dare use the lift for fear they would hear me. I'd have to tackle the six flights down to the third floor, which was no easy feat in my oversized boots.

The stairwell was stuffy and hot. By the time I pecked my way down and exited on the third floor, I was drenched in perspiration. Not very ladylike, I know, but wearing men's full kit in summer almost made me miss my corset. At least skirts allowed for airflow.

I peeked my head out the door to the hallway before exiting the stairwell. The hall was empty except for a maid's cart at the other end. I quickly ascertained the direction to room three-five-nine and hurried down the hall.

Standing in front of Fredrick's room, newspaper tucked under my arm, I gently gripped the door handle. Just as I suspected. Locked. Removing a hairpin from my hat—yes, even as a man, I used hairpins to keep my hat in place—I inserted it in the keyhole.

I thought of Sherlock Holmes in the Whitechapel murders. Using the ruse of shortness of breath, Sherlock summoned Dr. Watson, who blocked the view of possible onlookers while the sleuth unwrapped his picklocks and set to work picking the lock, left-handed no less. As a kid, I'd hole up for hours reading those Sherlock Holmes stories.

Unfortunately, unlike my literary hero, I had no lock-picking set to unwrap. And I had no Dr. Watson. But I did have my feminine ingenuity and a sturdy hairpin, not to mention a two-week crash course in espionage from the War Office.

"What the devil…" I let loose an expletive and whirled around to face Berthe, who'd just tickled me on the back of the neck. I must have been concentrating so hard on the lock, she crept up on me.

She laughed. "Cutie, you've gone red in the face." She curled a lock of hair around her little finger.

"What do you think you're doing sneaking up on me like that?" I tugged at the bottom of my jacket. "You could have given me a heart attack."

"What are you doing breaking into Mr. Fredricks's room?" She smiled like a badger who'd caught an ant in a honey pot.

"I'm delivering his newspaper." I straightened my cap.

"With a lady's hairpin?" She snatched the hairpin out of my hand and waved it over her head. "Who's the other lady?" She pouted. "Can't I be your *petite amie?*" She fingered one of the brass buttons on my jacket. "Don't you like me?"

"Of course, I like you." I stiffened and pressed myself up against the door.

She smiled and touched my cheek. I'd never met such a forward girl in all my life.

"Would you like to help me deliver this newspaper to Mr. Fredricks?" I held up the paper to shield my face.

"*Bien sûr*, Cutie." She pulled a large key from the dozens hanging from the belt around her thick waist and opened the door.

Now how was I going to get rid of her?

"Mr. Fredricks asked me to find his cigars and bring them to him." I smiled to myself, chuffed at my quick thinking.

"I'll help." Berthe stuck close by my side.

"Don't you have to clean the penthouse?" I tried to shake her loose.

"I already did. I'm the only housekeeper allowed inside." She said holding her snub nose in the air.

Interesting. No wonder that redhead was coming out of the penthouse in such a hurry. Whatever she had been doing in Mata Hari's penthouse, it wasn't dusting. I'd have to worry about her later. For now, I had to distract Berthe so I could search Fredricks's room.

"Mr. Fredricks also asked me to find his briefcase." *Why did I say briefcase? Now how would I justify looking in all the drawers? Fiona, sometimes you're such an idiot.* I glanced around the immaculate room wondering where to look first. It would help to know what I was looking for. "Why don't you find his cigars." *What sort of evidence would prove he is working for the Germans? A telegram in German from Kaiser Wilhelm?*

I watched Berthe out of the corner of my eye while I searched the drawers of the dresser. Fredricks's clothes—one pair of men's underpants, one pair of socks, and one undershirt—were folded with military precision. Nothing was out of order. Where would he hide secret documents? And where were the rest of his clothes? I lifted the corner of the mattress.

"Whatcha doing?" Berthe asked. "No one keeps their briefcase under the mattress."

"Right. Mr. Fredricks said he's missing a gold ring." I remembered the gold ring he wore on his pinky, the one with the panther insignia, his trademark. Mr. Fredrick Fredricks, otherwise known as the Black Panther. It was up to me to stop him from striking again. Striking what, I wasn't sure. But I aimed to find out.

The War Office suspected he was passing intelligence from the Allies to Germany. I suspected he was taking out double agents. He'd killed the countess at Ravenswick because she'd become a double agent, I was sure of it. Of course, I was the only one who thought so. Everyone else thought the murder was a domestic crime. If only I could find something incriminating and prove them wrong.

"I can't find any cigars," Berthe whined, closing the nightstand drawer. "Only gold cuff links and a tiepin. Very pretty ones." She held up something sparkly.

"Keep looking. Try that bureau." I pointed to a dresser I'd already examined.

While Berthe was occupied in Fredricks's sock drawer, I went to the closet. His spare pair of jodhpurs and a tweed hunting jacket hung above shiny high boots standing as if awaiting marching orders. I searched the pockets of the jacket.

"We shouldn't be going through Mr. Fredricks's things," Berthe said, sneaking up behind me. "It isn't right." She may be a flirt, but to my surprise, she had a conscience. Hopefully not enough to report me to the grumpy clerk. She obviously suspected me of something untoward.

"I'm only doing what he asked. But perhaps you're right." I pulled my hand out of the interior pocket of his jacket, palmed the folded paper I found there, and then discreetly slid it into my own trouser pocket. Pockets were certainly handy. If only women's clothing had more of them.

"You can't find the briefcase. I can't find the cigars. And I don't want to get canned." Berthe tugged at my sleeve. "Let's go."

"Very well." I followed her out into the hall, hoping the document I'd found was not just his laundry list.

I extricated myself from Berthe with a promise to meet her for a stroll after work. *Walking with Berthe this evening and then dinner with Clifford tomorrow.* Suddenly, I had a busy social schedule. For some undiscernible reason, she'd taken quite a shine to my Harold the helpful bellboy persona. Either the flirtatious maid wasn't very discriminating or she fancied the androgynous sort. I didn't know her well enough yet to know which, but suspected the former.

Once inside my room, I shut the door and, heart racing, hurriedly unfolded the slip of thin paper I'd stolen from Fredricks's pocket. Bewildered, I stood blinking down at it. It wasn't a telegram in code or a list of military maneuvers or any kind of secret correspondence. I reread it several times to make sure I hadn't missed something. Was this information worthy of a special telephone call to Captain Hall? I glanced at my watch. Golly. How did it get so late? Nine o-clock already. The call would have to wait until tomorrow.

The best I could make out, it was a copy of a claim submitted by Fredricks to the North America Insurance Company for the loss of mineral samples aboard three British supply ships en route from Brazil. *Why is Fredricks, a journalist and huntsman, shipping mineral samples from South America? What is the sneaky bounder up to?*

Chapter Six: The Evening Papers

The next day, unfortunately, the grumpy clerk had kept me running off my feet delivering luggage all day long... and I still hadn't gotten to the British Embassy to call Captain Hall. I glanced at my watch. *Blast, almost two-thirty.* Only thirty minutes until the embassy closed for the day. Given the war, embassies really should keep better hours.

Fumbling with the dozen bloody buttons on my jacket, I hurried to get out of my uniform and back into a sensible frock and my own well-fitting oxfords. I stepped out of the trousers. Short on time, I laid them on the bed instead of hanging them in the armoire along with my jacket and shirtwaist where they belonged. I quickly threw on my underclothes and a practical skirt set with a wide tan cinch belt. A quick glance in the dresser mirror produced a jarring sensation. My lovely spring outfit clashed with my mustache and bushy brows.

Ouch! Ripping the blasted things off left my upper lip and forehead stinging and red. I applied a dab of cold cream and face powder, and then tugged on my favorite wig, the strawberry-blond bobbed number. I topped off the ensemble with a close-fitting beige felt hat.

Fredricks's insurance claim and the transcriptions of Mata Hari's two telegrams were snug in my handbag, a *ménage à trois* of espionage and intrigue.

Luckily, the British Embassy was only a few blocks away on Rue du Faubourg Saint-Honoré. Still, it was closing in twenty minutes, so as the grumpy clerk would say, I couldn't dillydally.

It was a lovely afternoon, and if I weren't in such a hurry, I would stop and enjoy the warm sunshine at one of the outdoor cafés. Charming boutiques and cafés lined both sides of the wide majestic Champs-Élysées. The street was bustling with life. Women with scarfs covering their heads shopped for vegetables. Groups of soldiers in uniform drank wine and laughed. So different from London where people lived and breathed the war. The Parisians were in denial. They simply stepped over holes in the road, ignored paper tape across bombed-out windows, and shouted over the sirens. I guess they were determined not to let the Jerries keep them from enjoying life. *Maybe they're onto something... either that or they're kidding themselves.*

Stepping off the broad and fashionable Avenue des Champs-Élysées and turning the corner onto the narrow and nondescript embassy row was like leaving a *pâtisserie* for a breadline. But in wartime bread was more practical than pastries.

The British Embassy was a squat stone building, recognizable by the Union Jack flying out front. Of course, relations between Britain and the French Republic hadn't always been cordial. From the Napoleonic wars to the conquest of Africa, the main source of agreement between the two countries was fear of the Germans. United against the same enemy, we became allies, peacefully dividing up the colonies between ourselves. Egypt would go to Britain and Morocco would go to France. *I wonder what the Egyptians and Moroccans think of the arrangement? I doubt they were consulted.*

Taking long strides and concentrating on my mission, I approached the entrance to the embassy and marched up the stairs to the front door. I glanced at my watch. *Horsefeathers.* It was nearly three o'clock already. If the embassy closed early, I would have to find another way to get my information to Captain Hall. Then again, if all I'd found was some insurance claim, maybe it wasn't important enough to report.

An officer coming out of the building bumped my shoulder on his way past.

"I say, Fiona, is that you?" He took my elbow.

Blimey. Clifford Douglas. *What is he doing here? And why is he always grabbing my arm?* I had to admit he looked rather dashing in his uniform.

Flustered, I turned to greet him.

"Yesterday your hair was black, and today it's blond. You're the most changeable girl I've ever met."

He didn't know the half of it. "Clifford, what are you doing at the embassy?"

"The ambassador is a friend of mine. We had a smashing lunch at Ledoyen. I really must take you there one day. Delightful little terrace and delicious oysters."

I should have known Clifford would be hobnobbing with the toffs. "I'm not keen on oysters, but thanks."

"You don't have to eat oysters, you know." He looked hurt. "There are other options."

"Other fish in the sea?" I glanced at my watch. "Sorry, but I really must get inside before they close. My passport..."

"Right. I say, I hate to ask, but would you mind postponing our dinner tomorrow night until Thursday?" He blushed. "It's just that Fredricks has invited me to what promises to be a cracking garden party to see his friend dance."

"A garden party?" I was suddenly more interested in what Clifford had to say. "Where?"

"His friend Zelle has arranged the whole affair at a country house of another friend of hers. I'm told it's smashingly elegant and all that."

Why doesn't Clifford invite me to join him at this smashing affair? Does he have another date? Was the twinge I felt jealousy? Or a cramp from walking so fast? The poor sap was probably just as smitten as everyone else with Fredricks's friend Zelle—aka Mata Hari, aka Lady Gresha MacLeod, aka... she probably had a dozen other aliases. I'd add my name to the list, except there was no way she could pretend to be me, despite surely having my passport, as we looked nothing alike. For once my being more... plain seemed to be a plus. Blast it all. Maybe I could get Clifford to ask me to accompany him to the event. "Tell me more about Zelle, this friend of Fredricks."

"I don't know much, really. She's a Javanese princess or something. Jolly exotic and all that."

"That does sound like it will be a wonderful time." *Time.* I glanced at my watch. In my excitement about Mata Hari's garden party, I'd almost forgotten my mission—and my lack of time. I pulled my arm away. "I really must be going. Dinner tomorrow then."

"Thank you, old bean. But I do wish you'd let me pick you up."

I scowled at him. "I've already told you. I prefer to meet at the restaurant."

"Whatever you say, old girl."

As I opened the heavy wooden door to the embassy, I glanced back and saw Clifford watching me from the street. He was such a nuisance.

"Sorry, miss, the embassy is closed." The high-pitched voice hit me with such force I stopped in my tracks.

"But I need to place a very important call to the War Office."

"We close at three. Sorry." The desk attendant was coming at me with a hefty set of keys. "I was just about to lock up."

"It's urgent. I work for—"

"Sorry, you'll have to come back tomorrow." She pointed one of the keys at me and gestured toward the door. "We open at one tomorrow."

What kind of establishment was only open two hours a day? It may be the French way, but it didn't seem very British. I thought of an exchange between a Royal Navy officer and a French corsair. The Navy man reportedly said, "You French fight for money, while we British fight for honor." And the corsair replied, "Sir, a man fights for what he lacks the most." Right now, what I needed most was time... and a telephone.

I turned on my heels and left. On the bright side, perhaps I could search Fredricks's room again—this time *sans* Berthe—and learn the significance of the insurance claim, or find something more incriminating, something that would impress Captain Hall. This was my maiden voyage as a full-fledged British Intelligence agent, and I couldn't afford to muck it up. If I played my cards right, I just might uncover evidence of two German agents. That ought to impress Captain Hall. If I succeeded on this mission, they'd give me a permanent job in espionage. There was nothing I wanted more.

Since I couldn't make my call until tomorrow anyway, I strolled back to the hotel... this time enjoying the sights and sounds of the busy Paris avenue. I must have heard five different languages and seen people in all manner of clothes, from the drab khaki of the British army to colorful djellabas. The smells of bread and garlic emanating from the cafés made my mouth water. I would have loved to sit at one of the cafés and enjoy some crusty bread with a café au lait while people watching, but duty called. I picked up my pace.

Back at the hotel, I didn't waste any time. Fredricks could return from Mata Hari's penthouse at any moment, if he hadn't already.

Once again I transformed myself into Harold the helpful bellboy and then went directly to Fredricks's room. I should have checked first to see if his key was gone from the key cupboard. But I wanted to avoid any more encounters with the grumpy clerk. It was only a matter of time before the hotel staff caught on to me and chucked me out. I had to be careful that in my rush to impress Captain Hall, I didn't get reckless. Blowing my cover or being accused of spying myself would not endear me to the good captain, especially since he told me not to wear any disguises. But this was what I had to do to get the job done.

I removed a hairpin from my hat and was about to insert it into the lock when the door opened, and I was face-to-face with Fredrick Fredricks… or should I say with his hairy bare chest. He was wearing only a towel wrapped around his waist. His hair was wet and wild and he was attacking it with another smaller towel. Given his muscular physique, smooth tanned skin, and animal magnetism, I was beginning to see why women found him irresistible.

My cheeks afire, I took a step backward and quickly pocketed the hairpin.

"That's what I call service," Fredricks said, throwing the small towel onto the floor. "Anticipating my every need." He disappeared for a moment and then reappeared carrying a leather billfold. "Get me the newspaper and a dozen roses." He handed me several bills.

Stunned, I stood gaping at him.

He laughed and handed me another bill. "Okay then. You drive a hard bargain." He pulled at the towel around his waist.

I nearly fainted, and averted my eyes, trying to resist the urge to peek.

"I've got an important engagement tomorrow evening, so be back here at five sharp tomorrow." He gave me a quizzical look. "Got it? Five tomorrow

59

afternoon. Don't be late. I have an important date."

"Yes, sir."

"And get the papers from today and tomorrow."

"Yes, sir."

Thankfully, he shut the door before completely exposing himself.

I fanned myself with the bills. My heart was racing faster than my legs as I dashed off to find newspapers and flowers. I could get today's paper now, but I would have to wait to get tomorrow's… and flower would be better fresh too.

I'd just grabbed the evening paper and was on my way back through the hotel lobby when the grumpy clerk called out to me. I stuffed the paper inside my jacket and spent the rest of the evening carting luggage and helping the kitchen staff deliver supper. By the time the clerk ran out of things for me to do, it was nearly eleven and I was completely knackered. I wasn't used to running off my feet for hours on end. I couldn't wait to get back to my room, rip off my mustache, and sink into a bath—a warm one if I was lucky.

* * *

The next morning, after breakfast and as soon as the shops opened, I set out on my mission to find newspapers and roses. Or should I say Harold set out, for I'd donned by bellboy uniform since I was on official hotel business.

There were newspaper stands on every corner, but finding a dozen roses was blooming difficult. Flowers weren't exactly essential goods during wartime, except for those adorning gravestones that commemorated soldiers whose bodies were buried on far-away battlefields.

Beads of perspiration accumulated on my forehead as I rushed up and down, block after block, searching for a florist shop. Wearing a wool jacket and pants over a shirt-waist and men's boots was deuced uncomfortable in July. Grateful for a thunderhead blocking the summer sun and casting a shadow the length of the avenue, I stopped to dab my face with a handkerchief.

Breathing hard, I tuned out the hustle and bustle of the city and focused on regaining my equilibrium. Hands on my knees, I stood panting. Unsure of how many minutes had passed, I refocused my attention on my surroundings and noticed a sign across the street. *Durand Salon funéraire.* A funeral parlor. Perhaps they could help me find flowers.

Although I was neither overly religious nor superstitious, I crossed myself before entering. The room was dark and smelled of chemicals. Soft music played on a gramophone. Aside from a desk in one corner and a bench that looked like a church pew, the room was barren.

"Hello?" I called into the void.

A stout girl came rushing through the curtain that separated the front room from whatever ghastly operations they were performing in the back. "May I help you, sir?"

From her contralto voice to her intense green eyes, she was the spitting image of Berthe. If it weren't for her long mousy hair and clean face, I'd have thought she *was* Berthe. Uncanny.

"Are you by any chance related to a chambermaid at the Grand Hotel named Berthe?"

"She's my sister." The girl gave me a shy smile. "You work there too?"

"Yes and one of our guests is asking for a dozen red roses." I glanced around. Not a flower in sight. "I popped in hoping you might tell me where I could find flowers."

"What flowers we get these days, we get wholesale from a farmer." She shook her head and stared down at her feet. "Sorry I can't help."

"I can't get over how much you look like your sister." She didn't act like her though. Quite the opposite. Whereas Berthe was forward to a fault, her sister seemed timid.

"We're twins." She twisted the end of one of her frazzled braids around her index finger.

"I'm Harold." I held out my hand to her.

"Abby." She put her stubby-fingered hand into mine. "You're Harold the bellboy?"

I nodded.

She blushed. "Berthe told me about you yesterday at dinner."

Now I blushed.

"Just a minute." She dashed back behind the curtain and reappeared a minute later holding a single red rose. "This is the only rose we have." She held it out to me.

"I can't take your last rose."

She pressed it into my hand. "You're Berthe's friend and you need it. One rose won't help us any." Thankfully she'd wrapped its thorny stem in tissue paper.

"Thank you." I bowed slightly and then took my leave.

"Watch out for Berthe," she called after me.

Was she asking me to take care of her sister or warning me about her? How could two people who looked so alike be so different?

Success. Chuffed that I'd found a flower and the newspapers, I hurried back to the hotel and up the lift to my room. I piled the papers on the desk, and then unwrapped the single rose and put it into a glass of water. I still had all day to kill before five when Fredricks expected his delivery. I wondered why he wanted the newspapers so badly… I suspected I knew why he wanted the rose.

I decided to try to call Captain Hall again this afternoon as soon as the Embassy opened. A pleasant breeze accompanied down the avenue. I was buoyed up by the voices of hawkers selling their wares and soldiers buying them. The Paris streets were full of life and I was truly beginning to enjoy the sounds and sights of this fair city.

Unfortunately, Captain Hall didn't answer his telephone. I was starting to think he kept hours more limited than those of the Embassy. Sigh. I would have to try again later. In the meantime, I might as well enjoy some shopping. There was a darling hat shop on the way back to the hotel.

Just entering the shop and seeing so many delightful hats lifted my spirits even more. When I reached out for a lovely beribboned boater, the clerk asked, "Sir, may I help you?"

Fiddlesticks. I'd forgotten I was dressed as a man. "I'm just looking for a hat for my… sister. For her birthday."

The clerk rushed over, cooing about the boater I'd selected. I had no choice but to buy it. I gulped when I discovered the price. A month's wages. I really did need an expense account.

* * *

Standing outside Fredricks's room holding the papers in one hand and the single rose in the other, I waited until five on the dot and then knocked. He answered in a huff.

"Right on time," he said, sweeping a lock of hair from his forehead.

I had to admit, the Great White Hunter looked sharp in full evening kit, starched white high-collared shirt and black coat and tie. He held an engraved invitation in his hand. I stared at it, memorizing the details. Wednesday, July 4th, in honor of the blood moon, Mata Hari was giving a performance. *Tonight.* The smashing garden party. *Why was he dressing so early? Perhaps he was escorting Mata Hari from the hotel?*

"Sorry, sir, but roses are hard to come by these days." I handed him the single red rose. "This is the only one I could find."

"Only one rose?"

"Ladies often consider a single red rose more romantic than a dozen."

He smiled and looked at me as if seeing me for the first time. "And you have a lot of experience with the fairer sex?" He narrowed his brows and gave me a queer look. "Have we met before?"

"Perhaps you've been a guest at the Grand Hotel before?"

"I never forget a face, especially a pretty—" He stopped himself. "My newspapers?" he asked abruptly and pointed to the papers tucked under my arm.

I handed them to him, pleased that I'd managed to get both the morning and evening papers.

He put the rose between his teeth like a flamingo dancer and tore through the evening paper. His eyes lit up, and then he ripped out an entire page. I moved closer to get a look at the story. The headline read, "British supply ship sunk in Atlantic. Sabotage suspected."

When he noticed me staring at the paper, he stuffed it under his arm, took out his billfold, and handed me another note. "Right," he said through clenched teeth. "Here you go." He did an about-face and shut the door, forcing me to jump back out of the way.

Why was Fredricks so keen on news about a sunken ship? Could he have had something to do with its sinking? Or did he have minerals aboard and was he just looking to file another insurance claim? *Sabotage suspected.* I needed to report my findings to Captain Hall as soon as possible. If Fredricks was involved in the sabotage, the War Office needed to know. I couldn't wait until tomorrow afternoon when the embassy reopened. Where was there a telephone I could use?

Concentrating on the task at hand, I stepped into the lift, not knowing whether I'd go up to my room or back down to the lobby. There was no phone in my room, and I doubted the grumpy clerk would allow me to use his phone... especially if I was dressed as Harold the bellboy.

"Cutie!"

My hand flew to my chest. How did I miss her standing there in the corner of the lift?

"Madame Hari asked me to serve hors d'oeuvres at her garden party this evening." Berthe beamed. "Would you be my date?"

"To serve hors d'oeuvres?"

"Actually, you could help serve. Madame asked me to put together a team for the party." She played with a button on my jacket and gazed up at me with those same green eyes that had seemed so intelligent in the face of her twin sister. "Most men would give their *couilles* to see Madame dance."

"I'm not most men." I had to admit I was more than a little curious to see Mata Hari in action, even if I didn't have *couilles*. Undoubtedly Fredricks would be there. Perhaps I could gather a bit more information before calling Captain Hall. "Okay. I'll help."

"Really?" She clapped her chubby hands together. "Do you have a penguin suit?"

"Penguin suit?" Did she know my suitcase was full of disguises?

"A tuxedo, silly." She put her hands on her hips. "It's black tie."

"As a matter of fact, I do." I didn't tell her that I also had a maid's outfit that would rival hers.

"Where do you live? Can you change and get back here in an hour?"

I nodded.

"You can pour champagne while I serve canapés." She kissed my cheek. "So exciting."

All smiles, Berthe bounded out of the lift at the lobby level. I followed her out and then when she was out of sight, circled back, and to be safe took the stairs up to my room.

With plenty of time before I had to change and meet Berthe, I sat down at the small desk in the corner and took out my notebook. I had to gather my thoughts and take note of what I'd found out so far so I could present it to Captain Hall in an orderly fashion.

First, there was the matter of my missing passport and my suspicion that Lady Gresha MacLeod, aka Mata Hari, had stolen it. *But why?* And was this worthy of reporting to Captain Hall? Or would it just make me look clumsy and foolish?

Next, there were the two telegrams I'd found in Mata Hari's overnight case. The German telegram was particularly suspect. Why was Mata Hari receiving telegrams from our enemies? And more to the point, who was Heinrich? I made a note to try to find out more about Heinrich. Were any high-ranking officers in the German army named Heinrich? And was the telegram written in code or merely a message from another one of Mata Hari's many admirers?

The French telegram was signed G. Ladoux. Who was G. Ladoux? And why did he write that the information was useless? What information? Useless to whom? Was Mata Hari spying for the French or the Germans or both? *Golly.* Maybe she was a double agent. If I was right about Fredricks taking out double agents, then she might be in danger. Perhaps that's why Fredricks was in Paris. To dispose of Mata Hari. Should I warn her?

Would Captain Hall be interested in any of this? Or would he chastise me for getting distracted from my mission, which, as he'd so often pointed out, was watching Fredrick Fredricks and not playing Sherlock Holmes.

What had I learned about Fredricks that would be of interest to the War

Office? I made a list. First, he had an insurance claim with North American Insurance Company for mineral shipments lost on British supply ships coming from Brazil. Second, he had a special concern for at least one sunken British ship, the likely victim of sabotage. And third, he had a very special concern for at least one exotic dancer, Mata Hari.

Chapter Seven: The Garden Party

"**M**adame Hari" had given Berthe money for a carriage. The sun still high in the sky, the eager maid, her sullen sister Abby, and I rode to the outskirts of Paris. Charming stone cottages dotted fields of vibrant purple flowers, which Abby said were *"lavande,"* lavender. Again I marveled at the difference between the twins. Sitting between them on the journey, I felt as if I were trapped between parallel universes.

Except for the military lorries throwing up dust as we passed on the dirt roads, the countryside was so tranquil you'd never know there was a war on. One of my companions, on the other hand, was not. Berthe squirmed in the seat for the entire thirty-minute drive. She couldn't sit still to save her life. If Abby was squirming, it wasn't from excitement, but discomfort. Berthe had made her wear one of her spare maid's outfits. Dressed exactly alike, one with her face plain and natural, the other painted from chin to brows, created an uncanny effect of seeing double with a twist.

I tried to look past them both and enjoy the meadows and cottages along the way. As we got closer to the estate where Mata Hari was hosting her party, the chestnut trees lining the road got thicker while the road narrowed. A canopy of green covered the lane.

Mata Hari's garden party was at the country estate of wealthy industrialist Louis Renault, one of her many lovers. As we drove up, Berthe filled me in on the gossip. Apparently, Renault's wife had threatened to scratch Mata Hari's eyes out and relieve Renault of his manhood if he didn't give her up. Obviously, he hadn't and Berthe expected fireworks tonight.

Our carriage driver followed a line of carriages entering through a stone archway attached to a guard house. A guard in a blue uniform waved us in. When we pulled up in front of the sprawling chateau, a line of fine carriages and motorcars already circled the driveway.

I disembarked our carriage in awe. Wide-eyed, I started for the stately front entrance. When I turned back to check on Berthe, she was still sitting in the carriage with the door open, staring out at me with a sour look on her face. *Oh right.* I dashed back to the carriage and offered my hand. Even a maid expected to be helped from a carriage by a gentleman. I really needed to brush up on my masculine manners.

When I rushed around to the other side of the carriage, Abby had already alighted on the ground. With terror in her eyes, she seemed to shrink in on herself. She was practically shaking. I took her by the hand until we caught up with Berthe.

"I've never seen anything like it," Berthe said, gawking around. "Only in the moving pictures. So grand."

In the center of the stone driveway was a lovely little garden with rose bushes and a fountain. The fountain was dry, no doubt a concession to the war. But the roses were in full bloom, oblivious to the human folly all around them.

The house—or should I say mansion—had beveled-glass windows criss-crossed with dainty wooden lattice… nothing like the planks boarding up windows in the bombed-out areas of the city. On the second floor, high above the entrance, a small wrought-iron balcony overlooked the estate. I imagined the lord of the manor perched like a hawk taking stock of his property, which extended as far as the eye could see. My dark side imagined bankrupted aristocrats using the perch to launch themselves up to heaven, or the other place, to escape ordinary lives without servants, expensive whiskey, and imported cigars.

"You'd never know there was a war on," I said as I headed toward the front door again, this time concentrating on taking manly strides.

"Where do you think you're going, Mr. Hoity-toity?" Berthe grabbed my hand and pulled. "Come on." She led me around the mansion to a back entrance reserved for servants. Abby trailed behind, head lowered, obviously not enjoying herself.

Of course, we were there to serve and not to enjoy the party.

The enormous kitchen was bustling with cooks and parlor maids preparing fancy tidbits from whatever war rations—and the black market—would allow. The toffs may have had more than most, but even they couldn't completely escape the causalities of war. In England, this whole estate would have been turned into a military hospital or supply depot. Here it was a pleasure dome sheltered from the horrors of war.

Amongst the women in the kitchen busily preparing the party, I stood out like a fox in the henhouse. I was the only man in the bunch and as such received a lot of undue attention. The girls fussed over me as if I were a guest and not another servant. In fact, Berthe insisted I sit and eat canapés rather than serve them. If I weren't on a mission to find out everything I could about Fredrick Fredricks and Mata Hari, I would have been only too happy to oblige… although I doubt the master of the house would approve, unless French mores when it came to servants were different from the English standards of propriety. To humor Berthe—and because I hadn't eaten anything all day—I popped a delicate pastry puff into my mouth. The explosion of flavors was exquisite. The food on this assignment was much better than my last assignment at Ravenswick. After I snatched up a couple more canapes and gobbled them down, I poured champagne into fluted glasses lined up on a silver tray.

When I tried to carry the tray on one hand like I'd seen footmen do it in the moving pictures, the glasses started swaying like soused sailors after an all-night bender. I quickly steadied the tray and grasped it firmly in both hands. I may not be elegant, but at least I wouldn't douse the rich and famous.

I exited the kitchen and headed for the back garden. *Crikey.* A lush grass meadow stretched as far as the eye could see. On either side of the cut grass were manicured hedgerows lined with blue-green rosemary bushes, in front of which stood gorgeous beds of white lilies and yellow jonquil. In the center of the lawn close to the back entrance to the house a trellis laden with pink flowers and strings of fancy electric lights had been constructed, presumably for the performance.

I stood there gaping until a distinguished looking gent asked for a glass of champagne. From what I overheard of his conversation with two other gentlemen, he was the man of the house, Louis Renault, looking rather handsome in his crisp white shirt and tuxedo tails. He and the other two businessmen were discussing tank manufacturing.

"That *fils de pute* André Citroën has had explosions at his plant too," Renault said. "At least I'm not the only one menaced by accidents. *Zut* seventy-five millimeter shells." He shook his cigar at his guests. "I'll bet *le petit Juif* is selling munitions to the Krauts."

Amazing how hearing someone speak can change the way they look. When I first saw him, I thought Louis Renault a handsome man, with his angular features and noble carriage. But after hearing his cursing and insults, I found him vulgar and unattractive.

I continued to circulate with the drinks tray. Women in their finery chatted and sipped from champagne flutes, fanning themselves, and waiting for the show. Men in dress uniforms and penguin suits smoked cigars and rubbed their palms together. And in the center of a group of attractive ladies stood Clifford Douglas. I should have known he'd be admiring the *scenery*. He did have a more than healthy appreciation for the fairer sex. For fear he'd recognize me in spite of my mustache, brows, and eyeglasses, I moved to the far side of the lawn near the hedgerow.

What in heaven's name? I stopped short.

A strongly accented woman's voice wafted through the hedgerow. "Unhand me. What do you think you're doing?"

"You can't escape punishment after what you've done," another woman said. The voice was vaguely familiar.

I tried to peek through the hedge, but the greenery was so thick that all I could see was a flash of an emerald dress and what looked like the corner of a servant's apron. The hairs on my arms stood on end. Something about this party was a bit dodgy. Perhaps Berthe was right and there would be fireworks. The palpable tension in the air gave me an uneasy feeling.

As I turned back toward the kitchen to refill my tray, I saw a lovely woman dressed in a white gown arguing with Renault. Her flaxen hair fell loose around her bare shoulders and her pale cheeks were inflamed.

"Why don't you take *her* to Parade?" the woman shouted.

Parade? What Parade?

"If you don't quit making a scene, I just might do that."

When she slapped Renault's face, he grabbed her by the wrists. "Be a good girl darling and get us more champagne if you want to see *Ballet Russes* on Friday."

Aha. Parade must be a performance of the Russian Ballet.

She cursed at him. "The ballet won't make up for what you've done."

"I got us the best seats in the house, for Christ's sake."

I scurried past in time to hear him snarl, "*Chienne.*"

The woman wrested free from his grip, spit in his face, and stormed across the lawn and back into the house. I gathered she must be his estranged wife.

Blimey. It was turning out to be quite a party.

When I returned to the kitchen, Berthe and Abby were huddled near the icebox, whispering. I sat my tray on a counter and went to see if everything was okay. As I approached, I heard Berthe say, "Behave or I'll get the sack." *Strange.* If anyone needed to behave, it was Berthe. From what I'd seen, Abby couldn't misbehave if she tried.

"Is something wrong?" I asked.

Berthe shook her head. "My sister and her causes." She touched my sleeve. "You don't believe in such things, do you, Cutie?"

"What things?"

"Justice and equality," Abby said.

Not wanting to take sides in a sisterly argument, I said, "I'd best refill the tray and get back to the party."

"Good idea," Berthe said. "I'll come with you." Hands on her hips, she glared at her sister, who frowned in return.

The sun had set and the moonrise was a spectacular pinkish color. I was passing out more flutes of champagne when otherworldly music came from the center courtyard. The posh men and women stopped chatting and moved closer to witness the spectacle.

Under the trellis, four men dressed in robes and turbans sat on stools playing exotic stringed instruments that looked like giant gourds. A fifth man beat a bongo drum held between his knees. There was a mesmerizing quality to the high-pitched whine and whirl of the music. When it reached a certain frenzy, Mata Hari appeared, wearing a dress of long sheer veils and an ornate headdress that looked like the twisted horns of an exotic golden antelope. She swayed to the music. Arms gracefully outstretched, she sliced the air with her thin veils. Her breasts and upper arms were adorned with thick brass bejeweled plates that jangled as she moved. Beads and gemstones hung on strings around her neck. As she swayed, the gems swayed with her. The crowd was hypnotized.

When she dropped the outer layer of her veils, I nearly dropped the tray of champagne. Her midriff was bare and undulating. She had the most defined waist I'd ever seen... not that I'd seen many as exposed as hers. When she dropped the final veil, the women gasped and the men clapped with delight. Mata Hari stood arms stretched toward heaven wearing nothing but a brass brassiere and a seductive smile.

As I watched Mata Hari mesmerize the crowd, I realized that it wasn't just the brazenness of her nudity and the perfection of her body that seduced the onlookers. Rather, the intensity of her velvety brown eyes, lids partially lowered, that sealed their fate. No one, it seemed, was immune from Mata Hari's charms. When she finished, the crowd went wild with applause and she flashed a triumphant smile.

Fredrick Fredricks presented her with the single red rose and kissed her cheek, while Clifford Douglas clapped so hard he nearly fell over. My cheeks on fire, I scurried back to the kitchen. Part of me wanted to get back to England where all the women I knew kept their clothes on in public, but I had to admit the spectacle was thrilling.

When I heard the crowd calling "Brava! Brava!" I quickly filled another round of champagne flutes and made my way to the front for an unob-structed view of Mata Hari's encore.

I overheard a male spectator say to his mate, "She's so hot we need a fire extinguisher."

Judging by the rapt countenances all round, I'd say we needed an entire fire brigade. There was no doubt the lady had a certain allure.

After her dance, Mata Hari draped herself in a full-length fur coat, which seemed excessive given the July heat. "Butter on bacon," as my father would say.

I couldn't take my eyes off her as she made her way through the crowd to accept the congratulations and adoration of men and women alike. Following at a discreet distance, I distractedly offered champagne while watching several men press clandestine notes into Mata Hari's palm. Were they engaging in deadly espionage or dangerous flirtation? Were those furtive slips of paper state secrets hidden from warring enemies or romantic assignations hidden from angry wives?

In my opinion, the latter was as heinous as the former. If a man could be unfaithful to his wife, he could be unfaithful to his country. If he was capable of breaking the marriage contract, he was capable of breaking the social contract. If a man can't sustain his love for the person closest to him, how can he ever have compassion for those far away? And without compassion for others, aren't we doomed to perpetual war?

Such were my thoughts as I refilled champagne glasses, observed the high-toned Parisians, and circled the party trying to avoid Clifford Douglas.

A tinkling of glass caught my attention and I turned to see Fredricks lift his glass. Instead of a toast, he called out, "Garçon, a refill, if you please."

Since I was the only servant with a full champagne bottle, I had no choice but to wait on him. Of course, his sycophant friend, Clifford, was stuck to him like a barnacle on a hippopotamus's bottom. Luckily, caught up in drooling over Mata Hari, the men ignored me as I refilled their glasses.

"I say, what a smashing girl," Clifford exclaimed. "What poise. What elegance. What a figure."

"Yes, she's one of a kind." Fredricks lit his pipe and sucked on its stem.

"Good thing it's so warm out or the poor girl might catch cold dancing." Clifford sniffled as if he'd caught a cold just thinking about it.

"No need to worry about that." Fredricks laughed. "Vanity keeps an attractive woman warm."

Fredricks excused himself and left me standing face-to-face with Clifford. I averted my eyes and slinked off before he could get a good look at me. Clifford was such a gullible sort and certainly not the most observant of men. Fredricks was the one I should worry about. I tracked his movements through the crowd, watching for suspicious behavior. He flirted shamelessly with every woman present from newly minted debutants to widowed grandmothers. And to the lady, each basked in the warmth of his compliments. To my mind they were served up like reheated bangers and mash and it turned my stomach. But to each her own.

Fredricks came straight toward me, and I froze. He took two glasses of champagne from the tray I was holding and turned on his heels. A moment later, he alighted on a tall woman in an emerald dress with a matching feathered headband, and offered her a glass of champagne. I sauntered in that direction and stood with my back to them, listening intently while they made small talk about the weather.

With a strong Russian accent, the woman said, "It's unseasonably cool for July."

Horsefeathers. It was unseasonably hot for July. The beads of sweat on my forehead were proof.

When Fredricks replied "The bluebells should be in full bloom," I knew it had to be code. I glanced around in time to see him pass her a thin silver capsule... or was it a tiny fountain pen. I had to get my hands on that pen.

"I know what to do," the woman said.

Wait. That's the same voice I heard coming from the hedgerow. The accent was unmistakable.

"If you don't do it, the Germans will," Fredricks said. "It would be more pleasant for you if it didn't come to that."

I trailed the emerald woman through the throng. She circulated through the party making small talk with other guests. Eventually, she caught up to Mata Hari and congratulated her on her performance. I listened from behind a giant urn. The two of them started whispering and then headed into the house.

Trying not to draw attention to myself, I followed at a discrete distance. I went through the kitchen, but didn't see either the emerald lady or Mata Hari. I peeked out into the hallway. I heard a lady's heels tapping on the marble floor. I hung back in the foyer and hid behind a large Japanese vase. The tapping stopped. The lady must have entered a room at the end of the hallway. Was it Mata Hari or the emerald lady?

"Cutie, what are you doing?" the familiar voice came from behind me.

Straightening up and tugging on the bottom of my jacket, I averted my eyes from her accusing gaze. "Just waiting for the washroom."

She gave me a strange look. "The servants' lav is downstairs."

I changed the subject. "Who is the tall woman dressed in green with the peacock feather in her headband?"

"Do you mean Countess Pavlovna?" Berthe asked.

Not another bloody countess.

Berthe glanced around and then leaned closer and whispered into my ear. "She's a *Dame Blanche*."

Did I hear her correctly? "A white woman?"

She nodded. "That's what my sister says anyway."

"What is a *Dame Blanche*?"

"A political group or something." Berthe waved her hand as if she were shooing away a fly. "Abs knows about all those political causes."

Speak of the devil. Abby snuck up behind her sister and made Berthe jump.

"What do you know about the White Women?" I asked Abby.

Her countenance turned even more serious than usual. "They help us win the war."

"And the countess works with them?"

"Yes. But they call her Madame Bovary," Abby said in a low voice. "Why are you so interested in the countess?" She narrowed her eyes at me.

Good heavens! My contact. *Countess Pavlovna is Madame Bovary.* Why hadn't she answered my note?

"Do you know what's behind that door at the end of the hallway? I just saw the countess go in there." I had to follow her and find a way to introduce myself.

"I think it's the library, why?" Berthe said.

"You ask a lot of questions for a bellboy," Abby said. "What's your game?"

"I'm just a curious sort of chap. She is quite beautiful." That was the type of thing Clifford would say. Perhaps it would disarm Abby into thinking my interest was merely prurient. "Is the countess a good friend of the Renaults'?"

"Their cook says she's visiting from Russia and Madame Renault isn't happy about it." Berthe twisted a lock of hair around her finger. "Seems her husband is a philanderer, and she's had enough of his fooling around with the countess and the dancer both."

"What nerve." I was shocked. "He brings his mistresses to the house?"

"Rich people do lots of strange things," Abby said. "I wouldn't be surprised if they ate their own young."

Men do lots of strange things. I thought of Cronus eating his own sons so they wouldn't overpower him like he did his own father.

A series of thuds from down the hall interrupted our conversation. We stared at each other for a few seconds. Berthe's eyes widened. "I'd better get back to the kitchen." She took off in the opposite direction from the noise. Abby followed close on her heels.

Peeking into the empty hallway, I cocked my ears. *Blimey.* I swear I heard a muffled scream. Running down the hall in my oversized boots, I wasn't sure what I planned to do when I got to the source of the sounds. I slid to a stop at the door to the library. Not knowing what else to do, I knocked. "Countess?"

There was a rustling... and then a rattling... and then silence.

I knocked again. "Countess, are you okay?"

No answer.

Tentatively, I turned the doorknob and opened the door a crack.

The room was dark. "Countess?" Still no response. Thanks to the light spilling in from the hall, I could see a desk by the door with a lamp on it. I turned it on.

Good heavens. The countess was lying face up on the floor atop Mata Hari's fur coat, a dark red stain blossoming across the front of her green dress.

The faint smell of lilacs and something else—something sour—rode on the breeze. Walls of crammed bookshelves flanked the room on two sides. A third wall had curtained French windows. The last sported a giant stone fireplace. A large mahogany desk sat facing the fireplace. The body was sprawled on the floor behind the desk.

Hand across my mouth to stop from screaming, I entered the room. Stepping around the body, I checked the French windows. They were ajar. I pulled back the curtain, opened one the rest of the way, and looked out. The windows led out to the front of the house. If the assailant had left through the window, surely the chauffeurs waiting with their carriages and motorcars would have noticed… unless the killer was lying in wait here in the library. A prickling on the back of my neck made me whip around. The room seemed empty of life.

"Is someone here?" I asked. "Show yourself."

Nothing. Only the movement of the curtain and the silence of death.

I scanned the wooden floor for signs of footprints or other clues. Nothing. If someone had come in through the French windows from the front garden, there should be dirt or traces dust on the wood floor.

Squatting next to the body, I examined what I could without touching her. Warmth still emanated from her body, so she hadn't been dead long, which I'd already gathered from the commotion that drew me here and the rustling I heard just before opening the door. If I hadn't hesitated before entering, I may have caught the killer red-handed. But a servant never entered unannounced. Who knows what secret assignation they might happened upon. Perhaps the countess had such a rendezvous with her paramour, Monsieur Renault.

Countess Pavlovna's bottle-blond hair had come loose from her chignon, and there was a gash on her forehead. Could that indicate a struggle? I looked for telltale marks, bruises, or scratches on her arms. She had bruises on her neck. Someone had tried to strangle her.

I examined her arms. Strange. She had an angry red rash on her right wrist. I bent down for a closer look. There were tiny yellowish blisters in the rash. Could the rash have been caused by someone holding onto her wrist? The blisters suggested otherwise. A poisonous plant perhaps?

Wait. What's that in her hand? A tiny corner of white poked out of her clenched fist. I gritted my teeth and pried it loose. The torn paper had the Renault logo in the corner and looked to be a receipt. I held it up into the light. *Schmidt Industries. 1000 Papiermark. Papiermark?* Wasn't that German currency? I tucked the bit of paper into my waistcoat pocket and continued examining the body.

White foam bubbled between the countess's bluing lips. I shuddered. What a gruesome sight… and one that suggested poisoning. Had she ingested a poisonous plant? That might explain the rash and the foam. But why in the world would she eat a plant? I thought of the drink Fredricks brought her. Could he have poisoned it? And what was that silver capsule he'd given her? Something poisonous, perhaps?

I moved from her torso to her feet. One of her slippers had fallen off. On hands and knees, I moved closer. The hem of her dress and the soles of her shoes had a dusting of yellowish powder. Was it pollen? Blast. I wished I had something to scrape it with. I patted my vest pockets. *What could I use to get a sample?* Lacking a pocketknife, I had no choice but to settle on wiping the finger of one of my white gloves across the sole of her slipper. A yellowish stain appeared on my glove, and I removed the glove and tucked it into one of my oversized boots for safe keeping.

Why was she wearing Mata Hari's coat? It was deuced hot. I spun around on my knees and examined the coat. She wasn't actually wearing it. It looked as if she'd just had it draped over her shoulders. I put my face directly over the red stain on the front of her dress. The sour scent I'd sensed earlier got stronger. Blood would smell sweeter. I bent down and sniffed. Wine. The stain on her dress was wine and not blood. As I bent closer for another sniff to confirm my hypothesis, I saw it.

On the floor next to the body lay a dagger, bloody up to its pearl handle. Using my handkerchief, I picked up the instrument by the hilt and examined it. On closer inspection, it appeared to be a fancy letter-opener and not a dagger.

"I say. What are you doing?"

A hand caught my arm, and I dropped the knife, which clattered across the wooden floor, leaving red spots as it went.

Bloody hell. It was Clifford.

"What are you doing here?" I asked before realizing I was supposed to be Harold. I stared down at my oversized boots to avoid his gaze and to continue my examination of the crime scene.

"I came to get a book my friend wanted if you must know." Clifford picked up the knife. "Why did you do it?" He demanded, raising his voice. "Why did you kill the countess?"

"What's going on?" Fredricks asked from the doorway. "What's all the ruckus?"

"This dodgy waiter stabbed Countess Pavlovna," Clifford said, tightening his grip on my arm. "I caught him red-handed."

Blast it all. Clifford could be such a troublemaker.

"Hold him there. I'll fetch Inspector Gerard." Fredricks took off.

I covered my face with my palm. I wanted to cry. *How in the world will I get out of this mess without blowing my cover?* Harold was caught red-handed holding a knife over a dead countess. *Things don't look good for Harold... or me.*

"Why did you do it?" Clifford asked again, shaking me.

"I'm innocent, sir," I said in my deepest tenor. "Kindly quit manhandling me."

"I say. You're a cheeky sort of murderer, aren't you." Clifford huffed and loosened his grip.

"In here, Inspector." Fredricks reappeared in the doorway with a portly man, presumably Inspector Gerard, and the man of the house, Renault. "Captain Douglas caught this boy with the knife that killed the countess."

"That's right," Clifford said and puffed out his chest.

"Caught in the act," Renault said, holding one hand in the other. *Wait. Wasn't he wearing a white shirt and tuxedo jacket earlier?* Now he had on a blue shirt and smoking jacket. "How could something like this happen in my house?"

"Let's go." The inspector stepped into the room and grabbed me by the wrist.

"You must be joking." I tried to wrest my arm free. Cornered, I decided the best defense was a good offense. *Really, could they think I murdered the countess? Or that helpless Harold did it? Why would a mere bellboy kill a Russian countess?*

"Do I look like I'm joking?"

Actually, in his tight brown suit, he looked like five pounds of potatoes stuffed into a two pound bag.

I shook my head.

"What is your name?" he asked.

"Harold, sir."

"And your surname?"

The name of an old school chum of mine from primary school popped into my head. "Dukinfield Derbyshire," I said lifting my chin the way my little pal always did when he was caught stealing biscuits from my lunch tray.

"Monsieur Harold Dukinfield Derbyshire," the inspector said as he pulled on my wrist. "You're under arrest for the murder of Countess Pavlovna."

Chapter Eight: A Night in Jail

Resistance was futile, so I went along with the inspector until I could appeal to his superiors, which I hoped would be sooner rather than later. The inspector loaded me into a police motorcar and delivered me to the prefecture of police. The prefecture was housed in large former barracks smack dab in the middle of the Île de la Cité. *Why do the French ruin this beautiful island in the middle of Paris by marring it with a military barracks? Obviously, military strategy is beyond me.*

I hadn't visited this part of the city before. The island was lovely with arched bridges across the Seine, and of course the stunning Notre Dame Cathedral. Too bad I was being hauled off to jail. Standing between the cathedral and the police station, the word *mercy* came to mind.

Once inside the barracks, the inspector handed me off to a uniformed officer, who led me to a holding cell chocked full of men. Until now, I'd enjoyed greater freedom disguised as a man and often wished women were given the same liberties. But, at this moment, I longed for the protection of petticoats and a sturdy corset. The barbarity of being locked in a cage with a dozen ruthless criminals made me break out in a cold sweat.

As the officer shoved me into the cell, one hardened sort with an open gash across his temple looked me up and down as if I were the evening meal. Self-conscious, I glanced down at my trousers and realized I must look an odd duck in my penguin suit.

"*Une petite comtesse,*" the roughneck said with a chuckle.

Did he know I was really a woman? The thought terrified me. I might be a woman, but I certainly was not a *little countess*. I moved to the corner of the cell farthest from my new admirer.

I wrapped my arms around myself and realized I was trembling. All the men were staring at me. I felt like a rabbit cornered by a pack of wolves. They smelled like wolves too. The cell stank of excrement and urine. Most of the men were dirty and probably had lice. I shuddered at the thought of the various vermin lurking in their scraggly beards.

There were two lidded buckets in the back corner of the cell for necessities of nature. I couldn't even imagine using them. My bladder would have to burst first. I absolutely could not spend the night in this cell full of men, criminals no less. Of course, they probably thought I was a criminal too.

When a guard appeared with a tray of bread, I slid up to the front of the cell and waved my hand through the bars, trying to get his attention. "Excuse me, sir. I really must speak with the prefect. I don't belong here."

"*La Comtesse* doesn't belong here," Scarface said, mocking me. "And we do?"

The guard threw crusts of bread into the cell and the men attacked them like starving animals, fighting over the crumbs.

"Please, sir. It's a matter of national security."

The guard ignored me.

"I'm not who I seem. If only you'd let me phone the British Embassy. They'll tell you—"

"Hoity-toity," Scarface said in English, his nose in the air. "A regular toff are you?" His laugh sounded downright sinister.

"Call the War Office, Room Forty. They'll tell—" *I'm a terrible spy, spilling the beans at the first sign of trouble.* Captain Hall should have outfitted me with a cyanide pill to take in case of capture. Then again, I hadn't been captured by the enemy. I'd been jailed by our ally.

"Shut it, buster." The guard shoved a stale piece of dark brown bread into my outstretched hand.

A filthy, toothless bloke grabbed my bounty. Holding the bread in both hands, he gnawed on it like a starving raccoon.

Locking a heavy metal door that separated the holding cells from the rest of the station, the guard left us fighting over crumbs. My hopes of getting out of this stinking cell before dawn left with him.

Standing pinned to the wall, surrounded by male noises and male smells, I longed to be home in my second-floor flat with a nice cup of tea and a hot bath. Whatever compelled me to leave London? How did I end up in this rat hole? Fighting back tears, I spent the night making myself as small and invisible as possible.

The only way I'd get out of this devilish situation was to solve the murder of Countess Pavlovna myself. *But how?* I was locked up.

Sherlock Holmes may be an armchair detective, but I was a "mere file clerk and a woman no less." No doubt if I had the luxury of an arm chair—and a nice cuppa—instead of being crouched in a jail cell, praying the blokes leave me alone, I could do as well as he.

To distract myself from my wretched surroundings, I analyzed the clues at the scene of the crime and the strange events of Mata Hari's garden party. *First, what do I know about the victim?* She was Countess Pavlovna, visiting from Russia, possibly one of Louis Renault's lovers, a member of a political group called the White Women, and my War Office contact—Madame Bovary—which meant she was working for the good guys. Fredrick Fredricks handed her something just before her death, possibly a fountain pen or some other small silver object. If she was in cahoots with Fredricks, maybe she was really working for the bad guys. She was found lying atop Mata Hari's fur coat. *Are she and Mata Hari working together?*

And her death? She had white foam on her mouth and blue lips, which suggested poisoning. I'd guess a very fast-acting poison such as arsenic, cyanide, or strychnine. There was the strange rash on her wrist and yellow powder, probably pollen, on the hem of her dress and her slippers. She could have been allergic to the pollen. And of course, there was the bloody letter knife and the wine stain across the bodice of her dress to explain.

Second, what is the motive? Who had a reason to kill the countess? If she was a double agent, Fredricks may have been sent to Paris to kill her. My theory was that he worked for the Germans taking out double agents. Of course, the upper brass didn't believe me, a mere file clerk and a woman no less.

Then again, if the countess was having an affair with Renault—or even appeared to be having an affair with him—his wife had reason to do her in. Berthe said Madame Renault was insanely jealous of Mata Hari and threatened to gouge her eyes out. I wonder… What if the countess was wearing Mata Hari's fur coat and the assailant attacked her from the back, thinking she was Mata Hari? Perhaps Mata Hari was the real target.

So who would want to kill Mata Hari? Fredricks might if she too were a double agent. And of course, Madame Renault. Then again, if Mata Hari wanted Renault all to herself, she may have killed the countess.

What was the countess doing when she was killed? Why was she in Renault's library? Was she looking for something? Renault's factory made tanks and munitions for the war effort. If the countess was spying for the Germans, she might have been gathering intelligence on Renault's war manufacturing. In that case, Renault himself might have caught her in the act and killed her. He was such a bully and so disagreeable, I didn't doubt he was capable of murder. And the torn receipt I found in her hand suggested he was selling something to the Germans… Schmidt Industries to be exact.

The scratches and bruises on her face and arms suggested she'd been attacked and fought off her attacker. Could she have been poisoned *and* then attacked too?

Finally, was Countess Pavlovna the woman behind the hedgerow? And who was the other woman who had threatened her? The voice was so familiar. Mata Hari? No, it hadn't been sultry enough. Berthe? Why in the world would Berthe threaten the countess?

I had no shortage of questions. Now if only I had more answers. I needed to find a way to get back into that library… and to get tickets to Parade ballet on Friday… provided I got out of this hell-hole by then.

I must have dozed off leaning against the wall. I jolted awake when the guard raked the bars with his stick. I pushed my hand through the bars and my face up against them. "There's been a dreadful mistake," I shouted. "I'm Fiona Figg. I work for the War Office in London. I don't belong here." The phantom cyanide pill was calling again. If only I had one.

My pleas were drowned out by the coughing and whooping of the men as they gathered the mornings' rations of stale bread up off the floor.

"Please, Mr. Guard, call the British Embassy and they'll tell you. I'm Fiona Figg…"

It was no use. No one was listening.

At least the men had grown used to me. Scarface no longer leered and jeered. In fact, he offered me a crust of bread and a cup of water. I declined for fear of having to use the facilities, despite my stomach growling with hunger.

Eventually, they would have to haul me before a magistrate and charge me. They couldn't just keep me in this stinking cell indefinitely. Could they?

I sunk to the floor and hugged my knees to my chest. Warm tears rolled down my cheeks. I buried my face in my knees. Wrapping my arms around my head and making myself as small as possible, I tried to make myself disappear… or at least wake up from this nightmare.

* * *

Time stretched. I didn't know how many hours I'd spent locked up. I was becoming delusional from lack of food and water. The smells emanating from my own person were unspeakable. I'd never been so offensive in my life.

"*Comtesse*," the guard called out.

I stood up. I'd taken to answering to my new appellation.

"You're the boy continually going on about some gal called Fiona?" he asked, glaring at me.

Hearing my name lifted me out of the fog. "I'm Fiona."

"There's a *rosbif* here looking for a Miss Fiona Figg." The guard sorted through a jangle of giant keys and unlocked the cell.

A roast beef is looking for me? What does that mean? Oh, right. The French called the British roast beef just like we called them frogs. I hoped to heaven the roast beef, whoever he was, had come to rescue me.

"Move back," the guard commanded as the men rushed the door. "*Comtesse*, come with me." He gestured. "You're going to tell this gentleman where to

85

find your girlfriend or face a beating."

Hesitantly, I exited the cell and followed him through the heavy metal door. At least being in imminent danger had perfected my French. I understood every word.

At the end of the hallway, the guard ushered me into a tiny room and then shut and locked the door. I sat in a wooden chair and rested my head on the table. Exhaustion set in, and I was to the point that I didn't care whether I lived or died. I wagered I'd rather die than spend another night in that overcrowded cell.

When keys jangled at the door, I lifted my head.

The guard opened the door, and as a familiar lanky form appeared in the doorway, tears filled my eyes.

"I daresay a mistake has been made," he said. "Guard, this is not Fiona Figg. This is the man wrongly accused of murdering the countess."

But the door had already closed, and the guard had gone.

I broke down crying. "Clifford," I sobbed.

His eyes widened. "Good Lord. Fiona, is that you?" Clifford moved to my side. "What in heaven's name is that smell?" He waved his hand in front of his Roman nose. "What happened to you? Why are you in that getup?"

"I... I... I." I couldn't get a word out.

"And your hair!" Clifford sat down across from me. "You look like something the cat dragged in."

I touched the black spikes on the top of my head that passed for hair. Laughing gave me a coughing fit. "I feel even worse." Crying, laughing, coughing, and speaking at the same time, I was overcome with dizziness. Not usually one to faint, I opened my mouth in surprise, and then lost consciousness.

* * *

Even before I opened my eyes, I could tell by the strong smell of alcohol and bleach that I was in an infirmary. I shuddered. The last time I'd been in a hospital was back at Charing Cross the night Andrew died holding my hand.

As a volunteer nurse, I'd seen so many young men battered and bleeding, but watching my own husband—ex-husband—take his last gasping breath had been too much for me to bear. And now because of my foolishness I was taking a much needed bed that should go to one of those brave young soldiers.

I tried to sit up but was overcome by a wave of nausea and my head fell back against the pillow. I knew I was in a hospital, but where? *And how did I get here?* I'd always prided myself on my photographic memory, but now I couldn't remember what happened this morning. *Golly.* I didn't even know if it was night or day, and my head ached.

Documents, even ones in code or foreign languages, were burned into my brain like brands on animal hide. But the ebb and flow of daily experience were not as black and white as a memorandum or a telegram. Too bad. It would make everything a lot easier.

Steeling myself, I opened one eye and then the other. As the room came into focus, so did the whimpers and moans of women in beds on both sides of me. *Good heavens.* I was in the maternity ward. I couldn't have forgotten nine months, not to mention a romantic tryst. Unless I had amnesia, the last tryst I'd had was with Andrew before the divorce. And there hadn't been anyone interested in me since then, except that dolt, Clifford.

If men were like documents, I'd have been able to read my husband's infidelity. But if Andrew's dalliance had been written on his face, it was with invisible ink.

"Thank God you're awake." The voice came from my bedside.

"Clifford?" I turned my head toward him. *Clifford!*

"I was afraid you'd bought the farm, old girl."

My terrible memories of the jail returned, as well as the hope that had flooded my soul when Clifford had them fetch me from the cell. "If it weren't for you, Clifford dear, I believe I might have." It took all my strength to lift my hand. "You saved me."

"The nurses here helped a bit too. They gave you intravenous fluids. You were severely dehydrated from being in that horrible jail." He held my hand in both of his. The warmth of his touch was soothing.

"How did you find me there?"

"When you didn't show up for dinner last evening, I got worried and went looking for you." He gave me a crooked smile. "And when I couldn't find you last night and then again today, I went to the police."

"Good old reliable Clifford."

"You make me sound like a Vauxhall motorcar."

I removed my hand from his and sat up. *Blimey.* I wasn't wearing anything but a flimsy hospital gown. I pulled the sheets up around my neck. "Where are my clothes?"

"Hopefully burned."

I furrowed my brows. "That bad, eh?"

He nodded. "Full of critters I'm afraid."

"How did you spring me from that horrible jail?"

"Well… once I found you, I explained that you're a file clerk and not a murderer."

"I could be a file clerk and a murderer too. One doesn't exclude the other."

"True. But they were going to release you anyway. Countess Pavlovna committed suicide. She killed herself. So you couldn't be the murderer."

"What do you mean, killed herself?"

"The autopsy revealed she'd taken poison. And she left a suicide note."

"What did the note say?"

"It said something deuced odd. *The jig is up. I know what I have to do.*"

"That's all?" I narrowed my eyes at him. "What makes the police think it's a suicide note?"

"According to Fredricks, the countess was overwrought about events in Russia. She's a member of the aristocracy, you see, and those horrible Bolsheviks wanted her dead."

"Fredricks? What does he have to do with this?"

"Fredricks found the note. Darn clever of him, really."

Found it or wrote it, I wondered.

"By committing suicide, she gave them just what they wanted." I thought for a moment. "What makes you so sure one of those Bolsheviks didn't do it?"

"I say, I hadn't thought of that." He scratched his head. "Were there any Bolsheviks at the garden party?"

Abby came to mind. "I don't know, but I'm going to get out of this hospital bed and find out." I made to get out of bed but realized I wasn't dressed to leave. "Clifford dear, can you bring me some proper clothing?"

"What in heaven's name were you doing wearing a man's suit?"

"It's a long story. But if you bring me some clothes and take me out for a nice cuppa, I'll tell you everything." *Well, not everything.* "And then you can tell me what you know about the countess's death."

"You won't disappear on me again?" The concern on his face was sweet. I shook my head. "Not without any clothes."

Clifford had nearly reached the exit when I called out to him. "Can you get us tickets to the ballet while you're out?"

"Good Lord. You're thinking of going to the ballet at a time like this?" He doubled back to my bedside.

"I'll be forever grateful if you can get us tickets to the ballet for Friday." I don't know what I thought I could find out from spying on the Renault's at the ballet, but it was worth a try.

"If it will make you happy." Clifford smiled. "I'll be honored to take you to the ballet." He was whistling as he left the room.

Waiting for Clifford to return with clothes to spring me out of the hospital, I made a mental list of the tasks at hand.

First, I had to find out what really happened to the countess. I didn't believe the suicide story, especially if Fredricks "found" the suicide note. She may have been poisoned—and I needed to figure out who did that—but she also had that gash on her forehead and bruises on her neck, which suggested she fought with an attacker before she succumbed to the poison.

The countess was lying beside a pearl-handled letter opener covered in blood. But it wasn't her blood since she wasn't bleeding—the stain on her dress smelled like wine and not blood—which suggested someone who had regular access to the library had tried to kill her. But the countess got hold of the letter knife and stabbed the attacker. I doubted party guests regularly carried letter knives along with them in their handbags. The house belonged to Monsieur Renault. But who else lived there? And who else might have been a frequent enough visitor to know the whereabouts of a letter knife? Mata Hari came to mind.

Second, I had to find the silver pen—or whatever it was—that Fredricks passed to the countess shortly before she died. I was sure the clandestine handoff was involved with her death. Could Fredricks have passed her information and then tried to stab her for being a double agent? No, that couldn't be. I followed the countess from her conversation with Fredricks and watched her enter the library alone. No one followed her inside, which means the attacker had to have been in there already, possibly waiting for her.... Unless Fredricks circled around the house and came in through the French window. But could he have done that so quickly? And without tracking any soil inside? And why would he have done it, especially if he's the one who poisoned her? It seemed likely he had done that. He could have spilled something into the countess's champagne flute before he handed it to her.

Which reminded me, I never got the chance to call the War Office and make my report. I must call Captain Hall as soon as possible and tell him about Fredricks's insurance claim and the news clipping. *Could the invoice I found in the countess's dead hand have anything to do with the minerals Fredricks is shipping?* Was Fredricks working with Renault? Perhaps together they killed the countess. If Madame Bovary was a double-agent then that would support my theory that Fredricks was knocking off spies who'd turned against the Germans. Perhaps over tea, I could pump Clifford for information about Fredricks's mineral shipping business.

Third, there was the matter of Mata Hari. The dead countess was lying on top of her fur coat. Why? Had Mata Hari lured the countess into the library and killed her? *Which reminds me, I still haven't recovered my passport from the sneaky minx.* More to the point, I hadn't ascertained why she would want my passport and what she planned to do with it.

She and Fredricks were definitely involved. But was it more than a love affair? I daresay Mata Hari appeared to be the queen of combining business with pleasure. She was involved with so many officers and princes that, for all I knew, she could be the power behind the throne orchestrating the whole bloody war.

And then there was the file on Mata Hari in Room 40. *Why would British Intelligence have a file on her unless she was a spy or at least a person of interest?* Then again, it seemed most men found her a person of interest. And Room 40 might be uneasy about any woman who wielded her kind of power over men. On the other hand, if British Intelligence had a file on her, she must be up to something nefarious. Then again, for all I knew, they had a file on me too.

I closed my eyes and tried to conjure Mata Hari's file. I imagined myself back in Room 40. I was standing at my filing cabinet, the men were chattering on the other side of the partition, the smell of brewing coffee was wafting over from the kitchenette, I could feel the thick file folder in my hands. I opened the folder and glanced at the contents. *What in bloody Nora did it say?*

My meditations were interrupted by a nurse calling out to her compatriot, "Check on the patient in bed one."

Her compatriot answered, "I did twenty minutes ago."

Good heavens—21! That's it. Mata Hari was agent H21, the mysterious lady agent who was seducing officers in Paris and spying for the Germans. The one Mr. Grey mentioned before I left London. The file I saw in Room 40 named Mata Hari as German agent H21. Yet the telegram I'd found in her overnight case from G. Ladoux suggested she was working for the French. And if she was a double agent, that would certainly give Fredricks a motive to kill her. He probably poisoned the countess. Mata Hari could be next.

Chapter Nine: Sabotage

C lifford said he'd gotten the checkered poplin dress from his cousin. She must be more of a woman than I. The poplin print sagged in all the wrong places. Still, it was better than a hospital gown or a lice-infested tuxedo. He'd forgotten to get shoes, so I had to wear my oversized men's boots. As I slipped one on, I realized how lucky it was that he hadn't disposed of my boots since the pollen sample on my glove was still tucked into my boot.

I do wish he'd thought to grab a hat. I felt naked without a hat. A good hat was invaluable. A hat was more than a fashion accessory, it was a practical espionage tool. You could tilt the brim over one eye to stay incognito. And a hatpin had a multitude of uses.

Clifford persuaded the nurses to release me into his custody. And off I went, hatless and exposed, black spikes for hair, wearing a frock as baggy as a gunnysack, with my oversized men's boots on my unsteady feet.

I expected the café patrons to stare as Clifford led me to a table. In London they would have. Apparently in Paris outlandish dress was the norm because no one batted an eye.

Clifford wanted to sit outside and enjoy the sunshine. I insisted we go inside. I found a tiny table tucked into a dark corner in the back of the café to escape the scrutiny of our fellow diners, on the chance they chose to turn their attention my way.

Café Lyon was a cheerful little place with red-curtained windows and a black and white tiled floor. The checkered tablecloths and wine bottles in wicker holders put me in mind of a picnic, which made me think of the day Andrew proposed to me in Greenwich Park overlooking the Thames. My happy memory was instantly replaced by the last tragic image of poor Andrew, his beautiful face disfigured by mustard gas. On that night, a door to my heart had closed forever.

Even Clifford—not the most perceptive of men—must have sensed the depths of my melancholy, for we sat in silence until the coffee arrived. I longed for a nice cup of tea, but Clifford was right, the tea in this country tasted like dishwater. He convinced me to try the coffee, which he claimed was exquisite.

Famished, I ordered an omelet. The French may not know how to make a good cuppa, but they had perfected the omelet.

"So," he said, stirring his coffee. "What happened?"

I took a sip of my coffee and recoiled. "How can you drink this stuff without milk and sugar?"

"It is a bit stiff, isn't it?" He grinned.

"It's downright harsh." I took another tentative sip. "It'll put hair on your chest."

He blinked. "You say the darndest things for a girl."

I ran my fingers through the stubble on my head. "I'm not your ordinary girl."

"You can say that again." He took a drink. "You know what this needs? A shot of brandy." He gestured to the waiter, ordered two shots of brandy, and then turned back to me. "So—"

"So, why does your friend Fredricks ship minerals?" I decided to get right to the point before he could grill me about my stay in jail… and my disguise.

"Minerals?"

"He has several insurance claims for lost mineral samples."

"How do you know about that?" He poured a large splash of brandy into his coffee cup and a thimble into mine.

"I have my ways."

"I'm sure you do." He winked. "It's a funny story actually. About a year ago, Fredricks went to Brazil. He absolutely fell in love with—"

"Clifford." I gave him a stern look. "The point?"

"Yes, sorry." He blushed and stared down at his cup. "Right. So he opened a rubber plant and ships minerals from Brazil for the war effort."

"A rubber plant?"

"That's right. He's a darn clever businessman. You know he once ran a mill in South Africa. He's really a jack-of-all-trades. He can do anything he sets his mind to. He's an extraordinary—"

"He's the greatest thing since treacle pudding." Sometimes Clifford's nattering on was deuced annoying. "Tell me more about the mineral shipments from this rubber plant."

"Awfully bad luck, actually. Poor chap has had important samples blown up by the Jerries." He shook his head. "A shame really because he's an awfully resourceful fellow…" His voice trailed off. He must have noticed me rolling my eyes.

"So his minerals ride on ships that are bombed en route from South America to Britain," I said more to myself than to him.

"Well, some were on their way to France too." He pointed to my coffee cup. "If you're not going to finish yours, may I?"

I passed my cup to him, only too happy to get rid of the bitter swill.

"You still haven't told me what happened and why you were dressed—"

"How do the minerals help with the war effort?" I interrupted. I wasn't ready to explain my appearance and undercover assignment to Clifford the town crier. If word got back to Captain Hall that I was wearing disguises again, he'd probably sack me.

"Fredricks has some experiments going with rubber. He's inventing a new way to make tires or something. So that could be darn useful to our troops."

"Ours or theirs?" I stifled a yawn. Next to food, what I needed most was sleep.

"You don't still suspect Fredricks, do you?" Clifford scowled. "He's a darn good chap. You know he saved my life once. It's a funny story really. We were hunting elephants—"

"Really, Clifford, why must you go around killing defenseless elephants?" I dropped my fork. "It's appalling."

"You're not very sporting, old girl."

94

"Killing an innocent animal is not very sporting if you ask me."

He drank the last of the brandy straight and then stared down at his hands. "Do you think I should write about the war?" he asked earnestly. "At the Dingo bar, I met a young American chap last night named Hemingway. He's driving an ambulance and wants to write a novel about the war." He finished my coffee. "I gave him a few pointers."

"About the war or writing?" I asked, frustrated by Clifford's inability to stick to one subject or give direct answers.

"Both actually. I am a writer and a soldier after all. I've done a good deal more than drive a bloody ambulance." He patted his leg.

"Yes, your war wound." I reached over and patted his hand. "You're very brave, Clifford dear."

He smiled and blushed.

"You never told me how it happened." I knew if he started talking about the war, he'd never get around to asking me about my stay in jail or my costume.

"It was a bloody saboteur." His face hardened. "One of my own outfit too."

Sabotage! My heavens. That's it. I swallowed the last bite of omelet. "Clifford, you're a genius." I stood up and brushed imaginary crumbs from my dress. "I've got to get to the embassy."

"Whatever for?" He dropped his napkin on the table and stood too.

"I've got to call the War Office."

"What? Why?"

I tried to think of a good fib. "My passport."

"Must you go now?"

I glanced at my watch. "Good heavens. They close in thirty minutes." I scooted out from behind the table. "I'd better hop to it."

"I'll call a taxi."

"I'm fine. I don't need an escort." Actually, I wasn't fine. My head was spinning and I felt nauseated. I needed a hot bath, another full meal, and a good night's sleep. But first, I had to tell Capitan Hall my suspicions. I took a few steps, started swaying, and grabbed onto the back of a stranger's chair.

Clifford caught up to me and took my elbow. "I'm not letting you out of my sight." He insisted on escorting me to the embassy to *get a new passport*. It was as if he thought I was going to faint again simply because I'd already done it... twice that day.

For once, the embassy hadn't closed early. The receptionist smiled at Clifford but looked at me with suspicion. Perhaps it was my smell... or my shorn hair. Eventually, after much pleading, she agreed to allow me to use the telephone to call the War Office. Keeping her distance as if I were a rabid dog, she led me to an office and sat me down at a desk with a telephone. She placed the call and then handed me the receiver. I scowled at her, but she just stood staring at me, as if I might make off with the telephone.

"Do you mind?" I asked. "It's private."

She tightened her lips, turned on her heels, and headed for the door. At the threshold she turned back. "I'll be waiting just outside the door. You've got ten minutes."

Whether it was from exhaustion or my religious upbringing, I was overcome with an urge to confess.

When Captain Hall heard about my stint in jail, he blew a gasket. "I told you no disguises, no Sherlock Holmes. You're assignment is just to watch Fredricks and report back."

"Yes sir." My fingers troubled the lace collar of Clifford's cousin's dress. "There's another tiny hitch I should mention." I swallowed hard. "I'm involved in a murder investigation."

"Why am I not surprised?" He let out an exasperated sigh. "Not another countess." He chuckled.

"Actually, yes, another countess. She is—was—involved with Fredricks. He passed her what looked like a silver pen just before she was found dead."

"Don't tell me. You were there when she died. You're not playing doctor again, Miss Figg?" I could practically hear him shaking his head. "Don't interfere with the local constabulary. Stick with following Fredricks."

"I was trying to find the silver pen he gave her—"

"Follow and report back. Nothing more. I don't want you in harm's way."

Too blooming late to worry about putting me in danger. "But I thought if I found the pen then we'd—"

Captain Hall interrupted me again. "Look but don't touch. Keep your distance. I don't want Fredricks to know he's under surveillance. We need more solid evidence before we move in on him. And if he's just following orders, we need to find out who's giving them."

"Yes, sir. I have something to report, something very important."

"Go on."

I took a deep breath. "The murdered countess was Madame Bovary."

"Our sleeper agent? She was the one killed?"

"Yes, sir. And that's not all." I hurried my words before he could interrupt me again. "I found an insurance claim in Fredricks's pocket."

"What's so special about an insurance claim? And I don't want to know how you got into his pocket." I heard the rustling of papers on the other end. "You're supposed to be keeping your distance."

I repeated the names of the ships I'd seen listed on Fredricks's insurance invoice. "Bagdale, Dora, Firelight and Hartmann."

"Are you sure of those names? Twenty-three good men died on the Bagdale," Captain Hall said in a weary voice. "The Germans are sinking up to half a dozen British ships a day now."

"I think Fredricks may have something to do with ships sinking."

"What do you mean?"

"Well, when I delivered his newspaper—"

"Don't tell me why you're delivering his newspaper." He sighed.

"He ripped out a headline about a British cargo ship sinking."

"What ship?"

"Anatolia sunk on June twenty-third."

"The Anatolia hit a mine."

Sir, what if that ship didn't hit a mine? What if Fredricks planted explosives aboard disguised as mineral samples?"

There was silence on the other end.

"Did the other ships listed on his invoice hit mines too?"

"I'll check on the others." His voice perked up. "Why? What are you thinking?"

"What if Fredricks is sabotaging our ships and then filing insurance claims for his losses?" Clifford was right about one thing. His friend Fredricks was fiendishly clever.

"You mean he insures his mineral samples, plants bombs inside them, and then has the nerve to collect insurance for his lost property?"

"Yes, sir. That's exactly what I mean."

He whistled into the telephone. "If you're right, we've got to find out his next move. We've got to get ahead of him." I heard papers shuffling on the other end again.

"This is too important for an amateur. Along with cargo essential to the war effort, lives are at stake here. I'm going to assign another agent to Fredricks."

My heart sunk like a torpedoed ship. "But sir, I can do it."

"Miss Figg, you've done enough. This calls for someone with more experience, a professional… a man."

"But sir—"

"This is not a game. If what you say is true, then Fredricks—the Black Panther—may be one of the most dangerous saboteurs on the continent."

"I assure you, sir. I can finish my assignment. Please, sir. Don't take me off the case."

"Well…" A pencil or pen was tapping against a desk on the other end. I imagined Captain Blinker Hall keeping time with his eyelashes. "We'll see. For now, you're to meet the new operative when he arrives in Paris. Fill him in on everything you know."

"How will I find him?"

"He will find you. The code is *the acorn doesn't fall far from the tree*, to which you respond *so long as the tree is an oak*. Now just stay put in your hotel." The tapping sound stopped. "This isn't a fancy dress party, Miss Figg. The clock is ticking. We need to find out which ships Fredricks has contracted to carry samples and remove them before more precious cargo and lives are lost. Remember, *acorn and oak*."

"Acorn and oak," I repeated.

"Now if that's all, I've got work to do."

"But sir—" I hadn't told him about Mata Hari, agent H21. And that she

98

might be a double agent. And that she might be in danger.

It was too late. He'd hung up.

Chapter Ten: The Ballet

On the way back to the hotel, Clifford pestered me so much, I eventually had to make up a story about accidently bringing an important file with me on vacation to Paris to visit my Aunt Mable, which necessitated the trip to the embassy to call Captain Hall and report it.

"There's something not quite cricket about your story," he said, holding the hotel door open for me. "A missing file doesn't explain why you were disguised as a waiter at Mata Hari's garden party."

"Clifford darling, you deserve to know."

He nodded encouragingly.

"And someday, I'll tell you."

His face fell.

"But right now I need a hot bath and a lie-down." I patted his arm. "But tomorrow afternoon, you're taking me to the ballet."

"The ballet?"

"The matinee of Parade ballet, remember? Didn't you get the tickets yet?"

He shook his head. "Sorry, old girl. I forgot."

"Be a good boy and go get us tickets now and then come back for me at noon tomorrow." I don't know why I added "matinee." Given the blackouts, all performances were in the afternoons. In London, all shows were cancelled. But in Paris, the show must go on.

"But, Fiona…"

"I'll be fit as a fiddle by tomorrow." I shooed him away. "Go on. I'll be fine." After a night in that horrid jail, I didn't feel fine.

I left Clifford sputtering in the lobby and snuck into the service elevator behind the staircase in hopes that no one would see me in my baggy dress, men's boots, and crewcut.

Finally, back in my hotel room after what seemed like a lifetime, I stripped off my borrowed clothes and ran a warm bath. I was about to toss my foul socks into the waste bin when I noticed the white glove. Crikey. I'd completely forgotten about it. In fact, it seemed so long ago, and I'd been so caught up in my own ordeal, I nearly forgot about my fledgling investigation into the murder of Countess Pavlovna. I examined the yellow stain on the glove. Pollen, I surmised. But what kind of pollen? And what might it tell me about the murder? I carefully wrapped it in tissue paper.

First thing after my bath, I would send it off to my friend Daisy Nelson, a self-proclaimed "cunning woman" and practitioner of white magic, who ran the dispensary at Charing Cross Hospital and was an expert botanist. If anyone could determine what it was and where it was from, Daisy could.

I sunk into the warm water and closed my eyes. Thank goodness the hotel had hot water today. I'd never take a hot bath for granted again. Lathering my hair with jasmine-scented soap, I felt jolly lucky to be staying in such a luxurious hotel. Given the bugs I'd picked up in jail, I probably needed something stronger than jasmine soap, but it would have to do for now.

Still hungry, I splurged on room service and ordered a supper of potato and mutton stew. Captain Hall did tell me to stay in my room.

Clean and fed, now more than anything I wanted sleep. But as my father used to say, "No rest for the weary." I had to push on and find out which ships Fredricks planned to sabotage next. The lives of those seamen were more important than my kip. And if my suspicions were right, I could link Fredricks to the murder of the countess.

So, despite Captain Hall's strict orders to stay put, I had other plans. As he repeated so often, lives were at stake and the clock was ticking. We didn't have time to wait for another agent. Anyway, I was determined to prove that I could do the job as well as any man, professional or not.

First thing was to mail the parcel to Daisy. Next, I'd try to get more dirt on Fredricks. And tomorrow at the ballet, I'd see what I could find out about Renault. *Blimey*. The ballet. *What will I wear? My frumpy skirt sets aren't appropriate, but that's all I have... besides my maid's outfit.* I revised my plan. First mail parcel, second go shopping for a proper gown to wear to the ballet.

After my bath, I put on one of said skirt sets along with my practical oxfords and then set out to mail my parcel. Getting the glove properly wrapped, sealed, and posted, took me over an hour. By the time it was off to London, I was dead on my feet. I was so exhausted, just breathing took effort. There was no way I could go shopping in this state. I absolutely needed a nap.

Back in my hotel room, I fell back onto the bed without removing my clothes. *Ahhh.* It felt good to lay down. I'd been crouching in that jail cell for what seemed like an eternity. Unable to do otherwise, I surrendered to sleep.

* * *

Good heavens! I'd slept all night. My watch said it was after nine o'clock. I shook it. *Did it stop?* No it was ticking. *Golly.* I hadn't stayed in bed this late since my honeymoon... only then I wasn't sleeping.

Clifford was picking me up at noon for the ballet, and I still didn't have anything decent to wear. If I hurried I just might have time to bathe, wolf down some breakfast, and then go shopping for a proper dress. I'd have to hop it.

Instead of a nice bath, I washed quickly with a hand towel. I regretted looking in the mirror. My upper lip was red and blotchy from ripping that blasted mustache off so many times. At least today, I wouldn't have to wear it.

Shame I had to settle for a department store when Paris was full of custom designer boutiques. I wound my watch. But with just over two hours until show time, an off-the-rack frock would have to do. Scanning my handy *Baedeker's Paris*, I found *Au Bon Marché*, listed as the oldest department store in the world. Close to the Luxembourg Gardens and across the Seine, I'd have to take two trains to get there. I didn't have time. Closer was the *Grands Magasins du Louvre*, on the ground floor of the Grand Louvre Hotel, which was only one train-ride away and half as far.

I slipped on my practical oxfords and off I went.

The magnificent edifice of the Grand Louvre Hotel covered an entire city block. Baedeker's was right. Inside you could find any luxury your heart desired, from gorgeous rooms for reading to a scrumptious looking buffet where refreshments were dispensed gratis, along with haberdashery, laces, and all the accessories a lady would need for an excursion to the ballet with an officer... provided she could afford them.

I would have loved to have a leisurely look around, but I was on a time-sensitive mission. I located the ladies' eveningwear section on the second floor and made a beeline toward the gowns. Like a beggar before a banquet, my heart soared at the sight of such delicious dresses. Immediately my eye was drawn to lovely pillars of pale pink satin fringed with delicate bead-work draped from a vivid burgundy velvet boned bodice. I was in love. Afraid to look at the price, I swept it off the hanger and held it up to my waist. Even if it cost a month's wages, I had to have this exquisite gown. I really needed the War Office to give me an expense account. The damage I could do in a place like this.

The look on my face when the shop girl told me the price must have said it all. She took the gown from my hands and led me to the discount corner where last year's models had been marked down for quick sale. Like a suitor on the rebound, I grabbed the first decent one I saw, paid for it, and took off before buyer's remorse set in.

The dampness of my spirits evaporated when, on the way out, I spotted a darling straw lace hat with black chiffon on top. I tried it on. Yes, it would spruce up my ensemble nicely. I paid for the hat, and couldn't wait to get back to the hotel and put myself together.

As I walked down the avenue, an idea hit me. If the Renaults were at the ballet all afternoon, perhaps I could find a way to get back into their library. I did have my maid's outfit along. It would be a shame not to use it. I quickened my pace and hatched a plan. After the first act, I'd feign a headache, have Clifford take me back to the hotel, change into my maid's uniform, catch a cab out to the Renault estate, and present myself as a special type of cleaner—for accidents and such—hired by Mrs. Renault. I smiled to myself. *Yes. It just might work.*

* * *

Clifford was only ten minutes late. He looked dashing in his starched shirtwaist and black tails. His blue eyes blazing, he took my gloved hand. "Fiona, you look lovely."

"Thank you, Clifford dear. So do you."

He blushed.

* * *

Outside, Théâtre du Châtelet was a castle fortress on the bank of the Seine. Inside, the magnificent opera hall was filled with a who's who of Parisian society. Even with a war on, diplomates, statesmen, and colonels in dress uniforms escorted bejeweled society ladies decked out in their finest.

Our seats were in the nose-bleed section of the third balcony. I rented some opera glasses... not to see the performance, but to spy on the Renaults. The best seats in the house. Where might those be. I settled into my seat. Whether from the dizzying height, the impending ballet, or my mission, I was perspiring with excitement.

While I scanned the crowd with my opera glass, Clifford read from the program.

"Music by Erik Satie, choreographed by Léonide Massine, scenario by Jean Cocteau, stage design and costumes by Pablo Picasso, performed by *Ballet Russes*." Clifford touched my arm. "I say, listen to this. Scored for typewriters, sirens, airplane propellers, ticker tape, and a lottery wheel." He chuckled. "Good Lord, Fiona, you've brought us to a surrealist ballet."

Good Lord, indeed.

I spotted Mr. and Mrs. Renault sitting in a box near the stage. "Come on."

I stood up.

"But we just sat down." Clifford narrowed his brows.

"I want you to introduce me to the Renaults." I gestured across the auditorium.

"The Renaults? Now?" Clifford looked bewildered, not an unusual look for him.

"Let's go before the lights go down." I tugged at his sleeve.

He rose with a huff. "I say, you're a peculiar girl."

Mrs. Renault was wearing a pale blue gown with a beaded bodice. With her dark eyes, long neck, and thin lips, she looked like an elegant giraffe towering over her husband. She was a good head taller than he, and at least a decade younger. If she was surprised by our interruption, her aristocratic countenance didn't betray her.

After the requisite introductions and small talk, I dropped the bomb. "It was shocking to read about the Russian Countess found deceased in your library."

Mrs. Renault glanced at her husband and then back at me. "The library is Louis's habitat, not mine." The way she said *habitat* suggested her husband's library was a lair where he devoured unsuspecting prey.

"Did you know her well?"

"Louis knew her better than I. But that's true of most attractive ladies."

Ouch. Obviously, I'd hit a nerve. Mrs. Renault was not a fan of the countess. But did she feel strongly enough to murder her?

"Christine, darling, now is not the time," Renault said softly, "Let's not air our laundry…" He gave me an apologetic smile.

"My *culottes* are clean." Mrs. Renault smirked. "I don't know about yours."

"I need a drink." Mr. Renault grabbed his wife's arm. "Let's go see if we can find one." He pulled her past us and out of the box into the hallway. "If you'll excuse us," he said on the way by.

"That went well," I said.

For once, Clifford was shocked into silence.

The ballet was a bizarre spectacle of costumes, strange scenery, and atonal music. To my surprise, Clifford was enchanted. At least I wouldn't have to feign illness. The off-kilter backdrop and spinning bodies was making me motion sick. In fact, I wasn't sure I could wait until the end of the first act.

I leaned closer and whispered in Clifford's ear. "I'm not feeling well. I wonder if we could leave?"

"Now?" He balked. "It's almost over. Can't you hold out until the end, old girl?"

"But it's not even the end of the first act."

He held up the program and pointed.

Blast!

Parade, A Ballet in One Act. *As Thomas Hobbes said of life, it's "nasty, brutish, and short."*

There goes my plan to sneak into the Renault's library while they're away.

Chapter Eleven: The Microfilm

My trip to the Renault estate may have been postponed, but my mission to get the dirt on Fredrick Fredricks had not. I still had the rest of the afternoon. I'd might as well make the best of it. And while my dizzying trip to the ballet hadn't gleaned much, it had established that either Mr. or Mrs. Renault may have had a motive to kill the countess. I would have to find some excuse to get back out to their estate and search the library... and soon.

In the meantime, hopefully, no one had remarked on my—Harold's—absence for the last two days. Even bellboys get days off, after all. Then again, Berthe probably couldn't wait to tell everyone, including the grumpy clerk, that "Cutie" was arrested for murder. *By now they must know that "Cutie" is innocent.*

Dressed as Harold the helpful bellboy, I made my way to the lobby for my daily rounds. I'd missed the freedom of movement. And, as much as I disapproved of perfume-soaked ladies and noxious cigar smoke, I had to admit the heady mix was a monumental improvement over the nauseating smells of my jail cell.

On a satin sofa in a dim corner sat Mata Hari and Fredrick Fredricks, heads together, giggling. As long as they didn't get any notions to go upstairs, both of their rooms would be empty for the foreseeable future. Of course, there was the little problem of how to get in.

Wait. Should I be worried about Mata Hari? Should I try to warn her? If she *is* a double-agent, she might be Fredricks's next victim.

Mata Hari put her hand on Fredricks's knee.

I guess the seductress can take care of herself. I hope she knows what she's doing. Turning on my heels, I headed for the lift. I was in such a rush, I didn't see Berthe as I barreled out of the elevator on my way to Fredricks's room.

"Cutie, I've been so worried about you." Berthe played with her hair. "Did they let you out of jail?"

"I'm here, aren't I?"

"Why didn't you call me when you got out?" She stood in front of me, hands on her hips.

"We aren't exactly seeing each other or anything." I hoped I hadn't been leading her on, poor girl.

"That's good because the advert worked." She put her snub nose in the air. "What advert?"

"The widower looking for a wife. So I might be getting married, so long as he picks me over Suzanne," she said triumphantly as she stepped into the lift and disappeared.

Imagine. Marrying someone you met through a newspaper advert. How could you trust such a person? I shook my head. I was a fine one to talk. Look what happened to my marriage... and I'd met a nice respectable boy at a nice respectable house party.

Glancing down the long hallway in both directions, I removed a hairpin from my hat and began twisting it into the keyhole. In the movies it always worked. Struggling to keep the hairpin from bending in two, I poked and prodded until my fingers hurt.

The sound of a door opening down the hall made me redouble my efforts. As I was about to give up and seek cover, I felt the click before I heard it as the door lock gave way. I quickly opened the door and slid inside Fredricks's room.

Just as before, the room was so tidy you'd never know anyone was staying there. Whatever else he was, Fredricks was orderly and clean, which, after my experience continually cleaning the filthy kitchenette in Room 40, was more than I could say for most men.

I scanned the room. Where would I find information about what ships Fredricks planned to sabotage next? Where should I start looking? After my success with the insurance claim, I made a beeline to the wardrobe and began rifling through the pockets of all of Fredrick's jackets and jodhpurs. *Blast it.* Nothing but lint.

Next I searched the drawers of the nightstands. A pair of gold cuff links and a diamond tie stud sat inside a drawer in a tiny velvet tray. Otherwise, nothing.

Where would a journalist and huntsman keep records of his secret operations? I ran my hand around under the mattress. Again, nothing. He must have arrived with an attaché case or suitcase, but I didn't see any sign of one. In fact, if I didn't know better, I'd say Fredricks wasn't actually staying here. Aside from a tweed jacket, a linen jacket and a tuxedo jacket, one pair of jodhpurs, and tuxedo trousers, and a couple pairs of shiny black boots, the room was empty. More than that, it didn't have a lived-in feel… the way a room smells warm or sounds full with the lingering spirit of human presence.

After searching every corner of the room and finding nothing, I returned to the wardrobe. Staring down at the tall black boots, I wondered why Fredricks would sabotage British cargo ships. Why did he hate the British so much? Was he really a German and not South African? Then I remembered Archie's telegram from last month. "Fredricks's parents and siblings died in the Boer wars. His fault. More soon. Love, Archie Somersby." Fredricks's whole family was killed in the war between Great Britain and South Africa. Could that be why he hated the British? But why had Archie said the deaths were Fredricks's fault? I couldn't imagine anyone, even Fredricks, would try to get his whole family killed. But I did trust Archie.

Ah, Archie… and his telegram, which I still had. I never went anywhere without it. I carried it in the sole of my shoe. I liked to pretend it was a love note. It did say Love Archie, after all.

I lifted one of Fredricks's boots, turned it over, and gave it a good shake. Nothing. I did the same with its mate. Same result. My heart raced as I reached my hand inside the boot. I felt as if some creature were waiting inside to bite off my fingers. Just the thought of Fredricks's foot was off-putting to say the least. Still duty called. I was up to my elbow in boot when

I managed to loosen the insole with the tip of my index finger. I dropped to my knees to get some leverage and then really started digging. As I did, I heard a clinking coming from the heel of the boot. *Aha!* A false heel. I sat cross-legged on the floor and cranked on the heel to loosen it. My labors paid off. Three tiny silver canisters fell out and tinkled onto the marble floor. They were identical to the one I saw Fredricks pass to the countess.

I picked one up and examined it. It wasn't a pen at all, but more like a bullet or capsule with two halves pushed together. I carefully twisted one half free from the other. Inside I found a roll of microfilm, which I tucked into my vest pocket.

I opened another cylinder, which yielded a white pill. *Holy moly. Could that be a cyanide pill?* I'd heard that some spies carry them in case they're caught. Is that what Fredricks passed to the countess? A cyanide pill?

The third capsule held another tiny roll of microfilm, which I pocketed. I quickly repositioned the three tiny canisters back into the heel of the boot, refastened the heel, and replace the boot in the armoire.

Pleased with my work, I hopped up off the floor and rushed to make my escape. I had just reached the door and was about to turn the doorknob when I heard voices on the other side. *Blast! Now what?*

My heart leaped into my throat. I ran back to the wardrobe, jumped inside, and pulled the door shut after me. Holding my breath, I listened.

Keys jangled and the voices got louder. *Crikey. I was busted.* Even if I survived, I'd never get another assignment.

I pressed myself against the back of the wardrobe and hid behind one of Fredricks's riding jackets.

"In here," a woman said. *Is Fredricks bringing Mata Hari to his room this time?*

"Right behind you, darling," a man said. *That doesn't sound like Fredricks.*

I heard what sounded like a drawer opening.

"Look," the woman said, giggling. "For you, my love. Isn't it pretty?"

I was dying to peek out of the wardrobe and see what they were doing.

"We'd better be going now," the woman said. "Before someone comes and I get in trouble."

"I'll give you trouble, *mon chat*," the man said. "In all the right places." He had a slight accent I couldn't place. He definitely wasn't from Paris. Definitely not Fredricks. The voice was higher, more tenor than bass.

The woman laughed. "Désiré, you're so naughty."

Désiré? Who is Désiré? How I wanted to open the wardrobe a crack and take a look, but I didn't dare.

"What to make *crac-crac*?" the man asked. "Look at that nice bed."

I didn't know what *crac-crac* meant, but I could only imagine.

"Not here, you bad boy. Let's go."

Now, I recognized her voice.

I heard the door to the room open and shut and then silence. They were gone.

I exhaled, waited another minute, and then stepped out of the wardrobe.

Although tempted to run full speed out of the room and into the safety of the stairwell, I stopped to open the nightstand drawer. As I suspected, the gold cuff links and diamond tiepin were gone.

I had a hunch who the thief might be. But I couldn't exactly report it. *What would I say? I was disguised as a bellboy, hiding in Fredricks's wardrobe, when I heard a dodgy couple stealing his jewelry?* In any case, I had "bigger fish to fry," as my father would say.

I managed to get back to my room without anyone spotting me. It had been a very long day, and I was exhausted. I dropped into the desk chair and let out a sigh. It was only eight o'clock, but I longed for bed. But sleep would have to wait. Since the embassy was closed, I'd have to wait until tomorrow to contact Captain Hall and tell him about the microfilm. But that didn't mean I couldn't examine it for myself tonight.

Slipping the two coils of film from my vest pocket, I stood them on the desk. Pulling the lamp closer, I unrolled one and held it up. Shadowy script came into view. Some kind of list, but it was so small, I couldn't read it. I went to the lav to fetch a glass of water. Using the glass as a magnifier, I examined the film again, this time through the inch of water in the bottom of my glass. The list had names and dates, which I assumed were the names of ships and the dates they were scheduled to depart... or blow up.

How could I get word to Captain Hall? Even if I could use a private telephone, I don't know his home number. Would he be pleased or piqued? He'd told me to stay put in my room, and I'd disobeyed a direct order. On the other hand, I might have recovered information that would save crucial cargo and men's lives. Certainly, he would have to appreciate my ingenuity, *n'est-ce pas?*

Yawn. Overcome with exhaustion, I laid my head on the desk. I closed my eyes and weighed my options for finding a telephone. A few minutes of rest and then I'd go in search...

* * *

A knock at my door woke me up. I rubbed my stiff neck and glanced at my watch. Seven o'clock. *Good grief.* It was morning. I'd slept doubled over on the desk all night. *Blast.* Who was at my door?

I was still wearing my bellboy outfit, only a little wrinkled and worse for wear. But a bellboy only worked at the hotel. He didn't live there.

The knocking got louder and more insistent.

"Who is it?" I asked in a midrange, unsure of whether my visitor expected a man or a woman.

"Is this room Three-Four-Two?" a man answered.

"Who is it?" I asked again.

"Acorn." The voice sounded vaguely familiar in a way that sent chills up my spine.

I rubbed my eyes. *Did he say acorn? Double blast.* It must be the new agent Captain Hall had assigned to Fredricks.

"Oak," I said automatically. I opened the door.

Oh my lord. What is he doing here? I never thought I'd see him again.

"Am I too early? Do you want me to come back later?" he asked.

Speechless, I stood face-to-face with Archie Somersby.

Chapter Twelve: The Secret Agent

A rchie was even more handsome than I remembered. With his wavy chestnut hair and sea-green eyes he reminded me of a portrait of young Michael Faraday, the English scientist famous for work on electricity and magnetism. *Golly.* My heart fluttered. Talk about electricity and magnetism. The last time I saw Archie I felt the same current pass between us. Of course the last time I saw him, he was bare-chested and I was lying against said chest.

"Archie?" My hands flew to my burning cheeks.

"The acorn doesn't fall far from the tree," he said.

"So long as it is an oak," I repeated. *Is Archie Somersby the agent sent by Captain Hall?* I thought he was in South Africa.

"I'm afraid you have me at a disadvantage," he said. "The War Office didn't give me your name." He extended his hand. "Lieutenant Archie Somersby, at your service."

Good grief. I realized I was still in my bellboy getup. Speechless, I took his hand. The effect was electrifying.

"Is something wrong?" he asked.

Is something wrong? The man I'd been dreaming about since I met him three weeks ago was standing right in front me of. And I was dressed like an organ grinder's monkey with a shorn head and puffy eyes. Mortified, I wanted to disappear into my oversized boots.

"N-no," I stammered.

"Have we met before?" He tilted his head and pursed his perfectly formed lips.

Should I reveal my true identity? What would he think? What if he thought me ridiculous? I'd never wanted someone's good opinion so much in my life. I tugged on the bottom of my jacket. "I must look a sight."

"Should I come back later?" He held his field cap in both hands. "I shouldn't have come so early. But Captain Hall instructed me to contact you as soon as I arrived in Paris."

I stood gaping at him.

"I saw a nice little café across the street called the Leopold. Why don't we meet there in say thirty minutes?" He fitted his hat on his head, gave me a salute, and turned to go.

Paralyzed, I stood at the threshold watching the back of his well-cut uniform recede down the hallway.

Fiona, what have you gotten yourself into? Do I go to the café as Harold the helpful bellboy or as Fiona Figg the hopeless idiot?

In either case, I had less than half an hour to make myself presentable. I stripped off my clothes and then dashed into the washroom for a quick sponge bath. Hopefully the jasmine soap would wash away the sins of sleeping in my uniform. I slipped on my camisole and bloomers.

If only I'd brought my lovely lavender dress instead of my dreary espionage skirt-sets. I was tempted to wear my new gown, but decided that would be overkill.

With my crewcut and dirt-brown linen jacket, I hardly looked feminine, let alone alluring. But it was the best I could do, short of my maid's outfit. At least I didn't have facial hair—or none that was artificial anyway. And my upper lip didn't smell of spirit gum. What did it matter? *It's not as if Archie is going to kiss me after all.* For all I knew, he had a sweetheart back home... *I sincerely hope not.*

I tugged my strawberry wig into place and admired myself in the looking glass. Why couldn't I transform myself into a beauty like Mata Hari? Nothing I had in my makeup case could work that kind of magic. But some eye kohl and lipstick wouldn't hurt.

I lamented my lack of pretty hats. Thank goodness I'd grabbed my Parisian plum cloche at the last minute. It didn't match my outfit, but it did add a much-needed bit of panache… not to mention, its wide golden band provided the perfect place to hide the microfilm. I adjusted the cloche to a jaunty angle and then jabbed the hatpin through it. A good hat could cover a multitude of sins.

As I exited the elevator into the lobby, I ran smack into Berthe. Her face was puffy. Her hair was a mess. And her lip paint was smudged. Had someone attacked her?

"Berthe, what's wrong?" I asked in alarm.

"Excuse me, mademoiselle." She looked up at me with red-rimmed eyes. "Do I know you?"

Right. I forgot. She knew me as Harold the helpful bellboy, otherwise known as Cutie. "I'm a friend of your sister Abby."

"They sacked me," she whimpered.

"What?"

"For stealing." She let out a wail. Rivulets of Rimmel ran down her cheeks.

"Stealing?"

"I didn't take anything, mademoiselle. I promise. They think I took Madame Hari's necklace and Mr. Fredricks's cuff links. Just because I clean their rooms… I swear, I didn't do it." She broke down. "Now they blame me for all the thefts in the hotel. It's not right."

I took her arm and led her to a sitting area in a corner of the lobby. "Let's get you a nice cuppa."

"A what?" She glanced around. "I can't sit here, mademoiselle. I'm not allowed. I don't want to get into more trouble."

"I can prove you didn't steal from Madame Hari or Mr. Fredricks." I gestured for her to sit down.

"You can?" Her lips turned up in a weak smile but she remained standing, swaying more like.

"Sit down," I ordered, pointing at a satin-covered chair. I was in a hurry and didn't have time for pleasantries.

She stood staring at me.

"It's okay. I'll be responsible for the consequences. Now sit." I had to quickly resolve this issue with poor Berthe so I could get across the street to the Leopold café before Archie gave up on me.

Reluctantly, she took a seat.

"I know you didn't steal anything."

"You do?" Her eyes teared up again.

"I told you to get out!" The shriveled clerk appeared out of nowhere. Blast it all.

"Light-fingered maids are worse than grifters." He pointed toward the back entrance. "Out."

"But I didn't—"

"You did," he interrupted.

Berthe started bawling again.

"I've called the police." He huffed. "You can tell your sob story to them."

"Monsieur, Berthe may be a flirt, but she is not a thief."

"And who are you?"

"Miss Fiona Figg, room three twenty-two." I instinctively tugged on the bottom of my jacket, which to my surprise was not my double-breasted bellboy number. "I believe the maid you're looking for is the redhead. Why don't you ask her what she's been doing in Lady MacLeod and Fredrick Fredricks's rooms."

He narrowed his eyes. "Suzanne? She's not assigned to those rooms. Berthe here is."

"Call Miss Suzanne now, and the police can question her too."

"She didn't show up for work this morning or I would." The clerk scowled.

"All the more evidence of her guilt."

"But she doesn't clean those rooms," he insisted.

"Believe me, she doesn't clean any rooms, more evidence of her guilt."

"What do you mean?" the clerk asked.

"The redhead, Suzanne, is assigned to clean my room, and it hasn't been dusted since I arrived. Inspect Lady MacLeod's and Fredrick Fredricks's rooms and you'll find them spotless. Come to my room and you'll see dust shadows around every article on my dressing table and dust bunnies in the corners."

"Maybe Suzanne is just not a very good maid," Berthe said through her tears. "That doesn't make her a thief. She's new, that's all."

"You are too trusting. I'd say Suzanne is not a maid at all," I said. "She's a professional thief. And I think she has an accomplice. A man named Désiré."

Berthe blanched. "The man from the advert?"

"What advert?" the clerk asked.

"Never mind." Berthe shook her head. "I was thinking of something else."

I made a mental note to check the lonely-hearts adverts in the magazine in the break room as soon as I returned from meeting Archie.

The clerk waved to a police officer who had just entered the lobby. "Over here."

Blast and bother. Now I'll be late to meet Archie for sure.

The police interrogation was difficult, especially since the officer had a strong accent. Maybe he was from Belgium where their French was infused with Dutch. The egg-headed little man wore a perfectly waxed handlebar mustache and his uniform fit tightly around his large stomach, reminding me of a quirky character from a detective novel, which was not good under the circumstances. For it meant that the investigation took twice as long as it should have.

I couldn't very well tell the detective that I'd actually heard Suzanne and her accomplice and lover stealing Fredricks's cuff links and tiepin when I was hiding inside his wardrobe. But I did explain my theory that the redheaded maid was a professional thief, only recently hired at the Grand Hotel, who'd flown the coup when the police started closing in. I told the detective that Suzanne hadn't dusted properly—which didn't impress him in the least—and that I'd seen her dashing out of Mata Hari's penthouse looking ruddy suspicious.

By the time the officer finally agreed to free Berthe, and go looking for Suzanne to bring her in for questioning, I was an hour late to meet Archie. I stopped in the lav to touch up my lipstick and smooth my fake hair.

Hoping against hope that Archie was still waiting, and at the same time dreading the encounter, I hastened across the busy boulevard to the Leopold café.

The café was bustling and bright. The smell of burnt coffee lingered in the air, and the clatter of cups rang out from the kitchen. Nearly hyperventilating, I scanned the crowd for the fine soldier who'd made such an impression on me in our few short hours together. So many men in uniform, they all blurred together. My eyes alighted on a soldier in a back corner with his face buried in a book.

I knew so little of Archie, I realized I had no idea whether he liked to read or ride or hunt or dance or anything else. Riding, hunting, and dancing were not my fortes. In fact anything involving bodily coordination was a challenge for me. Give me words on a page any day. I much preferred mental exertion to the physical sort. Judging by the perfection of his physique, Archie must be physically active. *Just how active?*

A pair of gorgeous sea-green eyes peeked up over the book and returned my gaze. Cheeks afire, I made a beeline for his table.

"Fiona, is that you?" His countenance seemed both pleased and perplexed. "What are you doing in Paris?"

"I was about to ask you the same thing." I just couldn't bring myself to tell him I was in Paris dressing up as a bellboy. If Captain Hall found out, he'd sack me for sure. Blast. *What if Archie told the captain his contact in Paris was a bellboy?*

Archie stood up, extended his hand, and then kissed my cheek.

"I'm back from Africa and on a short holiday." He gestured for me to join him and pulled out a chair.

So, he wasn't going to tell me about his assignment either. Fair enough. How could he have gone to Africa and returned in such a short time? Unless he flew on one of those flying machines used by the military. *Can they fly all the way to South Africa?* Perhaps he never went to Africa. Perhaps the Africa story was just a cover for his true assignment.

He patted his recovered wrist. "At least I'm all in one piece this time."

"And fully clothed." The words just slipped out.

He laughed. "And you've changed your hair. I like it."

"Thank you." I didn't tell him I'd changed my own for someone else's hair. In fact, I wasn't certain that it was real human hair. I patted my wig.

He glanced at his watch and frowned. "I was waiting for an old friend, but

I guess he's not going to show up."

"Not a very reliable friend."

"Jolly unreliable. In fact, I probably should go check on him to make sure nothing's happened." He picked up his book. *The Collected Works of Edgar Allan Poe. I knew I liked this fellow.* "You never told me what you're doing in Paris."

"Visiting my aunt," I said, sticking to the story Captain Hall had invented for me.

"Would you like to have dinner with me tonight?" he asked, his cheeks a lovely pink.

Blast and double blast. I'd already agreed to have dinner with pesky Clifford Douglas. "I can't tonight—"

"Oh well, it was worth a try." He put on his hat and tucked his book under his arm. "I hope we meet again."

"I hope so too..."

When he smiled, I got the most peculiar sensation in my chest.

"I'd best go find out what happened to my mate. Goodbye Beautiful."

Just like that, he was gone.

And I'd best get back to my room and change in case Archie was going looking for Harold the bellboy. Racing back and forth, changing outfits—not to mention personae—was deuced difficult. *What had I gotten myself into?* To complete my mission, I had to work with the gorgeous Archie Somersby. *But how could I?* Every time I saw him, I felt completely lost. The easy way he comported himself drew me to him with a frightening force. Frankly, it scared me.

Chapter Thirteen: Kidnapped

I waited in my Harold outfit for the rest of the day, but Archie never returned to my hotel room. I guess he must have given up on his "old friend." I fretted about how to get the microfilm to him, but I had no idea where he was staying.

Anyway, I was scheduled to meet Clifford for dinner, so I'd best get ready. As much as I wanted to see Archie, I'd have to settle for dear old Clifford. I was to meet him across the street at *des Ambassadeurs*, a charming restaurant he'd found for us.

Des Ambassadeurs had large picture windows looking out on the boulevard. With its high ceilings, white linen tablecloths, and flickering candlelight, the ambience was a bit too romantic. In spite of the war, the patrons were laughing, drinking wine, and enjoying what promised to be a delicious dinner. Clifford had reserved a lovely table by the window and we watched the sunset while drinking a delightful fresh Beaujolais. The French may not have milk or tea, but by golly they still had wine.

I was just biting into a piece of warm war bread slathered with butter when I looked out the window and saw Archie looking in. When my eyes met his, he gave a little wave, turned on his heels, and walked away. *Oh dear. Now what must he think?*

Putting my emotional attachment aside, I thought of my mission. This might be my last chance to get the microfilm to Archie. I had to follow him.

"Clifford, excuse me for a moment." My napkin fell to the floor as I stood up. I picked it up and placed it on my chair. "I just saw an old friend, and I need to find out where he's staying."

"But Fiona—"

"I'll be right back." I squeezed my way through the crowded restaurant and then dashed out the door.

The wind was blowing, and I held on to my hat as I scanned the area for Archie. He'd taken off across the street in the direction of the hotel. Dodging carriages and motorcars, I headed that way. My Balmoral boots may not be fashionable, but they were practical, especially for giving chase. Once out of traffic and safely on the other side of the street, I quickened my pace.

Archie's striking silhouette ducked into a bistro, and I hurried to catch up.

Just as I reached the entrance, a gust of wind removed my hat in spite of its long hatpin and nearly took my wig with it. *The microfilm!* I turned to chase it when a hand clapped over my mouth and something sharp jabbed into my ribs.

"Archie!" My scream was muffled by large fingers, one of which I promptly bit.

"Try that again, Miss Figg, and I'll be forced to use this pistol."

I tried to twist around to get a look at the man handling me. He wrapped an arm around my waist and pulled me backward. Holding me in a tight embrace against his torso, he whispered in my ear, "Be a good girl and no one will get hurt."

Although I couldn't get a good look at his face, I recognized that voice... and those tall black boots. The fiendish Fredrick Fredricks.

"Archie," I yelled again.

"Tsk, tsk." Fredricks jammed the gun into my ribs.

A few passersby gave us strange looks, but no one came to my aid.

"My wife is a bit tipsy," Fredricks said to one couple as they passed. "Too much wine."

A husband pulling his wife down the street must be an everyday occurrence in this godforsaken city.

Fredricks dragged me into an alcove a few yards away. "Take the key from my pocket," he ordered.

"What?"

"My pants pocket. Reach in and get the key to the door." He tightened his grip on me as he twisted his hip to reveal said pocket.

"You want me to put my hand into your pants—"

"Pocket." He finished my sentence.

I reached around and slowly slid my hand into his pants pocket and pulled out a key.

"Open the door."

I did as he said.

"Let's go." He led me roughly by the hand to a lift in an old but swanky apartment building.

"Where are we going?"

"Some place quiet where we can talk." He shoved me into the lift.

"Why didn't you just invite me for tea?" *I might as well go along with him and find out what I can.*

"I have something stronger in mind."

"Clifford is going to wonder where I went and come looking for me."

"Clifford does have a soft spot for gingers, doesn't he?" Fredricks chuckled. "I can see why he likes you. You've got spunk."

Fredricks opened the door to a small flat on the top floor.

Aha! Now I knew why Fredricks's hotel room didn't look lived in. This flat was his true hideout. He invited me in with a push. I strolled around the circumference of the room, taking note of everything. One end of the room had a kitchenette and small table, while the other end seemed to serve as his office. Off the kitchen there was a closed door, which I assumed led into his bedroom and washroom.

An entire wall was filled with bookshelves, and the books were neatly arranged in what appeared to be alphabetical order. Fredricks had everything from literature and philosophy to physics and botany books. Above a large wooden desk in the far corner, a corkboard was adorned with newspaper clippings about mysterious explosions on British cargo ships, some in English and some in French. A letter pinned to the bulletin board caught my eye. It was in German. I bent closer to read it.

"That's from the German vice consul in Brazil congratulating me on my success."

"With your rubber business?"

He laughed. "Our mutual friend is a chatty fellow, isn't he?" He gestured to a chair at a small wooden table near the open window. The curtains fluttered, reminding me that my hat had blown down the street and with it, hidden in its band, the microfilm. *Did Fredricks know his film was missing? How had he found out I'd taken it? And I thought I'd been so clever.*

"He fancies himself a journalist." Fredricks scoffed. "Or is it a novelist?"

"And you? Aren't you a journalist?"

"I'm a jack-of-all-trades." He went to a cupboard and took out two stemmed glasses and a bottle of white wine. He twisted a knife into the cork. As he pulled it out, he glanced over at me. "I suspect you are too."

"Me? I'm a file clerk visiting my aunt in Paris."

"I would say you're a Jill-of-all-trades, except for your little cross-dressing performance back at the hotel." He poured wine into one of the glasses and held it out to me.

I ignored him.

He set it on the table in front of me. "Suit yourself. It's a Château Guiraud." He poured a glass for himself and then sat down across from me. "First it was Dr. Vogel, the visiting expert of female maladies, and now Harold the bellboy. You're incorrigible, Miss Figg. I admire you, I really do." He held up his glass. "To our various personae. May they get us out of as much trouble as they get us into." He took a sip. "You really should try this Bordeaux."

"Is Fredrick Fredricks one of your personae?"

"Did Chuang Tzu dream he was a butterfly?" He cocked his head. "Or was he really a butterfly dreaming he was Chaung Tzu?"

I'd heard of the Chinese philosopher Chuang Tzu. *Did Fredricks fancy himself a philosopher?* I narrowed my eyes and glared at him. "Is Fredrick Fredricks dreaming he's a low-down dodgy sod? Or is a low-down dodgy sod dreaming he's Fredrick Fredricks? That sort of thing?"

"*Exactement.* Now you're catching on." When he smiled, his incisors gleamed in the lamplight. "Is Miss Figg actually a British spy or is she merely pretending to be one?"

I tightened my lips.

"Anger becomes you, *ma chérie*." He moved his chair around to my side of the table. "It gives you a certain spark. Yes, I can see why Clifford is smitten."

"Clifford—" *Is smitten with anyone in a skirt who gives him the time of day*, I wanted to say, but restrained myself. After all, in the past month I'd known him, I'd witnessed his infatuation with Lady Mary at Ravenswick, read about his ridiculous proposal to Lilian Mandrake, and suffered at least two attempted proposals myself. *Dear Clifford. Such a sweet sop.* "What do you want with me?" I scooted my chair back until it hit the wall.

"I've heard you have a memory to rival an elephant."

"Yes, and I've heard you're keen on hunting those majestic creatures."

He twisted one end of his pointy mustache. "True. I am partial to majestic creatures."

"You're disgusting," I said through my teeth.

"Miss Figg, I'm really starting to like you." He took a sip. "Perhaps we could strike a deal."

"Not on your life." I crossed my arms across my chest.

"My life is not the one at stake."

I shuddered.

"You're a brave little actress, *ma chérie*. Your Captain Hall must be very proud. The things you're willing to do for your country."

How much does he know? How does he know about Captain Hall? Is there a double agent working for the War Office? "What do you have against my country?"

"Why do I despise jolly ole Blighty?" he said in a passable Cockney accent. "Let me tell you a story." He poured himself another glass of wine and then settled back into his chair.

In gory detail, he recounted how during the "Second War for Independence," as he called the second Boer War, the British army in South Africa killed his family, but not before raping his sister and burning their house down. Only a teenager, he'd watched from an outbuilding. In shock, and full of rage and fear, he couldn't remember how he'd escaped the blaze. He remembered only that on that "horrific day" he'd vowed to take his revenge against the British army for killing everyone and everything dear to him.

I had to admit, his story was very moving, if far too graphic. But if it were true, then why did Archie's telegram say it was Fredricks's fault? Whoever's fault, it was bloody awful. *Why do men wage bloody war against other men? If women were in charge, would it be any different?*

"My soul died that day." He stared down at his hands. After a few seconds of silence, as if awakening from a trance, he stood up. He pointed at my untouched wine glass. "If you're not going to drink that, mind if I do?"

I shrugged.

He picked up my wine glass and swirled the contents. "So Miss Figg, now you know what I have against your country." He started pacing back and forth across the small room. "Your country raped our women and raped our land, all so they could steal our gold."

"Gold?"

"Yes, Witwatersrand gold mine was a prized trophy." He sneered. "Why? Did you think your countrymen had more noble motives? Civilizing the savages, perhaps?"

"What does any of this have to do with me?" I felt sorry for him. I really did. Still, as my dear old dad always said, "Two wrongs don't make a right."

"I want to know what the British have on me." He rapped his fingers on the table.

"I told you, I'm just a file clerk."

"A file clerk with a photographic memory." He stilled his fingers.

How in the devil does he know that? "Classified documents are above my pay grade."

"Have you heard of the Black Panther?" He held out his pinky ring.

I recognized the insignia of a panther. I'd seen it before on his finger, and I'd seen the emblem on his calling card. I shook my head in denial. *Is Fredricks bragging about being the Black Panther?* His ego would be his downfall.

"They must have a file on me at your precious War Office."

"Not that I've seen." It was half-true. I'd seen the file on Captain Hall's desk, but I'd never read its contents. I sensed Fredricks's weakness. He wanted to be famous. "Perhaps you're not as important as you think."

"If that's the case, why did you follow me to Paris?" He stopped and gazed down at me. "And what about that handsome young lieutenant on my tail?"

I got a queer sensation in my stomach. "I don't know what you're talking about."

"He hounded me in Cape Town. He trailed me to New York. And now he's in Paris. He's been tracking me for months now."

"What's that got to do with me?"

"I saw you with him this afternoon at Café Leopold."

Is Fredricks tailing me? I wiped my palms on my skirt. *Is Archie tailing him?* My head was spinning. "Maybe I will have some of that wine."

"Smart girl." Fredricks retrieved another glass from the cupboard and poured. "Fortification, you're going to need it." He handed me the wine. "Did your friend Somersby mention he's a double agent."

I nearly spit out a mouthful of wine. "I don't believe you." *It isn't possible. Then again, what do I know about Archie Somersby?* I'd only met him once before. When push came to shove, I hardly knew the fellow.

"How well do you know him?" Fredricks asked as if reading my mind.

The Great White Hunter's skills of perception were unnerving to say the least.

I took another drink and averted his gaze.

"Ask him about the *Lusitania*. For that matter, ask him about the late Mrs. Derek Wilkinson. You attended her deathbed dressed up as Dr. Vogel as I recall."

What could Archie have to do with the sinking of the Lusitania *or the murder of Edith Wilkinson at Ravenswick?* The walls of the small room seemed to be closing in on me. I gasped for air.

"Are you all right, Miss Figg? You look a bit peaked." He went to the kitchenette. "How rude of me. I should have realized you didn't have time to eat your dinner." He opened the icebox and withdrew a platter, which, along with two small plates, cutlery, and cloth napkins, he delivered to the table with the dexterity of a head waiter.

I stared down at the cornucopia of fresh strawberries, ripe apricots, and dried figs surrounding a soft cheese. *Blimey.* I hadn't seen food as lovely since before the war.

Fredricks nipped back to the kitchen and returned with a beautiful loaf of bread... not dark coarse war bread but light fine French bread.

"Where did you get this?" My mouth was watering.

"I have my ways." He sat down beside me. "Especially for you." With a grand gesture, he waved his hand over the platter.

I wouldn't be bribed with food. Betraying me, my stomach growled audibly.

Fredricks laughed. "Go ahead. Help yourself."

I gazed longingly at the strawberries. *I really shouldn't but...* I started to reach for a berry and stopped myself. It could be poisoned. "You first."

He chuckled. "You don't trust me." He popped a strawberry into his mouth and then filled my plate with fruit, cheese, and bread, and did the same with his.

After I watched him eat bits of everything, I took a tentative bite of a berry. A heavenly burst of sweetness hit my tongue. I closed my eyes to savor the flavor. The bread and cheese were divine. And the apricots were to die for... which very well could be what Fredricks had planned for me. I took another bite of apricot. If I survived, I would have time to feel guilty later. If I didn't, I might as well enjoy my last meal.

I glanced at my watch. I'd only been Fredricks's captive for a little over half an hour, but it seemed like a lot longer. *What does he want with me? He didn't bring me up here just to ply me with apricots and fancy wine. So why?*

Whatever it was, he wasn't in a hurry. He sat next to me at the small table, sipping wine, nibbling on cheese, and asking me questions about my family, which of course, I refused to answer.

He was ruddy polite for a traitorous criminal. Under other circumstances, I even might say he was charming. Under the current circumstances, however—since he'd kidnapped me, was plotting the destruction of British cargo ships, and had accused Archie Somersby of high treason—I found him odious.

His hair was too thick, his lashes too long, his teeth too white, and that tight-fitting white shirt, open at the collar revealing... well, it just wasn't proper. In fact, in his tall boots and jodhpurs, he looked ridiculous. *Other women may find him irresistible but not me.* I set my wine glass down a wee bit too forcefully, and it made a loud bang.

Like a man suffering from shell shock, Fredricks jumped up from his chair. "You don't like this bloody war any more than I do. Why are we fighting? It's senseless."

He had a point. Why were we fighting?

"Because some Serbian patriot assassinated the archduke in Sarajevo?" Fredricks was pacing the room. "What does that have to do with Britain? Why is your country prolonging this violent idiocy?"

At the hospital, I'd seen so many boys shattered and broken, it made my heart ache. It was true. I hated the bloody war.

He stopped in his tracks and gazed at me. "Tell me, Miss Figg, does British Intelligence have a file on a German agent called H21?"

The wine must have been going to my head. Either that or he really had poisoned me. I had an overpowering urge to tell the truth, which was quite unlike me. I bit my tongue. Maybe the food was laced with truth serum.

"With your memory and my know-how, we can make a difference. But you've got to trust me." He put his hand over his heart as if taking an oath. "Please, Miss Figg, together we've got to try to stop the killing."

Yes, the wine must have been going to my head. I felt utterly confused by his sincerity. The man obviously believed what he was saying, but could I? Perhaps I should try to get some information out of him.

"You tell me what you know about Lieutenant Somersby," I said. "And I'll tell you what I know about agent H21."

"You're quite taken with the young lieutenant, aren't you?" He smiled. "I can see it in your eyes."

"Quid pro quo." My cheeks were hot. "You give me something and I'll give you something. That's all."

"You drive a hard bargain, Miss Figg." He sat down and took a sip of wine. "Let's just say, your young officer is not what he seems—"

A loud crash at the door sent Fredricks scrambling up from his chair. The door swung open and... *Wait. Where'd he come from? And what's he doing here?*

Archie flew into the room just as Fredricks was sliding out the window.

"Archie." I sailed across the room into his arms.

"Fiona." He wrapped his arms around me. "Are you okay?" he whispered into my ear.

A shudder ran up my spine. "How did you find me?" I pulled out of his embrace and gazed up into his lovely eyes.

"I heard you shout and saw Fredricks dragging you off." He held me out at a distance and examined me. "So I followed you, but I didn't know which building you'd gone in." He blushed. "I just wish it hadn't taken me so long to find you. Are you hurt?"

"Fredricks!" I pointed. "He went out the window." My stomach turned as I imagined him falling to his death. Even Fredricks didn't deserve that. After what he'd been through, I pitied him. Poor, tortured soul. *Fiona, get a grip. The man's a murderer and a traitor.*

Archie went to the window and stuck his head out. "I don't see him."

"Is he splayed on the ground below?" I grimaced.

"Not that I can see." Archie started to climb out.

"Be careful."

Archie kept one foot inside and the rest of him was crouched on the window ledge.

"Be careful," I repeated and held my breath.

"No sign of him. He must be a cat to climb along these ledges."

When Archie came back inside, I finally exhaled a big audible sigh of relief.

"I say, what's going on?" A familiar voice came from the doorway. I'd completely forgotten about poor Clifford.

"Clifford. What are you doing here?"

He was holding my hat, which, like all of us, had seen better days.

"When you didn't come back to the table, I went looking for you." He held up the hat. "This unmistakable gem made the detective work easy. Everyone I asked remembered the purple bucket on your head."

"It's plum not purple." I grabbed my hat. "Where did you find it?"

He glanced uneasily at Archie, who leaned against the window with a bemused look on his face. "On the street. Not far from here."

"Fiona, aren't you going to introduce me to your friend?" Archie asked.

The way he said "friend" made me cringe. He definitely had the wrong idea about my relationship with Clifford. Just because I was having dinner with the chap didn't mean I was in love with him.

"Really, old bean." Clifford huffed. "Leaving dinner was darn rude, don't you think?" He glared over at Archie and then back at me. "Are you giving me the brush off?"

I rolled my eyes. "Shouldn't someone go after Fredricks?"

"Fredricks? What's he got to do with this?" Clifford asked.

"I'll leave you two to sort it out," Archie said. He adjusted his cap and headed for the door. "I'll take care of Fredricks."

"It's not like that—"

Archie stopped at the threshold and then turned back to salute Clifford. He winked at me. "Goodbye, beautiful."

I opened my mouth to say goodbye, but he was gone.

Chapter Fourteen: Mrs. Henri Désiré Landru

In spite of the eventful night before, I was up at dawn. Still in my robe and slippers, I contemplated my options for the day. I was half tempted to don my maid's outfit and head out to the Renault estate and try my scheme. The more time that passed since the countess's murder, the less likely my plan to pose as a special type of cleaner would succeed.

Get it together, Fiona. What would Captain Hall say if he knew I was investigating another murder? My assignment was following Fredricks. I had to get the microfilm to Archie and then we had to get the information to Captain Hall. If I didn't find Archie soon, I'd have to call Captain Hall myself.

Pacing my hotel room, I racked my brain to come up with a plan. Circumnavigating the tiny room was difficult. I had to skirt the desk, dressing table, lamp, and bed, along with my suitcase, so I ended up walking in tight circles. Although I kept the room neat and tidy, there was barely enough space to turn around. How I missed my small two-bedroom London flat, which was downright spacious compared to this shoe-box hotel room.

I may not have the comforts of home, but at least I'd managed to get an electric kettle delivered to my room. I only wished I'd brought my own tea. Clifford was right. French tea tasted like ditch water. I filled the kettle with water from the lav and plugged it in. Ten minutes later, the water was boiling and I had my first cuppa of the day, such as it was.

Sitting at the dressing table, I examined my poor hat. I still couldn't believe

Clifford had chased it down. Although the lovely plum cloche was trampled and stained, by some miracle the microfilm was still safely tucked in the hat band. I carefully removed the two strips of film and held them up to the light. Using my water glass again as a magnifier, I committed the contents to memory just in case my hat blew off once more. I tucked the bits back into the hatband.

I've got to get the microfilm to Archie as soon as possible. Will he be back? Should I wait in my room or go out looking for him? And if I go looking, where? I had no idea where Archie was staying in Paris or if I would see him again. I pushed from my mind Fredricks's unthinkable insinuation that Archie was really a double agent and a traitor. Archie would be back soon. I was sure of it. It was ruddy confusing not knowing if I should go out and risk missing him, or wait and possibly put more lives in danger with every passing hour.

To save my hat—and calm my nerves—I retrieved a shoe brush from Harold the helpful bellboy's kit and brushed dirt from between the ribs of corduroy. The steady motion of the brush against the fabric was soothing. I lost myself in the rhythms of the strokes… and worried thoughts about my failed mission.

If I couldn't get the microfilm to Archie, then I must report it to Captain Hall today. *What would Blinker say when he found out I'd bungled it again?* At least I'd found the microfilm, for all the good it was doing tucked in my hatband. I dreaded explaining *how* I'd acquired it. Captain Hall had given me strict instructions to stay in my room and no more charades. Then again, maybe he'd underestimated Miss Fiona Figg.

I stopped my mediations long enough to admire my cloche. Not quite restored to its former glory, my hat was at least presentable again. I stored it on the top shelf in the wardrobe. I would get dressed, but I hadn't decided yet who I'd be today. Everything had gotten so confusing. It was time to make a list and order my thoughts. So many things had happened in my first few days in Paris, it was deuced difficult to keep track.

I gathered a pen and paper and sat at the small corner desk. I concentrated on my diary of events, arranging them in chronological order as best as I could recollect:

First there was my missing passport, stolen by the seductive Mata Hari, known to British Intelligence as agent H21. As subheadings, I wrote: Why did she want it? Where did she put it?

Next there was the matter of Mata Hari's missing jewelry. I'd seen the redheaded maid sneaking out of her room. And I'd heard the couple in Fredricks's room when I was hiding in his wardrobe. I surmised the girl had stolen the Great White Hunter's cuff links and tiepin for her accomplice, whose name was Désiré. *Only the French would name their son Désiré.*

Poor Berthe had been wrongfully accused of the theft. Luckily, I'd persuaded the detective to see reason. But he'd been unable to find Suzanne. The redheaded maid hadn't been back to work for days. She seemed to have disappeared. No doubt with the loot and her unscrupulous partner. *That reminds me, I meant to check the advert in that magazine in the breakroom.* Horsefeathers. I completely forgotten about it. I added it to my to-do-list. Hopefully it hadn't been tossed in the trash bin yet... where it belonged.

Let's see, what else had happened in my first few days in Paris? Ah, yes. I would never forget the night I spent in that awful jail cell with those hideous-smelling men. I thought the volunteer work I'd done at Charing Cross Hospital helping injured soldiers had prepared me for anything. I was wrong. And why had I been in jail? Because a Russian countess had had the bad manners to get murdered at a garden party. I'd read about the unrest in Russia. Maybe the murderer *was* a Bolshevik. *Abby?* I made a note to find out more about Berthe's twin sister, Abby.

Speaking of Berthe, what was it she said about the countess being involved with the White Ladies... or was it White Women? I made another note to find out more about the White Ladies/Women. I didn't believe for a second that the countess had killed herself. I wrote in bold capital letters, FIND COUNTESS PAVLOVNA'S MURDERER.

Back to the rest of my list... There was the reason I was in Paris in the first place, Fredrick Fredricks. At least now I knew why he hated the British. How in the world had he disappeared out that window? He was a deuced complicated and mighty clever fellow, but even he couldn't fly.

I glanced at my watch. The blasted embassy didn't open for hours. *What can I do with myself until then? I have to do something.* The information on those microfilms could save lives and important cargo, but only if I delivered them in time. With the embassy closed, I had no choice but to go in search of Archie Somersby. *But where should I look? And, more importantly, should I go as Fiona or Harold?*

He knows Fiona as a hopeless idiot, going around getting herself kidnapped, and then throwing herself at him. My cheeks burned remembering our embrace. *It had been reciprocated, hadn't it?*

He knows Harold the bellboy as his unreliable contact from British Intelligence. *Why in blazes hasn't he come back to check on me... Harold?* For all he knew, Harold had been kidnapped or worse. A strange thought crept into my mind. What if Archie and Fredricks were working together? I shook my head. *No blooming way.*

Come on, Fiona, get it together. I couldn't let my feelings for Archie cloud my judgment... or my commitment to the War Office. Back to the matter at hand. I folded my list and tucked it into my shoe for safe keeping, and then I went to my wardrobe and stood staring inside.

Now, the most important question of the day, what to wear? The navy blue trousers and monkey jacket? Or the dirt-brown skirt and fussy-librarian blouse? Trousers were more practical in case one had to make a quick run for it. And Harold the bellboy could go a lot of places Fiona couldn't, especially inside the hotel.

I pulled out the bellboy jacket and sniffed the armpits. I really needed to get my monkey suit cleaned soon or Fredricks would smell me coming.

Tugging on the trousers and tucking in the shirtwaist, I realized I liked being a man from time to time. It was a refreshing change from corsets, brassieres, and those newfangled girdles. Men were lucky they didn't have to torture their bodies into the perfect hourglass shape. The few women lucky enough to have natural curves were tortured in other ways. I thought of Mata Hari making love for a box of chocolates and a pearl necklace. Strawberries and lemons maybe... but jewelry never.

At my dressing table, I slicked back my hair with brilliantine and pinned the pillbox hat into place. I assessed my transformation in my hand mirror.

Blimey. I forgot my mustache. No self-respecting spy should go out without her mustache. Facial hair was not one of the things I liked about being a man. Imagine having to shave your face every day! How absurd.

The smell of spirit gum made my eyes water. But my little furry friend was firmly in place on my upper lip. One more gander in the looking glass confirmed that my transformation was complete. I tugged on the hem of my jacket, took a deep breath, and headed out to face whatever dangers awaited me in the hotel lobby... hopefully Archie Somersby... who posed a decided danger to my chastity.

No sooner had I stepped out of the lift than Berthe appeared. She was all smiles. What a change from the last time I saw her with makeup running down her sad puffy face. Had she gotten her job back?

"Cutie, you'll never guess what's happened." Bubbling over with her news, she swayed back and forth and then extended her left hand. "We're getting married."

Blimey. "Who's we?"

"Me and Désiré." She waved her ringed finger in front of my nose.

"Where did you get that ring?" I recognized the jade ring as one of Mata Hari's.

Berthe squinted at me. "From Désiré, of course. We're getting married."

"So you won the bet with your redheaded friend and the prize is Désiré Landru?"

"Suzanne? Cher Désiré dumped her when he met me." She smirked. "He says I'm twice the woman she is."

What did the scoundrel mean by that? "Don't marry him, Berthe. He's no good."

"Ah, Cutie, you're jealous."

"No. I mean it. He's a thief."

"That's not true. Anyway, I thought you said it was Suzanne."

True. She did seem like a professional. But I wouldn't doubt that *Cher Désiré* had recruited Suzanne to steal from the hotel. He was probably behind it all. And now he was trying to recruit Berthe.

"How long have you known this Désiré? You're young. What's the rush." I took her arm. "Please, at least wait until you know him better."

"Cher Désiré believes in love at first sight." She shrugged. "When you know, you know. He's so romantic."

What could the scoundrel want with Berthe? Was he recruiting Berthe into the jewel thieving ring? "Has he asked you to do anything?"

"What do you mean?"

"Anything you don't want to do?"

"You mean like hanky panky?"

"No, I mean like stealing." More than likely,

She glared at me. "I'm marrying him and that's that." She stomped her foot.

"Is there nothing I can say to stop you?"

"You could ask me to marry you," she said coyly, wrapping a lock of hair around her little finger.

"Believe me, you don't want to marry me." I didn't tell her I'd bungled my own marriage terribly. And that I was a woman. "Look, Berthe, men aren't always what they seem."

"What about you? You're a man."

"Case in point."

"What do you mean?"

"Never mind. Just be careful."

"I can take care of myself." She winked at me.

"I'm sure you can." I'm sure Suzanne had thought the same thing.... For that matter, I'd thought the same thing when I'd married Andrew, and he turned out to be a philandering cheat.

"Next time you see me I'll be a married lady," she gloated.

For her sake, I certainly hope not.

"Say, Berthe, have you seen a handsome British lieutenant with wavy chestnut hair and green eyes, broad shoulders and a perfect—"

"Why, Cutie, I didn't know you liked boys." She gave me a sly smile.

"No, that's not it—"

"No wonder you didn't want to help me make the bed." She clapped her hands together. "I feel so much better now..." She got a serious expression on her face. "Or do you like boys *and* girls?"

"Neither one," I said. "I'm looking for this soldier. I found something that belongs to him."

"So you're celibate? Like a priest or something?" She looked confused.

"Something like that." *Sigh.* "Just be careful with that Désiré chap."

She nodded. "Good luck finding your handsome soldier."

Good luck indeed. "Just because you'll be Missus… Missus…"

"Landru. Mrs. Henri Désiré Landru," she said with her nose in the air.

"Don't be a stranger just because you're Mrs. Désiré Landru."

"Don't worry. I'll always be your girl." She kissed me on the cheek. "You'll see me again soon, Cutie."

I hoped she was right. I had a very bad feeling about Mr. Henri Désiré Landru.

Chapter Fifteen: The Kiss

After a couple of turns around the lobby, I noticed a familiar mop of wavy chestnut hair atop a perfectly shaped head, which was poked into a book. Repressing a smile, I tried to appear nonchalant as I approached his chair.

Archie was grinning from ear to ear, which I didn't think was appropriate given the circumstances. I gave him a stern look.

"I'm afraid I don't know your name," he said putting down his book.

"Harold," I said in my lowest register.

"Pull up a chair, Harold." He had a mischievous look on his face that made me uneasy.

I patted my mustache to make sure it was still in place and glanced down at my uniform. I really didn't see what was so funny. "That's right. And you're Lieutenant Somersby from British Intelligence."

He nodded, obviously amused. "I'm sorry it didn't work out yesterday." He regained his composure. "I've been waiting for a decent hour to try again."

"I'm so sorry about missing our appointment." Even though I wasn't a real bellboy, I knew I couldn't sit across from a hotel guest, so I stood next to his table. "Something came up with one of the maids."

"As it does," he said with a smile.

I didn't want to know what he meant by that.

I bend down and whispered, "I have important information about Fredrick Fredricks and his sabotage operation." Archie smelled heavenly… like pine and citrus.

"Can I ask you something?" He didn't wait for an answer. "Are you an agent undercover as a bellboy? Or are you a bellboy working for British Intelligence?"

He was starting to sound like Fredricks with his butterfly nonsense. Anyway, I'd just told him I had gen on Fredricks and he was asking whether I was really a bellboy. "Does it matter?" I wondered what he was on about. I touched my mustache again.

"Just curious." His gaze was unnerving.

Was there something wrong with my disguise? I tugged on my jacket. *Had I forgotten something? Did he recognize me?* I cleared my throat. "As I was saying, I found a list of ships and dates in the heel of Fredricks's boot."

"In his boot?" He smiled up at me. "How clever of you."

"I think it's a list of the ships he plans to blow up."

"Can I see it?"

"It's on microfilm in my hatband."

He put his hand in front of his mouth, and whispered, "Do you want to take it out or should I?"

I touched my bellboy cap. "It's in my other hat, upstairs in my room." *Why in the world didn't I bring the microfilm with me? Now I'd have to take Archie back up to my room.*

"*Garçon!*" The grumpy clerk appeared out of nowhere. "Get back to work."

"Yes, sir." I glanced at Archie, who seemed amused by something again. He was a most unnerving fellow. I didn't remember him being so easily entertained back at Charing Cross Hospital… of course, then, he'd just been wounded.

"Shall we go upstairs?" Archie asked, a glimmer in his eyes.

The clerk huffed. "What's going on here?"

"Harold is helping me with my luggage," Archie said. He pointed to his limp arm. "War wound, I'm afraid. The bloody thing is completely useless."

"Of course, apologies." The clerk looked flustered. "Carry on."

I followed Archie to the lift. He pressed the button with his "bad" hand.

"You lied about your arm."

"Occupational hazard."

"War wounds or lying?" I asked.

"Both," he said, stepping into the lift.

I followed him in. As we rode the lift, I glanced over at him. He was so handsome in his uniform and cap, I felt strong desires I hadn't felt since my honeymoon. My cheeks burned as I battled fantasies of kissing him.

When the lift came to a stop, he pulled the iron gate open. "After you."

As I passed by, my arm grazed his and the warmth of his body sent an electric current up my spine. Walking next to him down the hallway, I had a nearly irresistible desire to take his hand.

I was about to open the door to my room when I realized there were signs of Fiona strewn about and enough feminine paraphernalia to give me away. "Give me a minute."

Alternating between Harold and Fiona was deuced confusing.

"Why? Are you hiding a maid in there?" A roguish spark danced in Archie's eyes.

"I'm not that kind of a man."

"What kind of a man are you?" he asked staring into my face with that uncanny gaze of his.

"Not that kind," I repeated. Rattled, I unlocked the door, opened it just enough to slip in, and shut the door in his face. *Why does Archie unnerve me so? Come on, Fiona old girl, control your emotions.*

Dashing around the room, I pitched all signs of Fiona into the wardrobe and slammed it shut.

When I opened the door again, Archie was leaning against the wall, smoking. "Do you mind?" he asked, waving the cigarette.

I shook my head. Vile cigarette smoke was the least of my worries.

Once inside, Archie sat down on my bed and removed his hat.

Cheeky devil, I thought… until I remembered we were just two blokes exchanging state secrets.

"Do you want to show me the microfilm?" He took a drag on his cigarette and blew out a foul cloud of smoke.

Blast! The microfilm was still in my hatband, and the hat was at the top of the wardrobe. *How can I open the blooming thing without my Fiona stash tumbling out? And I can't jolly well ask him to step outside again.*

140

"Do you have an ashtray?"

I pointed to a cup on my desk. "Use that." *Disgusting.* But at least it made him move out of the line of sight of my wardrobe.

I opened the wardrobe a crack and then glanced back to make sure he wasn't looking. Hiding behind the door to the wardrobe, I reached up for the hat. Peeking around to make sure Archie still couldn't see inside, I groped the top shelf until I felt the corduroy... and the stick of a hatpin. "Ouch."

"Are you okay?"

I had to maneuver the hat and remove the microfilm out of Archie's view. What would he think if he saw a lady's hat in my wardrobe? And not just any hat. The *unmistakable gem* I was wearing yesterday. I felt inside the band for the film. *Wait. Where is it?* I ripped at the band. Nothing. The microfilm was gone. "Oh no," I yelped. I cleared my throat. "Oh no," I repeated in Harold's voice. I backed away from the wardrobe.

"What's wrong?" Archie moved closer.

"The microfilm. It's not here."

"Could it have fallen out?" he asked.

If it hadn't fallen out when my hat blew off my head, tumbled down the street, and then suffered the crushing grip of Clifford's big paws, it wasn't going to fall out in the few seconds I'd been trying to pull the hat off the shelf. "No. It was stolen."

More accurately, my guess was it was stolen back. Had Fredricks broken into my room? How could he know which room was mine? He was a crafty devil, I'd give him that. He seemed to have eyes everywhere.

Archie came toward me. I slammed the wardrobe door shut and stood in front of it.

His face was just inches from mine. "Now what?" His voice cracked in a most appealing way.

I fought the urge to kiss him. *Fiona, really, you're in the middle of international espionage and all you can think about is...*

"May I kiss you?" he asked. Without waiting for an answer, he did it. He kissed me.

I felt weak in the knees. Even the pungent taste of his cigarette thrilled me.

"I've never kissed anyone with a mustache before," he said. "It tickles."

Good heavens. I'd forgotten I was wearing my bellboy disguise. *Does this mean that Archie is...* My mind was reeling. "We're supposed to be working. Lives are at stake. Fredricks..." I sputtered.

He wrapped his arms around me and whispered in my ear, "Don't worry. Fredricks was arrested an hour ago."

"What?" I pulled out of his embrace. "Why didn't you tell me?"

"I thought you knew." He took my hand and kissed it.

I withdrew my hand. "Really, Lieutenant Somersby, this is most inappropriate behavior."

He grinned. "You're very attractive when you're angry."

My cheeks were aflame. *What is he up to? Flirting with a bellboy? Or a man dressed as a bellboy? Should I come clean and reveal my true identity?* I longed for another kiss. It was all I could do to keep from throwing myself at him. "We need to get the information on those ships to the War Office. Another bomb could go off at any minute—"

He planted his lips on mine again.

"It's a matter of life and death," I said breathlessly.

"Yes, it is," he whispered in my ear.

I closed my eyes and wished this moment could last forever.

Archie loosened his embrace, and I gazed into his face. His eyes danced and he smiled, suppressing a chuckle.

"It's not funny." I moved away from him. "Men will die if we don't stop Fredricks."

"Of course, you're right." Archie cleared his throat and his tone became serious. "But you haven't got the microfilm. So where does that leave us?" He paced the room.

"I may not have the microfilm, but I do have the information."

He stopped in his tracks. "Where? Why didn't you say so?"

Because my lips were busy kissing you? I narrowed my eyes. "I was distracted."

"Where is the information?" His demeanor had changed as fast as a summer storm transforms a sunny sky. "We have to get it to Captain Hall immediately."

"It's in here." I tapped my temple.

"Your head?" He gave me a quizzical look.

"I memorized it."

"You really are something, you know that?" He laughed. "Let's get to work. Do you have a pen and paper? Can you write everything out?"

I withdrew writing materials from the desk drawer and sat down. I closed my eyes and allowed the microfilm to come into focus before my mind. Slowly and carefully, I made a list of the names and dates from the microfilm. It was a long list, but I was confident I'd remembered it all. I handed the paper to Archie. "This is everything."

"Brilliant." He took the paper, folded it, and put it in his jacket pocket. "I'll go telephone Captain Hall."

"I'll come with you."

"No, you stay here." He replaced his hat on his head. "I'll be back within the hour." He opened the door and then turned back. "Goodbye Beautiful." He winked and blew me a kiss.

After he left, a strange mix of emotions whirled in me like potent brandy, sweet treacle, and desiccated sultanas whipped into a Christmas pudding, ready to be baked and set on fire. I plopped onto my bed in the very spot where Archie had been sitting a few minutes ago. *What in blazes was he up to?* Did he know it was me under the bellboy disguise? Was he kissing me? My breath caught. Or did he go around calling boys "beautiful"?

Stunned, I just sat there paralyzed. Unbidden, Fredrick Fredricks's warning echoed through my head. *Your young officer is not what he seems.* I stroked the caterpillar on my upper lip. *Then again, neither am I.*

Fredricks claimed Archie was a double agent. I couldn't believe it. And yet... *Blimey.* I jumped up. If it were true, I'd just entrusted him to deliver crucial information to the War Office. *Blast.* I had to go after him. He'd distracted me with those delicious kisses and put me off my guard.

I dashed out into the hallway. Empty. No sign of Archie. I rushed to the lift and jammed on the button. The wait seemed to go on forever. Impatient, I gave up and raced down the stairs instead. I'd made it down one flight and half of a second when my oversized boots tripped me. I toppled down the stairs and thudded to a stop on the landing. I sat up and tried to catch my breath.

Everything hurt. No doubt glorious purple bruises would start sprouting everywhere. I stood up slowly and took several deep breaths. Gingerly, I started down the stairs again. With every step a sharp pain exploded in my right knee. I must have banged it up pretty badly.

Double blast. Now I'd never catch up to Archie.

By the time I reached the lobby, I was limping so badly people were staring. I hobbled through the curious crowd toward the entrance. I had to catch up to Archie.

"Harold?"

I did a double take. For a millisecond, I thought it was Berthe with longer hair and no makeup. Of course, it was her twin sister, Abby.

"Are you okay? You're bleeding." Abby rushed to my side.

"Bleeding?" I scanned my clothes for blood.

Abby took a handkerchief out from the wrist of her blouse and wiped at my cheek.

Bother. I might as well forget about trailing Archie. *What a mess.*

"What happened to you?"

"I fell down the stairs like an idiot."

"We should get a doctor." She put her hand on my sleeve.

What in the world? I stared down at her hand. Abby had the same angry rash with tiny blisters on her hand that I'd seen on Countess Pavlovna's dead wrist. Either Abby had been in contact with whatever gave the rash to the countess, or she'd been in contact with the countess herself. Maybe the rash was contagious. And maybe Abby was the Bolshevik who'd killed the countess.

It was too early to hear back from Daisy about the pollen I'd wiped off the countess's dress and slipper and onto my glove. Hopefully when I did, that would give me a clue to the origin of the rash.

"Should I call for a doctor?" Abby repeated.

I realized I was still staring at her rash. "No, no need for a doctor. I'm fine."

"At least sit down." Abby led me to a chair.

I glanced around to see if the grumpy clerk was watching before taking a seat.

"Are you sure you're okay?"

"Right as rain." I smiled weakly and rubbed my knee.

"Have you seen my sister?" Her cheeks were blotchy like she'd been crying... either that or the rash was spreading. "She hasn't been home for two days."

"I saw Berthe this morning. She said she's getting married."

"To that horrible man from the advert?" Abby troubled a handkerchief between her fingers.

I nodded.

"I told her not to. We had a fight and she stormed out." Abby's lips twitched. "I thought she'd come back when she calmed down, but she didn't."

"You don't suppose she's staying with him, do you?" I put my hand over my mouth.

"It wouldn't be the first time," Abby said, staring at her blistered hands.

Berthe was a terrible flirt, but I didn't think she would actually... *Don't be such a prude, Fiona. This is Paris, not London. Girls are different here.* I thought of Mata Hari. "I'm sure she'll return triumphant after her wedding," I said in my most reassuring voice.

"You really think so?" She sniffled. "I'm worried."

I reached across the table and patted her hand. *Me too.* Just in case that nasty rash was contagious, I retracted my hand and vowed to wash it with soap as soon as I got back to my room.

I may not be able to catch Archie, but I could call Captain Hall. I glanced at my watch. The Embassy didn't open for several hours yet. My knee hurt so badly, I didn't know if I could walk even the few blocks to get there. Could I ask Clifford for help? Or Abby? *Come on, Fiona, get a grip. Archie is not a double agent. He will call Captain Hall and be back soon.*

I went back to my room, washed my hands, and waited. To be safe, I transcribed what I'd seen on the microfilm again. I didn't want to get nervous and forget something when talking to the captain… if Archie didn't come back and I had to call Captain Hall myself. But I knew he'd be back. I glanced at my watch. He'd been gone almost an hour already. How long did it take to make the call and get back to the hotel? He couldn't be calling from the Embassy because it wasn't open yet. Of course, he probably had easier access to telephones than I did.

Pacing my room—or should I say, hobbling around it—I waited exactly one more hour. When Archie still hadn't returned, I went to Clifford's room and knocked on his door. No answer. I went to the front desk and asked them to ring Clifford's room. No answer.

Unable to get ahold of Clifford, I'd have to hobble to the Embassy on my own. I left the hotel just after noon to give myself plenty of time. I wasn't going to miss my chance to call Captain Hall and report what I'd found. If Archie wasn't a double-agent, and had done as he said and made the call, then the worst that would happen was Captain Hall would get the information twice. But if Archie really was a double-agent, then I needed to get the information to Captain Hall as soon as possible.

With my limp, it took me twice as long as usual to get to the Embassy. Still, I was there just before they opened. Relieved that I'd finally gotten here in time, I placed the call. The telephone rang, but there was no answer. Blast. Where was Captain Hall? Why wasn't he in his office? And why wasn't his secretary answering for him?

I waited another hour and tried again. Still no answer. Just before three o'clock, the Embassy staff warned me they would be closing in a few minutes. I tried one last time. *Sigh. Now what?* I had no choice but to hobble back to the hotel and vow to try again tomorrow. I hoped to heaven Fredricks was lying about Archie being a double-agent. I still held out hope he'd be back. If Archie was a double-agent, I'd just sabotaged my country and let him sabotage my heart.

Chapter Sixteen: Berthe is Missing

W racked with worry, that night I barely slept. The next morning, I got up early, made a cup of tea—such as it was—and tried to clear my head. I spent most of the morning pacing my room, trying to figure out what to do.

Archie had said he'd be back within the hour. That was yesterday. I wondered what else he'd lied about. Maybe Fredricks was right and Archie really was a double agent. Sigh. I felt doubly used... as Fiona the hopeless idiot and as Harold the helpful bellboy.

As I rounded my bed for the hundredth time, my eyes burned with tears of heartbreak and rage. *How could he kiss and run? And what if he didn't like girls?* I couldn't be Harold the bellboy forever. *Is Archie like Dilly Knox, an inveterate flirt who beds both men and women?* I knew such people existed, but I never thought I'd be involved with one. "Never underestimate the whimsy of nature," my grandmother used to say when watching the animals on the farm. "They get up to all sorts of things." Fredricks claimed humans are animals too. *I guess he's right.*

At least Archie had told the truth about one thing. Fredricks had been arrested, which is probably why Archie had been so cavalier about the missing microfilm. The French were holding Fredricks at La Santé Prison in Montparnasse. I was determined to find a way to get to Fredricks in prison. He had two key pieces of information crucial to my survival as an espionage agent. First, he knew the connection between the tiny silver canister and Countess Pavlovna's murder—in fact, I wouldn't be surprised if Fredricks was the murderer. And, dearer to my heart, he knew the truth about Archie Somersby.

As much as I wanted the gen on Archie's personal life, my top priority was finding out whether he'd called Captain Hall with the information from the microfilm. I had to put my personal feelings aside and do my job.

Waiting for the embassy to open was making me a nervous wreck. To distract myself, I went to the break room looking for Berthe. Another maid told me Berthe hadn't come in to work. Had she gone through with it and married that dodgy Désiré from the advert? *I sincerely hope not, for her sake.*

For lack of a plan, I went back to my room to pace. Although my ego was bruised, I'd more or less recovered from my stupid tumble down the stairs. My knee still hurt, but after a night's rest, my limp was barely noticeable. Walking in circles was actually making it better. If only I could say the same for my bruised ego. *Archie, where are you?*

It had been twenty-six hours and twenty-three minutes since Archie had left to call Captain Hall and he hadn't been back… and neither had Berthe.

I checked my watch. The blasted embassy didn't open for over two hours. I wished I could just get it over with… confess the royal mess I'd made and let Captain Hall sack me over the telephone. It was better than facing his blinking eyes in person. Then again… If I cracked the case of the countess and proved it was linked to Fredricks, I'd be back in Captain Hall's good graces. *Don't give up now, old girl.* Everything decisive in life comes against the greatest obstacles. I was resolved to figure out who killed the countess and what her murder had to do with Fredricks and with military secrets.

Since the embassy didn't open for hours, I had plenty of time to visit the library on my way and do some research. A trip to a library just might calm my nerves. I'd always loved libraries. I made another list of info I could gather at the library.

1. La Santé Prison. Find out everything to plan my strategy to get inside and find Fredricks and then pump him for gen on Archie… and the countess… and his sabotage operations.
2. The *Dames Blanches*, White Women. Who were they and what might they have to do with the countess's death? Was Abby involved with

these White Women too? And what about her rash? Info I couldn't get at the library but nonetheless was of interest.

3. Henri Désiré Landru and his adverts in the lonely-hearts column. Surely the library would have copies of the magazine. How long had the bounder been placing ads? Who, besides Berthe, had answered the ads? I'd have to go to the advert agency for that information.

Bibliothèque Mararine was the oldest library in Paris. Turns out, it was across the Seine near Ponts des Arts, and very close to the prison where Fredricks was prisoner.

Walking through the coral stone archways and standing in the grand foyer of the library, I felt that I'd entered a sacred place... and not just because somewhere behind its grandiose façade, and hidden deep inside its belly, was a secret vault that housed a Gutenberg Bible.

The magnificent reading room with wooden columns, floor-to-ceiling bookshelves, and ornate chandeliers, put me in mind of my days at North London Collegiate School. Back then, I used to spend hours in the British Museum Library enjoying people watching and the heady smell of old books instead of studying.

Sitting at a large wooden table with a hefty encyclopedia in front of me, I wished I'd spent more time perfecting my French. I flipped through the pages until I found La Santé Prison. Interesting. In 1867, it replaced the Madelonnettes Convent, where the Marquis de Sade was imprisoned during the French Revolution. The prisoners were still visited by nuns, who cared for them. *Aha!* My chest tingled with excitement. *What luck.* I had the perfect disguise.

I continued thumbing through the pages until I found *Dames Blanches*, White Ladies. In French mythology they were female spirits. I squinted. *Female spirits?* The countess may be a female spirit now that she's dead, but while she was alive? That didn't make sense. I'd have to try a more reliable source... a reference librarian.

The reference librarian was a small silver-haired woman sitting behind an orderly desk. She glanced up as I approached.

"*Excusez moi*, do you know anything about a political group called the White Women?" I asked in my best French accent.

"La Dame Blanche is an intelligence organization started last year in Belgium," the librarian answered, her eyes bright.

"Why is it called White Lady?" I asked. "Are they all women?"

"Some of them, but not all," the librarian whispered. "The White Lady was a ghost who cursed the ancient German Hohenzollern dynasty."

"And they work for the allies?"

"That's right." She nodded. "Mostly watching the train tracks and holding political meetings." She knew so much, I wondered if she were a White Woman too.

Political meetings? Didn't Berthe complain that her sister was too political? And Abby had that same rash as the dead countess. I remembered the argument between two women behind the hedgerow that I'd overheard at the garden party. *"Unhand me. What do you think you're doing?"* and then *"You can't escape punishment after what you've done."* Yes... the other woman must have been Abby. Abby knew the countess was a White Woman. But what had she done? Escape punishment for what? *Perhaps my hunch is right and Abby really is a Bolshevik.* What an absurd thought. Abby was a nice French girl who worked in a funeral home.... Actually, she was kind of creepy.

"Is poison ivy or poison oak native to these environs?" I asked the librarian.

"No. Poison ivy was imported from the Americas. Joséphine Bonaparte had it planted in her ornamental garden." She sighed as if nostalgic for the days of Bonaparte. "And it is still found in a few ornamental gardens. But it is not native to France."

Did Renault's garden grow poison ivy? A question too specific and too empirical for the reference library... or even the reference librarian. I would have to find another means of research. I crossed two items off my list, a map of the prison, and the White Ladies. Next, the lonely-hearts adverts. "Where might I find back issues of *Le Journal* magazine?"

The librarian raised her eyebrows. "That would be in the periodicals section downstairs."

The periodical reading room was cozy with six leather chairs forming a semicircle around a low wooden table. The sitting area was surrounded by shelves of magazines and newspapers arranged in alphabetical order, with the most recent ones on display and the older ones stacked behind them. I gathered up the stack of *Le Journal*, which was quite an armful, and made my way to one of the chairs. Sitting with the magazines in my lap, I thumbed through them. The stack of weeklies went back three months.

The lonely-hearts column was near the back of the magazine. To my surprise, there were column after column of adverts from soldiers asking for *marraines de guerre* to write them letters, send them care packages, and comfort them on their leaves in Paris. I'd heard about these *godmothers of war* and their tender mercies, which often included giving soldiers the "French disease" along with knitted socks and scarfs.

Iris Matrimonial Agency had its own dedicated column with dozens of adverts from lonely men and women seeking liaisons. I couldn't imagine meeting a strange man I'd found through an advert. Although given my luck with men, perhaps I should try it. I couldn't do much worse. My marriage had ended in betrayal and divorce, and my all-too-brief dalliance with Archie had been a total disaster.

About halfway down the adverts from the Iris agency, I spotted it.

Widower, aged 43, with two children and comfortable income, serious and moving in good society, desires to meet amiable woman with a view to matrimony. Address inquiries to Henri Désiré Landru, Box 78, 22 rue Saint-Augustin.

I jotted the address down.

In every single issue of *Le Journal*, I found similar adverts from Henri Désiré Landru. The bounder had been at it for a while. I gathered up the stack of magazine and returned them to the shelf. On a whim, I picked up the latest issue from yesterday and flipped through it. As with the others, the lonely-hearts columns went on for pages. *Wait. What?* Surely, if Désiré

Landru had married Berthe and taken her off to some comfy family home, he wouldn't need to continue advertising. Yet there is was, at the top of the second page of adverts, "Widower, aged 43..." I knew there was something suspicious about that bloke.

I hoped for Berthe's sake that my suspicions were wrong and Désiré Landru was on the up and up. Perhaps it had been too late to pull the ad from the weekly magazine? A queasy feeling in my stomach told me otherwise. I checked my watch. I still had some time before the embassy opened, time enough to inquire at the matrimonial agency.

Next stop, Iris Matrimonial Agency, 22 rue Saint-Augustin. Hopefully it wasn't too far out of my way. The map in my trusty *Baedeker's Paris and its Environs* indicated that it was halfway back in the direction of the embassy, the closest Metro stop was Pont Neuf Station back across the Seine, and the best way to get there was to walk across the Pont des Arts bridge to the train station.

Although what I'd discovered about Désiré Landru's advertising habits seemed ominous, the trip to the library had done my spirits good. The stillness of being surrounded by books was like a trip home. I hated to leave, especially if what I suspected about Désiré Landru was true. I dreaded what I'd learn at the agency. Adjusting my cloche, I stepped outside into the sunshine.

It was a lovely day. If it hadn't been for the rotting-fish smells coming from under the bridge, it would have been a perfect walk. Although they weren't stylish, I was glad to be wearing my well-worn Oxfords instead of my cute Mary Janes... or my oversized men's boots. I enjoyed being myself for a change.

Strolling across the boardwalk, I rehearsed what I'd learned and what I still needed to find out. Most important, Fredricks had been arrested for espionage, which confirmed my suspicions from early on back at Ravenswick Abbey. Yet I knew there was more to the story, and I was determined to find out what. Tomorrow morning, I would present myself at La Santé Prison and learn what I could from the prisoner himself. He may be a crafty devil, but I still had a few tricks up my sleeve... my long black sleeve. I smiled to myself. *I can't wait to try out my new disguise.*

More immediately, I'd get the gen on Henri Désiré Landru from the Iris agency, and then go to the embassy and call Captain Hall. I was dreading that call. I should have tried harder to get through yesterday, but I was still half hoping Archie would come back. My country was more important than my heart. What an idiot I'd been. For all I knew, Archie had skipped town with the information… and another bellboy.

Half an hour later, I stood in front of a large wooden door with a small gold plaque that read "Agence Iris." Inside, the office was dark and smelled of cooked onions. A middle-aged woman sat behind a desk knitting. Otherwise, the room was wall-to-wall postal boxes. I scanned the boxes for Landru's. I could see through the tiny window that it was stuffed with responses. Henri Désiré was *desirable* indeed.

"Can I help you?" The woman looked up from her knitting. "Would you like to place an ad?"

"No thanks." My mind was racing to come up with a story to get information out of her about Désiré Landru. *Am I a reporter? A policewoman? A jilted lover? His sister? Why didn't I think about this in advance?* "I'm Henrietta Landru, Henri Landru's cousin, and I've come to collect his mail. He's in England now with my parents."

She eyed me suspiciously. "We only allow clients to pick up their own mail."

I pointed to her knitting. "Your yarn is gorgeous." My father always said, you catch more flies with honey than vinegar. "What are you knitting?"

"A scarf for my Maurice. He's fighting at the front."

"I'm sure he'll appreciate a warm scarf. Is Maurice your husband?"

She nodded. "My son."

"When was the last time you saw Maurice?"

"It's been months." Her eyes filled with tears. "The way the war is going, I don't know if I'll ever see him again."

"Oh, I'm sure you will." I tried to think of something to cheer her up. "Now that the Americans have joined, I'm sure it will be over soon."

"Psssht. Doughboys think the war is one big party." She sat her knitting on the desk. "They come here and sample our wine and women and then leave. What do they care about us?"

"I volunteer at the hospital, and I've seen doughboys injured in battle just the same as the Tommies and poilus." I sighed. "In the end, they all cry for their mothers."

"My Jacques has two little ones to think of. Those children need a father, not a folded flag."

I thought of poor little Georgie growing up without a father. No matter what I thought of his husband-stealing-tart of a mother, Nancy, it wasn't Georgie's fault. A pang reminded me that I'd promised Andrew on his deathbed that I'd help look after little Georgie. I vowed to look in on them as soon as I got back to London.

"And women need their husbands," I said without thinking. "Mine died in my arms. Mustard gas. Those horrid Germans..."

"Sorry to hear that." She wiped a tear from her cheek. "Too much suffering in this world as it is. Why do we need to kill each other?"

"I couldn't agree more." I picked up a copy of *Le Journal* that was sitting on the desk. "Do a lot of war widows place adverts with your agency?"

"Soldiers, war widows, lots of people.... Loneliness isn't a crime."

"Of course not." I put the magazine back. "Well, I should let you get back to your knitting." I smiled. "My brother is sick and wanted me to collect his mail for him. But I'll tell him—"

"Well, I suppose if he's sick. Just this once you understand." She stood up. "Were you wanting the mail from all of his postal boxes then?"

All? I narrowed my eyes. *How many boxes did he have?*

I left Iris Matrimonial Agency with a stack of letters to rival my armful of magazines at the library. I felt bad for deceiving the poor woman who was so worried about her son. But Berthe's life was at stake.

Weighing the stack of letters, I'd say Henri Désiré Landru was a very busy bloke. What would happen when he came looking for his mail and discovered his long lost cousin from England had collected it for him? I chuckled to myself and made a beeline to the nearest trash receptacle and dumped the letters with relish. The dodgy pillock.

Poor Berthe. I shuddered to think of what might have happened to her. The funeral parlor was on my way to the embassy. I'd stop off and ask Abby if her sister had come back yet.

Since I still had some time before the blasted embassy opened, I decided to walk instead of take the train so I could enjoy the sunshine, something I saw little of back home in London. And on the way, I could grab a bite to eat.

Strolling along the avenues, I passed a woman beating a rug in front of a furniture shop, and another washing the windows of her dress shop, and a third standing in the doorway of a patisserie wiping her hands on her apron. Like London, Paris was a city run by women... women hoping their husbands, brothers, and sons would make it home. *What will those men think when they get home and see how women have taken over the world? If they don't like it, maybe they'll think twice about starting another bloody war.*

Deep in thought, I nearly missed the entrance to the funeral parlor. Crossing the threshold was like stepping from the light into the darkness. Inside, the funeral home was dank and smelled of mildew and chemicals. I rang the bell on the counter, and a minute later Abby floated into the room like an apparition. Her face was pale and wan compared to her sister's rosy rouged cheeks and bright-red mouth.

I skipped all pleasantries and got right to the point. "Have you heard from Berthe?"

She gave me a quizzical look. "Who's asking?"

Bother. That's right. Abby knew me only as Harold the helpful bellboy.

"My name is Fiona Figg. I'm a friend of your sister's. We met at the Grand Hotel."

She blinked at me like a mole coming into the daylight for the first time in months.

"I have information about her intended, Henri Landru... Désiré."

"Berthe isn't here."

"And you haven't seen her?"

She shook her head.

How to present my suspicions? "Mr. Désiré Landru may not be... what he

155

seems."

"Dressed like a dandy, with that polka-dotted bow tie, his sweaty bald head, and streaked black beard..." She flipped a braid over her shoulder. "He seems like a rotter."

"Yes, well, perhaps he *is* what he seems." Polka-dotted bow tie, streaked black beard. I'd seen him hanging around the lobby of the hotel, stalking his prey no doubt. "Do you think Berthe went off with Désiré Landru and got married?"

"Wait here." She disappeared into the back room and reappeared a moment later. "I got this." When she handed me the postcard, I noticed the nasty rash on her hand was scabbed over and a bit less inflamed.

I examined the postcard. Postmarked Gambais, yesterday. "Gambais. That's not far from Paris." I wondered if that's how the card arrived so soon. With the war on, the post could be deuced unreliable.

"Gambais is very close to the city. But I don't think Berthe is there."

I read the card out loud. "Dear Abby. I'm so happy with Désiré. Miss you. Love, Berthe." I glanced at Abby, who was scowling. "At least she's okay. Right?"

"She's not okay." Abby grabbed the card out of my hands. "This isn't her handwriting. And she never calls me Abby. She's called me Abs ever since we were small. She didn't write this postcard."

"Why would Désiré Landru forge a postcard from Berthe?" I said more to myself than to Abby. The hair on my arms stood on end. "Is there a train to Gambais?"

She nodded.

"Get your hat. We're going to the train station."

"What?" She scratched at her hand.

"We're going to find your sister." This may have been a situation where my determination outstripped my abilities.

"Okay." Abby ducked behind the curtain into the back room. When she floated out again, her braids tucked up in a boater, she was the spitting image of a clean-faced Berthe.

"Do you have a photograph of your sister?"

Abby shook her head.

"Never mind. I have an idea." I rummaged through my handbag for a lipstick. "Here, put some on."

"I don't want to look like a *putain*." She waved away my offer.

"It's part of my plan. Trust me."

She took the lipstick and reluctantly applied some to her full lips. The transformation was uncanny. I would swear she was Berthe. Now if she would just flirt, she could pass for her twin sister.

I'd asked her to trust me, but can I trust her? I remembered her voice coming from the shrubbery at the garden party, and I screwed up my nerve to ask, "What happened to your hand?"

She glanced down. "Poison ivy. Idiot rich people plant it for decoration."

"Renault's garden party?" I asked.

She looked surprised. "How did you know?"

"I saw you there." I didn't tell her I was Harold, the helpful bellboy and champagne server.

Abby blew on her hand. "Imported ivy hedgerow. Ridiculous."

So Abby had been with the countess behind the hedgerow. It *was* her I heard threaten the countess.

"Yes, isn't it though." I had to find out why Abby was behind the hedges threatening the countess. I'd heard her say, *"You can't escape punishment after what you've done."* What had the countess done? "That lady who died, Countess Pavlovna, did you know her?"

"She is—was—Russian royalty. A spoiled rich lady who plays bridge and feeds truffles to her poodles while people are starving. We did away with our monarchy over a hundred years ago. Russia is finally following suit. About time." Her voice rose.

Her passion surprised me. Maybe Abby wasn't so timid after all.

"I heard she was a member of a political group called the White Women, and was actually working for the allies." I patted my wig and tried to sound nonchalant.

"She only pretended to be working for us. Rich ladies like her dapple in politics as a hobby." Abby tightened her lips. "Vladimir Lenin, we need more men like him. He is my hero."

Lenin. Of course, I'd heard of Lenin, the Marxist revolutionary. I knew from his file at the War Office that he often went by N. Lenin, which wasn't his real name, and the N stood for nothing. "Why are you so invested in what happens in Russia?"

"Don't you care what happens in the rest of the world?" She rubbed her hand.

I wanted to tell her not to scratch at it, but I bit my tongue. I wasn't her mother after all.

"My mother was Russian," she said. "My grandparents left rather than starve."

Blimey. So she did have a motive for murder. And she had access to the food and beverages served at the garden party, so she had the means. But did she have the temperament? I decided to play along. "Yes, the aristocracy have to go. By the sounds of it, Countess Pavlovna deserved to die. You probably wish you could have murdered her yourself. After what you've said, I know I do." I was laying it on a little thick, but I didn't know what else to do. After all, only in detective movies did criminal actually admit to their crimes when asked.

"No." She got a horrified look on her face. "Are you mad? I wouldn't face Madame Guillotine for killing the likes of her. She's not worth it."

"Of course not." I believed her. Flustered, I adjusted my hat. "At the party, did I overhear your sister worrying about getting the sack? Could the countess have had something to do with—" *What am I saying?* The last time I'd seen Berthe she'd been too busy husband hunting to worry about a snobby Russian countess. Then again, if she had been involved in the countess's death, maybe that's why she'd disappeared.

"Berthe wouldn't hurt a flea." Abby scowled. "She's a good girl."

I wondered how good. Berthe was a terrible flirt. But flirting wasn't a crime. "Let's go find your sister. Come on." I took her elbow—careful to avoid the rash. "We're going to the train station."

"Why should I trust you?"

"Your sister's life may be in danger. I want to help her as much as you do."

I glanced at my watch. Just after one. I had less than two hours to find out what happened to Berthe and then get to the embassy to call Captain Hall. "Hurry. We don't have much time."

Abby bit her lip and then grabbed her hat.

* * *

The Gare de Paris-Montparnasse was bustling. Soldiers had commandeered most of the trains and the station looked like a military outpost. I dragged Abby from window to window asking the cashiers if they'd seen a girl who looked just like her accompanied by an older man with a bald head and streaked black beard. I'd almost given up when a fussy little teller with a glass eye said he'd seen the pair a few days ago. He recognized the man, who often bought return tickets for himself and one-way tickets for his lady companions.

Why did he buy the ladies one-way tickets? Does he have a harem in Gambais? Or had he… I shuddered to think.

"Did he buy a return ticket this time? Was a girl who looked like her with him? Did he buy her a one-way or return ticket?" The words came tumbling out.

"I believe he bought himself a return and the girl a one-way as usual," the cashier said.

"When was this? Do you remember what date was on his return ticket?"

"I'm sorry, Mademoiselle. I can't recall. I think it was an open return."

I had to talk Abby out of jumping on a train to Gambais right then and there. I glanced at my watch. *Blast!* Two-thirty. The embassy was closing in half an hour. *Do I continue to help Abby and try to find out what has happened to Berthe? Or do I abandon Abby to make the dreaded phone call?*

Hundreds of soldiers' lives could be at stake. But so could Berthe's life. A purely utilitarian calculus of lives didn't seem appropriate. *Can you really calculate the value of a life? Isn't each life a world? And with every death comes the end of a world?* Although she was only one person, Berthe's life was as important as any soldier's. And she was in real imminent danger while those hypothetical soldiers were in possible future danger.

Abby had tears in her eyes. "Why would he buy a one-way ticket for Berthe? What has he done with her?"

Enough with the philosophical questions. I had to act. My call to Captain Hall would have to wait… yet again. "Come on." I pulled Abby by the hand. "We have work to do."

"Where are we going?"

"Back to the hotel to turn you into Berthe."

I sincerely hope my gut feeling about Archie is spot on and he's already called Captain Hall with the gen from the microfilm.

Chapter Seventeen: The Ghost

When we arrived at the hotel, the lobby was abuzz with reporters. *What in heaven's name is going on?* Men in suits and women in skirts jostled each other trying to get closer to the staircase. Had someone tripped and broken their neck? I had tripped a time or two myself. A cacophony of voices echoed through the cavernous lobby and the excitement of the moment was palpable. Was a princess or king visiting? Or maybe an American film star?

With Abby in tow, I pushed my way through the crowd. When I got to the bottom of the stairs, I looked up and saw Mata Hari, resplendent, standing at the top of the stairs like a princess about to make a grand entrance. Instead of footmen or ladies-in-waiting, she was flanked by two uniformed police officers. She flipped a fox stole around her neck, put her head in the air, and then slowly descended the stairs, wagging her ample hips as she went. The policemen trailed behind, no doubt enjoying the view.

When she reached the landing, a symphony of reporters yelled out questions. "Mata, is it true you're a spy?" "Mata, whose side are you on?" "Mata, why did you do it?"

"Darlings, I'm not a spy. I'm a dancer." Mata Hari waved to the crowd. "You know me. I love Paris and Paris loves me."

I watched, open mouthed, as the police escorted Mata Hari past the first gaggle of reporters. She was so close, I could have reached out and touched her. When she saw me, she got a surprised look on her face.

"Miss Lemons." Mata Hari grabbed my hands. "Please tell these good people that I'm not a spy." She slipped a small key into my hand. "You know it's not true."

What's she up to? I surreptitiously pocketed the key.

"Do you know her?" Abby whispered in my ear.

I nodded and gaped like a fish. I wanted to ask Mata Hari the whereabouts of my passport, but now was not the time.

"Georges Ladoux has it in for me. He's jealous of my Vadime," Mata said as the police pulled her away from me. "I'm working for Ladoux... for France. Why won't you believe me?"

Georges Ladoux. I remembered that name from the telegram I'd found in Mata Hari's room.

"Ladoux and his Deuxième Bureau can go straight to hell," Mata Hari called back to the crowd of reporters. "He double-crossed me. He's the spy, not me."

The police whisked Mata Hari out of the hotel and into a waiting police lorry. I couldn't believe it. Mata Hari was being arrested for espionage. Agent H21 had been caught. *What gave her away? Am I an accomplice for accepting that key?* First Fredricks and now Mata. Georges Ladoux and the *Deuxième Bureau* espionage unit must be on a mission to round up spies. I hoped I wasn't next. *Come on, Fiona, old girl, you're working for the good guys.* Of course, that's what Mata Hari said too.

"Who is that incredible lady?" Abby asked. "Another rich woman treading on the poor?"

Hmm. Perhaps Abby really is a Bolshevik. "I'll tell you upstairs." Swimming upstream against the reporters rushing after Mata Hari, I headed for the lift. "Come on."

As I rounded the corner, I saw the telltale black beard streaked with gray and shiny pate. *Oh bother. He's here already. I can't let him see Abby until we transform her into Berthe.* "Hurry, Abby." I pulled on her arm. "We're taking the stairs." I led her back to the main staircase and dashed up as quickly as I could.

"What's going on?" Abby asked trying to catch up.

"I saw him." I glanced back at her.

She'd gone as white as a sack of flour. "Henri Désiré Landru?"

I nodded. "Come on. I have a plan."

Abby looked suspicious. "What sort of plan?"

I told Abby my plan. She was nervous, but agreed to give it a try. After all, if the dastardly Désiré Landru was here at the hotel, where was Berthe? We planned to find out, even if it meant conjuring a ghost.

Back in my hotel room, I pointed to my dressing table and instructed Abby to take a seat while I hauled my makeup kit out from under the bed, where I kept it hidden. I set the case on the table, opened it, and withdrew a pair of scissors.

Abby's eyes got wide.

"It will grow back," I said.

"What will grow back?" she asked, her face a mask of fear.

"Your hair, silly."

"My hair!" She jumped up from the chair. "No. I won't let you."

"You want to find your sister, don't you?"

She nodded. "But my hair."

"Sit." I pointed at the chair.

"Are you mad? Who are you? How do you know my sister? Why should I trust you?" Abby was on the verge of tears.

"Your sister cleaned my room. We talked as she did. You could say we were fond of each other." Not all of it was a fib.

Abby blinked at me with those big earnest eyes.

"Abby, I'm just trying to help you find out what happened to Berthe." I handed her a tissue. "You want to find your sister, don't you?"

She nodded and blew her nose.

"Okay then, you've got to trust me."

She sat down. Silent tears fell as I cut off her hair into my best approximation of Berthe's fashionable bob.

Next, I applied the heavy green eye shadow favored by Berthe, along with kohl, mascara, and more lipstick. The transformation was complete. I handed Abby a looking glass.

She gasped when she saw herself.

"You're the spitting image of Berthe."

She put her hand to her mouth.

"Don't smear your lipstick."

"Now for your clothes." I went to my wardrobe and removed my maid's outfit. It wasn't identical to those worn at the Grand Hotel but close enough. The trouble was, Abby and I had very different body shapes. My costume might not fit her. "Try this on."

"Turn around," she said as she took the dress and apron.

I did as she asked.

She grunted. I could only guess that she was trying to tug the dress over her bosom, something I never had to worry about.

"You can turn back around now."

Oh dear. The dress was straining at the seams and Abby looked ready to burst out at any minute. "That won't do." Berthe had worn her uniform tight, but not *that* tight. "Let's go back to your gray dress, and I'll spruce it up with some silk flowers or something."

Abby changed clothes again, and I pinned a silk rose to one shoulder. The effect wasn't bad. The dark red against the dark gray set off the crimson of her lips. Her twin would have had painted her fingernails bright red to match, but neither Abby nor I had ever painted our nails, and I didn't own any nail paint.

"That will have to do," I said, adjusting the flower. "You'll have to be convincing as Berthe. Can you?"

"Flirting doesn't come naturally to me." Abby bit her lip.

"Perfect." I clapped my hands together. "That's the look. Very seductive."

"Really?"

"Now practice flirting." I sat down on the end of my bed. "Pretend I'm Henri Landru. What would you say to me?"

"Where's my sister you *bâtard?*"

Sigh. "You're Berthe, remember? Try again."

"Mr. Landru, your dress is very pretty." She smiled.

"Very funny." I shook my head. "Remember, Berthe calls him Désiré."

"Désiré, your sweaty head and lice-filled beard really get me going."

Abby had more spunk than I'd given her credit for.

164

"Seriously, you have to make him think you're Berthe."

Abby put her hands on her hips and twisted the end of a lock of hair around her little finger. "Cutie, want to come upstairs and help me make the bed?"

My mouth fell open. The effect was astounding, eerie even. She sounded exactly like Berthe. "You're ready." I shuddered. I felt as if I'd seen a ghost. "Be careful. And don't leave the hotel with him no matter what he says."

We headed back to the lobby to set the trap for Désiré Landru. As we exited the lift, I asked Abby to give me a head start. I circled the lobby, looking for our target. When I spotted him, drinking a demitasse coffee and chatting up one of the hotel patrons, I signaled Abby. The setup was perfect. She could play the jealous lover come to read him the riot act for taking coffee with another woman.

I hid behind a pillar nearby and listened. The dodgy blackguard was using a sad story about his dead wife and orphaned children to seduce his prey. Why some women fell for such drivel, I'd never know.

"Désiré, why did you do it?" Abby shouted. *Good girl.* She was making a scene just as we'd planned.

I peeked around the pillar to see his reaction. His round face paled to match the ivory marble floor, and his eyes flashed. "Berthe. Impossible!"

"Why did you leave me?" Abby put her hand on her hip, imitating Berthe.

The woman sitting with him asked, "What's going on, Henri? Who is this girl?"

"Impossible," he repeated. "You're dead... I disposed..." He gasped.

Dead? Disposed? I stumbled back a couple of steps and my stomach flip-flopped. Just as I figured. He'd killed Berthe. How awful. I'd hoped he'd say something else—something about where Berthe was supposed to be. But in my heart I'd feared the worst. How many other girls had he killed? I put my hand on the pillar to steady myself.

There was a commotion at the table. I peeked around the pillar again in time to see Désiré Landru barreling toward me. As he rounded the pillar, I stuck my practical oxford-clad foot out. He tripped and fell flat on his face.

"Security," I shouted. "Police!"

Landru peeled himself off the floor and made a break for the exit.

"Stop him!" I ran after him.

Trying to tackle him, I managed to grab his jacket. He pulled away, leaving me flat on my face on the floor while he zipped out the door and ran off down the street.

Abby helped me up. Her face was ashen and her eyes sprouted tears.

"I'm so sorry about your sister," I said, brushing off my skirt and adjusting my blouse. "We've got to go to the police."

I bundled a distraught Abby off to the closest police station.

* * *

At the station, I had to do the talking since Abby was sobbing and couldn't speak. I told the police about my suspicions... Henri Désiré Landru had been luring unsuspecting women to their deaths using the lonely hearts adverts in *Le Journal*. He had four postal boxes under four different names at the Iris Matrimonial Agency. He'd sent a forged postcard from Berthe to her sister Abby. He'd bought return train tickets for himself, but one-way tickets for the women he'd taken to Gambais to murder. When he'd seen Abby made up like her sister, he all but admitted he'd killed Berthe.

"Was this Berthe woman a streetwalker?" the policeman asked.

"No," Abby said through her tears. "My sister worked at the Grand Hotel."

"What difference does it make?" I asked.

"We don't have time to check on all the prostitutes or runaways, now do we?" the policeman said.

"Why not? They have rights too." I narrowed my eyes. *What kind of police station is this? They don't care about murdered women if they are prostitutes or runaways?* "Murder is murder."

"We'd be better off without those dregs of society."

I was fuming. "Without clients there would be no prostitutes."

"Are you a working girl, yourself?" the policeman asked.

"Well, I never!" I shook my finger at him. "If you won't do anything, I will."

"Have at it, lady," he said with a chuckle. "We have enough crime to deal with here without getting ourselves involved in things that happen in Gambais."

"Despicable." I turned on my heels. "Come on, Abby. We're getting nowhere."

I took Abby back to the hotel for a brandy. My nerves were shot, and with makeup running down her face, she was a blooming mess. If the police wouldn't do anything about Berthe's murder, we would have to take matters into our own capable hands.

Chapter Eighteen: The Call

D ue to circumstances beyond my control, I was way overdue for my call to Captain Hall. For that reason, I was dreading it even more than usual.

I nibbled on my croissant and sipped my milky coffee. *Should I tell him that Archie Somersby is a possible double agent?* What evidence did I have besides Fredricks taunting me and the fact that Archie had disappeared? Best to let Captain Hall do the talking and see what I could find out. This afternoon, I would get to the embassy in time to call, no matter what. Berthe's death wouldn't stop me. Abby wouldn't stop me. Nothing was going to stop me from making that call.

I finished my breakfast and glanced at my watch. Blast. I'd forgotten to wind it. I pulled the stem and twisted it round and round.

"Excuse me," I signaled the waiter. "What time is it?" I felt like a schoolgirl practicing my French.

"Nine-thirty, madame." The waiter made a little bow and disappeared.

Sigh. I had hours to kill until I could call Captain Hall. If only I could convince the grumpy clerk to let me use the hotel telephone. *It doesn't matter. The Captain already has the information.* I knew in my heart Archie had made the call already. I knew it. He wasn't a double agent. I was sure of it.

As tragic as it was, at least Berthe's disappearance had distracted me from Archie's vanishing act. What a cad. He'd used me—or Harold the bellboy—something terrible. Memories of his strong embrace and soft lips still caused a sharp pain in my chest. He was the only man I'd admired since I met Andrew, five years ago now. *Fiona, quit feeling sorry for yourself. You aren't the only young woman who lost a husband or a sweetheart. At least Archie is still alive... I hope... even if he like boys and not girls.* My heart sunk. What did it matter? I'd never see him again.

My top priority today was making it to the embassy during the slim two hours they were open. Abby had wanted to start our search for Henri Désiré Landru at dawn. But I was not going to miss another chance to call the War Office. Captain Hall was probably getting ready to send the cavalry after me. Anyway, now that we knew Berthe was dead, rushing after Désiré Landru wouldn't bring her back... although we might just save some other lonely woman from meeting the same fate, whatever it had been. I shuddered to think.

I'd persuaded Abby to get tickets to Gambais for this evening. We would spend the night and have plenty of time to snoop around tomorrow. I just wish we knew what we were looking for. I glanced at my watch.

Blasted embassy. Not open until one in the afternoon. I spent the morning pacing my hotel room and wondering how I'd managed to get involved with not one murder, but two. First the countess and now Berthe. At least I wasn't a suspect in Berthe's murder. Given their relationship, maybe Harold the bellboy would be though. I hoped not or Harold would get quite a reputation. Maybe with both Fredricks and Mata Hari in prison, I could retire Harold the helpful bellboy for good.

Mata Hari... the key! I went to my wardrobe and patted the pocket of the skirt I was wearing yesterday. Sure enough, the little key she slipped to me was still there. I removed it and examined it. It looked too small to be a key to her room. Was it a key to a suitcase... or a safety-deposit box? I turned it over in my palm. Too bad Berthe wasn't here to help me get into the penthouse. Poor Berthe.

With time to kill before the embassy opened, I went up to the penthouse to try my luck. I should have known. The place was swarming with police. I knocked on the door.

"Can I help you, Mademoiselle?" asked a portly officer with a great bushy mustache.

"Lady MacLeod borrowed one of my..." *One of my what?* "A pair of my...

169

earrings," I stammered. "I wondered if I might look for them in her room?" I was becoming a practiced prevaricator. Given my Protestant upbringing, the ease with which I fibbed was disturbing.

"Let me ask my supervisor." He disappeared into the penthouse.

I followed him inside. *What in heaven's name!* Gorgeous fur coats were ripped from their linings, beautiful beaded dresses were heaped on the floor, precious jewels were jumbled in the middle of the sitting room table, and another policeman was sitting on a sofa examining Mata Hari's lace underthings, which he had piled up next to him.

I dashed over and grabbed the undergarments from his hands. "Is fondling ladies' knickers part of your job?"

"Who are you?" The policeman stared up at me red-faced.

"A friend of Lady MacLeod's."

"What are you doing here?"

"Lady MacLeod asked me to collect her underwear and a change of clothes," I fibbed again. Jolly clever, actually. The lady would *need* clean underthings and a change of clothes. It would give me a good excuse to visit her and find out why she gave me the key and what it was for. I grabbed a handful of garments from the pile next to him. I wished I had somewhere to put them. For now, I rolled them up and tucked them under my arm.

"You can't take those. They're evidence."

"Evidence of what? That the lady has good taste?"

"They might be hiding state secrets."

"State secrets in Lady MacLeod's knickers?" I scoffed.

The portly officer I'd encountered at the door returned from the bedroom. Given what I'd witnessed in the sitting room, I hated to think what damage they'd done in there.

"My superior says you'll have to leave. If you describe your earrings, we can keep an eye out."

"Never mind." I grabbed another handful of underwear. "I'll take it up with your superiors." I turned to go.

"Where are you going with those?" the portly policeman asked.

"I'm delivering them to Lady MacLeod."

"But—"

"The lady needs her knickers and that's that." I marched out of the room.

In the hallway, I nearly broke into a run. Giddy with the excitement of standing up to that lecherous policeman, I hurried back to my own room.

Mata Hari's fancy underclothes must be worth at least a week's wages. I carefully folded the lacy silks and wrapped them in tissue paper. I would find out where they'd taken her and go on an errand of mercy.

I glanced at my watch. Only eleven. The blooming embassy still wasn't open. I might as well get some lunch. I put on my cloche and gloves. There was a lovely little café off the promenade des Champs-Élysées near the embassy that I'd been meaning to try.

Walking to the café, I passed several gorgeous boutiques. I was tempted to do some shopping… just to calm down, mind you. A beautiful turquoise linen dress and a wide-brimmed hat with matching turquoise band caught my eye. I stopped in front of the boutique window. *Did I dare?* I popped inside and inquired about the dress. When the shop girl told me the price, I had to bite my tongue. *A whole year's wages for one dress!* No shopping for me. I'd have to be content with window shopping, or *lèche-vitrine*—window-licking—as the French called it.

Café Soleil had a cheerful awning over sidewalk tables where patrons enjoyed coffee and quiche in the sunshine, apropos of its name. I sat at a small table under the awning, enjoying the warmth of the sun, something we rarely saw in London. With all the direct sunlight, I was surprised the French women weren't sunburned and wrinkled. No wonder so many of them carried parasols. I should have thought to bring mine. Perhaps I would have to go shopping after all… but not in this posh part of town.

I longed for a nice strong cuppa, but having learned there wasn't a decent cup of tea to be had in Paris, I settled for café au lait. With enough milk, and a bit of sugar (when available), it was actually quite tasty. And I'd become very fond of the warm French bread lathered with butter, which was still available in the fancy cafés in this part of town. I much preferred the French breakfast of bread and coffee to the full English with eggs, bacon, kidneys, and beans. So much more elegant, if not as hardy.

While the French had wonderful pastries, they still couldn't compete when it came to English tea. Give me a strong cuppa and a sweet biscuit and I was happy.

For now, bread and warm milk with a splash of coffee would be plenty. I thought of all the poor boys shivering in the trenches, eating cold tinned beef and stale brown bread. Surely, it wouldn't hurt me to go without tea until I returned home.

I was munching on warm crusty bread followed by sips of sweet milky coffee, thinking again of that stunning kiss, when a familiar voice interrupted my daydreams.

"Fiona, old girl, mind if I join you?" Clifford sat down across from me before I could answer. "Where have you been hiding? I haven't seen you in days."

"I haven't been hiding." I hadn't even donned my Harold the helpful bellboy outfit since... the kiss.

"Did you hear? They've arrested Fredricks." Clifford shook his head. "Seems they're rounding up journalists."

Spies and murderers, more like. "Are you sure he's just a journalist?"

"Whatever else he is, he is at least a journalist. He's even won awards."

"Do you know any other journalists who've been arrested?"

"Yes, actually, quite a few." He waved to the waiter and ordered a demitasse. "Censorship may be necessary to protect our troops, but do they really need to pressure newspapers to publish all that balderdash? German bullets pass through the skin without a tear, my eye." He slapped his wounded knee. "Satire is fine, but real news is banned. What are we fighting for, after all if it isn't freedom, including freedom of the press?"

"Well said, Clifford dear." I sipped my milky coffee.

"They've arrested Fredricks because he's working for an American newspaper and he's writing real news stories and not just patriotic rubbish."

"You mean propaganda?"

"That's exactly what I mean."

The waiter delivered his coffee.

"Would you like some bread and butter?" I asked. "It's scrummy."

"Don't mind if I do." He tucked into the bread with gusto.

"The men in Room Forty were talking about censorship… and arrests, come to think of it." *Maybe Clifford is right and Fredricks isn't a spy but a journalist just doing his job.* Everything Fredricks said the other evening at his secret apartment had made me certain he was a spy, but he could have known the things he knew and asked the questions he asked because he was a journalist seeking the truth and wanting to stop the war. *Right?… No, I'm certain he poisoned Edith Wilkinson at Ravenswick Abbey, and he has something to do with Countess Pavlovna's death.* "I'm sure of it."

"Sure of what?"

"Oh, did I say that out loud?" I patted my wig.

"So what have you been up to? I haven't seen you since I had to chase down your hat and found you with that young lieutenant." He gave me his hangdog look. "I say, you never told me what that was all about."

"I've been helping a friend whose sister went missing," I said, changing the subject. "Remember that bright young maid at the hotel, Berthe?"

He shook his head. "Can't say as I do."

"Berthe answered an advert in a lonely-hearts column and then went missing. Her sister and I tracked down the dodgy bounder, and…" I paused, not quite sure how to put my suspicions into words. "I think he's a psychotic killer murdering the girls and women who answer his advert."

"Good Lord. You can't be serious."

I nodded. "Unfortunately, I'm deadly serious."

"Good Lord," he repeated. "How dreadful."

"Quite."

"Did you go to the police?"

"Yes. But they're too busy to care about a missing chambermaid."

"You know, I'm a bit of a detective myself." He cocked his head. "If you need any help, I'm at your service."

"Thank you, Clifford dear." I reached across and patted his hand. "Abby, Berthe's twin sister, and I are going to Gambais this evening to do some detective work of our own."

"By Jove, I'm coming with you." He sat up straight in his chair.

"That won't be necessary."

"Are you barmy? I won't let two girls go on their own to find a dangerous killer."

I could tell by the glint in his eye there was no getting rid of Clifford. "Oh, all right. Meet us at Gare de Paris-Montparnasse at six this evening."

"I'll be there," he said with a smile. "You can count on me, old girl."

I glanced at my watch. Blast. Two o'clock already. I had best get to the embassy before they closed. "I've got to go."

"Where are you going? I'll walk with you."

"I can take care of myself."

"I just... I mean... I thought..." He stammered.

"It's okay, Clifford. Thanks anyway."

I opened my handbag to pay the check.

"Oh no. Let me," Clifford said, reaching across the table and putting his hand on mine.

I gave him a stern look.

"Right," he said, retracting his hand.

I dropped a few silver centimes on the table and stood up. "See you at six o'clock sharp. Don't be late."

I had a full hour to walk the five minutes to the embassy, but I quickened my pace just to be sure. I was determined to get there in time.

Standing on the steps to the embassy, I couldn't believe I'd finally made it during business hours. I pushed the heavy door open and readied myself to face the embassy staff... and the dreaded call to Captain Blinker Hall.

The embassy staff was actually quite helpful and led me to a telephone in a back room. Captain Hall was another matter.

"Miss Figg, you were supposed to check in two days ago," Captain Hall said, his impatience traveling through the telephone wires all the way from London.

"Sorry, sir. The agent you sent..." *The dreamy but disappointing Archie Somersby.* "He was supposed to call—"

"Yes, Lieutenant Somersby said he was impressed with your stiff upper lip in spite of the pressure," Captain Hall said. "He was particularly—what

174

was the word he used—*fascinated* by the way you handled Fredricks."

Gobsmacked, I held the receiver to my ear, wondering what in blazes Archie had said about me. Cheeky cad. *Stiff upper lip, my fake mustache.*

"Said he couldn't wait to see what else you can do undercover."

I just bet he can't. Unfortunately, my mind immediately went back to the image of Archie bare chested under the sheets in the hospital bed at Charing Cross. *Blast.* I had to purge him from my thoughts, the rogue.

"Arch… Lieutenant Somersby didn't come back." My voice cracked in a way that may have betrayed my feelings.

"Don't worry about him. Now that Fredricks has been arrested, your job is done. You can go back to filing papers in Room Forty, where you belong."

"But, sir—" I didn't relish going back to my old life filing papers. I preferred the excitement of my new life.

As if reading my mind, Captain Hall said, "Yes, I know. You're enjoying Paris. No one ever wants to come back." He chuckled.

"No, sir. That's not it. I would like—"

"Okay, take two weeks holiday. You deserve it for a job well done."

"But sir—"

"See you back at the War Office in two weeks."

"But sir—" I wanted to ask him about Archie. But I couldn't get a word in.

"And Miss Figg?"

"Yes, sir."

"Stay out of trouble."

"Yes, sir," I repeated into the dead receiver. Captain Hall had already hung up.

Chapter Nineteen: Gambais

L ike every train station, the Gare de Paris-Montparnasse was packed with soldiers. Abby was shivering even though the station was sweltering. Her eyes were puffy and she looked like she hadn't slept a wink.

I scanned the station for Clifford. It was so crowded, I didn't know how I'd find him, even if he was on time for a change. Hopefully, he'd find us. I bought two return-trip tickets for Gambais, and then treated Abby to a hot chocolate while we waited to be called to the platform. *I have to admit, the French know how to make hot chocolate.* The bittersweet liquid happiness was the perfect accompaniment to a flaky croissant, which by some miracle the station café had on offer. Although Paris was feeling the effects of war, unlike the English who embraced scarcity with the fervor of a martyr's hair shirt, the French seemed in denial. They were determined to enjoy life in spite of the bloody war.

The loudspeaker announced the train to Gambais.

Clifford was still nowhere to be seen. Figures he would be late. I should have told him the train left earlier. I'd learned from past experience that if you wanted Clifford to be on time, you had to adjust the hour by at least fifteen minutes to account for Clifford-time.

We were just stepping up to board the train when I heard the familiar voice. "I say, Fiona, is that you?"

I turned to see Clifford, red-faced from running. "I made it just in time," he said triumphantly, and offered his hand to help me board. The color in his cheeks offset his brilliant blue eyes, which sparkled in the dim lights on

176

the underground platform. He really wasn't a bad-looking sort.

"I say, who's this?" he asked, smiling at Abby.

"Abby," I said. "The missing girl's twin sister." I turned to Abby. "I realize I don't know your family name."

"Canard," she said.

"Duck?" I asked.

She nodded. "I'm afraid so."

"A darn pretty duck too," Clifford said.

I rolled my eyes. *Here we go.* Clifford couldn't resist a damsel in distress.

He held out his hand to Abby and helped her aboard. *I really hope that rash isn't contagious.*

The trip to Gambais was only an hour, but I was glad to have Clifford along. His nonstop nattering was a good distraction for poor Abby. He regaled her with stories of big-game hunting in Africa with Fredrick Fredricks, and told her his secret desire to be a true-crime writer, the next Arthur Conan Doyle. I didn't bother pointing out that Conan Doyle wrote mysteries and not true crime.

"Clifford Douglas, the next Sherlock Holmes," I said.

He grinned. "Why not?"

Because, contrary to popular belief, Sherlock Holmes is a fictional character? Clifford was charming in his own clueless way.

While Clifford entertained Abby, I enjoyed the scenery. The city gave way to lush green hills and fields of glorious yellow wildflowers. The sky was as blue as I'd ever seen it. Nothing like the drab gray skies of London.

The countryside of Northern France was so lovely, it was hard to imagine just two hours north of here, the British had lost nearly twenty thousand souls in one day in the Somme Offensive. Weren't the horrors of war enough? It was unthinkable that profiteers and murderers alike used the war for their own nefarious ends. I thought of the man who was caught stealing single shoes from display windows and selling them to amputees. If my suspicions were right, what he did was tame compared with Landru.

Without even enough time to take a watery cup of tea, we pulled into the station at Gambais. Unlike the cavernous stations in Paris, the small platform was nearly deserted. We alighted the train without much sense of what to do next.

Clifford and Abby looked to me for direction. After all, I was the mastermind behind our depressing search for Berthe… or what was left of her. First stop, find a hotel. Second stop, dinner. And then we could begin our reconnaissance. But where? What was my master-plan? I really should think things through before rushing off half-cocked. *What kind of spy am I? Judging from recent events, not a very good one, I'm afraid. And I'm an even worse detective.*

Abby and I each carried a small overnight case, while Clifford had a full-sized duffel bag. You'd think he was staying a fortnight. As we wandered toward the heart of the village, I spotted a lovely country inn. *Yes, that would do nicely.* I pointed. "Let's try that."

The stone building housed a cozy sitting room with a homey restaurant just off the reception area. The savory aroma coming from the kitchen was divine. My stomach grumbled, reminding me that except for the croissant at the station, I hadn't eaten anything except bread all day.

"Smells absolutely scrummy," Clifford said. "I don't know about you two, but I'm famished."

After storing our luggage in our rooms—Abby and I in one room and Clifford in another—we settled in for a delicious bowl of fish soup served with crusty bread, a local specialty. I indulged in an extra glass of wine to fortify myself for the night ahead.

At dinner, I asked the waitresses if they'd seen a girl who looked like Abby with a dapper forty-ish man with a bushy black beard. One waitress looked Abby up and down and then said, "Yes. I saw them. They came in here together all giggly. He's a regular rotter, he is. Brings a different girl in here every week."

"When were they here last?" I asked.

"Dunno. Maybe a few days ago."

So Berthe was here with that scoundrel Landru.

We'd learned from the innkeeper that Henri Landru owned a modest villa on the edge of town. With a full moon rising and the scent of wild lavender in the air, it would have been a beautiful evening for a stroll if our mission hadn't been so gruesome. We set out on foot across the village. With the nightly blackouts, we had to get there and back before dark.

On the way, I stopped passersby and asked if they'd seen a girl who looked like Abby. Having Abby along was a good as having a photograph. A woman dragging two children along beside her told us Henri Désiré Landru was infamous around town for his philandering ways and she wouldn't be surprised if he'd promised the girl to marry her. Seems half the town knew about Désiré Landru's racket.

Henri Désiré Landru's villa was a box of a building with a rounded mansard roof with a large redbrick chimney at either end. Except for a tile inlaid triangle at each upper corner, the façade was plain. A hedgerow shielded the house from the dusty street.

I was a bundle of nerves as we approached the front door. I wished the blasted police would do their job so we didn't have to. With Abby and Clifford in tow, I ascended the front steps and then gave the heavy door knocker two quick raps. *What would we do if Landru answered armed with a butcher knife?*

"J'arrive," a woman's voice said from inside.

A pleasantly plump woman wearing a cotton cap answered the door. "Can I help you?" Her accent was different than that of the Parisians, and I had more trouble understanding than usual.

"We're looking for Monsieur Henri Landru," I said.

I heard a clicking sound and turned around to see Abby's teeth chattering. Poor girl.

"My husband isn't home," the woman said.

Husband! Désiré Landru is married?

"He's in Paris on business."

I bet he is. "When will he return?"

"Tomorrow or the next day." She wiped her hands on her apron. "I don't keep track. He's away so much for work, I usually just stay at my sister's. You're lucky you caught me."

"Yes, very lucky," I said, trying to peek around her to see inside.

"Would you like to come in for *palets de dames*?" she asked. "They're fresh from the oven."

I stood, staring at her. *Palets de dames? Ladies' what?* Whatever they were, now was our chance to look around. "That's very kind of you." I nodded to Abby and Clifford. "Why not?"

Abby took Clifford's hand as she crossed the threshold.

"I say," Clifford said, blushing.

Shivers ran up my spine as I imagined Berthe here in this house. Did Landru's wife know about his murderous tendencies? Was she in on it? Was this the scene of the gruesome crime? I needed to find out all I could from his wife and his house.

Mrs. Landru led us into the sitting room. I sat on an upholstered chair and Abby and Clifford took a corduroy sofa. The house smelled like fresh-baked bread with an undercurrent of smoky burnt wood. Heavy drapes and wood walls gave the room a dark masculine feel.

Mrs. Landru excused herself, disappeared into the kitchen, and then returned carrying a tray, upon which sat a teapot, four cups, and a plate of golden biscuits. *Palets de dames* turned out to be crispy, buttery biscuits topped with raisins. Mrs. Landru served them with the tea, good strong tea, not the usually watery French version. For a murderer's wife, she was very cordial.

"How do you know my husband?" Mrs. Landru asked as she passed around the plate of biscuits again.

"We... we... I..." I stammered.

"We met at the Grand Hotel." Clifford came to my rescue. "My sisters and I were dining in the café when your husband kindly offered to show us around Paris, where he works, that sort of thing."

Jolly clever, Clifford dear.

"Are you collectors too?" she asked.

"Collectors?" Clifford repeated.

"Do you collect antiques too, you know, furniture, paintings, *objets d'art*?" Mrs. Landru asked. "Henri just loves collecting old things."

What else does he collect? Wives?

"I'm a bit of a collector," Clifford said. "Nothing serious, just as a hobby, mind."

"Henri loves to take visitors to the antique shops. He specializes in widows."

"Widows?" I glanced at Abby, who had an alarmed look on her face.

"That's our little joke." Mrs. Landru giggled behind her hand. "Widows often have to sell their furniture." Her countenance became somber. "It's sad, really. Henri tries to soften the blow."

I bet he does. "That's why we're here." I put my arm around Abby's trembling shoulders. "My sister just lost her husband and the death duties are too much. We need to sell some furniture."

"I'm so sorry, dear. Was it the war that took him?" Mrs. Landru poured more tea for Abby. "More milk?"

At least the story about Abby being a widow would explain her sulky and nervous behavior. Poor Abby looked as if she might burst into tears at any moment.

I nodded to Abby encouragingly and eventually she spoke. "Yes." Her voice was barely audible.

"I'm sorry Henri isn't here to help you." Mrs. Landru nibbled on a *palet de dames.* "Would you like to see some of his collection?"

"*Bien sûr.*" I nodded to my companions.

Mrs. Landru placed the half-eaten biscuit on her saucer and wiped her hands on her apron. "I'm sure he won't mind me showing you his storage room."

"Yes, we would very much like to see his tools of the trade." *And the antique trade isn't the one I have in mind.*

"Follow me." Mrs. Landru led us from the front sitting room, down a long hallway with several closed doors, to the door at the very end. She jangled a key ring attached to her belt, plucked a key, and inserted it into the lock. "Henri loves beautiful things." She opened the door. "See."

From wall to wall, the room was a jumble of furniture, statues, lamps, paintings, vases, and bric-a-brac. Chairs attached to hooks hung from the upper portions of the wall, giving the room an eerie feel, as if ghosts floated up there to have tea parties.

Hoping to explore more of the house, I asked to use the lav. Mrs. Landru pointed to a door down the hall on the right. While she was describing her husband's various treasures, I dashed down the hall, peeking inside doors as I went... the ones that weren't locked. I tiptoed into the kitchen, and that's when I saw it. My palms broke out in a sweat. A giant oven, big enough to dispose of a woman's body.

Fiona, get a grip. You've read too many gothic novels. The kitchen was cavernous and several iron pots hung from hooks above the stove. A sink large enough to wash a calf was full of dirty dishes... the ones Mrs. Landru had used to make the biscuits? A dusting of flour covered the floor.

Glancing around to make sure no one was watching, I slid across the planked wooden floor to the oven and opened the heavy door. *I had to check.* It was filled with ashes.... A glimmer of silver caught my eye. I was reaching for it when I heard footsteps from the hallway. I slammed the oven door shut and dashed out of the kitchen.

Mrs. Landru was leading the rest of our party back to the sitting room. "Did you find the facilities okay?" she asked.

"Yes, thank you," I said, hiding my ash-covered hand behind my back. This place gave me an uneasy feeling. Whatever was going on here, I was sure Landru was up to no good. I needed to find a way to get back and investigate properly.

As we were leaving, Mrs. Landru extended her hand. *Holy mother of pearl.* She was wearing Mata Hari's jade ring, the one Désiré Landru had given to Berthe.

Chapter Twenty: Saint-Lazare Prison

Although the trip to Gambais had been enlightening, we hadn't uncovered any hard evidence, at least not enough to get the Paris police to pay attention. A large oven filled with ashes, a silver glimmer, and my uneasy feeling, weren't enough to convince them to investigate. Even Mata Hari's ring on Mrs. Landru's ring finger didn't do the trick. Since I was officially on holiday, I decided to take the case on myself. I owed it to poor Berthe and her sister.

Pacing around my small room back at the Grand Hotel, I hatched a plan. If Landru was using the lonely-hearts adverts to lure unsuspecting war widows to their deaths, then there was only one way to catch him in the act. I had to answer Landru's lonely-hearts advert. I didn't relish the idea of using myself as bait, but given that the police weren't taking the disappearance of poor women seriously, I had to do whatever necessary to catch the murderous pillock myself.

I sat down at the desk, took out a piece of hotel stationary, and wrote a letter, describing myself as a rich war widow looking for security and a man I could trust to manage my fortune. That should get his attention. In a sense, I was a war widow, though not rich by any means, and after my failed marriage and Andrew's infidelity, I didn't know if I'd ever trust a man again. I sealed and addressed the envelope. I would drop it in a postbox on the way to the prison.

I was excited to try my new disguise, which should gain me entrance to the women's prison where Mata Hari was being held. I only hoped I could find her cell and get some time alone with her. First things first.

The prisoners were cared for by nuns from the Marie-Joseph order. Even before my assignment in Paris, I'd assumed a nun could get away with murder—so to speak—and my prized possession was a nun's habit from Angels Fancy Dress shop, which I'd purchased before I left London. I pulled the heavy disguise off a hanger and examined it. It didn't have much shape and it looked hot. But it certainly would give me ample cover.

I layered the black robe over the white dress robes and attached the wimple. There was plenty of room under the habit to stuff Mata Hari's underclothing into my own. Scrutinizing the result in my looking glass, I was shocked to see the stark face framed by the heavy cloth. I looked like a man dressed up as a nun. At least I didn't have to worry about my hair since it completely disappeared into the wimple.

By some lucky surprise, I'd found a bible in the dresser drawer of my hotel room. The cover was embossed in gold with "Placed in this hotel by the Gideons." As I recalled from my early bible classes, Gideon was an Old Testament military hero. Who were the modern Gideons? Warriors for God? I hoped they didn't mind my borrowing their bible.

I tucked the bible under my arm, made sure no one saw me leave my room, snuck into the service elevator, and then exited the hotel by a side door. A brisk walk to the train station on a warm summer morning left me perspiring under the weight of the fabric. In summer, a nun's kit was even worse than a man's three-piece suit. The advantage was that one could hide an entire trousseau underneath.

Saint-Lazare women's prison was only a few blocks from the Gare du Nord station. The imposing façade of the prison was made even more somber by the jagged spire of an adjoining chapel. A guard at the gate merely nodded in response to my greeting. It was surprisingly easy to pass without suspicion dressed as a nun. I made a mental note to consider the nun disguise for future assignments... assuming I'd get any.

Inside, the prison was dark, dank, and oppressive. I was glad that I could leave whenever I wanted. The thought of being locked up in here was unnerving at best and downright terrifying at worst. To keep the walls from closing in on me, I took deep breaths as I explored the cavernous hallways.

The smell of excrement and other unsavory bodily fluids hung in the damp air. I only wished my nose was as protected as the rest of my body.

The guards generally ignored me as I passed by. When I needed one of them to unlock a door or let me into a passageway, I simply nodded and they nodded back and let me in. Seemed I had the run of the place. Of course, the guards weren't my only worry. There were the other nuns to consider. They were probably a tight-knit community and undoubtedly would recognize an interloper immediately.

Judging by the human tragedy I saw lying in lumps on what looked to be flea-infested straw mattresses, my guess was the prisoners would welcome any visitor who might bring them solace… or better yet, a sweet treat and some clean knickers. Glancing into the tiny windows in the doors of every cell I passed, I saw all sizes and shapes of pathetic women, but not Mata Hari. With all her grace and splendor, it was hard to imagine Mata Hari in a squalid place like this.

Where is she? Maybe they kept treasonous prisoners in a special wing. I continued my explorations, searching for the most secure part of the prison, hoping I'd find Mata Hari.

I didn't find Mata Hari, but I did find a cramped kitchen that smelled of sour milk. One elderly nun was ladling thin soup into bowls while another even older nun scurried back and forth putting bowls of soup on trays. The one stirring the giant caldron had a wart on her nose that reminded me of a fairy tale my mother used to read to me at bedtime about a witch and a gingerbread house.

"Hurry, Sister," the ladler said. "We don't want the soup to get cold."

In for a penny, in for a pound. I'd come this far. I might as well help serve lunch to the lady prisoners. What better way to look for Mata Hari?

"Can I help?" I asked in French with my best Irish accent. After two weeks in Paris, I was nearly fluent, and had been told that my English accent was barely discernable, which came in handy in the espionage business.

"Oh, Sister, you startled me," the older nun said, putting a shriveled hand to her chest. "Can you put a slice of bread on each tray?" She used the ladle to point to dark brown loaves piled on a large tray. "There's a bread knife in that drawer." She pointed in the other direction toward a long counter with drawers underneath.

I found the knife and went back to the bread. The loaves were heavy and dry, more like corkboard than bread. I sawed off a thick slice and set it on one of the trays next to the bowl of watery soup.

"Oh dear," the other nun said as she delivered more bowls of soup to waiting trays. "You'll have to cut smaller slices or we'll run out."

Smaller slices. *What do these poor women live on?* I thought of Mata Hari's quip about the women on the Titanic who refused the dessert tray. Could memories of life's sweetness sustain anyone in this hellish place?

I helped the older nun put the trays on a wheelie cart for delivery.

"There's a new prisoner, a Lady MacLeod," I said. "I prayed with her earlier, but now I don't remember her cell number. I'd like to pray with her again."

"Is that the fancy lady complaining she doesn't belong here? Asking for her furs and perfume and such?" The elderly nun puffed as she pushed the cart.

"Let me do that, Sister." I took her place behind the cart. "Sounds like her all right."

"Cell block C, last door."

I didn't dare ask her the location of cell block C, or I'd give myself away. If I accompanied her delivering soup, eventually, I'd have to find Mata Hari.

"What's your name, Sister?" she asked. "I don't believe we've met."

"Fiona."

"That's not a French name."

"I grew up in Ireland." It was close to true. My mother was Irish, bless her soul. She died of tuberculosis when I was sixteen. From then on, I'd had to take care of myself and my dear—now departed—father, who was so hopeless he couldn't even boil an egg.

"I'm Béatrice." She put her hands together in prayer and gave a slight bow. I mirrored her gesture.

"I can manage now," Sister Béatrice said. "Why don't you go back and help sister Noelle in the kitchen."

"I'd like to deliver lunch. I do so enjoy praying with the prisoners."

She gave me a queer look. "Suit yourself. I need a smoke break anyway." She pulled a package of cigarettes out from under her habit. She tapped out a cigarette and smiled at me. "Would you like one?" She held out the pack.

"No, thanks. I don't smoke." I didn't know nuns were allowed to smoke. Judging by the color of her teeth, I'd say Sister Béatrice smoked like a chimney.

I was glad to be making the lunch rounds alone. It would have been difficult to deliver the lingerie and ask about the key with Sister Béatrice looking over my shoulder.

As I pushed the cart from cell to cell, a guard opened each door in turn, and I delivered the meager tray of soup and bread. Some of the women tore into the food like starving dogs Others ignored me and didn't move from their beds. One woman who smelled like she'd already died threw her crust of bread at me and cursed. Another young woman with a dirty face and big eyes begged me to stay and keep her company while she ate.

You'd think after volunteering at the hospital and seeing so many boys fragmented and broken, I'd be used to human suffering. But I wasn't. And I hoped I'd never become complacent about the misery of others. Criminals or not, these women deserved better than this.

The case that pushed me over the edge was a young mother who, with tears in her eyes, implored me to make sure her children were still alive. Her husband beat them and her until one day she took a butcher knife to him. He survived. She was afraid her children wouldn't. As I left her cell, I wiped my eyes on the back of my sleeve. Each woman had her own tragic story.

I'd been delivering cold soup for the last hour and still hadn't come across cell block C. Eventually, I broke down and asked a guard.

"I have lunch for cell block C."

Without a word, he led me to a locked door. Inside was a hallway, at the end of which was another locked door. He opened that one too.

"Have at it," he said, and left me there.

Another guard opened the cell doors for me.

"Why is this wing under double locks?" I asked.

"High-security prisoners."

I nodded. Just as I suspected. They had a special place for treasonous spies.

I skipped the other cells and went straight to the end. Peeking through the window, I saw Mata Hari lying on her cot.

"I have lunch for this prisoner," I said to the guard, who opened the cell.

He stood outside the door, waiting.

"I'd like to say a prayer with the penitent, if you don't mind." I waved him away.

He nodded.

I wheeled the cart inside, and he shut the cell door behind me. Now I was locked in too. Immune to the smells, I took a deep breath and pretended I wasn't even a little bit claustrophobic.

Mata Hari rolled over and stared at me with swollen eyes. She looked ten years older than the last time I saw her. Her hair was disheveled and her skin was blotchy. "Sister, help me." Her voice was a soft lament. "I can't stay here. I'll go mad."

I glanced around to make sure the guard wasn't watching through the window. "I've brought you something." I pulled the contraband out from under my habit. "Two pairs of clean knickers and a chemise." I laid the underthings on the bottom of her bed.

She sat up and smiled. "Thank God. I've been asking for clean clothes." She grabbed her underwear and hugged them to her breasts. "How did you get these? My lingerie. Sister, you are a saint." Her face fell again. "If only I had some water to wash. I've never been so filthy. I'll die of filth. Please, Sister, get me some wash water, I beg you."

"I'll see what I can do." I knocked on the door to the cell and the guard appeared at the little window.

With a great jangling noise, he unlocked the door.

"Where can I find wash water?"

He laughed. "The great lady is crying because she's dirty. So sad," he said in a mocking tone. "She can rot for all I care."

"By the smell of her, you'll get your wish," I said under my breath. With hands on hips, I stood up straight, adjusted my habit, and chastised the guard. "Sir, cleanliness is next to godliness. You will help me get this woman cleaned up."

"Me?" He looked stunned.

"Yes, you." I wagged my finger at him. "Now direct me to the wash water."

"Yes, Sister."

When I returned with a pitcher of water, a basin, and a rag, Mata Hari was sitting on the edge of her bed, eagerly waiting.

"Oh thank you, Sister." She clapped her hands together. "I have been going out of my mind. My skin is crawling from this filthy place." She ripped off her shirt and dipped the rag in the lukewarm water.

I whirled around to give her some privacy, not that she seemed to mind. After all, she'd displayed her body in all its natural glory on stages all over Europe. But after three days in prison, its natural glory was a bit too natural. Seeing the magnificent lady reduced to a desperate sponge-bath with a dirty rag made clear the advantages of make-up—not to mention soap and water—a nice jasmine soap, a rose-water perfume, a bit of lipstick and kohl and that mysterious tin of Lash-Brow-Ine.

"I asked for my clothes. Why won't they bring them? And my makeup."

I turned to answer and saw she was nearly naked and swung back around.

"A woman can't live like this. It isn't right. I've done nothing wrong." She was breathless from bathing and talking as if she were running a race. "They say I'm a spy for the Germans. No, that's not right. It's the French I work for, just ask Ladoux. Why won't he tell them?"

"G. Ladoux, the head of the espionage unit in Paris?" I asked.

"He asked me to get information from a German prince. He promised he would give me a pass to visit Vadime in the hospital in Vittel. He lied to me. I'll go mad in here. They have to let me out. I'm a lady, not a common thief." She continued her rant throughout her sponge bath. Only when she'd changed into the clean underthings and replaced her clothes did she settle down.

"Who is Vadime?"

"My fiancé. He's a Russian soldier. He was wounded. All I wanted was to see him again…" Her voice trailed off. She sat on the edge of her cot. She invited me to sit next to her, but I remained standing for fear of lice or whatever other vermin the mattress held.

"So you're working for the French and not the Germans?" I asked.

"I took money from the German government but only because they confiscated my furs and jewelry. I was performing in Berlin when the war broke out. They took my belongings, and I barely got out of the country." Her shoulders slumped in a way that made her look like a dowager instead of a courtesan. "When the German consul in Amsterdam offered me twenty thousand francs to spy, I figured they owed me." She gave a little laugh. "Karl Kroemer handed me three bottles of invisible ink. I took the money and threw the bottles into the canal. I never had any intention of working for the Germans. I just wanted what they owed me. Is that a crime?"

Actually, taking money from the German government during war might very well be considered a crime. I shook my head. "So you never sent them any information or used the invisible ink?"

"Invisible ink is undignified. I never sent any information of value. Only trifles they already knew."

"Do you know an officer named Heinrich?" I thought of the German telegram I'd seen in her handbag.

"I know many officers named Heinrich," she said with a coy smile. "My favorite is a general and personal friend with the Kaiser."

Aha. She was spying for the Germans. My nun's habit seemed to bring out the desire to confess, so I took advantage of it. "And what about G. Ladoux?"

"He double-crossed me. He promised to pay me enough that Vadime and I could get married. Instead, he's had me arrested." Tears welled in her eyes. "Please, Sister, I'd rather die than stay in this place. You've got to get me out of here. I swear, I'll go mad." She tore at her hair and let out a pitiful wail.

Poor woman. She was so forthright and sincere in recounting her story, I began to think her only crime was being naïve. Men liked to have their fun with pretty women, but the same qualities that attracted them to alluring ladies also repulsed their sense of honor. I knew very few men who didn't have double standards when it came to love. Perhaps Mata Hari's only crime was loving men too much... and too many.

Chapter Twenty-One: Paralyzed

After nearly an hour of listening to Mata Hari recount her tragic life story, my feet were tired and I longed for a place to sit. I pushed the lunch cart against the wall and leaned up against it.

I'd tried to coax Mata Hari to eat something, but she said the food wasn't fit for dogs. She had a point.

The poor woman really did have an extraordinary life. Her mother had died when she was fifteen. Her father had shipped her off to live in the small Friesian town of Sneek with an uncle who ignored her. At the age of eighteen, she'd answered an advert in Amsterdam's *News of the Day* placed by Dutch soldier Rudolf MacLeod, just home from the Dutch East Indies. Six days later they were married. On their wedding night, he gave her syphilis.

"He was a beast. He drank and beat me and went with other women." Mata Hari's voice was small and defeated. "One night he came home drunk and broke my jaw. The next day, I fled to Paris where I reinvented myself as Mata Hari, sacred Javanese dancer." She gave a weak smile. "I lived off the kindness of men."

"Men's kindness is fickle," I said, thinking of my own disastrous marriage.

"I know that better than anyone. Look at me now. None of my friends will help me." She troubled the hem of her blouse. "Ladoux trapped me. I only agreed to spy for him because I needed the money to marry Vadime." She stared across the room at me as if looking right through me. "Fighting for the allies took his eyesight. He's blind, poor lamb. He needs me now more than ever. That's why I have to get out of here." She tore at her shirt. "Please, Sister," she begged. "You've got to help me."

I didn't know what else to do. I pulled out a sweet from a pocket under my habit. "Here, have a sweetie." I went to her bedside and held it out to her.

She looked up at me with such gratitude, my heart ached for her. Without her veils and headdress, the powerful seductress had become as helpless as a sick child.

The guard knocked on the door, signaling my time was up. I risked the vermin and sat next to Mata Hari on the bed. I removed the little key she'd given me from a pocket inside my habit.

"You gave this to me when they arrested you." I held out the key in the palm of my hand. "Why? What's it for?"

She stared at me with a puzzled look on her face. As recognition took hold, a knowing smile graced her lips. "Miss Lemons, is that really you?" She took my hands. "You've come to help me. I knew I could count on you."

"I have to go. The guard is getting suspicious. But first, tell me about the key."

"A safety-deposit box at the hotel," she whispered. "Can you get it and bring it to me?"

"I'll try."

"Can you bring some clean clothes and my makeup kit?" She gazed at me full of hope. "I have two dresses ready at the dressmakers. Might you pick them up for me? And my fur coat is at the cleaners."

She'd gone from confessing her sins to asking me to run errands for her, as if she had fancy parties to go to in this prison. "The fur coat you wore at the garden party?"

"Yes. How did you know?"

"Never mind that." Mata Hari didn't need to know that I was also Harold the helpful bellboy and served champagne at the garden party. "Tell me, why was Countess Pavlovna wearing your coat when she died?"

She stared down at her hands, which were folded in her lap. "Dear Nakita was not feeling well. She was shivering. So I gave her my coat."

The poison. When Mata saw the countess after the performance, she must have already ingested the poison and had started feeling the effects.

"She was going to the library to lie down... and then some waiter found

193

her…" Her voice trailed off. She glanced up at me. "Do you think you could fetch my coat from the cleaners? It's frightfully cold in here at night."

"I'll see what I can do. But I think it best not to arouse suspicions, don't you?" I patted her hand. "Otherwise, they may not let me come back."

She nodded, and then she squeezed my hand. "Oh, Fiona, promise me you'll come back tomorrow."

"I will on one condition."

"What?"

"You tell me what you did with my passport."

"Your passport? Why in heaven's name would I have your passport?"

"Didn't you take my passport from the train?"

"Why in the world would I take your passport?"

"I dropped it while I was sleeping and you picked it up."

"I never saw your passport." She gazed at me with those deep brown eyes, so sincere and pleading, she looked like a baby seal begging for a sardine.

"I was sleeping and then I saw you…"

"You looked so sweet that I wanted to make your acquaintance." She gave me a weak smile. "I'm a very good judge of character."

"You picked up something from the floor. Are you sure it wasn't my passport?"

"As I recall, my shoe had come untied. That's all."

"Did you see anyone else nearby while I was sleeping?"

"I had an assignation with my friend Fredrick. I met him in the dining car. And then he went off to do something mysterious, as usual, in the second-class compartment, and I took the seat next to you."

"Fredrick Fredricks?"

"That's right. Do you know him?"

So I really did see the rascal on the train.

"Sister, is everything okay in there?" The guard banged on the door.

"I'd better go." I handed my last piece of chocolate to Mata Hari.

Her face lit up.

"See you tomorrow." I patted her hand again.

"Tell them I'm innocent," she pleaded. "Tell them to let me out."

"Don't worry. If you're innocent, they'll have to let you out." I hoped I wasn't being naïve in thinking that was true. Surely, if she really was innocent and this was all a colossal misunderstanding, they'd have to release her.

"Yes," she said softly. "When I make them understand, they'll let me out."

I stood to go, adjusted my habit, and returned to the cart. I knocked on the cell door, and the guard let me out.

"I'll see you tomorrow, my child," I said as I left.

I quickly delivered the rest of the cold soups, and then returned the cart to the kitchen. Luckily, the place was deserted. I tidied up a bit, wiped my hands on a dishrag, and left before I was recruited into making whatever slop they had planned for dinner.

After my morning rounds at Saint-Lazare women's prison, I was ready to graduate to La Santé Prison in Montparnasse. If my disguise fooled Mata Hari, then hopefully it would fool the Great White Hunter.

According to my trusty Baedeker's, La Santé Prison was a trek back across the Seine. I made my way back to the Gare du Nord station. The three-block walk already had me sweating. After spending the morning in the women's prison, I felt as if I were covered in an invisible film of despair and hopelessness. I doubted the men's prison would be any better. Given that men's habits could be disgusting even in the best of situations, I expected it would be worse... much worse. In fact, I was dreading entering a place designed to hold the most hardened criminals.

A man on the train offered me his seat. Being a nun had its advantages. Indeed, it was surprising how differently people treated me just because I was wrapped in yards of broadcloth.

When I exited at the Royal-Palace station, I realized I was just a block away from the famous Luxembourg Gardens. I glanced at my watch. I still had several hours before dark. *Why not take a peek at the garden?* I needed to come up for air. Something beautiful and fragrant would fortify me before my next dive into the bowels of despair.

I read from my Baedeker's: "Known for its lawns, tree-lined promenades, flowerbeds, model sailboats on its circular basin, and picturesque Medici

Fountain built in 1620, the gardens cover twenty-three hectares. The terraces around the parterre are embellished with twenty modern statues in marble of celebrated Frenchwomen, the stiffness of which does not harmonize well with the garden."

My curiosity piqued, I went in search of those twenty stiff Frenchwomen. I thought English gardens were the best in the world, but Luxembourg Gardens was magnificent. The scent of lilac and lavender filled the air, and the color of summer exploded against the manicured green grass. In the midst of this splendor, one could completely forget about the war, and spies, and prisons.

The twenty stiff ladies, most of them queens of France, stood around the circumference of a large pond in front of the palace. I was admiring the statue of Margaret of Anjou, a fifteenth-century queen of England, when a ball hit my foot. I picked it up and tossed it back to a small boy who came running after it. The park was crowded with women and small children enjoying the warm sunshine and fresh air. The lovely scene did my heart good after the dark, dreary prison where so many women languished alone, wondering what had become of their children.

And to think, now I was on my way to another prison where the prisoners were men, some of them rapists and murderers.

After the gorgeous gardens, stepping into La Santé prison was like descending from heaven into Dante's inferno. It was hot as Hades and smelled of death. I stretched the collar of my wimple over my nose and mouth to keep from gagging. *Whew.* I didn't know if I could ever adjust to the putrid smells of this place. And I wasn't about to go from cell to cell distributing watery soup to unwashed men to find Fredricks. I needed a more direct course of action.

I approached the front desk where a uniformed guard sat reading a newspaper. "Excuse me, sir," I said in my best Irish brogue. "I was told that Monsieur Fredrick Fredricks has requested someone to pray with. Can you direct me to him?" I asked in French, tinged with a proper Irish accent.

"Fredricks?" He looked up from his paper. "Ah, that paralyzed fellow they brought in last week."

196

"Paralyzed?" I clutched my bible to my chest.

"As you Brits would say, legs as useless as a chocolate teapot."

"Really?" I guess my Irish accent was lost on him.

"Doc stuck needles in him and everything. He didn't even flinch."

"Needles?" *How barbaric.* "Where can I find Mr. Fredricks now?"

The guard signed me in as Sister Maggie Malone from Dublin assigned to minister to sinners in Paris—from what I'd seen there were quite a lot of them—and then directed me to the infirmary.

The infirmary was a narrow windowless room with a line of a half dozen cots on either side. Next to each cot was a small table on top of which stood a water pitcher and various medical supplies. When I told the head nurse I was there to pray with one of her patients, she invited me to take one of the two wooden chairs sitting next to the entrance.

Fredricks was sitting up in bed, chatting with the man in the adjoining bunk. His dark hair was slicked back, his mustache waxed to perfection, and he was wearing crisply pressed striped pajamas. *How does he manage to be so well groomed in prison?* The men in the other beds were unwashed, disheveled, and some had scabs or open wounds on their broken skin. In spite of his depressing surroundings, Fredricks's countenance was lively, even chipper. Had he sweet-talked a nurse into giving him special treatment?

Dragging the chair in one hand, I approached his bedside. "I'm Sister Margaret." I held up the bible. "Would you like me to read to you?"

He eyed me suspiciously.

My stomach lurched. Had he seen through my disguise already?

"Take a seat, Sister," he said, gesturing to a space next to the bed. "I'm not a devotee, but perhaps you can start with my favorite verse from Leviticus twenty-four."

I sat down. "Certainly." I wished I'd paid more attention at bible study. I remembered Leviticus was in the Old Testament. I flipped through the front of the bible until I found it. "Which verse?"

"Nineteen through twenty-one." He folded his hands on his lap and waited.

I scanned the page and then read aloud, "Anyone who injures their neighbor is to be injured in the same manner: fracture for fracture, eye

197

for eye, tooth for tooth. The one who has inflicted the injury must suffer the same injury." I glanced over at him.

"What do you think of that principle, *Sister?*" he asked, smiling like a wolf about to devour a lamb.

"Wasn't it Gandhi who said an eye for an eye makes the whole world blind?" I closed the bible and laid it on my lap.

"Are you Catholic or Hindu?" He raised his eyebrows. "Don't you believe the scripture? You're a free thinker, then."

"I don't believe in violence or repaying violence with more violence."

"The Old Testament is epic in its violence. And your faith is founded on death."

I narrow my brows. "What do you mean?"

"Jesus was crucified. Christianity is a religion founded on the death penalty." He gave me a questioning look. "Surely, Sister, if you don't believe in repaying violence with violence, you can't endorse capital punishment... or this bloody war."

"The cost of the war is paid for with the lives of innocents."

"So killing is fine for the guilty?" he asked.

I didn't want to debate the merits of capital punishment, especially since that was his fate if he were found guilty of treason. "Gandhi—"

He interrupted. "I met Mohandas Gandhi in South Africa, before he became Mahatma, *venerable one.* He was a London-educated lawyer working in Durban and fancied himself British, but the white South Africans had other ideas." He shook his head. "He saved my life. He was my enemy, but he saved my life."

"Gandhi was your enemy?" I asked, wondering about this remarkable man who was happily carrying on a philosophical conversation, unfazed by imprisonment.

"He drove an ambulance for the British during the war. He was trying to prove Hindus were fit for manly duties just as much as any British soldier. But, unlike the bloody British, he had compassion for the Afrikaners. He could have left me on the battlefield to die, but he put me on a stretcher instead." Fredricks glanced over at me as if coming out of a daze. "After that, he gave up war and embraced peace. Noble if unrealistic."

"You don't think peace is possible?" I wished I'd kept up with the Boer war. I knew the British had colonies in South Africa. But were we really fighting the Afrikaners over a gold mine?

"All animals kill to eat or to protect their young. But humans are the only animals capable of true beastliness."

"Not all animals are carnivores. Horses—"

"Horses bite and kick to establish dominance and who gets fed at the trough first. Humans do the same. Look at the British and their colonies. The British get fat by kicking the rest of the world to the back of the feed line."

I remembered what the British had done to his family and decided I'd better change the subject. "What happened to your legs?" I asked. My cheeks flamed when I realized how untactful I'd been in just blurting it out. But I was deuced curious.

He got a twinkle in his eyes and twisted his torso to face me. "Defenestration at the hands of a beautiful woman."

"A woman threw you out a window?"

"Not exactly." He wound the end of one side of his mustache around his finger. "The lovely lady had accompanied me back to my flat." He paused and gazed at me. "Does that shock you, Sister?"

I shook my head. "Of course not. I may be a nun, but I'm not naïve."

"I've admired this lady since I made her acquaintance a few months ago. We got to know each other and became more intimately acquainted at a charming English abbey." He pointed at my bible. "As an Irish Catholic, I imagine you don't approve of the English."

"I may be a nun, but I'm not a fanatic."

"As I was saying, I rather fell for this woman, Fiona is her name."

I gasped.

"Are you quite all right, Sister? Do you need a drink of water?" He called out to a nurse, who came running.

"Hélène, be a dear and get the sister a glass of water? I'm afraid I've given her a shock." He flashed a toothy smile. "You know how incorrigible I can be." He winked at her.

Nurse Hélène giggled and then trotted off to fetch the water.

"You seem to have the nursing staff at your beck and call," I said stiffly.

"Do not neglect to show hospitality to strangers, for thereby some have entertained angels unawares." He pointed to my bible again. "You need to brush up on your Old Testament, Sister."

Nurse Hélène returned with my glass of water, which truth be told, I very much needed after Fredricks's revelation.

After an exchange of flirtatious glances with Fredricks, Hélène finally left, and he continued his story. "My own angel and I were enjoying a cold supper with an excellent Château Guiraud when a jealous lover—a lieutenant in her majesty's army no less—broke in and interrupted our bliss. I had no choice but to go out the window." He waved his hand over his legs. "Complete paralysis of both legs. I may never be able to walk again." He sighed dramatically. "Those few minutes alone with *ma chérie* Fiona were worth it."

My face burned. I was completely appalled. *Is Fredricks in love with me? Am I the cause of his paralysis?* I was at once mortified and filled with pity. Perhaps he was pulling my leg. I mean, he was laying it on pretty thick. I pulled a long hatpin out from under my wimple and stabbed him in the right leg.

"Why on earth did you do that?" he asked without flinching. "You're as bad as those bloody sadistic doctors. Perhaps you should go now, Sister, and come back when you're in a better humor."

"Yes, perhaps I should." I was shaken by the encounter and didn't know if I could face him again.

"Do come back. Apart from your attack with a hatpin, I've enjoyed our chat."

With his preposterous story, Fredricks had completely thrown me off my game. Next time I'd have to be better prepared if I hoped to find out what he'd given the countess minutes before her death… and what he knew about Archie Somersby. *Jealous lover, my eye.*

Chapter Twenty-Two: Love Archie

When I arrived back at the hotel, completely knackered from visiting not one but two prisons, I asked for Lady MacLeod's safety-deposit box. The grumpy clerk gave me the evil eye.

"The lady asked me to bring its contents to her." I pulled the tiny key out of my pocket and held it up. "She gave me the key."

The clerk looked me up and down and then begrudgingly retrieved the box and gave it to me.

Being a nun had its advantages. I thanked him and took the box, which was surprisingly heavy.

"Did Miss Fiona Figg receive any letters?" I asked. "She's my sister and I'm on my way to her room now."

"Actually, Miss Figg did receive a telegram." He pointed toward the cubbies behind him.

"A telegram for my sister? I'll take it to her." *Aha! Henri Landru has answered my letter.* I tucked the box under my arm and held out my hand.

The clerk hesitated.

I tightened my lips and bit my tongue to stop from saying something rude.

He glared at me and then pulled the telegram from one of the key cubbies. *What is his problem? Are all French clerks so unpleasant?*

I slipped the telegram into a pocket inside my habit. I couldn't wait to get back to my room, remove the blasted heavy garment, and slip into a nice bath to wash away the prison grime, and then open Mata Hari's deposit box and read Landru's response. First things first. A bath.

As I lay back in the bathtub, I closed my eyes and tried to empty my mind.

I didn't want to think of those poor women and men in prison or their cries for help—or their smell. I just wanted to disappear into the warm water. *If only I could wash away the memories of all the tragedy I've seen. Sigh.* In the last year, I'd seen enough death and suffering to last several lifetimes. The bloody war. The overflowing hospitals. The ghastly prisons. Two countesses. Why couldn't I have a normal life with a husband and kids where my only concern was what to cook for dinner and which hat to wear to church?

Buck up, Fiona. Lots of girls would kill to be in your shoes, working for British Intelligence, living a life of adventure and intrigue. *Who needs a flat full of dirty dishes and even dirtier nappies?* And, thanks to Angels Fancy Dress shop, my hat collection was more interesting than most.

I lathered myself from head to toe with the fancy jasmine-scented soap. One advantage of shorn hair was it was easy to wash in the bathtub. I held my breath, closed my eyes, and slid under the water to rinse the soap out of my stubbly hair. Resurfacing, I lay back in the bathtub, and tried to wash all the unpleasant thoughts from my mind. But the image of Countess Pavlovna prone on the floor of Renault's library haunted me. Something wasn't right, aside from the dead body. A bloody paperknife, a missing silver capsule, suspected poisoning, a suicide note, the torn receipt, Mata Hari's fur coat... It just didn't add up. I wished I could do right by the countess and solve her murder, but until I heard back from Daisy Nelson about the pollen on the countess's hem and shoes, or until I could get Fredricks to reveal what he knows about the silver capsule—and perhaps more, I was at a loss of where to start.

Tepid water and wrinkly skin finally forced me out of the tub. Refreshed, I toweled off and slipped on the hotel robe and slippers. *Ahhhh... it feels so good to be clean.*

Now to examine the contents of Mata Hari's safety-deposit box. I set the metal box on my desk, prepared a cup of tea, and then settled in to savor the excursion into Mata Hari's most prized possessions, or at least those that could fit into a nine-by-twelve-inch box. Perhaps now I'd learn what made her tick.

I took a sip of watery tea and then inserted the tiny key in the lock. Laying on top was a photograph of Mata Hari—looking gorgeous—standing next to a short plain man in uniform with a patch over one eye. What an odd couple. *Was that her beloved Vadime?* Given that Mata Hari could have any man she desired, her beloved Russian soldier wasn't what I'd expected. I admired her even more. I lifted the photograph to examine the rest of the contents.

Good heavens! An ivory-handled miniature revolver. *Not that it will do her any good locked in a safety-deposit box.* I handled it with care. The ivory handle was cool to the touch. I weighed it in my palm. The little fellow was heavier than you'd think. I had a worrying thought. Was it loaded? I didn't have the foggiest idea how to open it to find out and didn't want to accidently blow off a finger. I laid it on the desk next to the box and continued my exploration.

A diamond broach, a strand of pearls, a fancy fountain pen, and another photograph. This one of a young woman with two children, a little girl and a baby. I held the picture under the lamplight. There was no doubt. The woman was a young Lady MacLeod. Were those her children?

I thought of Andrew. Four years of marriage and I had never been able to conceive. Little Georgie was proof that it wasn't Andrew's fault. *Was I barren? Destined to mourn the loss of children I never had?* If we'd had children, maybe Andrew wouldn't have turned to Nancy. Maybe there wouldn't have been a divorce. *Who knows?* Maybe Andrew would still be alive. But we hadn't and he wasn't. Nothing was more certain than the absolute absence of Andrew. My first and only lover, my best friend, my confidant, gone forever.

I pushed my melancholy thoughts aside and gathered up Mata Hari's belongings. I would take them to her tomorrow… except for the gun, of course. *What in heaven's name should I do with it?* I glanced around the room looking for a good hiding place. Taking a page from Fredricks's book, I hid it in one of Harold the bellboy's boots.

Did she really need diamonds and pearls in prison? Perhaps the photographs were enough for now. I slid the mementos of her beloved Vadime and her children into a pocket of my habit.

As I did, I felt the corner of the envelope the grumpy clerk had handed to me earlier. I removed it from the pocket and took it back to the desk. My heart was racing as I tore open the envelope, which must contain the time and place for a possibly deadly assignation with the murderous Henri Désiré Landru. I knew it was risky, but since the police wouldn't arrest him, I had to catch him red-handed. An image of his hands covered in my blood flashed through my mind. I shuddered as I removed the telegram from the envelope.

Good heavens! The telegram was not from Désiré Landru, but from Archie Somersby. I read it quickly and then read it again… and again.

Dearest Fiona,
Sorry I didn't come back.
Blinker sent me on an urgent assignment.
Next time, lose the mustache.
Love, Archie

The rogue. My cheeks caught fire. *Wait.* Did this mean he knew it was me all along? The little blighter. I read the last lines out loud, "Next time, lose the mustache. Love, Archie." I laughed through my tears. "*Love*, Archie."

He hadn't been kissing Harold the helpful bellboy… he'd been kissing me, Fiona the hopeless fool. My eyes filled with tears. *Oh, darling Archie. When will I see you again?*

I knew he wasn't a double-agent. *I mean, I couldn't be in love with a double-agent, could I?* I felt myself blushing again. Certainly I couldn't be in love at all… I barely knew the man. *Oh Archie, I want to get to know you.*

Where had Archie been sent this time? What kind of agent was he? I had the feeling he was high up in the ranks of secret espionage. He probably found my attempts at spying ridiculous. If I wanted to keep up with Archie, I'd have to up my game.

I went to bed exhausted but happy. *Love Archie*, I repeated as I drifted off to fiery dreams of our reunion.

Chapter Twenty-Three: A Tethered Goat

For the next two weeks, I made my daily rounds at the prisons, spending as much time with Mata Hari and Fredrick Fredricks as I could without arousing suspicions.

Mata Hari thanked me for the photographs, but complained bitterly about the dreadful living conditions. I didn't blame her. She'd lost confidence that her innocence alone would be enough to liberate her. With each passing day, she became more despondent. In the prison, there was even talk of execution. I shuddered to think.

Fredrick Fredricks was moved from the infirmary to a regular cell after doctors concluded his paralysis was permanent. In spite of his immobility, and the filthy surroundings, he remained in good spirits and only too happy to tip the wink on Archie Somersby's supposed "double life,"—which I didn't believe for a second, at least not after my recent telegram—his affair with Mata Hari, and his hatred of the British. He only occasionally mentioned his admiration for Fiona Figg, but when he did, it made me deuced uncomfortable. To my relief, my flaming cheeks hadn't given me away… yet.

After spending every morning at one or the other prison, in the afternoons I checked on Abby, who was still grieving the loss of her sister. I was beginning to think my imagination had run away with me. These days, it seemed murder was always the first thing on my mind. Coincidently—or not—there were no more reports of missing jewelry at the hotel since Berthe and her redheaded friend disappeared. Perhaps they weren't victims at all but a pair of thieves preying on guests at fancy hotels… And, nearly caught in the act, they'd decided to move on.

I remembered what the grumpy clerk told me when I first checked in. Jewelry was missing from the hotel... and so were girls. Maids were going off to get married without any notice. I hoped to heaven they weren't all marrying Henri Désiré Landru. Getting to the bottom of the jewelry theft and the missing girls was on the top of my to-do list... just after finding out who murdered the countess, and getting more information out of Fredricks.

I had to admit, in the last two weeks, I hadn't made much headway with my list.

In the evenings, when I wasn't too tired or impatient to listen to his nattering, I met Clifford for dinner. Tonight, he was taking me to Café de Flore near the Sorbonne, where some poet and artist chaps met to talk about something called surrealism. Given Clifford's general squeamishness, I hadn't figured him for the avant-garde sort... although I was coming to realize, he was a bit of a voyeur. He always acted shocked by the latest trends—women wearing men's cravats, kimono-style evening gowns, war crinolines showing bare ankles. But secretly, he loved to gawk. I giggled to myself thinking of all the times I'd shocked Clifford. I could hear him saying "Good Lord!" or "I say!" Dear old Clifford. I could do worse than a marriage proposal from a not-bad-looking and thoroughly decent fellow.

* * *

This evening—as I did every evening after my visits to the prisons—I took a quick bath to wash off the smells of confinement and solitude. Wearing the hotel robe, which had become one of my favorite articles of clothing of late, I padded over to the wardrobe to select an appropriate dress for a late supper with an officer. *Why didn't I bring my favorite lavender frock?* I was still kicking myself. A nice linen skirt and blouse would have to do. Even with my fashionably bobbed wig, I looked more like a stern librarian about to shush a noisy patron than an international espionage agent on a top-secret mission.... Technically I wasn't on a mission since Captain Hall had relieved me of duty, but still I was determined to continue serving my country and prove my usefulness.

I tucked my favorite wig into my cloche, and attached the hat with its handy extra-long hatpin. On the way out the door, I remembered Mata Hari's revolver hidden in Harold the bellboy's boot. On a whim, I slipped the little gun into my handbag... just in case.

I tried to sneak past the front desk without attracting the attention of the grumpy clerk, who, for some reason, seemed suspicious of me. It was no use.

"Miss Figg, Miss Figg." He chased after me. "Another letter arrived for you."

My heart skipped a beat. *A letter from Archie?* I hoped for a return address so I could write back. I took the envelope, thanked the clerk, and made my way through the lobby to the nearest sofa and sat down to wait for Clifford. I was so excited, I could hardly sit still. I glanced around to make sure Clifford hadn't arrived yet—which was unnecessary since he was never on time—and then tore open the envelope. *Wait. There is no return address.* The envelope had no postmark. It must have been delivered locally. My heart sunk... unless, of course, Archie was back in Paris.

Blast! After over a week with no response, I'd almost forgotten about answering Henri Désiré Landru's lonely-hearts advert. Désiré Landru was requesting a meeting... tonight! *Oh dear.* Now I'd have to put Clifford off.

"Fiona, you look lovely."

I gasped. "Don't sneak up on me like that." My hand flew to my chest. "You want me to pop my cogs?"

"Sorry, old girl. Didn't mean to frighten you." He sat down next to me. "What's that?" He craned his neck to see Landru's letter.

"That beast Henri Landru wants to meet me—"

"Good Lord!" He snatched the letter out of my hand. "I say, you're not planning to go, are you?" He scanned the letter. "Café d'Orléans, eight o'clock." He glanced at his watch. "That's an hour from now." He looked at me in alarm. "The man's dangerous. Let the police handle it."

"They say they're too short-staffed to investigate every *runaway* woman." I grabbed the letter back. "If they won't, I will."

"At least let me go with you." He reached out and took my hand. "Please."

"Really, Clifford, you think just because we're in Paris he wants a *ménage à trois*?"

"Good heavens, Fiona." He blushed bright red. "You say the darndest things."

I smiled. There was nothing I enjoyed more than giving Clifford dear a hard time. "I'm sorry about our dinner. Can I take a rain check until tomorrow?"

"I'm happy to dine with you any evening. But must you go now?"

I nodded. "Yes, I owe it to Berthe... and to Abby."

"Will you at least call me from the house telephone when you get back?" He squeezed my hand. "No matter what time it is."

"I'm not a schoolgirl, you know." I returned his squeeze. "Okay."

"Promise?"

"I promise." Touched by his concern, I realized he might be the only person on the planet who truly cared if I lived or died... a sobering thought. After all, I hardly knew Archie Somersby, although I knew him well enough to know he wasn't a double-agent. At least I hoped he wasn't. "I'd better go or I'll be late." I put on my gloves and rose to leave.

Clifford looked up at me with those basset hound eyes.

"Don't worry." I kissed his cheek. "I can take care of myself." I hoped I was right.

* * *

The Café d'Orléans sported festive orange-and-white checkered chairs sprinkled around wooden café tables under a cheerful red-and-white awning. It was just before eight o'clock, and I didn't see Désiré Landru, so I took a seat with a panoramic view of the walkways and ordered a coffee. I felt like a tethered goat waiting to trap a lion.

After a few sips, I realized the coffee was a mistake. I was already jittery enough. I folded my hands in my lap, took a deep breath, and willed myself to calm down. No wonder I'd never answered a lonely-hearts advert before. It was deuced nerve-racking. *You're not trying to catch a husband but a murderer,* I reminded myself.

A tall bearded figure wearing a top hat and a bow tie approached the café from across the street. My mouth went dry, and I gulped down the rest of my coffee. As he got closer, there could be no doubt. The well-trimmed beard, the bushy eyebrows, the tailored suit. It was Henri Désiré Landru.

Good heavens! Who was trotting along behind him? Captain Clifford Douglas. *What on earth is he doing here? He's going to ruin everything.*

"You must be the lovely Fiona." Henri Landru extended a manicured hand. When I took it my blood ran cold. *Am I shaking hands with a murderer?*

"And you're Henri Landru. A widower, is that right?"

"May I?" He gestured toward the chair. "Please call me Désiré."

I nodded. To my mind, there was nothing *désiré* about him. As my father would say, a pig in a silk suit is still a pig.

"Yes, my poor wife died last year." He sighed. "I can barely function without her." His voice broke. "She was the love of my life."

I could swear he was about to cry. *Blimey. He's good.* "It must be very hard for you." Out of the corner of my eye, I glimpsed Clifford waving at me. He was seated at another table behind Landru. I ignored him. "I'm a war widow myself. My dear Andrew was killed not long ago." I didn't bother telling him that Andrew was already married to someone else by then.

For another twenty minutes, Désiré Landru gushed about his dead wife, which I had to admit was an effective strategy to gain a woman's trust. His grief did have a certain charm. Meanwhile, Clifford's attempts to get my attention were deuced distracting. I was glad when the first course of his meal arrived and kept him otherwise occupied.

"Would you like another cup of coffee?" Désiré Landru asked.

"Actually, I prefer tea, but I can't get a decent cup in Paris."

"Ah, a fellow tea drinker. We have something in common."

He reached into his pocket and dropped a few coins on the table.

"Would you like to go someplace quieter?" he asked. "This crowd is grating on my poor nerves." He continued to play the pity card.

I swallowed hard. "Sure." I placed my napkin on the table and stood up.

"Where shall we go?"

"I have a pied-à-terre two blocks from here." He stood too. "I could make you a cup of tea, lest you think Parisians don't know how." He grinned like a wolf sizing up a lamb.

As I left with Landru, I saw Clifford desperately fumbling with his wallet. He probably regretted having ordered the full prix fixe menu. Now he was going to have to choose between me and his pudding.

Désiré Landru's pied-à-terre was a run-down third-floor flat above a butcher's shop that smelled of stale cheese and pungent sandalwood cologne. A small kitchenette was nestled against the back wall, and up front a sitting area was furnished with a tiny wooden table and two wooden chairs, a standing lamp with a dark-green fringe shade, and a wide satin divan with claw feet, where I suspected Désiré Landru entertained his ladies before he did them in. *What a gruesome thought.*

Désiré Landru invited me to take a seat and then proceeded to the kitchenette where he added water to a teakettle and put it on the flame. While we waited for the water to boil, he told me that his late wife was a tea drinker too, but she favored "exotic" oolong from China. He poured boiling water in two cups, swirled it around, and then dumped it out, warming up the cups. He did the same with the pot before he added tea and more hot water. The man knew how to make a cuppa.

He delivered the cups and teapot to the table and sat down across from me. If it weren't for my suspicions about Berthe and the other girls—and the fact that I was in the flat of a man I'd just met and didn't know from Adam—I could have enjoyed the strong tea with a splash of milk... the best cuppa I'd had in Paris by far. Désiré Landru carried on a pleasant enough conversation and—for a murderer—seemed like an amiable bloke, in spite of his tendency to lick his lips as he gazed across the table at me.

As we drank our tea, he told me about his house in Gambais, leaving out the inconvenient detail that he had a wife there. The conversation was so mundane and his mannerisms so banal, I was beginning to wonder if I had it wrong. Maybe Désiré Landru wasn't a murderer but merely a serial adulterer who lied to women to gain their confidence and take advantage of them. Though that didn't explain why the clerk at the train station had said Landru often bought tickets to Gambais, roundtrip for himself and one-way for female traveling companions. Or why he turned pale upon seeing Abby, disguised as Berthe, and blurted out that she couldn't be standing in the hotel lobby because she was dead. I couldn't wait around all night to find out.

I glanced at my watch. "Goodness, it's ten o'clock already. I should be going."

"I know we just met, but I feel a connection. I hope you do too." He rose from the table. "Will you permit me to give you a small token of my esteem?"

My cheeks burned. "What kind of token?"

He pulled a small heart-shaped locket necklace from his vest pocket. "I'd like you to have this. It was my mother's."

Good grief! I felt like a rock had dropped to the pit of my stomach. I recognized the locket. It belonged to Berthe. I swallowed hard. "How kind..."

Before I could say any more, he'd swooped behind me. "I'll just help you put it on."

I felt the cool locket dangle on my breastbone, and then Landru's warm hands wrapped around my throat. I screamed.

Oh my heavens, I walked right into this, and now I'm going to die, just like Berthe.

I tried to twist free, but he was too strong, and I couldn't get my balance. My handbag fell off my lap to the floor. The bag—and Mata Hari's gun—were out of my reach. I struggled to pry his hands away. But he tightened his grip. As I wheezed, I heard thumping. Was that my heart threatening to give out? Flailing, I felt for my cloche. If I could just grab its extra-long hatpin.... Yes! My fingers curled around its ivory tip. I dislodged the hatpin and stabbed it into the beast's torso. He yelped and loosened his chokehold. Panting, I managed to break free and stand. Then I kicked him in the shin.

The door burst open with a bang. Clifford exploded into the room. "Unhand her!"

Landru made a break for it, but Clifford was blocking the exit. Landru pulled a switchblade from his vest pocket and slashed at Clifford.

"Stop," I screamed. I ducked under the table to collect my purse. I grabbed Mata Hari's handgun and pointed it at Landru. He was struggling with Clifford. Even if I knew how to shoot a gun, I couldn't get a clear shot. As they wrestled, I waved the gun back and forth trying to aim at Landru. If I pulled the trigger now, I'd risk shooting Clifford instead of Landru. "Stop," I yelled again. "I've got a gun!" I aimed it at the ceiling and fired. Click. Click. *Blast!* It wasn't loaded.

Landru glanced over at me. Clifford took advantage of the split-second distraction and socked him in the jaw. Désiré Landru crumpled to the floor.

I flew to Clifford.

He wrapped his arms around me. "Are you all right, old girl?" he asked into my wig.

"I had everything under control," I said. But the tears streaming down my cheeks said otherwise. I was never so glad to see good old reliable Clifford in my life.

Chapter Twenty-Four: Awaiting Execution

Seeing no phone in Landru's flat, Clifford and I ran to the street to alert the police. One of us should have stayed there with him, but Clifford would not leave me alone for a moment. In the few minutes we were gone, Désiré Landru escaped.

Fortunately, my run-in with Henri Désiré Landru finally convinced the police—in Paris and Gambais—to investigate. Unfortunately, when they searched his house in Gambais, they found human teeth and bone fragments in his oven, including the redheaded jewelry thief cum maid, Suzanne's. We were waiting to hear if any of them belonged to Berthe. I didn't need official confirmation. I knew. Berthe's heart-shaped locket had given him away.

The police had recovered Mata Hari's jade ring from Landru's wife. And since they no longer needed it as evidence, I promised to return it to Mata. They had also found other jewelry missing from the Grand Hotel stashed in a well behind Landru's house. Turns out, I was right. Suzanne was a known jewel thief and the police surmised she'd fallen in with Landru by accident.

The police had to admit that I was right about Landru too. Henri Désiré Landru was using the lonely-hearts adverts to lure lonesome women, many of them war widows, to their deaths. So far, the police had discovered over two hundred romantic liaisons and dozens of missing women. The French newspapers called Landru "The Bluebeard of Gambais."

Two days after my near strangulation, they caught him in a flat with his twenty-four-year-old mistress, an aspiring cabaret actress. The blackguard had a wife and a mistress and still collected lonely women. What women saw in him, I'd never know. Was a man, any man, such a desirable commodity these days when most men were away at the front?

It was too gruesome for words. At least the monster was locked away now and couldn't hurt anyone else. Poor Berthe... Abby had been inconsolable when the truth came out.

To forget about the whole horrible affair and my brush with death—or worse—I threw myself into my mission. While I'd helped catch the evil Désiré Landru, that would not impress Captain Hall, quite the contrary. To get back into his good graces and prove myself as a spy, I had to get some useful information out of Fredricks... or Mata Hari. And I had only one more week to do it. I'd been visiting the prisons daily, and, luckily, my nun's outfit worked like magic to loosen tongues. Even Fredricks had lowered his guard and confided in me.

This morning, I decided to visit Fredricks first. I was determined to find out more about his sabotage operation. And I was determined to find a way to get him to confess to killing the countess... or both countesses.

Whereas Landru went for war widows, Fredricks went for double-dealing countesses. If only I could get something useful out of him, Captain Hall would forgive my disguises and bumbling ways and keep me on as an agent. My stint in jail aside, I rather enjoyed espionage.

When I arrived at La Santé Prison, Fredricks was sitting up on his cot, leaning against the stone wall, his lifeless legs covered with a blanket and stretched out in front of him. As usual, he was reading. A stack of books sat next to his bed. In the infirmary the nurses delivered his books. Now, he had me doing it for him. I'd made several trips to his Paris flat to retrieve volumes in French, German, English, and Spanish. The man was a wonder.

I narrowed my eyes to see the spine of the book in his hands and get a glimpse of what he was reading today. Sigmund Freud, in German no less. *Zeitgemäßes über Krieg und Tod*, whatever that was. *If I remember correctly,* tod *means death.* I shuddered, remembering my own near-death experience.

"Sister Maggie, I was hoping you'd visit." He smiled. "Pull up a chair."

Of course, there was no chair. And I wasn't about to join him on the bed.

"I brought you last month's issue of *Forest and Stream*." I laid the magazine on the top of his stack of books. "Do you know how difficult it is to find an American magazine in Paris?"

"You're a miracle worker," he said taking up the magazine.

"Your *friend* Theodore Roosevelt has an essay in this issue." I pointed to the magazine.

Several times in the last week, Fredricks had regaled me with stories of big-game hunting in Africa with the former American president. Their bloodlust was almost too much for me to bear. But I was trying to get information out of Fredricks, not offend him, so I kept my gob shut.

"Did you know when Teddy was shot while campaigning in Milwaukee, the tough old lion finished delivering a ninety-minute speech with blood seeping through his shirt." Fredricks chuckled. "That bloody bullet is still lodged in his chest."

I fiddled with the cord to my habit, trying to recollect anything I'd heard about the tough old lion. "Did you know, during a trip to the Amazon he became so feverish all he could do was recite the first lines of *Kubla Khan*?" I only remembered this trivial tidbit because I'd had to memorize that same poem at North London Collegiate School. On my deathbed, like an incantation, I'd probably be reciting Coleridge too.

"Have you ever killed a man?" Fredricks asked out of the blue.

"Me?" I blinked. "Is that a rhetorical question?"

"I was only twelve when I killed my first man, if you can call him a man." Fredricks stared off into space. "A bloody Zulu who attacked my mum... I gutted him with his own assegai sword."

"Your first." I stared at Fredricks in disbelief. "It's a wonder you've escaped prison this long."

"Oh, but I haven't." He grinned. "I've escaped prison many times."

My mouth fell open.

"Don't underestimate Fredrick Fredricks."

"I don't think you're going anywhere for a while." I pointed to his legs and then regretted it. Calling attention to his infirmity wasn't polite. *Hadn't my mother taught me not to point and stare at other people's misfortunes?*

"You never finished telling me about your nemesis," I said to change the subject... and to find out what Fredricks knew about Archie, "that British lieutenant what's-his-name, Somerset."

"Ah, the good Lieutenant Somersby." He dropped the magazine on the bed and then closed the book he'd laid across his lap and sat it on top of his stack. "I knew him in South Africa during the war... or, I should say, I knew *of* him. We were on opposite sides. That is, until we found his price. Every man has his price."

"I don't believe that. Some people—even men—value principles more than money."

"Every woman has her price too. Whether or not it's money... I'd bet there is something that would make you give up your habit and leave the nunnery."

"Like what?" I adjusted my wimple.

"The handsome Lieutenant Somersby perhaps?" He grinned mischievously. "You're very keen to find out more about him." He stroked his bold chin. "I wonder why."

"I've never even met him," I said a bit too defensively. "You're the one who keeps waffling on about him."

"Yes, well, *I* haven't taken a vow of celibacy." He pointed to the book he'd just been reading. "Anyway, Freud's bisexuality thesis aside, my fancies lie in another direction." He winked at me.

I scowled. I'd gathered that from the scores of women he'd told me about over the last week and a half, including my own good self. "You mean like the dancer, Mata Hari?"

"Ah, Mata is a beautiful creature. As dark and sleek as a panther. It's a shame she will be executed."

"What do you mean executed?" My heart was racing.

"She's scheduled to be shot." *How in the world does he do it?* The sneaky cad had eyes and ears everywhere. Even in prison, he had more information than he was letting on. Obviously, he'd charmed—or bribed—one of the guards.

"Surely even the French won't execute a woman." I crossed myself and hoped I was right. I'd taken a liking to the lady, even though I didn't always approve of her means of supporting herself. Poor woman. Desperate times call for desperate means.

"I've heard her trial didn't go well and that scoundrel Ladoux dropped her like a hot potato." He sighed. "Bloody shame."

Is the trial over already? Last I'd heard, her trial just started yesterday. I checked my watch, as if it would somehow tell me the date and whether the trail was over. "If it's God's will..." I touched the rosary around my neck. Although I was acting the part, my prayers for Mata Hari were real. "Ladoux, is that one of her paramours?" Mata Hari constantly complained about the head of the French espionage unit, but I never completely understood why. I'd gleaned that he'd double-crossed her somehow, and it had something to do with her fiancé, Vadime. "He's a policeman, isn't he?"

"He's the head of French espionage, and I know for a fact he hired her to spy for the French. But now he denies it. Why?" He shook his head. "Georges Ladoux is the double agent, not Mata Hari."

"You think everyone is a double agent," I said without thinking. I adjusted the cord around my waist and tried to sound more Catholic. "You need to have more faith, young man."

"Like I said, everyone has their price... even you, Sister Maggie."

There, the scoundrel was wrong. I wondered, *what could make me turn on my own country and work for the enemy?* Nothing. There was nothing that could turn me.

"You think there's nothing that could turn you." He flashed a crooked smile. "But you're wrong."

Uncanny bounder. *Can he read my mind?* Just in case, I decided I'd spent enough time with the irritating Fredrick Fredricks and best move on to Mata Hari. If he was right and her trial had ended and she'd been found guilty, she would need moral support.

* * *

I made the now familiar walk across the Pont des Arts bridge to the Pont Neuf station, took the train to the Gare du Nord station, and then walked the few blocks to Saint-Lazare women's prison. The trip took longer today than usual—almost an hour—because a woman had thrown herself onto the tracks... probably another war widow. The tragedy did not bode well for my visit to Mata Hari. As if sensing my mood, the sun went behind a cloud and hail started hitting me just as I reached the prison gate.

Shaking pellets off my clothes, I ducked inside. The guard recognized me and waved me in. I no longer made the rounds delivering meals, but went directly to Mata Hari's cell. When I arrived at cell block C, the officer stationed there told me Mata Hari had been asking for me. I hurried down the hallway to her cell at the end.

Mata Hari was motionless on her bed. My breath caught. *Is she dead?* Had she killed herself? She'd threatened to do it often enough. Every time I visited, she told me, "If I have to stay in this awful place one more night, I'll die." Could she have willed herself to die? I stood at the threshold watching to see if her chest was moving.

"Lady MacLeod?" I moved closer to the bed. "Gresha? Are you asleep?" Stupid question, I know. But I couldn't jolly well ask if she was dead.

She stirred and groaned.

"Are you all right?" I whispered.

In the past week, she'd aged another decade. Her once jet-black hair was faded with graying roots exposed. Her once silken skin was wrinkled and blotchy. Her once bright eyes were puffy and dull. She'd gone from a great beauty to a sad old lady in a matter of two weeks. Prison would do that to anyone... except Fredricks, the annoying cad.

"Lemons, is that you?" Her voice was hoarse.

"I'm here." I gingerly sat on the edge of her bed and took her hand. "Has something happened?"

"I begged them not to..." Her face twisted into an anguished mask and she turned her head aside.

"Not to what?"

"Call Vadime to testify." She sobbed. "I didn't want him to see me like this. I wanted his last memory of me to be as I was... beautiful, dignified... clean."

"If he loves you, I'm sure he understands—"

"That's just it," she interrupted. "He denied we were engaged to be married." She rolled over, her shoulders heaving. "He's the only man I've ever loved," she said into her filthy pillow.

"I have something for you." I removed the jade ring from my pocket, hoping to cheer her up. "The police found your ring."

She turned over and wiped her eyes. "Where?"

"You don't want to know." I held out the ring.

She took it and slipped it on her finger. "Vadime gave this to me." She started sobbing again.

Poor woman. I knew what it was to be betrayed by the man you loved. I rubbed her back to comfort her.

"I want to die..." Her words were muffled, but I'd heard them so often that I recognized the familiar refrain. "This place is torment. I'm going mad...." Her voice trailed off into more bawling.

After a few more minutes of trying to comfort her to no avail, I asked, "What happened at the trial?"

She sat up in bed. I handed her a handkerchief and she dried her eyes. "Bouchardon read off a list of the names of officers I've known as if it were a crime to love officers."

"Bouchardon?"

"The prosecutor. A small man with a small mind. He and Ladoux both. Whereas I see grandness, they see only pettiness." She sniffled. "Yes, I have taken, but I have also been taken. But I swear I have never committed an act of treason against France." She gazed at me with those endless brown eyes. "You have to believe me.... You believe me, don't you, my little Lemons?"

I nodded. "Yes, Gresha, I do." It was the truth. I did believe her. In her every confidence, never had she betrayed any espionage against the Allies. She'd told me many things, some of them shocking, but never anything involving state secrets. For her, pillow talk was an art. Her talent for seduction had been used to gain financial independence, not war intel. Surely the French authorities couldn't execute her for loving luxury and officers, could they?

The answer came soon enough.

Later that very afternoon, Bouchardon concluded his case against Mata

Hari by describing her as a predator who "descended on the Grand Hotel, where she set her snares for Allied officers, one by one, as they came along." Clearly the man was a patriarchal prude who condemned Mata Hari more for her sexual activities than for actually being a spy.

Her trial started on July 24th and ended on July 25th. The all-male jury deliberated for less than forty-five minutes. That evening, Mata Hari was moved to cell number twelve, which was reserved for those awaiting execution. She was scheduled to face a firing squad tomorrow. I wished I could stay the night with her at the prison. But I promised to come back before dawn.

Men and their double standards. It was okay for them to take lovers, but any woman who enjoyed the same was considered loose. And while I personally didn't approve of philandering in either men or women, I didn't think it worthy of capital punishment. Although I had to admit, there had been times when I'd felt like poisoning my own unfaithful spouse.

Chapter Twenty-Five: The Firing Squad at Dawn

T he next morning, I arose long before dawn. I'd promised Mata Hari I'd accompany her to the end. The whole thing seemed like a bad dream. How could they execute a woman for espionage without any proof?

The only evidence they had was a suspicious telegram supposedly intercepted from the Germans naming H21, the very telegram Mr. Grey had mentioned before I left England. I thought of the conversation between the code-breakers at the War Office the day I left. Mr. Knox said even the frogs had broken that code. So why was that telegram sent in a code the Germans knew the Allies had already broken... unless someone was trying to frame Mata Hari? Why would anyone want to frame her?

She never should have admitted to taking money from the Germans. Not that I endorsed prevaricating. But she could have kept that little detail to herself. Anyway, I believed her when she said she'd only taken the money from the Germans because they had confiscated her furs and jewelry the last time she was in Berlin, and they owed her.

And what about the French? She'd also received money from them. Ladoux himself had paid her to go to Amsterdam and spy on German diplomats. Of course he denied it. *Is he scapegoating Mata Hari to show he's tough on spies? Is she his low-hanging fruit?* I despised the man and I'd never even met him. Small-minded, Mata Hari had called him.

Using the electric kettle, I boiled water and made myself a strong cuppa...

too strong since I didn't have any milk. The bitter tea worked as an antidote to the ridiculously early hour. I put on my watch to verify the time. It was so ungodly early, I wondered if the blasted thing had stopped again. I held it to my ear. No. It was ticking.

The last time I'd seen three in the morning was the night Andrew died at Charing Cross Hospital. The whole hospital had been overflowing with men suffering from mustard gas poisoning, a horrible and cruel blow dealt by the Germans. Hadn't killing thousands been bad enough? Had they needed to make them brutally suffer too? And now an innocent woman would be executed. Maybe Fredricks was right. Man was the cruelest animal.

I took another sip of tea and then assembled my habit and wimple. The garment needed a good cleaning, but I hadn't had time. I pulled the tunic over my head, smoothed my bristly hair with a brush, and then adjusted the coif on my crown. I drew the wimple over my head, slid a rosary over the ensemble, and positioned it around my neck. Finally, I tied a long cord around my waist. The cord had four knots, which represented the Franciscan values of chastity, poverty, obedience, and enclosure, the antithesis of Mata Hari's life—and not my favorites either. I'd had quite enough of all four, especially chastity…

My thoughts drifted to Archie. I drained my teacup. Now was not the time to indulge in romantic fantasies. I quickly put on my sturdy oxfords, and then went back to my wardrobe to pack an outfit for Mata Hari. I'd managed to confiscate more clothes from the penthouse before the police packed them all away. She deserved to look nice today. I folded an elegant fur-trimmed jacket and then a matching dove gray skirt and laid them out on the bed. I gathered stockings, a cream silk blouse—rather too low-cut for my own taste—and handsome ankle boots, along with a jaunty tri-cornered hat. I smiled to myself, pleased with the ensemble I'd put together. I hoped Mata Hari would like it too.

I carefully packed the clothes and some makeup into my overnight case, picked up my bible, and took a last look around my hotel room. *Is there anything else I can bring to the poor woman?* I dashed back into the bath, retrieved a bar of Jasmine soap, wrapped it in a handkerchief, and tucked it into my pocket. On a whim, I slid my new evening gown off its hanger and add it to my care package.

It was still dark when I arrived at Saint-Lazare prison. The cool morning air was a reprieve from the usual summer heat. Although it wasn't cold, a shiver ran through me as I approached the gate. I tightened my grip on the bible. As I crossed the threshold, I said a little prayer for Lady Gresha MacLeod. My disguise may be fake, but the prayer was real. Only God could save her now.

Mata Hari was already awake, sitting on the edge of her bed, her eyes glazed over and her look faraway.

"I brought you some clothes," I said, trying to sound upbeat. I set the overnight case on the end of her bed.

She gave me a wistful smile.

"Some makeup and hairpins and fresh clothes and you'll be right as rain." I busied myself opening the case and laying out the clothes. I hated to put them on the dirty bedding, but there was no place else any better. "I brought jasmine soap!" I pulled the bar from my pocket. "I'll go fetch some water."

She nodded.

When I returned with a basin of warm water, Mata Hari had already stripped off her dirty prison dress. Standing tall in her undergarments, her head high, her posture was that of a grand lady waiting for her lady's maid to dress her.

I yanked the blanket off the bed, spread it out on the floor, and then put the basin down in the center. I unwrapped the bar of soap and handed it to Mata Hari.

She held it to her nose and inhaled. "Lovely." When she sniffed the scented soap again, the old spark came back into her dark eyes. "Thank you, dearest Fiona." She knelt in front of the basin, plunged the soap into the water, and rubbed up a luscious lather.

I turned around to give her some privacy, although at this point, prison had stolen whatever modesty she'd had and I'd grown used to seeing her in various stages of undress and ill health.

"I'll never take soap for granted again," she said splashing.

"There are clean underthings in the case." I pointed at the bed without turning around.

"A corset," she said with genuine joy in her voice. "You're a saint, Lemons."

Just because I'm wearing a habit, doesn't make me a saint... or even a nun. "The cover is not the book," I said, glancing around at her and then quickly turning away again. I'd never seen anyone so happy about wearing a corset.

"Not me," she said. "What you see is what you get."

Although her veil dance had been revealing, and I had no doubt many an officer had *gotten* her, I didn't believe for a second that Lady Gresha MacLeod—aka Mata Hari, also known as Madame Zelle—was an open book.

"A gown!" She sounded like a schoolgirl going to her first dance. "How enchanting." She giggled. "How do I look?"

I turned around. "Lovely."

Although the gown was tight on her, she looked almost young again, vibrant even.

"Let me fix your hair." I took a brush and some hairpins from the overnight case. I held the pins between my teeth and wielded the brush.

She sat on the edge of the bed, reminiscing about her high-powered lovers, while I brushed out her hair. Her scalp could use a good wash with disinfectant, but there was neither time nor space for that complicated operation.

Removing the hairpins from my mouth one by one, I began to pin up Mata Hari's thick black hair. Even my creative chignon couldn't cover the gray sprouting from her roots. I wished I'd brought a looking glass so she could see her transformation. Then again, since she hadn't seen her reflection for weeks, she might not be as impressed with the improvement as I was.

"Dear Lemons," she said, "you've performed a miracle. I feel like I'm on my way to see *La Boehme* at Théâtre du Châtelet instead of facing a firing squad." She patted her hair. "Now for some face paint."

La Boheme, how apt. Another opera where the poor woman is martyred.

Like a nurse assisting a surgeon, I handed her rouge, kohl, and then mascara, all of which she applied liberally.

"My final performance." Her ample hips undulating seductively, she hummed an eastern melody as her graceful arms fluttered above her head.

Good heavens! A knock at the door had startled me. My hands flew to my chest, where my heart was pounding as if it wanted to escape the prison of my body.

"Ten minutes," a guard said from the other side of the door.

"I'm ready," Mata Hari said, her voice full of resolve.

"I'm not," I said, wiping tears from my eyes with the backs of my hands. I'd never admired her as much as I did at this moment. Even facing death, she was poised and dignified.

"Oh, Lemons, don't cry." Mata Hari wrapped her arms around me.

"I'm sorry," I sniffled into her beautiful fur collar. "It's not right."

"Might makes right, my dear." She held me at arm's length, as if I were a sulky child. "And all of my mighty friends have forsaken me." She kissed me on the cheek. "Men are as fickle as fate. Never trust a man."

I nodded, too choked up to say another word.

"Dear Fiona, don't cry for me." She tucked a loose hair back into my wimple. "I'm not worth it."

"Don't say that." I sobbed. "You're worth a thousand Ladouxs and ten thousand Bouchardons." I wiped my eyes on the sleeves of my robe. "You're the bravest woman I know."

"Courage, my friend." She took my hand. "I would rather die than spend one more moment in this horrid prison. Don't you see? Now, I'm—"

Another knock interrupted her. "It's time," the guard said, unlocking the cell. "I'm sorry, ladies. It's time."

Mata Hari slipped the jade ring off her finger and pressed it into my palm. "I want you to have this. You've been so kind to me."

"I couldn't—"

"Nonsense." Her hand enveloped mine. She closed her fingers around mine and pressed the ring into my palm. "I'd rather you have it than the mistress of the man who shoots me." She lifted the tri-cornered hat off the bed, and I helped her pin it into her hair at a becoming angle.

* * *

Outside the prison, the first blush of dawn was filtered through a gauzy fog. The guard led us through a throng of reporters to a black motorcar that looked like a hearse. Behind it, five other identical cars stood at the ready, no doubt transporting the firing squad and their commander.

The guard opened the back door of the first hearse and helped me in. I scooted to the edge of the seat to make room for Mata Hari. Before getting in, she turned back to the journalists and photographers gathered outside and waved, an actress on her way to the theater for her premiere. Once inside the car, she drew the blinds over the windows and took my hand.

"Where are you taking us?" I asked the driver.

"*La Caponnière*," he answered in a gruff voice.

What in blazes? My French wasn't great, but I could swear *la caponnière* meant chicken coop.

We rode in silence to the chicken coop, which turned out to be a military installment near Vincennes. The motorcade stopped in front of an expansive field, which the driver informed us was used for drill practice by the cavalry.

"I've always loved the cavalry," Mata Hari said playfully.

The driver escorted us from the hearse to the edge of the field. Men in khaki uniforms with red fez hats streamed out of the other cars. One officer wearing a blue uniform and a black beret barked orders. A priest carrying a bible in one hand and a rosary in the other said something to the black beret.

"They're so young," Mata Hari said as she gingerly stepped over a puddle. "Poor boys."

Two khakis approached us and flanked Mata Hari on either side. She took their arms and smiled as if they were suitors escorting her to the opera.

I followed behind, picking my way through the muddy field. The priest caught up to me.

"Sister," he said. "We must pray for the soul of this fallen woman whose sins know no bounds." He fingered his rosary beads.

I just glared at him and continued walking.

When we reached a lone tree in the middle of the field, one of the khakis unfastened a rope he was carrying over his shoulder. *Does he mean to tie Mata Hari to the tree?*

I stifled a gasp.

The priest nodded approvingly.

"You naughty boy." Mata Hari threw her head back and laughed. "Perhaps some other time." She waved off the rope and stood tall, her back against the tree.

The second khaki offered her a blindfold, which she also refused, saying, "But darling, I want to see your handsome face." When she reached up to touch his cheek, he flinched and took a step backward.

"Does the woman have no shame?" the priest asked.

"Perhaps we should let God be the judge," I answered.

He huffed and sniffed, but said nothing.

The black beret commanded his men to line up. Twelve men stood at attention with rifles at the ready.

A man in a dark suit stepped out into the center of the field and read out the charge. "By order of the Council of War, Lady MacLeod, also known as Mata Hari, has been sentenced to death for high treason and espionage against the French government. For these crimes, she now faces the firing squad." He quickly walked back to stand behind the armed brigade.

The black beret lifted his saber, signaling the firing squad to shoulder their rifles.

I began to tremble. Tears streamed down my face. *Is this really happening? Are they actually going to shoot her? Would they really shoot a woman? An innocent woman?*

Mata Hari must have noticed my distress, for just then, she blew me a kiss.

The black beret shouted, "Aim!"

Mata Hari didn't flinch. She looked as elegant as ever, a woman waiting for her lover under a sycamore tree.

I wiped the tears from my eyes and looked away.

"Fire!" the commander yelled.

I held my breath. When I glanced back, Mata Hari was crumpled on the ground under the tree.

The black beret approached her body. To my horror, he withdrew his pistol and shot her in the head. "She may not have known how to live," he said, "but damned if the lady didn't know how to die."

I wiped a tear from my cheek. He was right. *And facing death is the hardest part of living.*

Chapter Twenty-Six: The Escape

After spending the rest of the morning hugging my pillow and wallowing in my own sorrow, that afternoon I finally pulled myself together, took a warm bath, and resolved to continue my mission. Wrapped in my habit, bible in hand, I forced myself to go back to La Santé Prison to interrogate Fredrick Fredricks.

My heart wasn't in it, and perhaps that's why I let my guard down.

* * *

The walk to the train station seemed especially oppressive. My heavy robe pulled on my shoulders like the weight of the world, and perspiration soaked my wimple. Squinting into the bright Parisian sun, I trudged through block after block of soldiers eating in cafés, buying newspapers, smoking on corners, and catcalling pretty girls. I was sick of this bloody war, and I was sick of this overly cheerful city. I wanted to go home and hide in my flat until the war was over.

I hadn't planned to leave Paris for another five days, but upon entering the Gare du Nord train station, I decided I'd had enough of Paris. I was desperate to get back home, sleep in my own bed, wear my own clothes, and enjoy a nice cuppa. I bought a ticket for a morning train back to London for Monday, the day after tomorrow. After the agent handed me the ticket, I let out a great sigh of relief. I would be safe at home soon and could put the whole beastly Paris affair behind me... poor naïve Berthe, the martyred Mata Hari, and even the blackguard Fredrick Fredricks. That left only the unfinished business of the countess's murder. I had one more day to find out who'd killed her. Her death was no more suicide than I was a bellboy. And I had a sneaking suspicion of who was the guilty party.

As I walked across the Pont du Neuf with the sun beating on my back, I thought of Mata Hari's slap in the face to death. If only I could have been as composed as she was. I was still fighting back tears. It all seemed so pointless. I was sure she'd been scapegoated by the French espionage unit. Ladoux had a reputation to uphold. With reports of French battalions mutinying daily and troop morale so low, he needed to round up spies and execute them. As if killing more people would somehow cheer on the soldiers.

I'd never believed they would execute a woman. *Is killing a woman a sign of progress in the fight for suffrage?* I'd heard the rallying cry of anti-suffragists in America. "Bullets for ballots." Mata Hari had taken a bullet, but women were no closer to having the ballot. It wasn't fair.

Mata Hari, whose only crime was loving officers, was dead while Fredrick Fredricks, a saboteur of the first order, was happily studying German philosophy in his prison cell.

I entered the prison with a sense of doom. *Buck up, Fiona, old girl. This is it, your last chance.* As usual, the first guard waved me inside. As usual, the second guard opened Fredricks's cell.

I took a deep breath. This would be my last interview with Fredricks… and my last chance to get information out of him about his spy ring, the murder of the countess, and Archie Somersby's so-called "double life." I'd better make it good.

As usual, Fredricks was stretched out on his bed reading.

"Ah, Sister Maggie, come in, come in." He was all smiles.

"What are you reading?"

"*Creative Evolution* by the French philosopher Henri Bergson." He closed the book. "He says creativity is the motor of life. What do you think of that?"

"If creativity is the motor, who are the mechanics?"

"Not the clergy." He smirked. "No offense, Maggie dear."

I really wasn't in the mood for his games. I wanted him to finally tip the wink on the countess and Archie so I could get back to my room to pack my suitcase and prepare to get out of this hole of despair.

"I'm afraid this will be my last visit." I fingered one of the knots on the cord around my waist. "I've been called home."

"Back to Ireland?"

I nodded. "Is there anything you'd like to tell me before I go?"

"Such as?"

"Something you want to get off your chest perhaps…"

"Ah, I see. You want a confession?" He tilted his head and pursed his lips. "Did I kill the countess? The truth about your boyfriend, Lieutenant Somersby? That sort of thing?"

Good heavens. *Did he know who I was? Had he recognized me? Was he just toying with me all this time?* Not sure what to do, I cleared my throat to regain my composure. "Whatever you'd like to talk about, I'm here for you."

"Whatever *you'd* like me to talk about, you mean." He slapped the philosophy book down on top of the pile of books next to his bed. He glanced around as if looking for something. "All right, you're on." His eyes flashed like those of a big cat on a scent. "I want you to be satisfied, *ma chérie.*" He patted a spot on the bed next to him. "Come sit down and Uncle Fredrick will tell you everything you want to know." He flashed his canines.

They didn't call him the Black Panther for nothing.

Reluctantly, I crossed his cell. *What can he do? He's paralyzed.* Still, I wasn't keen on getting too close. *What if he had recognized me?* I'm leaving soon. *What does it matter?* He's in prison and I'm going back home. I stood by his bedside blinking.

He nodded and patted the spot again.

Trying not to take up any room, I sat on the very edge of his bed. With both feet squarely on the floor, I folded my hands in my lap and averted my gaze.

"Good girl. Come closer and Uncle Fredrick will tell you a story that will make your hair stand on end."

I didn't doubt that he could. I inched a tiny bit closer to him on the bed.

He gazed at me, an inquisitive look on his face. "Closer," he whispered.

I didn't relish getting any closer to the fiend. "I'm close enough. What did you want to tell me, my child?"

He threw his head back and laughed.

I glared at him. "What in heaven's name is so funny?"

"You are delightful, *ma chérie*." He kicked the blanket off and wrapped his arms around me.

"No!" I gasped and my hands flew to my throat. Fredricks had me in a chokehold. I could barely breathe. Desperate, I clawed at his hands and tried to twist free.

Struggling for air, I gave him a sharp elbow to the ribs. "No, please!" I shook my head back and forth in a panic. *How had I let myself get so close to another murderer that he's trying to strangle me too?*

He stuffed a wad of cloth in my mouth. *Was it a sock?*

Tears welled in my eyes. I felt like I was suffocating. *Calm down, Fiona. The guard is right outside.* "You'll never get away with it," I said into the sock.

"Calm down, Fiona, *ma chérie*. I'm not going to hurt you." He pushed me back into the bed and sat on top of me. Then he untied the cord from around my waist, flipped me over, and tied my hands behind my back. I was now lying face down over the bed, my feet still planted on the floor.

Blast! The blackguard knew it was me all along. And what the devil. He isn't paralyzed either? He'd fooled the doctors… and me. But I'd stabbed him with my hatpin, and he hadn't even flinched. He was bloody good, the fiend.

Using all the strength of my legs, I pushed my practical oxfords into the floor and attempted to launch myself back off the bed.

Fredricks grabbed me around the waist and pushed me down against the bed again. "Oh no, you don't." He stretched the cord from my wrists to my ankles and hog-tied me. "You wanted to know everything. Relax, and I'll tell you the whole sordid story." He chuckled. "Nothing like a captive audience." He sat on the edge of the bed next to me. "Ah, it feels good to stretch my legs."

I tried to flip myself over and get up, but it was no use. Gagged, face-down on the bed, and hogtied, I could only flail around like the proverbial fish out of water.

"I've already told you the sad story of my family and why I hate the British.

Now, let me tell you how much I hate them." As he talked, he removed my wimple.

He must have seen the terror in my eyes. He interrupted his story and said, "I'm not going to touch you... not that I wouldn't like to, but this isn't the time or the place for romance. And I'm not in the habit of forcing myself on my paramours." He loosened my garments. "Speaking of habits, I need yours."

I struggled in vain.

Fredricks was twice my size and extremely muscular and strong. He untied me long enough to remove my robes, and then tied my wrists and ankles to the bed, leaving me sprawled on the bed in only my smalls.

If it hadn't been so blasted hot outside, I would have worn a proper dress under my habit. Trousers would have been even better. I grimaced. *What is Fredricks up to? Why is he taking off my clothes?* Good heavens. He can't be serious. The cad must plan to use my disguise to break out of prison.

Even in my current predicament, facing this murderous traitor and saboteur, all I could think about was my shame at being undressed. The only man who'd ever seen me disrobed was Andrew, and then only in dim candlelight. *Bloody barbarian. Let me go!* Every time I tried to scream or talk, I gagged on the sock in my mouth. It was no use. I gave up trying to wriggle out of the rope and turned my head so I could watch Fredricks... and breath through my nose.

"You wanted a confession, dear Fiona, and you shall get one." He was fiddling with my bible. *Now what is he doing?* He ripped out an entire section of the new testament.

"You found my insurance claims, so you know about my clever little scheme to blow up British ships and then collect the insurance money." He chuckled as he went to his stack of books, slipped a fat tome out of the center of the pile, and opened it.

The large book had a secret compartment inside. It wasn't a book at all, but a storage safe. *Clever devil. How in the world did he get that past the guards? Knowing Fredricks, he'd somehow persuaded the guard to fetch it for him from his flat.*

"What you don't know is I'm working with Renault to help him sell machine parts to the Germans."

"Very lucrative business. We couldn't let Countess Pavlovna ruin our plans, now could we?" He smiled. "You know she was working for us in the beginning. Too bad she betrayed us. Renault caught her in the act." He laughed.

The torn invoice I'd found in the countess's clenched fist. That's why she was murdered. She'd found that bill of sale. Renault must not have realized he'd left part of the evidence behind, clutched in her hand.

"The vixen stabbed him with a letter knife. Bloody mess." He stared down at me. "I trust you will keep our little secret?" He waved his hand in front of his face as if shooing a fly. "No matter. Your precious War Office won't catch up to me. And as for Renault... well, let's just say we've dissolved our partnership."

I knew the blood on the paperknife didn't belong to the countess. Now I knew whose it was. It belonged to Louis Renault. *Aha!* That's why he had hidden his right hand when he came to the library at the garden party. It must have been bandaged. And that's why he had to change out of his white shirt and tuxedo. He must have been covered in blood. He must have found the countess going through his desk. In the struggle, she stabbed him with the paperknife... and then what? Had she already succumbed to the poison? Or had Renault strangled her? Or accidently thrown her into the corner of the desk? Who killed the countess? Fredricks or Renault? Fredricks had just admitted they were working together.

Fredricks put my habit on over his clothes and adjusted the robes. "I didn't murder her, if that's what you're thinking. Not that I didn't try. The clever woman only sipped enough of her drink to make her ill, but not enough to kill her." He held up a silver capsule like the one I'd seen him give the countess. He tapped out two tiny white capsules. "Cyanide pills."

Just as I suspected. Cyanide. I was right. He was involved in the countess's death. So Fredricks had poisoned her drink. And just like Edith Wilkinson from Ravenswick Abbey, the countess had been a double agent. She'd turned from the Germans to the allies. And just as he'd done with Edith Wilkinson,

Fredricks had taken her out. Or, to hear him tell it, Renault had done it for him. *Why is he telling me all this? Either he's the cockiest murderer I've ever met—not that I've met many, mind—or, he's lying and he does plan to kill me.*

"I tried to convince her to do the honorable thing and take it herself." He chuckled again. "Planning ahead, you see, I'd already dumped one into her drink."

"So you dispose of double agents?" I asked. Blasted sock in my mouth.

"What was that, Fiona, *ma chérie?*" He put his hand behind his ear. "I can't hear you." He wrapped the wimple over his head and tucked the ends into the robe. *Golly.* Except for his mustache, he made a more attractive nun than I had. He went back to his book safe and rummaged through the contents.

"You see, Fiona, it's always a good idea to plan ahead." He held up a pocket watch, which was clunky and not as elegant as I would have expected for Fredricks. "This little fellow is a Ticka Expo camera," he said proudly. "It takes photographs through the stem." He gave me a demonstration by taking my picture, prostrate and severely underdressed, cheeky cad.

A spy camera. *Why doesn't the War Office give me one of those? Because my photographic memory is a sort of built-in spy camera?* I watched Fredricks with interest.

Next, he removed two silver capsules like the ones I'd taken from his boot, lifted the habit, and tucked them into the waistband of his prison pajamas. He must have engineered a secret pocket inside the band.

Just as I suspected. He stole them back from my hatband. *But how did he know I'd taken them?* His cunning was deuced annoying.

"Check out these little gems." He unscrewed the top off a small silver pill box, revealing tiny opaque beads. "Invisible ink." He picked out one of the little pellets and tapped it under his fingernail. "Tricks of the trade."

He hid the invisible ink in plain sight. Jolly clever. *Tricks of the trade, my eye. When—IF—I get back to London, I'm going to ask Blinker Hall for more spy tools. I want nifty gadgets too.*

"Does this look familiar?" Fredricks asked. *How in the world did he get that?* He held my passport wrapped with a blue ribbon.

Mata Hari wasn't the passport thief after all. She'd been telling the truth.

Fredricks must have picked it up off the floor of the train while I was sleeping, the sneaky scoundrel. For all the good it would do him.

"It's going to be amusing being you, *ma chérie.*" He removed the ribbon and held the passport picture up to his face. "You're not the only master of disguise." He ripped off his pencil mustache. *Good heavens!* "What do you think? Can I pass for Miss Fiona Figg—?" He glanced at the passport. "...excuse me, Mrs. Andrew Cunningham—file clerk and British spy?"

Infuriating man. There was no way a six-foot, two hundred-pound man would pass for a five-foot-six-inch, one hundred twenty-pound woman.

He slouched his broad shoulders into my nun's habit. "Covers a multitude of sins, doesn't it, *ma chérie?*"

"You'll never get away with it," I said through the sock.

"*Excusez moi?*" He leaned closer and cupped his hand behind his wimple-covered ear. "Did you say something?"

"You'll never get away with it," I repeated.

"Oh, but I will." He flashed a devilish smile. He tied the loose end of the cord that was wrapped around my wrists and ankles to the bed frame. "I always do," he whispered into my ear. He stuffed the new testament into his book safe, and then put the watch-camera, the pillbox, and my passport between the pages of the bible and wrapped it with the blue ribbon. "A sweet for my sweet." He sat a little silver ball next to me on the bed. "In case you need to reach me."

I strained to see what it was. A chocolate? How in heaven's name would a chocolate help me reach him? What was he playing at?

"You know Fiona, if you had more confidence, you'd be dangerous. Now, I'm afraid I really must be going." He winked. "Until we meet again, *ma chérie.*"

Devilish blackguard.

My bible under his arm, he rapped on the cell door. As soon as the guard started to open it a crack, Fredricks slipped out, and closed it behind him. He was gone, leaving me to languish nearly naked on the blasted flea-infested mattress in the bloody roach-infested prison. Hot tears sprouted from my eyes. If it weren't for the dirty sock in my mouth, I could scream bloody murder. Fredricks was getting away, and I'd completely cocked up my assignment. Now Captain Hall would demote me back to "mere filing clerk" for sure.

Given my state of undress, and the bloody painful ropes around my wrists and ankles, demotion was the least of my worries.

Chapter Twenty-Seven: Going Home

I lay on that filthy mattress in my underclothes screaming and choking into the gag for the longest two hours of my life. Finally, when a guard opened the cell door to deliver Fredrick's dinner, he found me hog-tied on the bed.

"What's going on here?" he asked, his ruddy face turning pale. Instead of liberating me from my bonds, he blew into a whistle. The high-pitched shriek echoed off the stone walls and pierced my ears.

I struggled to move and to speak but gave up. As I'd learned hours ago, it was no use. *Come on, bloke, untie me, for heaven's sake.*

The blooming guard stood by the door—as if I was going anywhere—until his colleague appeared, a cup in his hand and coffee dripping down his shirt. "What's the ruckus?"

The first guard pointed at me. "I think it's a girl."

What a dolt. Of course I'm girl. I'm nearly naked. Isn't it obvious?

"What the..." Stained Shirt had the good sense to rush to my side and loosen the cord.

I waved my head back and forth, grunting through the gag. *Get this bloody thing out of my mouth!*

As soon as the sock was out of my mouth, I said in a hoarse voice, "Fredricks, he escaped wearing my nun's outfit... my habit and wimple."

"Jean-Luc, you idiot," Stained Shirt said. "Can't you tell a man from a woman? And a holy sister. How could you let this happen?"

"Sorry, boss." The red-faced guard looked like a scolded puppy. "Who looks at a nun?"

Who looks at a nun, indeed. That's what Fredricks was counting on. A nun's habit worked as a sort of carte blanche. Fredricks was right. The flowing robes of the habit cover a multitude of sins.

I asked the guards to call Captain Clifford Douglas at the Grand Hotel and tell him to bring me some clothes. They looked at each other and then at me.

"You don't want us to call the convent?" Stained Shirt asked.

"No," I said a bit too abruptly. "That won't be necessary. Captain Douglas is my..." I almost said husband, but then remembered I'd taken a vow of chastity, "...my brother. My given name is Fiona and not Margaret, the name I took when I took my vows, so he'll know me as Fiona." The lies were piling up. I only hoped I didn't get buried under them.

* * *

An hour and a half later, Clifford appeared with my clothes bundled in a paper sack. "Good Lord, Fiona, what happened to you?" he asked.

I was sitting in the guards' break room wrapped in a prison blanket.

"Your *friend*, the Great White Hunter, stole my habit."

"Fredricks? But isn't he in prison?" Clifford blinked a few times. "I say, stole your what?"

I forgot, he doesn't know I was impersonating a nun. I glanced at the guard in the room, who was slouched in a chair, reading a magazine and looking like a sack of flour with arms and legs. Thank heavens he didn't seem to have noticed what Clifford had said. "Did you bring my clothes?" I held out my hand and wiggled my fingers.

"Oh right." He handed the paper bag to me.

"Can we move our dinner plans to London?" I asked, rummaging through the contents of the bag to see what Clifford had brought. "I've had enough of Paris. I'm going back to London on Monday morning."

"You're sitting there..."—he fumbled for the right word—"*exposed* and in this dodgy place and you're worried about our plans?"

"Sweet, isn't it?" I wrapped the blanket tighter and stood up. "Where can I put on these clothes?" I asked the guard.

"We don't have facilities for ladies." The guard didn't even look up from his magazine.

"Yes, I know." After having avoided drinking anything for hours on end to forestall the necessity of using the facilities each time I came here, I knew very well that the prison didn't have a washroom for ladies. "That's why I'm asking."

"How about this storage closet?" The guard pointed to a door on the other side of the break room.

"I'll watch the door to make sure no one comes in," Clifford said.

The paper bag tucked under my arm, I shuffled into the closet. At least Fredricks hadn't take my practical oxfords. Obviously, they'd been useless to him. My feet were big but not that big.

Is Clifford color-blind? He'd brought a brown skirt, a pink blouse, and a navy jacket. A green hat was smashed in the bottom of the bag. I should be glad he thought to bring a hat, especially since I didn't have a wig. The habit and wimple I'd worn—I thought again of Fredricks—had hid a lot, including the dreadful black porcupine quills that passed for my hair these days. Thankfully, Clifford hadn't said anything this time. But I had seen the anxiety on his face. He was missing my auburn locks, and, frankly, so was I.

I was seriously considering resigning as a spy and going back to being Miss Fiona Figg, boring file clerk and spinster divorcé… that is, if Captain Hall hadn't already demoted me… or worse. After he heard about my latest debacle, he probably would sack me. *Can I swear Clifford to secrecy?* He was such a chatterbox.

Clifford gave a little chuckle when I exited the closet. *Is he laughing at me?* He was the one who'd picked out the ridiculous outfit. "I think I've had enough of Paris too." He took me by the elbow and led me out into the hallway. "If you permit me, I'd like to accompany you on the boat-train home. It's not safe for a girl to make the trip alone."

I stopped in my tracks. "In the first place, I'm not a girl. And I made the trip here alone and managed to get here in one piece"—*all but my passport.* "I'm perfectly capable of taking care of myself."

The guard followed us out into the hallway and called after us, "Take care of her, Captain."

Clifford gave him a thumbs-up and then said under his breath, "If you're so ruddy capable, then why is this the second time I've had to rescue you from jail?"

I scowled at him.

"I would say it's not you I'm worried about... but that's not true." He hurried me through the prison gate. "You're a catastrophe waiting to happen."

Maybe Clifford was right. Once we reached the street, the adrenaline surge that had kept me upright and talking gave way to sweeping sobs. My shoulders shook as I tried to rein in my tears. *What a ninny.*

"Fiona, old girl." Clifford put his arm around me. "I shouldn't have said that. I'm dreadfully sorry. Please don't cry."

"It's not you." I sniffled and patted his hand. "I've had the most dismal day."

"A nice cuppa will fix you up."

"And where can we find that in this absurd city?"

"Darn if I know." He laughed.

Looking up into his kindly blue eyes, I knew everything would be okay.

* * *

Monday morning at dawn, Clifford and I boarded the train together. Even his incessant nattering on couldn't ruin my good mood. Truth be told, I was glad for his company.

Three women in knee-high boots, billowy overalls, and matching puffy hats looked like three puffball mushrooms as they worked on the train tracks. I wouldn't be surprised if the conductor were a woman too. If this blasted war had a silver lining, it was that women were getting opportunities previously reserved for men.

To think... I was working for British Intelligence as a spy all because some clumsy man had broken his leg while boarding the train to Ravenswick

Abbey. With a shortage of men to replace him, his rotten luck had been my big break. I had to admit, after the last few weeks, I was beginning to wonder if it wasn't the other way round—his big break was my rotten luck.

As we settled into our second-class seats, Clifford turned to me, his eyes alight. "I say, maybe I should write an article about your adventures in Paris for the *Daily News*." Clifford looked pleased with the idea. "They were darn happy with my last piece."

His last piece about the murder at Ravenswick Abbey was an inflated bit of self-aggrandizement that nearly deified his *brilliant friend* Fredrick Fredricks and misrepresented some of the most salient aspects of the case. Most notably, Clifford had reported that the Great White Hunter had solved the crime and not committed it.

"My misadventures, more like," I said, removing my gloves. "I was arrested for the murder of Countess Pavlovna and spent that horrible night in jail."

"Until I rescued you," he said triumphantly.

I could see already that in his version of the story, he would be the hero.

"Yes, and I thank you." I tucked my right arm into my side to avoid touching the man in the window seat whose arm was on my armrest. He wasn't even trying to keep to himself. I saw now why people who could afford it went first-class. "Then after my arrest, poor Berthe disappeared. Such a tragedy. All those women." I shook my head. "I know the police are short-staffed, but their cavalier attitude toward missing girls is shocking."

"You did the job better than any of those bumbling bobbies could have, old girl." Clifford smiled. "You're quite a girl... I mean, woman."

"At least the horrible Landru is in prison and can't harm another unsuspecting war widow. What a loathsome man." I picked at the finger of my glove. The police had found some of Berthe's teeth in Landru's oven and thereby confirmed what I already knew. *Utterly ghastly.* I shuddered. *What if we're called back to Paris to testify?* I was hoping never to set foot in that sinful city again.

"Indeed," Clifford agreed. "I say, I can write a story for the newspaper about how you caught the Bluebeard of Gambais... with my help, of course."

"Of course." I patted his arm. "But under no circumstances can you write about my stint as Harold the bellboy or you'll ruin..." I almost spilled the beans and said *my cover*. Surely by now, even Clifford was catching on. "Instead, why not write about your *brilliant* friend Fredrick Fredricks. He's always good fodder for a true-crime story."

"I still can't believe he's a spy... and that he escaped in your clothes. Good Lord. How in the world could he get away with it?" Clifford stretched his long legs until his knees hit the seat in front of him. "And he took your passport? What is he on about? He can never pass for you or any woman. It's ridiculous."

"Apparently he succeeded." I used my sharp elbow to give the smelly bloke next to me a hint. The pillock responded by taking up more room. "They still haven't found Fredricks. He's probably halfway around the world by now." I turned to Clifford. "You don't know where he went, do you? Since you're such good friends and all."

"Heavens no," he sputtered. "You don't think I'm in cahoots with Fredricks?"

"Are you?"

He gave a nervous chuckle. "You can't be serious."

"You pick some jolly questionable friends."

"And some jolly nice ones too." He glanced down at me and smiled.

"And what about Lady Gresha MacLeod?"

He gave me a strange look.

"Mata Hari, the dancer Fredricks—and you—were so enamored with... the one executed for being a spy."

"Stunning."

I didn't know if he meant Mata Hari or her execution.

"I can't believe they shot her." The gruesome memory came flooding back. Her defiance in the face of death. Her crumpled body under the tree. I pitied her. A tightness in my chest revealed more. I had been fond of Mata Hari, admired her even. She'd lived not just by her beauty but by her wits.

"How could such a beautiful woman be a spy?" Clifford exhaled wistfully.

"So only ugly women can be spies?"

"Of course not, no..." he sputtered. "It's just that spying is dangerous and ladies are so… so…" He searched for the right word.

"Delicate?" I asked.

"Yes."

"Fragile," I said.

"Yes."

"Treacherous?"

He squinted at me. "You're treacherous, old bean." He pretended to flinch as if I'd hit him.

"Mata Hari's only crime was trusting men."

"Are you saying men aren't trustworthy?"

"Present company excepted, Clifford dear." I fiddled with my gloves. "If Mata Hari was a spy, she wasn't a very good one."

"Why do you say that?"

"Because all she got out of the German prince was a box of chocolates. I hope it was worth it."

"I might commit treason for a box of chocolates." Clifford grinned. "I haven't had chocolate for over a year now."

"But would you risk a firing squad?"

"Only if the chocolates came with Christmas pudding and a nice bottle of single malt Scotch," he said, beaming.

"Speaking of chocolates…" I plucked the chocolate from my handbag and examined it. "What do you think of this?" The colorful wrapper said *Mozart Bonbon*.

"Austrian chocolate." Clifford's eyes got wide. "Where'd you get that?"

"From your mate, Fredricks." I turned the bonbon over in my hand. Fredricks had given it to me in case I needed to find him. *Maybe it contains a clue or a secret message.* I unwrapped it. The smooth milk chocolate tempted me, but I wasn't about to eat anything offered by that murderous scoundrel Fredricks. After all, he'd poisoned at least one countess and maybe two.

"If you're not going to have it, I will." Clifford held out his hand. "May I?"

"What if it's poison?"

"Steady on. Fredricks may be a spy, but he's not a murderer."

"That's what you think."

"I say, you don't think he killed the countess, do you?"

"Not directly..." I held out the bonbon. "If you dare."

Clifford's face lit up. "Gee, thanks." He popped the bonbon into his mouth.

I examined the wrapper. Inside the foil there was a small white postage-stamp sized piece of blank paper. *Wait a second.* "Clifford, do you have a match?" I'd learned in my crash espionage course that there were two kinds of invisible ink, chemically reactive and heat reactive. I was hoping for the later.

Clifford dug in his jacket pocket and offered me a small bronze square. "What is it?"

"A lighter. Haven't you seen a lighter before?" Clifford snapped it open, hit a flint with his thumb, and a flame appeared. "Sargent Ambrose gave it to me in the trench at Verdun." He snapped the lighter shut. "He didn't make it and I ended up wounded." He tapped his bum leg.

"Can I borrow that lighter?"

Clifford handed it to me. It was heavier than it looked, and the bronze was decorated with a carving of a tree. I flipped it open and tried to hit the flint in the way I'd seen Clifford do it. Nothing.

"Here. Allow me." Clifford took the lighter, hit the flint, and the flame appeared again.

"Hold it steady," I said, passing the wrapper over the flame, careful to keep it far enough above the flame so it wouldn't catch fire. After two passes, letters began to appear. "It's working!" My heart was racing.

"I say, it's invisible ink." Clifford leaned closer to get a look at the letters. "H-O-T-E-L-S-A-C-H-E-R."

"Hotel Sacher," I said. "Where's that?"

"I-N-N-E-R-E-S-T-A-D-T," Clifford continued reading. He looked at me with questioning eyes. "Stadt means city in German. Inner city."

"Inner-city where?"

He shrugged.

Hotel Sacher, inner city. What does it mean? I'd heard of a Sacher torte, the famous Austrian pudding. And the Mozart bonbon was from Austria. *"You don't suppose Fredricks could be going to Austria?"* Behind enemy lines. How in the world could I follow him there?

"Why in the world would he do that?" Clifford asked.

"Because he's working for the Germans."

"Poppycock." Clifford waved his hand in front of his nose as if he'd smelled something foul.

For the next hour, we sat in silence as the train chugged along through the French countryside. I tried to ignore the big bloke next to me and looked past him out the window. The blue sky was brilliant against the green fields. I had to admit, I was going to miss the sunshine but not much else about France.

"I say, look at this." Clifford held up a newspaper. "Georges Ladoux, the head of the French espionage unit, has been arrested for being a double agent."

I knew it. If only he'd been caught a week ago. Mata Hari might still be alive. "Poor Gresha," is all I could say. "Poor Gresha."

Chapter Twenty-Eight: A Royal Ball

I'd never been so glad to be home in all my life. The gray London skies and soot-filled air welcomed me back to Northwick Terrace. In spite of the summer heat, I threw open the windows of my second-story flat. After several weeks away, the place was beyond stuffy. The air wafting up from Warwick Avenue wasn't exactly fresh, but it wasn't stagnant either. The familiar sounds from the street below—a flower girl hawking violets, a paperboy yelling headlines, motorcars honking, horse hooves clopping—reminded me I was home. Thank goodness.

I could have kissed my tea kettle and my Smith & Philips gas stove. Finally I could make a proper cuppa. The water gurgling out of the tap was brown and rusty. I let it run until it went clear—more or less—and then filled my kettle. London water could be a bit dodgy, so I made sure to boil it for an extra minute.

Blast. I should have stopped on the way home to get some milk. Oh well. I was completely knackered and couldn't bring myself to go back out. I'd have to drink my tea black. And to top it off, my cupboards were bare except for half a package of stale biscuits. Still, it was good to be back.

Once I'd steeped the tea extra strong, I poured a cup and I sat at my cozy kitchen table dunking a biscuit into my steaming cuppa. *Ahhh.* I closed my eyes and tried to wash away the image of Mata Hari beneath that tree, the horrible conditions of the prison, and the gruesome death of poor Berthe. So much suffering in the world. I wanted to retreat from it but knew I couldn't. I still had two days left of my forced vacation. And as much as I'd like to rest, I was needed at Charing Cross hospital. As Captain Hall said, the war didn't rest, and neither could we.

Tomorrow, I'd go back to volunteer for the first time since Andrew's death. Those poor boys. It was the least I could do. And I could stop by to see Daisy Nelson and find out if she'd learned anything about the pollen on the hem of Countess Pavlovna's gown.

I ate the last dry biscuit and then drank the dregs of my tea. Not a very hearty dinner, but it would have to do. I was too tired to even run a bath. In fact, I was nodding off at the table. I dragged myself up and forced myself to wash my face before heading for bed. It wasn't even dark yet, but I was too knackered to stay up any longer.

I had just flipped off my shoes and flopped onto my bed when the telephone rang. *Horsefeathers. Who's calling me? Who knows I'm back?* Clifford. He was the only one. And I just left him not two hours ago… when once again he rescued me at passport control and then called a cab to bring me home.

I lingered in bed for a few seconds more and then got up to answer the telephone.

"Miss Figg. You're back." *Blimey.* It was Captain Hall.

"Yes, sir. I just now got back."

"So I've been told."

By whom? Blabbermouth Clifford, no doubt. But why would Clifford be talking to Captain Hall immediately after returning from Paris? Especially at dinnertime? I glanced at my watch. It was after six o'clock. More to the point, why was Captain Hall calling? I waited for the other shoe to drop.

"I need to talk to you. It's urgent."

"Yes, sir." *We're talking now, aren't we?* I bit my lip.

"Be at my office at O-seven-hundred tomorrow." He hung up.

"Yes, sir," I said into the dead receiver. *Crikey.* What could be so urgent that Captain Hall needed to talk to me in person in his office so early? Had he found out about my two stints in prison? Or that I'd let Fredricks escape? Or that I'd posed as a nun… and a bellhop? Goodness. He must want to fire me face-to-face. That's the way men of honor did things, face-to-face. *Blast it all. Now what will I do?*

I'd be out of a job. *Fiona, old girl, you should have thought of that before you went gallivanting off to Paris and defied orders at every turn.* What would I live on? *No husband. No job. No hope.*

I shuffled back to my bedroom and threw myself down on the bed. I was too exhausted to cry. I missed Andrew.

* * *

The next morning I woke at dawn with a dark taste in my mouth. My blouse was sticking to my back and my skirt was twisted around my legs. Needless to say, I was not feeling refreshed. I glanced around the room, wondering where I was. *Right. I'm back home in my own bedroom.*

Yawning, I staggered into the washroom and turned on the bath. With a ruddy lot of clanking noise, rusty water chugged out of the tap. I peeled off my clothes. And before the tub was full, I climbed in. Shivering, I splashed warm water up onto my torso. It was going to be a beastly day, I could tell already.

After a quick bath, I toweled off, gathered clean underclothes, and went to my dressing table. Sitting there in my knickers, I took up my hand mirror, wondering what to do about my hair. *Eeeh gad.* I looked like a bruised badger with the purple bags under my eyes and my spiky dyed hair. Yet again I mourned the loss of my most feminine feature, my long auburn locks. It would takes months to grow them back.

I still had some of Mata Hari's makeup... not to mention her petite handgun. Not yet desperate enough for the gun, I chose the makeup. It may not help, but it couldn't hurt.

I applied face powder to conceal my blotchy skin and puffy eyes, and then I carefully added some kohl. I checked my progress in the looking glass. *Crikey.* Now I looked like a vampire, so pale with dark kohl around my eyes. I quickly added some rouge to liven up my cheeks. I picked up Mata Hari's small tin of Lash-Brow-Ine, unscrewed the top, and used the tiny brush inside to apply the black paste to my lashes and brows.

Next I tugged on my bobbed wig and then examined the results. I was no Mata Hari, but plain old Fiona Figg would have to do.

I went to my wardrobe and stood for a few moments admiring my dresses and hats. Yes, it was good to be home. Finally, I could feel like myself again. Putting on my favorite lavender summer frock and some strappy Mary Janes lifted my spirits considerably. I may as well look my best when I got sacked.

I might not be facing a firing squad, but I dreaded meeting with Captain Blinker Hall all the same. Hopefully I could convince him to let me keep my job as a filing clerk. I wondered if Mr. Montgomery would intervene on my behalf. It wouldn't be so bad to go back to being regular old Fiona Figg, shuffling papers and typing up memos. At least I would have my familiar routine—taking the train to Whitehall, tidying up the kitchenette, bringing coffee to the men, perfecting my filing system, and having lunch with Clifford in the canteen. *Not a bad life... and a tad less excitement sounds pretty good right about now.*

I left an extra hour early. The last thing I wanted was to be late to meet Captain Hall. *Although if I'm going to be sacked, what does it matter?* Punctuality was a matter of pride, and even if I was going to be fired, I was going to be on time. Andrew used to tease that I'd be early for my own funeral. *Oh, Andrew, where did we go wrong?*

On my way out the door, I gathered the mail from my box. Given I was away for a month, there wasn't as much as I expected. But one letter stood out. I recognized the handwriting. It was from Daisy Nelson. She must have learned something about the pollen on the white glove I'd sent her before I left Paris.

I tore open the letter. Well I'll be… The pollen on the hem of Countess Pavlovna's dress was from *Leontopodium nivale*, Edelweiss, a flower native to the mountains of Austria and not native to France. What in the world had the countess been doing behind enemy lines in Austria? That pollen had traveled a long distance on the hem of her gown. Fredricks must have been telling the truth. The countess had been working for the Germans and then became a double agent. I couldn't wait to tell Captain Hall what I'd found out about the operative he'd called Madame Bovary.

Countess Pavlovna had come to Paris from Austria. And now, if I was right, Fredrick Fredricks was on his way to Austria. *What does it mean? Given my imminent demotion to "mere file clerk," I doubt I'll get the chance to find out.*

As I exited Westminster station, the rising sun was a blurry streak of orange low on the horizon burning through the mist. I'd say it was a real pea-souper. But the eerie glow made the thick fog more of a carrot-souper. I glanced at my watch. Not even six. I had over an hour until my meeting with Captain Hall. To clear my head, I decided on a stroll through St. James's Park.

Duck Island in the center of the park had always been one of my favorite spots. My dad used to take me there to feed the ducks crusts of bread. That was back when we had crusts to spare. Now it was hard enough for people to get bread let alone feed the ducks.

I stopped in the middle of the wooden bridge connecting the park to Duck Island. Watching the swans and geese pecking at the water was soothing. *Do they miss flying?* Like them, soon I would have my own wings clipped. I inhaled the smell of water lilies and dodgy fish and told myself it would be okay. *Clipped wings or not, I'll land on my feet. I always do.* My pep talk to myself wasn't working as well as I'd hoped. I was still dreading my meeting with Blinker Hall.

Lost in meditation, time slipped away and by the time I thought to check my watch, I was nearly late. Another of Andrew's favorite jabs, "You're so early you're late." If I didn't hop to it, he'd be right.

Taking long strides as if walking in a race, I made a beeline for the War Office. The streets were buzzing with businesses opening up and women going to work. Even the butcher's shop was being run by all women these days. It was still jarring to see a woman standing out front, her apron covered in blood.

I turned the corner onto Horse Guards Avenue and then filed in behind a group of uniformed officers making their way through the main arch of the Old Admiralty Building. These days, the only place thick with men was the entrance to the War Office. As Captain Hall always said, the war didn't take a day off so neither could we.

Still rushing so as not to be late for my sacking, I climbed the stairs to the third floor. Beads of sweat threatened to ruin my makeup. I stopped outside Captain Hall's office door. Using my handkerchief, I dabbed at my face before entering the reception area.

His secretary offered me a cup of lukewarm tea, which I accepted, if for no other reason than to keep my hands busy while I waited.

"Captain Hall will see you now." The receptionist gestured toward a big wooden door.

I quickly drained my cup and handed it to the receptionist. I straightened the skirt of my dress and took a deep breath. *Showtime. The sacking of Fiona Figg in one hair-raising act.*

As usual, Captain Hall was sitting behind his large wooden desk. His office was neat and tidy, but his person was disheveled. He looked as if he'd spent the night in his clothes. He glanced up from his papers and blinked at me. "Take a seat, Miss Figg."

Expecting I wouldn't be staying long, I sat on the edge of the chair, ready to bolt. I forced a smile, which wasn't returned.

"What happened in Paris?" He glared at me. "I told you to stay out of trouble... and to give up those ridiculous getups."

My getups *as he called them are jolly brilliant.* I bit my tongue and fiddled with the pair of gloves I was holding in my lap. "But sir—"

"Don't *but sir* me." Eyelids fluttering a mile a minute, he shook his head. "If it was up to me, you'd be back in Room Forty shuffling papers."

What did that mean? It isn't up to him? I'm not going back to filing papers? I tightened my lips and stared at him.

"Unfortunately, we need you on another assignment."

Another assignment. *Golly. So I'm not being sacked?* My spirits brightened considerably. I ignored the *unfortunately.* "I won't let you down, sir."

He sighed. "Miss Figg, don't make promises you can't keep."

"Yes, sir." I troubled the finger of my glove. It was no use arguing with him. I'd only dig myself in deeper.

"I'm not at all happy about this, but it seems you're in a unique position to help with the Fredricks case." He held out an envelope.

I took it and examined it. Although it was addressed to me, it had been opened. I glanced up at him. *How odd. Who is sending me a letter addressed to the War Office? And why is it already open?* I turned the envelope over. The paper was thick, very fine stock. This was no ordinary letter. Inside was an embossed card. I slipped it out of the envelope and read it.

My face was burning. "What does it mean?" *The cheek of the blackguard. What game was he playing at?*

Captain Hall tapped his pencil on his desk. "Apparently you made quite an impression."

I reread the card.

On August 17th, 1917, Mr. Fredrick Fredricks requests the honor of Miss Fiona Figg's company at the birthday celebration for His Imperial and Royal Apostolic Majesty, The Emperor of Austria, Apostolic King of Hungary, Croatia, Slavonia, and Dalmatia, King Charles I. A formal dinner will be followed by a royal masked ball. Vienna, Austria.

Good heavens. A formal dinner and a royal ball. "What does it mean?" I repeated, more to myself than to him. Fredricks really was a cad. The image of a black panther—Fredricks's insignia—was embossed on the bottom of the invitation.

"It means, Miss Figg, you're going to a Hapsburg ball." He stopped tapping and started blinking. "Behind enemy lines."

"But, I can't—"

"It's dangerous, I know, but we're depending on you."

"I don't—"

"No one wants to go behind enemy lines, but we must if we're going to win this damned war."

"No, I don't have a—"

The blasted captain interrupted me again. "We'll get you to Vienna." He wouldn't let me get a word in edgewise. "Don't worry about that."

"But, sir—"

"You're not getting cold feet, are you, Miss Figg?" He scowled. "I thought you thrived on espionage and deceit."

Steady on. Deceit? I wasn't sure I liked the sounds of that. "You don't understand—"

"Well, quit dithering and spit it out then."

"I need—" *A gown.* I was trying to tell him I need a ballgown. Too bad I'd given my only evening dress to poor Mata Hari.

"Will you do it? Will you go to Vienna and… get *close* to Fredricks?"

What in heaven's name does he mean, get close? Does he want me to become England's Mata Hari? A bit of rumpy-pumpy reconnaissance? I don't think so.

"What do you mean, get close to him?"

"With your first assignment at Ravenswick, you proved Fredricks is the infamous Black Panther. In Paris, you found the list of ships he helped sabotage. So, I understand if you feel you've done your part. Your information saved lives." He tapped his pencil on the desk. "But if you could do this one last assignment. We can find out how far up Fredricks's connections go and what he's doing in Vienna. If you can get more information out of him, he just might be of more use to us on the loose than locked up." For once he stared at me unblinkingly. "Look, we'll get you everything you need. Will you do it?"

"Everything?"

He nodded.

"Including a ball gown?"

He gave me a quizzical look and then smiled. "Well I suppose you *will* need a dress if you're going to a royal ball now, won't you."

"And spy gadgets?"

"Spy gadgets?" His lashes fluttered.

"You know, the tricks of the trade. Invisible ink, pocket-watch camera, that sort of thing."

"Costumes, now gadgets." He shook his head and scoffed. "Miss Figg, you do have a flair for the dramatic." He stood up. "So you'll do it then?"

I followed suit and stood too. "Yes, sir."

Whatever I need. What are the latest styles in Vienna? My pulse quickened. I would need a ball gown, and a formal dress for dinner, and clothes for royal events during the daytime, a smart suit with a matching hat for a garden party luncheon… I started making a mental shopping list.

"So the War Office will outfit me with everything I need?" *Yes, I'd need at least three new hats. And a new passport!*

"Whatever you need." He nodded encouragingly.

"Everything?"

"Everything."

"A spy camera?"

"Steady on, Miss Figg."

"How about a new hat... or two?"

"Yes, fine."

"A new passport?"

"Of course. Will you do it?"

If the War Office was paying, I'd forgo my usual pedestrian Liberty and go straight to the best, Harrods. "I'll do it."

"Brilliant!" He held out his hand. "Let's quit chin wagging. You've got to buy those hats, get your new passport, and pack."

"Sir, about Madame Bovary—"

"Yes, a shame. She was a good agent."

"I think Fredricks—"

Blasted man interrupted me *again.* "We know all about Fredricks and Madame Bovary. Now, off you go." He waved his hand in front of him like he was shooing a fly. "Go back to Room 40, write up your report on Paris, deliver it back here, and then go get whatever you need for that royal ball and get yourself ready for your next assignment."

I stared at him in disbelief. I was being sent on another assignment... to Vienna, Austria, no less.

"That's an order, Miss Figg." He pointed toward the door.

"Yes, sir." I stood up and gave him a salute.

He shook his head and chuckled. "Captain Douglas will pick you up at fifteen-hundred hours tomorrow. I trust Douglas. He will see you get to Vienna safe and sound."

Clifford is driving me to Vienna? This is going to be interesting. After several days in a motorcar with Clifford nattering on nonstop, even if I arrived safe, I didn't expect to be sound... or on time. *Does this mean Clifford knows I'm spying for the War Office?* I'm not sure if that will make my assignment easier or more difficult.

Captain Hall picked up the receiver of his telephone. He barked out orders to get me a new passport, and then hung up. "Your new passport will be ready within the hour. You can pick it up when you drop off your report."

"Did you say tomorrow?" My palms were sweating. I had darn little time to prepare for my first trip to Vienna. I was revising my plans. First stop, Foyles Bookshop to pick up Baedeker's Vienna, and then across town to Harrods, and then Angels Fancy Dress. Or should I go to Angels before Harrods? *Oh dear. I'm discombobulated by a trip across town. How am I going to make it across Europe?*

"Fifteen-hundred hours. Now you'd better get going."

"Yes, sir."

As I crossed the threshold, I heard him call after me, "No disguises this time. A ball gown, that's it."

"And a mask," I called back. Afterall, it was a masked ball.

I tried to contain my excitement. I hurried back to my desk. Avoiding any chitchat with the men in Room 40, I ducked into my alcove, and typed up my report. I delivered it to Captain Hall's secretary. Then I sneaked out of the Old Admiralty Building as if I were a spy. *By golly, I am a spy, and a jolly good one.*

And next I was going to Vienna, behind enemy lines. But first I was going shopping at Harrods... and then a clandestine trip to Angels Fancy Dress shop. Captain Hall may not approve of my *getups*, but if you asked me, they came in ruddy handy.

* * *

Harrods's art nouveau windows and giant dome always made me think I was about to enter Parliament. *Everyone who is anyone shops at Harrods.* You never knew who you might see at Harrods, princes and queens, lords and ladies, or film stars and dancers. And, in the exotic-pets department you might see the kings and queens of the jungle, monkeys and parrots, lemurs and lions, or exotic snakes and reptiles.

Perhaps I could buy a man-eating boa constrictor as a gift for Fredricks. *Of all the dirty tricks. Inviting me to a royal ball.* I did have to thank him for saving my job. If it hadn't been for Fredricks's invitation, I was sure Captain Hall would have sent me back to my filing cabinet... or worse.

I had to ask directions to the ladies evening wear section of the store. Entertaining Andrew's flying mates and co-workers hadn't required formal wear, so I'd never been in the evening-gown department. A receptionist directed me to the west wing of the third floor. With some trepidation, I boarded the moving staircase. I would never get used to the newfangled contraptions. Give me an old-fashioned lift or a set of stairs. I was afraid my foot would get caught and I'd be sucked into the works.

On my way to the west wing, I passed the hat department. A lovely mauve cloche caught my eye. I stopped and admired it. Given what happened to my favorite hat in Paris, I was in the market for a new one. I really should concentrate on finding an evening gown. Then again, if I had to attend a royal luncheon or garden party, I would need a new hat... or two... or three. Forget about spy gadgets, fancy hats were more my speed. I lifted the cloche off its stand and gently caressed the ostrich feather attached to its gorgeous silk band. *Lovely.* Careful not to ruin the moment by looking at the price, I tried it on. After all, I was officially on an expense account.

I eyed myself in the mirror. *Not bad.* Smiling to myself, I put my nose in the air. *Miss Fiona Figg, guest of the king and queen of Austria.* I tilted the hat to a jaunty angle and removed the hatpin. Nice and long, just the way I liked them. I couldn't wait to use it on Fredrick Fredricks, the rotter. I turned the hatpin over in my hand and then pressed the point against my index finger. Nice and sharp. *Yes. That's the ticket.*

Never underestimate the power of a good hat... or a sharp hatpin.

Afterword

Chronology of Events

Fiona's nemesis, Fredrick Fredricks, is based on the real life Fredrick "Fritz" Duquesne, South African soldier, huntsman, journalist, and spy, known as the "Black Panther," who used various aliases, including Fredrick Fredricks. Duquesne was a spy for the Germans in both WWI and WWII. He really did escape prison by feigning paralysis and dressing as a woman. For more information on the colorful life of Fritz Duquesne, read Clement Wood's *The Man who Killed Kitchener; the life of Fritz Joubert Duquesne* (1932) and Art Ronnie's *Counterfeit Hero – Fritz Duquesne, Adventurer and Spy* (1995).

The character of Mata Hari is based on the real Mata Hari, Dutch born Margaretha Geertruida "Margreet" MacLeod (née Zelle; 7 August 1876 – 15 October 1917). Mata Hari did live at the Grand Hotel. But by July 1917, she was already in prison. She'd been arrested in February. Her trial did take place on July 24th and 25th. And she was executed by firing squad on October 15, 1917. My characterization is based on the excellent biography by Pat Shipman, *Femme Fatale: Love, Lies and the Unknown Life of Mata Hari*.

The famous car manufacturer, Louis Renault, sold machinery to the Germans in WWII, and not in WWI. In fact, he was decorated with the Legion of Honor for his service to France in WWI. He was known to be a harsh character and had a running competition with André-Gustave Citroen, both of whom made tanks during both World Wars. In 1938, he visited Adolf Hitler, whom he admired. And he died before he could be tried for treason. His wife Christine claims he was murdered. And although he was reportedly a vulgar and obnoxious man, he was not necessarily a womanizer as he is portrayed here.

The men in Room 40 of the Old Admiralty Building are also based on real WWI code breakers, Alfred Dillwyn "Dilly" Knox, Rev. William Montgomery, and Nigel de Grey. Room 40 became MI5, which eventually became MI6.

The novel is full of other historical tidbits based on true events. But everything and everyone has been fictionalized for your enjoyment.

Acknowledgements

Thanks to my friend and "rough" editor, Lisa Walsh. She's been with me from the beginning of my journey into the world of fiction, and I really couldn't do it without her. Thanks to my wonderful "fine" editor, Barb Goffman for whipping Fiona into shape. And thanks to Verena and Shawn at Level Best Books for putting Fiona through her paces. As always, thanks to my companions, Benigno, Mischief, Mayhem, and Flan, for preventing me from totally losing myself in the fictional world of Fiona, Clifford, and Fredrick Fredricks, while at the same time encouraging me to spend as much time there as I want.

A Note from the Author

If you enjoyed *High Treason at the Grand Hotel,* please consider leaving a review on Amazon or Goodreads. Those reviews mean a lot to indie authors like me.

LINKS:
  https://kellyoliverbooks.com/
  https://twitter.com/Kellyoliverbook
  https://www.facebook.com/kellyoliverauthor/
  Newsletter: https://hello.kaospress.com/welcome/

About the Author

Kelly Oliver is the award-winning and Amazon Bestselling author of *The Jessica James Mystery Series*, including *Wolf, Coyote, Fox, Jackal,* and *Viper*. *Wolf* won the *Independent Publisher's Gold Medal* for best Thriller/Mystery, was a finalist for the *Foreward Magazine* award for best mystery, and was voted number one in Women's Mysteries on Goodreads. *Coyote* won a *Silver Falchion Award* for Best Suspense. *Fox* was a finalist for both the *Claymore* and the *Silver Falchion Awards*. *Jackal* won the 2020 E-Lit Award for Best Mystery-Thriller, and was a finalist for the *Mystery and Mayhem Award* and for the Silver Falchion Award.

Kelly is the author of the middle grade mystery trilogy, The Pet Detective Mysteries. *Kassy O'Roarke, Cub Reporter*, the first in the series, won a Reader's Choice Award for Children's Mysteries.

When she's not writing novels, Kelly is a Distinguished Professor of Philosophy at Vanderbilt University, and the author of fifteen nonfiction books, and over 100 articles, on issues such as the refugee crisis, campus rape, women and the media, animals and the environment. Her latest nonfiction book, *Hunting Girls: Sexual Violence from The Hunger Games to Campus Rape* won a Choice Magazine Award for Outstanding title. She has published in *The New York Times* and *The Los Angeles Review of Books*, and has been featured on ABC news, CSPAN books, the Canadian Broadcasting Network, and various radio programs. To learn more about Kelly and her books, go to www.kellyoliverbooks.com.

9 781947 915909